The Very Secret Diary

Everyone's done it - gone to bed with a book, opened it, found their place, read a few pages then fallen asleep. The following day you reread the pages, but first go back to the start of the chapter to remind yourself of what's been going on. Before you know it you're asleep again. By the end of the week you seem to be going backwards.

This is where Horace Horrise comes in.

Written primarily for grown-ups who don't always have time to read a whole book, The Very Secret Diary of Horace Horrise is 366 micro stories, one a day, that can each be read in a matter of

minutes if not seconds. Most days are standalone so although there are continuing themes throughout the book you can dip into almost any day at random and still have a story to enjoy.

Nearly all the days are illustrated, or as Horace says, "doodlestrated," by his own hand, with drawings that are mainly relevant to the stories.

Horace Horrise is the UK's funniest, liveliest and naughtiest young person with "grown-up stories for grown-up kids" but older kids will love them too.

And remember - no one falls asleep with Horace's diary in their hands...

© Searchline Publishing 2019
First edition 2019
ISBN: 978 1 897864 56 2
British Library Cataloguing in Publication Data available
Published by Searchline Publishing, Searchline House
Holbrook Lane, Chislehurst, Kent, BR7 6PE, UK

Tel: +44 (0)20 8468 7945
www.johnhemmingclark.com

Printed in England by www.catfordprint.co.uk

The Very Secret Diary of Horace Horrise is mostly a work
of fiction. Names, characters, businesses, places, events
and incidents are either the product of the author's
imagination or used in a fictitious manner. Any
resemblance to actual persons, living or dead, or actual
events is purely coincidental.

Acknowledgements: Rachel Ferrand for some fab
quotes; Michael R for the pheasant; Georgette Baldet for
a great team name; Katie Harris for the "campfire"
memory; Ali and Liam for a couple of the vicar stories;
Pauline Deacon for "the patch"; Will for the straws; Sam
Griffiths for the umbrella incident; Billy for the "Old Crow"
and hamper episode; Sarah Gray for the joke brandy
glass; Charles, Zoe and the rest of 5th Chis. for just
talking - even when they're not supposed to...

The *Very* Secret Diary of Horace Horrise

John Hemming-Clark

Dedicated to Shane and his friends and carers / leaders at 46th Norwich Special Needs Scout Group.

"Do not fritter away your life, like a fool. Life is short – live in the moment and make the most of every day."
Nicky Gumbel

Introduction by the author
"The *Very* Secret Diary of Horace Horrise" is mostly in his eleven-year-old words although it's been through a few grown-up editors just to tidy it up a bit and to make it a little more readable in places. Some of Horace's unusual words, phrases, expressions and spellings have however been left in.

Horace appears to have an adventure a day so I have tried to make the book into 366 micro stories - aimed at those who never seem to have enough time to read a whole book. Each entry can be read in minutes if not a few seconds.

Introduction by Horace
Let me tell you about my family and friends...
Karen and David Horrise: Mummy and daddy
Sam and Olivia: Older brother and younger sister
Tanya: Sam's girlfriend and scout leader Skip's daughter
George: Cat
Ravings (aka Ravens): My patrol that includes me, Archie, Edward, Charlie (Best Friend), Mel(anie), Em(ily) and now Sonny
And with this lot my life is in turmoil as you're just about to discover...

Sunday 31st December

The children need to be in charge.

All I can say is, I think we'll be glad to see the back of this year. Things can't be any worse next year. My new year's resolution is to do my best. Again. And I hope that I won't be saying this in a year's time. Again. The end of next year will be a Monday just to confuse us all. Or maybe it will be a Saturday. I can never remember which way round it is. If you have an extra day after you've done all the weeks then does the day go forwards by one or back? Whatever it is, all the days will have changed. If I'm right Christmas Day will be on a Tuesday which is a really silly day. Easter Day's always on a Sunday so why can't Christmas Day be the same? Whoever made up the days should have made sure that we had a number in a year that was divisible by seven and not seven with one left over. And why do we have days and weeks and months anyway? Why don't we just have numbers? Like today is day 365. I'm sure that if children were in charge things would run much more smoothly and we could also have equal numbers of days in each term and equal numbers of days in each holiday.

Mummy's made a new year's resolution to join a book club. I did suggest that she would probably be more comfortable with a magazine club but she just ignored me. Mummy reads loads of magazines; I don't know how she's going to find the time to fit in any books.

I got up on Boxing Day in England and went to bed on Boxing Day in Austria. And here I still am for a couple of days more. It's been quite an eventful time already but I expect things will calm down after this evening.

Monday 1st January

Things aren't quite what they seem in Saalbach.

A new year and we're on the slopes in Saalbach for the last day of this holiday. We went down a really long run this morning and ended up lost 'cos daddy refuses to look at the piste map. I wanted the toilet, mummy was thirsty and Sam said he needed something to eat. Daddy didn't seem to want or need anything. On and on we skied with me wanting the toilet more, mummy getting extremely thirsty and Sam starting to starve. Just when we thought that we would have to 'phone the piste patrol for a helicopter mummy saw a big building with a large picture of a wine cup outside like an outsized medieval goblet. "This'll do," she said. Thank goodness. We left our skis outside and all  tromped inside whereupon we found ourselves in long hallway. Mummy went off to find the bar, Sam the restaurant and me the toilet. And I found the toilet, just the one and inside there was a little stained glass window and a Bible on a table. I thought that this was a bit odd 'cos I didn't think that there were any Christians in Austria 'cos all the missionaries came by sea and there's no sea in Austria just snow and they couldn't have come by ski 'cos they hadn't been invented. When we met back in the hallway after a couple of minutes, mummy said that she had found a bar and asked for a gluhwein but was told that there were no alcoholic drinks. Sam had found the restaurant but was told that there was no menu. It was all a bit odd and I was beginning to think that the Austrians don't like the English. Just then a lady appeared from a side room. She looked like the Mother Abbess in "The Sound of Music." Mummy said to her that she fancied a mulled wine and that Sam and I would like some food. "I am afraid zat zat iz not possible," the lady said with a slight smile. "Why not?" mummy asked. "Because," the lady explained, "vee are not a restaurant, vee are a religious order. But you are velcome to join uz for matins."

Tuesday 2nd January
Sam takes a dislike to Spacey.

Just back from a few days' skiing in Saalbach. It was great fun. We listened to a DJ called Spacey. He was great fun as well. Daddy was a bit suspicious of him 'cos his name is an anagram of "Ace Spy." Sam doesn't like him. Spacey asked Sam how we'd got to Saalbach - had we driven or flown? Sam told him that we had flown. Then Spacey asked him who he had flown with and Sam said, "How am I supposed to know the names of all the other passengers?" Spacey just laughed.

Wednesday 3rd January
Is mummy trying out "suggestive texting?"
Mummy had a new 'phone for Christmas and she's been playing with it today now we're back at home. She is so slow texting that it's almost painful. When she was trying to text daddy this afternoon I asked her why she didn't use suggestive texting. She looked at me a bit oddly then smiled then said that she might be but she wasn't 'cos she was jabbing at the letters and not stroking them. Sam said that he thought that I meant "suggested texting, more commonly called 'predictive texting.'" When

daddy came home mummy told him that I had said that mummy should use "suggestive texting" and daddy laughed and said, "That would be most welcome," so it looks as though I was right all along and Sam was wrong - not for the first time.

5

Thursday 4th January

Melanie gets her team name suggestion banned.

Archie, Charlie, Emily, Melanie, Edward and I, a.k.a Ravings, have been trying to think of some great team names for when we do the activities that have been planned for this year in scouts. Our top four are:

1.Bear Girls (for the girls).

2.Soup-a-Stars (for when we're doing cooking competitions).

3.Ready, Aim, Splat (for when we're paintballing).

4.Cereal Killers (for when we're on camp and eat all the Coco-Pops).

Melanie also suggested "Womb Raiders" but scout leader Skip banned it.

Friday 5th January

Skip gets told off - and not for the last time I'm sure.

Skip was really told off tonight at scouts. He's put a combination lock on the gate that we share with the stables. When he went down to tell them he said that the combination was "ten sixty-

six." When the stables person asked, "How on earth am I going to remember that?" Skip said, "It's the year of your birth."

I've come home with a bag of slows from Skip that he said, "are for your father."

Saturday 6th January

Emily renames the chopping boards.

We have six new different coloured chopping boards for camp. We have red for raw meat, blue for raw fish, yellow for cooked meats, green for salads and fruits, brown for vegetables and white for dairy products. Skip has marked the back of each one in large letters so we know. However, whilst Skip was speaking to the stables and getting the combination changed so that the stable person can make out that she's only twenty-one, Emily renamed them in even larger letters.

Red is now chopped finger, blue is hypothermia, yellow diarrhoea and vomiting, green is cub's sneaked in, brown is hands not washed and white is winter camp. Skip hasn't seen 'cos Emily put them back in the rack and there they'll probably stay 'cos we'll most likely still use the wooden ones now we have our health and safety sticker.

Daddy said that the slows are for making slow gin and he's been pricking them all to release the juices before putting them in a demijohn with loads of sugar and gin. He said that it has to be shaken daily for two months then strained and bottled.

Sunday 7th January

Sam desperately needs some more muscles.

Sam got a voucher for Christmas and finally decided on what he was going to spend it - some more weights for his home gym bench press thing in his bedroom. He went into Bromley on the bus and bought two twenty-kilo dumbbells but daddy had to go and pick him up as he couldn't lift the package off the counter. Now we've been sworn to secrecy and Sam's told me that if ever

Tanya mentions it he'll know who told her and I'll be dead. I'm still weighing up the pros and cons 'cos it would be very funny if she knew although death is quite a big con so I probably won't tell.

Monday 8th January
Mummy tries to get home closed.

It snowed this morning! There was absolutely no snow on the

way to school but during morning break it was so bad that we all had to stay inside. At lunchtime mummy sent an email to the school that said, "Due to the recent snowfall I regret to inform you that the Horrise home has been closed and pupils are to remain at school until the weather improves. I am sorry for this short notice but you will know that the snow has caught everyone unawares and the safety of parents and grandparents is paramount."

Tuesday 9th January
Mummy feels she's been ignored.

No school today due to the snow. Mummy said that had the school bothered to read her email lessons could have continued with or without any teachers although school without teachers sounds a bit odd, although it would be most welcome.

We were all a bit bored but at lunchtime mummy was going out so we were allowed to make our own lunch. She said that we could have what we liked, so long as it was already in the house. I fancied soup but we didn't have any and mummy wasn't going to make it before she went out so then I decided on a toasted sandwich but unfortunately the toastie maker was broken after Sam had used it to try to make waffles but flooded it. However I had an idea. I got two slices of bread, buttered them and put

8

them together with the butter on the outsides having put some grated cheese and a slice of ham and sliced tomato in the middle. I then bashed it down a bit, put the toaster on its side on the work surface and stuck the sandwich in the toaster and pulled down (or along) the switch thing. I thought that I would give it a couple of minutes but the toaster gave itself only one minute and twenty seconds before it shot the gloopy mess out across the kitchen. The cat litter tray

took a direct hit and there it stayed until mummy came home and I told her that George had been sick 'cos I was going nowhere near it. I had some cereal instead.

Wednesday 10th January

Melanie loses an airloom.

No school today again due to the snow and now ice. The Ravings all met at the scout hut 'cos the steep slope on the far side that we usually use for a water slide in the summer makes a great sledge run. The snow was really soft and fluffy, like skiing off-piste (although I've never done that, not on purpose anyway). We had to go straight down and then turn sharply at the bottom to miss the gas cage and to slow down. Charlie decided to go as fast as he could, then do a minimal turn. He went so fast that he was unable to stop until the fence did it for him. Melanie has, I mean "had" a

lovely old sledge. It was a wooden one with metal rungs and it had belonged to her grandad. She said that it was a "airloom" whatever that is. She said that she wanted to make her own tracks so took a line on the far side by the wall. She flew down the slope then screamed then face-planted. When she stood up all we could do was laugh. She looked like a walrus that had been shoving its face in the snow. She wasn't happy. She was even less happy when we couldn't find her sledge. It just disappeared. We searched everywhere for it. Emily said that it may have just taken off under the snow and gone miles until we pointed out that the fence would / should have stopped it. In the end we just gave up and Mel is going to be in so much trouble although we'll find it when the snow melts.

Thursday 11th January
The fire brigade make an emergency visit.
Ravings were asked to help at the combined beavers / cubs (the younger sections) meeting tonight in the snow. They were having an A to Z campfire singsong on the steps at one end of the fire circle whilst Ravings were in charge of gently feeding the fire with wood from the woodpile. No chance! Wood is for burning and not gently! As the beavers and cubs started to sing "Animal Fair" we began to load the fire up. By the time they had reached

"Pizza Hut" we had most of it on and when they arrived at "You'll never get to Heaven..." we had a proper fire going. At this point, as the branches way up on high on the huge tree that hangs overhead started to crackle, cub leader Akela turned round and said to us a little bit more than firmly, "I asked for a campfire, not a bonfire." You just can't please some people can you? Archie started singing, "Campfire's burning, campfire's burning, fetch the engine, fetch the engine, fire, fire..." but was told off - until we really did have to 'phone the fire brigade. At least they put out the fire for us which is usually the most boring and time-consuming bit.

Friday 12th January

Chaos and confusion with Scout Hunt.

We had a bit of an incident at scouts tonight. Skip had arranged for us to play Scout Hunt in the woods by the common. Through the woods there is a path that connects two pubs. Assistant scout leader Patrick took four scouts to one end of the woods and Skip blew his whistle. The four scouts had to get to the large oak tree at the other end without being tagged.

Skip told us all about how to be furtive: no torches, no chatting - that sort of thing. In the woods it was almost pitch black with it being nearly a new moon. Melanie had positioned herself in the undergrowth, ready to pounce on any scout that foolishly decided to walk up the path.

 We had rounded up three of the scouts and there was only Archie left to go when Mel saw him coming slowly up the path - a tall, shadowy figure. Mel waited until he had just gone past her when she leapt out of her hiding place and jumped on his back.

"Got ya!" she cried as "Archie" let out a blood-curdling scream. Patrick and Skip and the scouts all came running and torches were switched back on.

It wasn't Archie, it was Vera from the allotments - going to meet her husband in the Lion's Head! Once we had calmed her down and apologised Skip did a count. There was one scout missing - Archie. We walked slowly up the path to the scout hut to prepare our "Missing Scout" leaflets and for Skip to make a difficult 'phone call. Fortunately we found Archie on the way. He was standing by the oak tree with a large smile on his face.

"Well done Mel," he said. "That was a fantastic distraction technique, one of the best. Everyone thought that you were on the other team."

"So did I," said Mel lamely.

Saturday 13th January
Mel gets falsely accused and Sam's partying.
Mel's in such big trouble! 'Cos Mel is always complaining that she has no money or not enough her daddy has accused her of selling the sledge on an auction site.

Sam's gone to a fancy dress party with Tanya. It's a superheroes party and Tanya's gone as Wonder Woman and Sam's as Spiderman. When she came round earlier I said that at least Sam hadn't gone as The Incredible Hulk 'cos no one would believe him after you know what but I didn't say what to her.

Sunday 14th January
Mel's sledge mystery deepens.
The snow melted considerably overnight so I went up to the scout hut to see if I could see Mel's sledge but there was no sign of it. The mystery deepens.

Monday 15th January
Most drunk people live in Chislehurst.
Daddy said that he read a statistick today that was that Public Health England stated that just 4% of the population drink nearly a third of all the alcohol sold in England.

Judging by the number of drunk people that I can see in the pub as I walk past on the way home from scouts I reckon that most of them must live in Chislehurst.

Tuesday 16th January

Neither candles needed and cause confusion.

Skip asked if we could all bring some candles to scouts this week. Mummy said that we don't have any at home so I walked down to the supermarket to buy some. I asked one of the ladies in the shop if they sold candles and she said, "Boy or girl?" so I said "neither" and she just laughed. I went and saw Mr Lillie in The Workshed instead. He had "neither" candles.

Wednesday 17th January

Tanya school skirt policy issue.

Tanya came round for tea today and she's not very happy. Her school has imposed a skirt policy. Apparently the hem has to be below where your fingertips reach on your legs when you're standing up and your arms are dangling. What about if you have really short arms? 'Cos that will mean that when girls wear miniskirts to school the other girls won't say, "Oh look, she's wearing a mini," they'll say, "Oh look, she must have really short arms," and then she'll be bullied. And what if you don't have any arms? They can't have you walking around in your knickers can they?

I'm glad I wear shorts and trousers.

Thursday 18th January

Daddy makes a joke that someone doesn't find very funny.
Daddy was really told off tonight. Thank goodness. Otherwise it would seem always to be me. Daddy had bought a new razor in the supermarket 'cos his old one was getting rather blunt and daddy's face was getting stubbly. It was a very nice looking razor as far as I could make out but it hadn't cost very much. When he got home and pulled it out of its packaging he saw that a bit of the handle had fallen off and was rattling about in the box. "Oh well," said mummy, "you get what you pay for." Daddy likes to make a joke sometimes so said back, "Yes, why do you think I married you?"

then looked like he had realised that that didn't sound too good. When mummy exploded daddy tried to make out that he meant that mummy was priceless but it didn't work and now daddy's in his shed. I hope he's making the effort to have a shave whilst he's in there.

Friday 19th January

Skip's not careful of possessions and property this evening.
A camp fire and sing song and skits this evening. Sitting round

the camp fire was a bit dangerous for Skip, his chair at least, 'cos it was a bit windy. The scouts were all sitting on lumps of wood so we were okay, but when Skip stood up his chair blew onto the camp fire. Fortunately Charlie managed to pull it out but there wasn't much

left of it.

Skip lost his car keys and had to walk home after telling the scouts that anyone who found them would get a reward. So far they have not been found.

Saturday 20th January
Assembling tent instructions for scouts and leaders.
Skip has written out and handed round instructions for,

Assembling your Tent
1. The scout way: Arrive at camp late, get the poles out, run around, light some tinder for the camp fire, go and get some wood because the tinder's gone out, return after twenty minutes with two twigs, put them down, tip the canvas out into the mud, put the fly sheet under the canvas, lose the mallet, light some kindling because there's no more tinder, whittle a tent peg even though there are fifty in a bag, put the canvas up inside out without pegging out the guys, let go, disappear off to the toilet for twenty minutes, return having not been to the toilet, set light to the tent pegs, tell scout leader that there are no tent pegs, go to the toilet again for another twenty minutes, return to find the scout leader has put the tent up, have some hot chocolate that scout leader has prepared on gas stove in mess tent that scout leader has put up in twenty minutes, unpack rucksack and go to bed at about midnight and talk for four hours.
2. The scout leader way: Start on your own tent at five past midnight.

Sunday 21st January
We find Skip's keys but he doesn't keep his word.
A scout is to be trusted? No chance.
Charlie and I went up to the scout hut to look for Skip's keys so that we could earn some brownie points. We found them in the fire ash. They were all bent and melted.

We took them round to Skip's and told him that we had found them in the fire. I don't think he believed us and he was looking at us very suspiciously when his wife came to the door and told us that when they're on holiday he always puts his keys in the cup holder on his chair for safe keeping. "Not very safe on Friday though, was it?" Charlie told Skip. Needless to say we didn't get any reward.

Monday 22nd January

Cat hair conflict.

We had a stir-fry tonight. It was very yummy. Mummy's good at stir-fries. Tonight we had chicken and noodles and coloured bits. When daddy was eating Sam pointed out that he had  a hair sticking out of his. Daddy pulled it out, examined it and said, "It looks like a cat's hair." Mummy sometimes says things without thinking and this was one of those sometimes 'cos she then said, "I wonder where that's come from?" to which daddy replied, "A cat I would imagine." Now mummy's not speaking to daddy.

Tuesday 23rd January

A potential problem with a beaver badge.

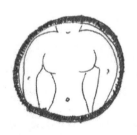 Mummy took me to the scout shop in Orpington to get a new shirt. Whilst we were there a beaver leader came in and asked Evelyn, who is in charge, "One Naturist Activity Badge please." "And where exactly is the parent going to sew it?" was Evelyn's reply. Where does she think it's going to be sewn? On the uniform of course like all the other badges but I didn't say anything 'cos the grown-ups were all smiling.

Wednesday 24th January
Mel's sledge found!

I think Mel's sledge has been found! Tanya told Sam that the cesspit man went to the scout hut to empty the cesspit yesterday.

He put his big tube into the manhole cover thing but couldn't get it down 'cos there was a blockage. He then put a huge, huge hook thing into the hole and pulled out - a sledge! How were we to know that the cover was the wrong size and didn't fit properly? I suppose that we should all be grateful that we still have Mel with us 'cos she's a bit thinner than her sledge and a bit more streamlined so she wouldn't have caused a blockage, she would have gone straight in and that could have been a real problem - going home and telling her daddy that we had lost Mel in the scout hut snow.

Thursday 25th January
Sledge needs a deep clean.

Mel's got her sledge back but it's staying in the garden until her daddy has time to disinfect it followed by a jet wash.

Friday 26th January
The fire brigade return.

We got really told off at scouts this evening. Skip said we could make some hot chocolate so Charlie, Mel and I went into the kitchen to heat up the milk on the hob. It was taking a really long time so Mel said, "Why don't we put the milk in the kettle 'cos it heats up water quickly enough so it'll do the same for milk?" So that's what we did. Anyway the milk did heat up quickly but kept on going then the kettle started to smoke and then the smoke alarm went off and we all had to evacuate the scout hut and then the fire brigade came (again!) by which time the kettle had turned itself off. But when we were allowed back in the kettle wouldn't even heat the water up and it was all black inside and so we had

cold hot chocolate. We won't be trying that again will we Mel? Skip's been told by the chief fireman that if the fire brigade have to attend the scout hut once more this year then they will charge.

Saturday 27th January
Tie challenge amongst the oldies.
Grandad's friend Wayne has come to visit for the day and we took him out for lunch. They're both getting a bit confused these days. They were in the sitting room at elevenses and Wayne asked grandad if he had had any good Thais. "I still have a very nice red silk one with white polka dots," grandad told him.

Sunday 28th January
Gender issues cause daddy consternation.
It was a bit of a mucky day outside so we were all in the sitting room not doing much when Sam jumped up and said, "Let's play gender." Daddy put down his paper and said, "For goodness sake, Sam, I read enough of all that stuff in the news. Can't we just agree that we're born either male or female and that's all there is to it? If a male feels that he should be a female then there's

not much than can be done biologically because you can't mess with what nature has given you unless you want to spend your life in even more misery than you are already in. We all don't like some things about our bodies but if we start trying to change them then where's it going to end? And just suppose I wanted to be a cat, how would that work? Would I have to see a doctor or a vet? It wouldn't surprise me if..." By now mummy had heard enough. "David darling, I think you're going a little bit deaf. Sam is suggesting that we play a game of 'Jenga.'"

Monday 29th January
Continuing gender issue grief.

Emily has found a fantastic use for what she calls her "laborious gender lessons" at school. Counselling her mummy. When she got home she found her in tears 'cos her mummy had just found out that she was getting a lot less money at work than a man that she works with who is doing the same job. Emily told her that if she changed her name and had gender realignment surgery then she could ask for a pay rise.

Tuesday 30th January
Sam gets paid for looking after George.

Mummy found a dark curly cat poo under the kitchen table this evening and totally freaked out. She really told George off before opening the back door and shooing him out. "Why didn't you ask to go out?" she asked him. Poor George. It wasn't his fault. Sam offered to clear the mess up which he did. "At least

19

it wasn't a runny and sticky one," said mummy as she cut a large slice of cake and handed it to Sam. "This is for your trouble." Alright for some.

Wednesday 31st January

Sam gets unpaid for not looking after George.

This morning mummy came down to breakfast and totally freaked out again when she found another dark curly poo this time on the kitchen table. She was a bit confused because George had stayed out all night and it could hardly belong to a family member. When Sam appeared he offered to clear the mess up in return for a large slice of cake. It was then that mummy became a little suspicious. She approached the poo with a bread knife, gave it a tentative poke and sighed when the poo moved a few centimetres instead of sticking. "SAMUEL," she cried. She needn't have bothered 'cos Sam was hiding  behind the kitchen door. He came in smiling. "What's the meaning of this?" Sam explained that they had been practising wild camping at explorers (the older section) on Monday and how to go to the toilet in the middle of nowhere. Their leader had brought along a fake poo as a prop and had let Sam take it home. "I don't want to see it again and you owe the kitchen a large slice of fruit cake," mummy informed him.

Thursday 1st February

The biscuit tin runs dry - but who's to blame?

I was really looking forward to a biscuit or two when I came home from school. Mummy wasn't in the kitchen so I would be able to take one or two more. I put down my bag and picked up the biscuit tin that was sitting on the table. Quietly I pulled off the lid. Disaster! There were no biscuits. Not one! Not even any fig rolls. I would even eat a fig roll in an emergency and this was one. I made myself a glass of squash and sat down and pondered. What was I going to do? Olivia came into the kitchen. "No biscuits," I told her. "I don't believe you," she said so I showed her the tin. Then she accused me of hiding them. There was a slam of the front door and Sam came in. In one step he was in the kitchen. "No biscuits," I told him as he grabbed the tin and looked inside. "Who's been eating them all then?" he demanded. "All of you," said mummy as she appeared in the doorway. "But we've run out," I told her. And what was her response? It was, "If you ate them slower then there would still be some left." In silence the three of us sat and thought about what mummy had just said. Something didn't quite add up but we couldn't put our fingers on it. After all, they would still all have been eaten, it's just that we would've spent more time eating them. We wouldn't have thought, "Oh, I can only have one biscuit today 'cos my five minutes allocated for biscuit-eating has been used up."

I had some toast.

Friday 2nd February
A new doormat appears.
I don't think daddy's too bothered about what I get up to at scouts - although he has just put a doormat outside the front door on which has been printed:

SCARF
WOGGLE
PENKNIFE
PLASTERS

Saturday 3rd February
Potential pizza topping predicament averted.

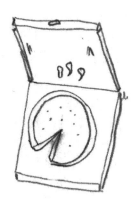

Pizza night tonight! I had my favourite which is a Veneziana and I'm allowed to have one all to myself now and so is Olivia and we can eat them straight from the box so it's a bit like being on camp with no knives and forks and plates. When Olivia opened hers she squealed, "There's no topping on mine, it's just pizza base!" Sam patiently explained that if she closed the pizza box back up, turned it upside down and then opened it again she might find that her topping would magically appear. She did and it did.

Sunday 4th February
Helmet and go-kart wars somewhere in London.

The explorers went go-karting this afternoon and some of the scouts were allowed to go to make up the numbers, including yours truly. It was outdoors and a bit chilly but we survived 'cos we're scouts. We went to a huge field in London somewhere. It was like a football pitch only it was concrete. The people had made a race track and we had to wear protective clothing and we were allowed to drive really fast cars like at probably twenty miles an hour. We had heats

and finals and trophies and stuff like that. Sam's friend (the one who's a show-off) brought along his Christmas present - a big and expensive shiny black helmet with red flame stripes on it that looked so much better than the ones that we were given. He said that he was an expert go-karter and would no doubt be in the top three if not the winner. He soon shut his mouth up when Archie arrived 'cos Archie had not been given a black helmet for Christmas - he had been given a go-kart. What's more Archie was allowed to drive it! But he didn't tell the men that he hadn't driven it before. In the first heat it was red flame stripe helmet versus go-kart. On the straight bit Archie was in front but couldn't turn in time so smashed into the wall of tyres and made a big hole, then he reversed out. Helmet came flying down behind Archie but Archie hadn't yet got going and was blocking the track and helmet couldn't stop in time and went straight through the hole in the tyres. He was then disqualified for leaving the track and came last. Archie came second. I didn't do too badly but I'm not sure of my position. It doesn't really matter though. It's the taking part that counts.

Monday 5th February

'Phones get banned at explorers.
Sam's not very happy at the moment as his explorer leader who's called Chrissie has now banned 'phones from meetings completely.
Sam: I need it to take photos.
Leader: Get a camera.
Sam: I need it to tell the time.
Leader: Get a watch.
Sam: I need it for the light.
Leader: Get a torch.
Sam: I need it for the satnav.
Leader: Get a compass.

Tuesday 6th February
More poo issues. Olivia to the rescue.

There was a scream from daddy's study this evening. He came rushing out and said that the dirty cat had made a disgusting mess on his beloved captain's chair. Olivia was first to offer to clear the poo up and was given ten pounds!

Wednesday 7th February
Poo issues continue. Olivia in the dock.
Daddy asked Olivia for his ten pounds back this evening. Olivia

said that she had spent it. Daddy is not happy but Olivia said that she had cleared the mess up and that it wasn't her fault that the poo wasn't as much of a mess as it could've been. Daddy's still not happy.

Thursday 8th February
Susie enters the poo fray.
We had a very rare visit from Susie from next door this afternoon. I answered the door and let her in as mummy rushed upstairs to "do my hair." I showed Susie into the sitting room and sat her down on the sofa and gave her a magazine and told her that mummy was just coming. Someone had put the fake poo in the middle of the carpet but Susie didn't say anything. Eventually mummy emerged. Not only had she done her hair but she had got changed from what she was wearing, had put on a pair of her most expensive shiny red high heels that daddy bought her in France last year saying, "Hang the expense," and she smelt different. Normally she's rushing around the house like crazy but now she sort of glided into the sitting room. "Oh, hello Susie," she said, putting on her silly posh voice. "How are you?" "I'm fine and I won't waste your time," said Susie stiffly, "so I'll come straight to the point. But before I do," Susie pointed at the fake

poo with a grimace, "I think you ought to know that there's a, um, thing on the carpet that you'll probably want to clear up." Mummy glanced over, saw the poo and said dismissively, "We don't worry about that sort of thing in this household. This is how we deal with that type of non-event." Mummy walked over to the poo and whilst keeping her eyes fixed on Susie she trod on it forcibly and squished the mess into the carpet with the sole of her shoe, smiling at Susie all the while. Susie's grimace increased. She stood up and wiped her hands over her stomach as if wiping them clean of any non-existent muck. Mummy looked down at

her shoes. Mummy was the first to scream. She had smeared poo all over the carpet, all over the sole of her left shoe and it was squidging out and over her shiny red upper. Then Susie screamed. She ran to the door, opened it and without a "Goodbye" ran out and down the path. I don't expect we'll find out for some time what it was that Susie actually wanted. No one offered to clear this particular mess up and George has had his Christmas catnip mouse confiscated until Easter.

Friday 9th February
A scout is to be trusted? I don't think so.
Skip is sneaky. Official. "No 'phones at scouts," he says then tonight we're making pancakes. Skip's brought all the ingredients but has forgotten the recipe. "Anyone got a 'phone?"

he asked. Seven scouts brought out their 'phones from various pockets and other hiding places and looked up a recipe. Then Skip confiscated all the 'phones.

Saturday 10th February

Skiing in Samoens.

We're on our half-term skiing holiday and we've been driving all day to Samoens which is pronounced like you're saying "someone" if you're very posh. We're staying at a hotel that's full of teddies. We have half-board which means that we don't have to go out to eat and we don't have to choose which makes things a lot easier. Tonight we had a very cheesy thing with sausage and then a hot tart. They eat different food in France. Daddy says they eat horses. Daddy has eaten a lot of food in France and the only thing he can't stand is something called "salade de gesiers" which he says is chicken innards and it stinks. Mummy and daddy drank a magnum of rosé between them this evening. Mummy asked me what I was staring at as she finished off the last glass. "It's rather a lot of wine," I said to her. "Don't be schilly," she said, trying to sound French. "Ish only a bottle."

Mummy's

Daddy's

Sunday 11th February

Poo issues abroad. Now daddy's involved.

Our first day on the slopes this holiday and it didn't go too well for daddy. He was trying to avoid all the ski schools so he took us miles away to a very quiet slope that didn't have many people on it. The weather was really bad and it took us a long time to get anywhere 'cos we couldn't see beyond the end of our noses. We didn't know where we were and so were just following the marker poles on the sides of the slopes and making sure that we were between them and not on the wrong side. Mummy was complaining that she was very cold, Sam said his goggles weren't working properly and Olivia just wanted to "go back to the hotel" so daddy said that "if" we found somewhere that was open we would stop. No one went past us all morning and just as mummy was threatening to call the piste people to get us rescued a building came into view with no wine glass outside. It was called "Alpine Hotel and Restaurant." "Rejoice," said mummy. Daddy said that it looked a bit expensive but mummy told him that whatever she ate would be cheaper than a helicopter rescue.

Inside there were a few people around but it wasn't very busy. We sat down at a very welcoming table with cotton napkins that mummy loves and loads of glasses and decorations and a candle. Daddy said that he wasn't particularly hungry and went off to the toilet. Whilst he was gone mummy called for a waiter. This man appeared and he was dressed "immaculately" according to mummy, with a large starched white apron and a smart smile. Mummy smiled back. She managed to get hold of a menu and a wine list that boasted over one thousand wines. I think that if daddy hadn't disgraced himself mummy would have been happy staying there all day and getting a skidoo down in the evening. Mummy ordered a bottle of wine, and some drinks for us and some nibbles. Whilst we were waiting, daddy appeared from the toilet but instead of coming over to the table he went over to our waiter and there was loads of pointing and then another man went over to daddy. He wasn't dressed like the waiters but was very smart indeed and had a name badge. Daddy then disappeared back into the toilet with both the waiter and the other man. After a couple of minutes all three emerged and daddy came up to our table and told us we had to leave as our wine and nibbles arrived. Mummy said that she was going to drink her wine and have her nibbles first but daddy said that we had to go "Now! And leave the wine and food" but mummy wasn't going anywhere. When daddy repeated what he had just said mummy told him how much the wine had cost and daddy looked very cross and asked mummy why she couldn't have picked a cheaper bottle. "Because that was the cheapest bottle," she explained whereupon daddy told her to put the cork back in and shove it in her rucksack along with the nibbles "because we have to go now!" daddy said again.

We did finally get down the mountain and we had a cheaper lunch but daddy didn't stay up this evening, he went to bed. It was only then that mummy told us what had happened at lunchtime. Daddy had had "a bit of a tummy" and had gone to the toilet and done a number two. Quite a large number two, in fact. When he tried to flush it away he couldn't 'cos the water pressure was so low. He tried a couple of times but the cistern was taking ages to refill and there was no loo brush and the poo was really stuck. In the end, when daddy reappeared, it was to do the right thing and inform the waiter and then the owner that his poo was stuck. The only problem was daddy speaks not much French, mainly food French only and no poo French and so the waiter and owner couldn't work out what the problem was so daddy beckoned them both into the toilet. The three of them crammed into daddy's cubicle; daddy lifted the lid and pointed at his enormous poo. The waiter and owner looked at it and then each other. "Watch," daddy said as he pressed the flush button whereupon a cascade of water came down the bowl and took daddy's torpedo off on its onward journey. The waiter and owner looked at each other, shrugged their shoulders and left. I don't think we'll be going there again.

Monday 12th February

Parlez-vous English?

Mummy came up on one of chairlifts behind us this morning as she wasn't concentrating. We watched in horror as she didn't realise that she was at the top 'cos she was texting and started to go back down again. The lift attendant had to press the emergency button and the whole lift stopped in order to let mummy off the chair. She only had to jump about fifteen centimetres but even then she squealed and fell over and so the lift man had to go over and rescue her. He said something to her in French which were words we didn't understand 'cos we had never heard them before but he wasn't very happy so we had some idea what he was

saying. Mummy tried to tell us that she didn't lift up the bar on the chairlift 'cos there was a sign on the last pylon that said "CLOSE" but daddy had to explain that "CLOSE" obviously means close as in "near" not "close" as in the opposite of "open."

Tuesday 13th February

Mummy gets ignored on the chairlift.

Big queues today. Mummy forgot to get off the chairlift again today. It was the same lift as yesterday AND it was the same lift attendant AND mummy was texting again. This time mummy looked up as the chair started to go back down again and she shouted "Help" at the lift attendant and waved but he just shrugged his shoulders, said something that we didn't understand (again) and went inside his little hut. Mummy had to go all the way back down again but they wouldn't let her stay on at the bottom and so she had to get off and then queue up from the back again. She missed her mid-morning coffee and when she got back up to the top of the lift (still texting) the attendant blew a whistle at her just as she was supposed to be lifting up the restraining bar so she dropped her 'phone in fright and then couldn't find it in the

deep snow when she went to look. Daddy tried ringing it but we couldn't hear anything. However we ascertained that there is a "CLOSE" sign on the last pylon but it also has a picture of a person lifting up the restraining bar so it should be obvious although mummy says that they could be closing it apart from the fact the arrow's pointing in the wrong direction. Mummy told me that if I go on a chair in front of her tomorrow and trip the emergency stop she will give me fifty Euros. I don't know what she's up to but I've agreed.

Wednesday 14th February
Mummy gets her 'phone back.
We all came up on the chairlift again today with me in front. I jumped off and when the lift attendant wasn't looking I kicked the emergency brake stick thing and skied round to the side of the lift. As the lift person went over to reset it I saw mummy leaning out of her chair about three down. Sam told me later that

they had stopped right next to the "CLOSE" pylon. Mummy produced a thick black Sharpie, leant out of the chair, crossed off

"CLOSE" and wrote "OPEN - NEAR" underneath. At least she was able to get off at the correct time with the rest of the family with her. As they went over where mummy had dropped her 'phone yesterday mummy commented that there was a big dip in the snow like someone had been digging. They got off the lift and mummy went to the attendant's office but it was a different person. Mummy explained that she had dropped her 'phone the day before and pointed to the place. The attendant went inside and came out with an envelope with "Fou femme anglaise" written on it which the attendant looked at and didn't give to mummy. The attendant opened the envelope and inside was mummy's 'phone. Mummy said, "Thank you very much," but the 'phone doesn't work now and she won't give Olivia her Sharpie back so

mummy has to get on chairlifts first now and not last. I got my fifty Euros though.

Thursday 15th February

Chairlift conversations with daddy.

Today daddy and I jumped on a six-man chairlift. Mummy was ahead of us. Daddy had me on one side and a little boy who was in ski-school on the other. We had been asked by the lift attendant if we would accompany him to the top of the lift just to make sure that he didn't fall off.

Daddy's always speaking to people whom he doesn't know and little boys are no exception. "Are you English or tu-es Francais?" daddy asked. The little boy was very polite and he said, "I am English." Then he added, just in case daddy wanted to speak in French (which he didn't), "I do speak a few French words also." Fortunately daddy didn't ask him which ones they were just in case they were a few that the little boy may have picked up from the lift attendant.

"And how old are you?"

"I'm eight."

"And are you staying in Flaine?"

"I'm not sure. Somewhere near here but I'm not exactly sure."

"That's useful. Have you skied before?"

"No, this is my first time."

"Are you enjoying it?"

"Yes. It's good fun."

"And you're having lessons?"

"Yes."

"Are you with your friends?"

"Yes. I have my sister Harriet and our friend Noah. All the other children are French."

"Do you have a French teacher?"

"Yes. His name is Christophe."

"Do you understand him?"

"No. He speaks English but it's not the sort of English that the three of us understand so we just follow the French children."

"That's a good idea."

"Not always. Because sometimes we follow them when they do the wrong things."

"That's not so good. Are you staying in a hotel or a chalet?"

"We're in a chalet. There's me and my mummy and daddy and me and Harriet. Then we have the Billinghursts. They have a mummy and a daddy and there's Daniel and Jack and Katie. We also have the Eyres family and their children. We did have Jamie as well but he's been sent home and he's staying with his auntie."

"Oh dear, poor Jamie. Has he been a naughty boy?"

"No, not really. Someone skied into him on the first day whilst he was at ski school and broke his leg." That stopped daddy talking for a moment but he soon regained his composure.

"Oh dear, that's terrible," said daddy who looked genuinely shocked. "And is he eight also?"

The little boy thought for a second then he said, "No he's not. I think he's forty-seven."

"Oh, I see. That's still pretty dreadful."

"Mummy says that the only dreadful thing is that when it's time to go home his wife will have to drive their family which is a bit of a concern to mummy because mummy say's that Jamie's wife is normally plastered."

"It sounds as though they're both plastered," daddy suggested but the little boy didn't say anything.

Fortunately we were at the top of the lift by this stage so daddy raised the bar and the little boy skied off to find his friends, but daddy spent the whole of the afternoon keeping his eye out for a group of children with a woman who was ever so slightly wobbly on her skis and looking more than a little out of control.

Friday 16th February

Bother on the black.

We met some friends of daddy's today. Their daddy is called Matt and he is an excellent skier. The weather was very misty but he said that if we just follow his black ski suit and orange helmet we would be okay. We might've been okay but I don't think anybody else thought that he was okay - from a distance he looked like a matchstick.

We went down a blue run which are the easy ones and then a green run which can be quite difficult 'cos they're almost flat and then a red run which are so called 'cos you normally see loads of blood on them, according to daddy. He says that red runs are the worse 'cos they're full of (mostly English) skiers who should be on the blues and French skiers that are good enough for blacks but who treat the reds as if they are practice slopes but still go as

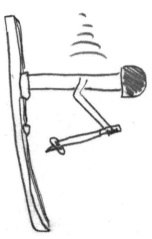 fast as if they were on a black. And daddy said that blacks are not allowed if you're young like me 'cos, "You don't see blood on black runs, just limbs." I had never been on a red run before and I soon fell over and no one saw me and my ski came off so I had to put it back on all by myself and it took ages. Then I looked up and Mr matchstick Matt was waiting for me a bit further down the slope and he started off again and I followed him. He went down a run that was called "Veroce" and it was really steep. Then it got even steeper and steeper and Matt was going faster and faster. Then I fell over again but I didn't stop this time and I just slid down and down and down. There was just no way that I could stop. I just kept on going - sliding then rolling and going really fast and someone was screaming so loudly as I went past. Then I hit a big softish bump and I took off then landed in some very deep snow which slowed my down. When I finally did come to a halt at the bottom of a lift there was another run going across me with loads of people on it. Then Matt came over to me but didn't say anything, he just waved up the mountain but no one could see him 'cos it was too foggy. Then more people came and stood round me and they

were all talking to themselves in not English. Then mummy suddenly appeared from out of the mist and through the crowd and she pushed everyone aside and lifted me up off the snow and asked me if anything was broken and I told her I didn't know but if it was it was a bit late now. Then she asked me where I had been and I said, "Following Matt" and then she picked me up in her arms and started to cry. Then she asked me where I had skied from and I pointed up the mountain and I said, "From up there," and Matt gasped and said that that was the blackest of black runs in Flaine and he sounded all squeaky. Mummy asked me why I had gone down it and I said that I was following Matt and then I looked over as Matt took off his helmet and it was a "her" and I said, "Oh dear," and mummy hugged me some more. Then she asked me where my skis were and real Matt appeared and pointed up Veroce and said, "Up there probably." Mummy started to get very cross and told me that I knew that they were hire skis and that she would probably have to pay a big fine and I said that I didn't do it on purpose. Matt said that it would be fine because the skis would reappear at the bottom of the run when the snow melts but mummy said that she wasn't going to stay in sweary word Flaine until May just for a pair of sweary word skis and then she just skied off and left me with Matt so Matt said, "We might as well do the black now, and do it properly, if it's okay with your mum and dad." I said to him that the only way that I could do it at present would be by walking down. Then we went and found mummy and decided that it was time for lunch.

After lunch Matt disappeared for twenty minutes with one of my boots and came back with a pair of skis for me that looked just like the ones that were on Veroce somewhere. He told mummy that he had hired them from his local shop and I should return them at the end of tomorrow. We

didn't do the black run again though and mummy skied next to me.

We had salade de gesiers for dinner tonight. Daddy went hungry.

Saturday 17th February
Mummy sorts out the skis to her satisfaction.
We skied this morning before packing and starting our drive home. Mummy took the barcode labels off my skis and took them back to our hire shop and told the man that the labels had peeled off by themselves. The man said that the labels do not peel off as they are heat-glued on but he took the skis anyway and didn't say anything else so mummy was happy. She told me that if Matt is bothered by the fact that it's now his and the other hire shop's problem and that if he's so concerned HE can come back in May to retrieve my skis. We've stopped at a place called Bourg en Bresse for the night.

Sunday 18th February
Dining disasters in Bourg en Bresse and a visit to Six Burgers of Calais.
We drove home today from Bourg en Bresse. It was a very long drive and quite boring. In fact very boring. At one point daddy was doing one hundred miles an hour. Mummy told daddy that the speed limit was one hundred and thirty kilometres (not miles) but because our car has no markings other than miles daddy wasn't sure what one hundred and thirty kilometres was in miles so he just guessed. We were overtaking loads of other cars though. Sam said that so long as there were more than one hundred and thirty hundredths of one hundred we were fine, but no one even knew how to calculate it so in the end daddy just slowed down. Whatever speed we were supposed to go at, we reached Calais sooner than expected. Daddy went on the motorway all the time which is quite expensive 'cos you have to pay which means that the only people on the motorways are lorries and the English who are in a hurry. Every so often we had

to take a ticket from a booth at a payage and then pay up at the end of that particular section. At one busy payage daddy went to the machine right at the end 'cos the queue was a bit shorter. Even though there were loads of lorries around there were fewer actual vehicles so daddy said, "Result!"

When mummy pressed the button no ticket came out. Then we didn't know what to do. Drivers spend a good few seconds trying to work out which queue is the shortest as they approach so to be stuck behind a car, especially an English one, causes all sorts of problems. People behind started bibbing their horns very loudly and mummy was now pressing all the buttons, including a red one which meant that someone started speaking to us but no one knew what the person was saying so all mummy said, well shouted actually, was, "Your [very sweary word] machine has not given me a [very sweary word] ticket!" The person behind the red button said, "En haut! En haut!" and it sounded like she was saying, "Oh no!" Daddy then got out of the car and went and told the man behind (who was English) that he would have to reverse 'cos the machine wasn't working. Unfortunately the man couldn't reverse 'cos there was a man behind him in a lorry who was French. Daddy went up to his cab and stretched his head up as far as he could at the driver but there was no one there. So he then had to go to the other side 'cos daddy had forgotten for a moment that drivers in France are in the wrong side of their vehicles. "NO TICKET!" said daddy when the man leant out of the window. The man said "Oh no!" also but was a bit more helpful in that he pointed at the machine, about two metres up.

There, sticking out of another slot was - a ticket. "That's very clever," said mummy. "The machine has a ticket height for cars and another for lorries." "Not if it thinks I'm a lorry," said daddy crossly. I don't now expect we'll be putting the roof box on the car again next time we drive to France.

We had plenty of time before our ferry sailed or whatever ferries do so daddy took us into the town for what he called "a bit of culture." I didn't think that there was any culture in Calais seeing as it was once owned by the British according to Sam and my opinion was confirmed when daddy said that we were going to the "Six Burgers of Calais" which Olivia and I reckoned was a fast-food restaurant. I didn't mind as I hadn't had a burger for a week so I was looking forward to a cheeseburger and chips. Sam wondered whether he could get one with a tex-mex sauce and Olivia was looking forward to a chicken burger. Unfortunately, when we found the burgers they weren't in the posh hotel that looks like Big Ben and the Houses of Parliament 'cos they were a statue of six bronze men dressed in bed sheets. So we got a bit of culture after all - but not much. We didn't fancy burgers after that so we went down the high street to a French-looking restaurant serving French food called Café de Paris. (The "é" in "Café" means it's pronounced like an "a" so why they can't just spell it "Cafa" I don't know. Maybe it's 'cos it would then be pronounced "Caf-ah" rather than "Caf-ay." Gosh, English is so difficult. No wonder the French people don't speak it very well. They still did burgers though. Mummy and daddy ate with us after the incident last night.

Last night we had stayed in a very modern hotel that mummy found on Hotel Hunter. Everything was bright colours - reds, yellows and greens - the walls, the furniture, the reception area. It was everywhere. Daddy said that it felt like he was in a pre-school nursery. Mummy said that she needed to go for a walk so she disappeared off and tried to book a table for us for the evening 'cos the hotel didn't do food, just breakfast, and we didn't want that for dinner. She couldn't find anywhere that was reasonably priced but not fully booked so, in despair, on the way back she went into the restaurant on the corner which was part of the theatre and which was called Brasserie de la Theatre and very expensive she told us. She said that they only had one table for two available and so she booked that for her and daddy and us children were sent to a pizzeria next door to the hotel that wasn't particularly cheap but had space. Sam had mummy's debit card. I don't know why mummy and daddy couldn't have had a pizza with us. Mummy said that it was because she had already booked the posh place but given what happened she probably wished that she had come with us.

Mummy and daddy went out looking all smart and the three of us children went next door wearing the same clothes that we had been in for the car journey so we looked like the sort of people who would appreciate a pizza.

We all left at seven o'clock as mummy didn't want us out late. When we arrived there was no one else in the pizzeria so we could choose which table we wanted. We chose the biggest one which was just as well. The lady who served us was Italian but she didn't speak any English and the menu was all in French and Italian so we decided just to have a bit from every section. The first was called "Primo" and it was mostly salads so we ordered one each. The lady kept putting one finger up like she wanted us to have one between three but we were hungry so we had a salad each. Then the next section was "Bruschetta" and Sam knew what that was. He told us it was like pizza toppings but on bread so we ordered one of those each as well and the Italian lady kept smiling at us still waving her one finger in the air. We felt very sorry for her 'cos there was no one else in the restaurant and so she wasn't going to make much money so we then looked at the menus some more and found pizzas. We ordered one of those each and then she made a drinking sign so we ordered some lemonade by making fizzy noises but something went wrong and Sam got a bottle of grand Prosecco. We ate the salads okay but they were quite big and when the bruschetta came they were like pizzas only bread instead of pizza base which is like bread anyway. We managed to eat them and then pizzas turned up and they were enormous so we ate them very slowly and we were really stuffed and Sam had to help Olivia out but we managed them all apart from the crusts so we hid them under the tablecloth. By the time that we had finished Sam had drunk all the Prosecco and said that the room was moving which it wasn't and there still weren't any other people at the other tables so we asked for pudding. Then the lady took the tablecloth off and looked at our crusts and we said that they weren't ours but they were still warm.

The lady said that pudding was "glace" and we knew what that was and she said it was "homemade" 'cos she managed that word in English so Sam had lemon sorbet and I had a berry one and so did Olivia. Then the lady held up one finger but Sam held up three on each hand but he had no idea what she was on about 'cos we weren't going to share an ice cream. We found out soon enough when they turned up and we had six scoops each and then a man came over with a bottle of vodka and poured loads of it over Sam's sorbet. We didn't really need a drink after that but we felt sorry for the lady and the man and their empty restaurant so we ordered a hot chocolate each 'cos we can do those in French and when they turned up Sam said he needed to go to the toilet. He didn't know how to ask for the toilet in French or Italian so he just stood up and pointed at his willy and the lady smiled and showed him a door down some steps. When he returned a few minutes later he was giggling and he said that downstairs there was another part of the restaurant that opened onto another street 'cos we were on a hill and we must have come in the back way and there were loads of people down there so Olivia and I then both had to go to the toilet and it was true - downstairs was full up and very, very busy so then we were happy and felt that we didn't need to order anything else - except the bill. The lady understood "bill" alright though. When it came up and Sam looked at it he went very pale 'cos we had spent about four times what mummy had suggested but we had to pay it. Then the lady brought us another drink each and I've no idea what it was but we drank it. Anyway once we were all finished and just about to leave mummy and daddy came in. Sam gave the receipt to mummy and said that he had been on a bit of a bender and mummy gave the bill to daddy who asked Sam if the total was in Euros and was the dot in the wrong place? Sam said that he had no idea and he was just helping the lady out. When daddy said that our meal was more than double per head what he had just paid in one of the most expensive restaurants in Bourg en Bresse Sam said, "I'll put some of it back then," and promptly threw up.

Looking back I think Sam should've asked for a doggy bag at some point, maybe several points, but knowing France that's exactly what we would've got in our bag - doggy.

Monday 19th February
A quiet day - for Sam.
Back to school today for Olivia and me. Sam didn't go to school today. He stayed in bed.

Tuesday 20th February
"Horace" is in danger.
Mummy told me today that the name "Horace" is in danger of extinction. Sam said that he had looked up in Numerology and found that "Horace" is number 5. Apparently 5s are explorers who love to connect with others. "Curious and impulsive, they're free-spirited, enjoy travelling, and adapt easily to new situations. They're philosophers at heart and make new friends easily."

So, as most people seem to spend their lives sitting on a sofa watching TV or getting a twitchy finger on their electronic games, it's hardly surprising that there aren't many of us Horaces left. Sam reckons that there aren't many people called Horace 'cos it's an anagram of "Chorea," whatever that is.

Wednesday 21st February
The balling of paint or the painting of ball.
Three days until paintballing. Emily said that she wasn't going to go 'cos it didn't sound very nice.

Thursday 22nd February
Charlie and his emergency pants.
Charlie's hair looked normal at school this morning but by lunchtime it was sticking up in the air like he had seen a giant ghost. When I asked him what the problem was he told me that he was wearing the emergency pants 'cos his mummy was behind with the laundry. He said that they were nylon which meant that every time he walked down a corridor he generated loads of static electricity which made his hair stand on end. It's just as well he's not running anywhere 'cos he might set light to himself.

Friday 23rd February
Scouts aren't horses Skip.
Charlie doesn't appear to be wearing his nylon pants today.

We were all standing outside the scout hut this evening when a very badly behaved horse clip-clopped past with its owner down to the stables. Skip said to the owner, "They're just like naughty little children, aren't they?" The owner said, "Yes, but at least I can lock Ralph up in his box for the night and throw a bit of straw at him," to which Skip replied, "Now there's an idea." Charming.

Charlie said to me in a loud voice, "Horace what sort of mad person would call their horse, 'Ralph?'" Unfortunately the owner heard and so she said to her horse but I think mainly to us, "Ralph what sort of mad person would call their child, 'Horace?'"

Saturday 24th February
I spy. Such a stupid game.
We had a great scout trip today to go paintballing and we went in a minibus. Emily came after we realised what her problem was which was that she thought that it was called "painballing." It was such fun and I think I've found a great way to redecorate our sitting room. I'll suggest it to daddy. Buy a paintball gun each and a load of paintballs, clear out all the furniture and then have an enormous great battle. We all got some great bruises and Mel's got one that's apparently really big but she wouldn't show anyone apart from Emily 'cos of where it is. Having thought about it, maybe it should be called "painballing" after all.

On the way home Archie suggested we play "I spy." It was going fine until Charlie had a go. No one could guess his "N" so he said, "Knee." Then Mel had to explain that that was "K" but he said that wasn't fair and demanded another go and said, "L and it's also on your body." No one could guess that either so he said, "Elbow." Then Mel had to explain that that was "E" and Charlie said that that wasn't fair either and so had another go and said,

"R." No one guessed "Wrist" and he started to sulk when Mel said that that begun with "W" so Emily suggested he stayed away from body parts. Emily was then allowed a go and said "I" and Charlie said, "Eye" and we all laughed but Charlie didn't. When we got back to the scout hut we were still playing and Edward was on "W." When no one knew what it was he said "Worm." "I can't see any worms," Archie said but Emily just pointed at the ground. "You can't see them but we know they're there." Whilst we were waiting for our parents it was Archie's turn so he chose "G." When no one got the right word he said, "God," and Emily said, "I can't see

him," and Archie replied, pointing to the sky, "I can't see him either but we know he's there," and with that point Archie won. I don't think we'll be playing I spy again anytime soon. Or painballing.

Sunday 25th February
Spoilsport daddy strikes.
Daddy has vetoed the paintballing decorating idea.

Monday 26th February
Daddy needs to realise that the world has moved on, but he hasn't.
Daddy decided to go to the gym today which is not something that he does very often. However I don't think he'll be going back soon after he came back dressed in only his towel. Actually, although he went to the gym he didn't do gym stuff he did swimming. When he came out of the pool and went to get dressed there were a load of other men by his padlock and a

manager with a pair of bolt-cutters in his hands. One of the men pointed at a padlock next to daddy's and said, "That's the one." Apparently the man's combination on the lock didn't work. The

manager bolt-cutted the padlock and inside the locker there was - nothing. "Where's my 'phone and where are my clothes?" he wailed. "Are you sure that you have the correct locker sir?" the bolt-cutter manager asked. "Yes, of course. Someone's stolen my gear and put another lock on. Get the CCTV out and let's have a look." "I'm afraid that there's no CCTV in the changing rooms, sir," said the bolt-cutter manager, "for, ahem, personal reasons." At this point daddy butted in and said that despite cameras being everywhere in the gym the one place where they would be of most use is the one place where they're not. After all," he continued, "I wouldn't be too worried about one of the young ladies on reception looking at me in the changing rooms..." At this point bolt-cutter manager walked off and came back with security and daddy was asked to leave "Now!" even though he tried to explain that he was trying to say that the greater good was identifying the locker thief over one's person being filmed whilst in the altogether but it was too late, the damage had been done.

Mummy's not very happy either and said, "Oh the shame. I can't go back there. I'll have to change membership to another club," but then she started fretting over what she would have to put as the "extenuating circumstances" in order not to have to pay a three-month cancellation charge. Daddy suggested "Pregnancy." Mummy said, "How about, 'Husband in prison?'"

Tuesday 27th February
Sam's showering routine is a little unconventional.

Sam had a shower this morning before school which was a bit odd. Then he told me that he was seeing Tanya after school which wasn't so odd. Then he put on some after-shave, ha ha, which was only a little bit odd. When he came home after school and after Tanya he said that he was having a shower 'cos "I smell of after-shave and perfume and I don't want to smell like this for football practice." So he had another shower. When he came home from football practice he was soaking wet and muddy 'cos of the weather. He also smelt really sweaty. He came in the back door

and took off (most of) his clothes and left them on the mat with his boots. "I'm going to bed now mum," he said. "Aren't you going to have a shower first?" mummy asked him. He said, "No, I don't need one." That was until mummy said that Tanya had called and she was popping round with something that he had left at her house.

I'm glad I don't have a girlfriend. I can have a shower when I need it, not when anybody else thinks I do.

Wednesday 28th February
World Book Day - almost!
The day that I have been looking forward to for weeks - World Book Day! I went dressed as my favourite book character which is Tintin. I went as Tintin in "Tintin in America" and I was really pleased that mummy had helped get my costume ready. I had some baggy trousers, a checked shirt, a scarf like a scout scarf but worn the wrong way round and a big hat. I also took a long stick with a shoelace attached to the end. This was my whip. "I'll be

the best-dressed character in the whole of the school," I thought as I walked into my classroom. Why did no one tell me?

Unfortunately I was the only book character in the school as I was a day early for World Book Day. Today was the school photo day. You won't miss me in the photo, that's for sure. Everyone is wearing very smart school uniform apart from me. I'm the only one dressed as a cowboy. Sir put me in the back row and I put my hat on Charlie's head 'cos he said that he didn't want to be missed either.

Thursday 1st March
World Book Day - actual!
World Book Day. Stuff Tintin. I went as myself. "Forget, did we?" asked sir sarcastically. Little does he know that my Tintin uniform less the hat will be around for much longer than he will be.

Sam had one of his Christmas bath bombs this evening. Unfortunately it was a twinkle one. It does say on the bag "Stand out from the crowd at the party" but Sam didn't read that or question it and now he's covered in thousands of little sparkly flakes that have stuck to him which he can't get off. Tomorrow should be fun at school for him.

Daddy has strained the slow gin mixture this evening and will bottle it tomorrow.

Friday 2nd March

Please Mr Postman has no winners.

Sam was sent home from school today. His teacher told him that World Book Day was yesterday and "No, you can't come today dressed as a glitter ball."

Skip was really told off tonight at scouts. We played "Please Mr Postman" which is a wide game that we do in the woods. Skip hands out envelopes and we have to go and find leaders in turn (who might be hiding) to get the envelopes addressed, then return addressed then stamped and then the envelope has to be posted in a box before starting all over again. It all has to be done in order and the scout with most envelopes posted at the end is the winner. Skip said that to remember "Address, Return address and Stamp" in that order we had to think "ARS" and he wrote it on the white board in large letters. Apparently Ars is, according to Skip, a village in Iran. Charlie suggested that once we had stamped the envelope we needed to post the envelope and so should add an "E" which Skip did. Unfortunately the game was a draw. Everyone drew with a total of zero envelopes posted. The problem was that Charlie's daddy was on stamps but no one could find him. We were a bit late back to the scout hut and when we were doing flag down Charlie's

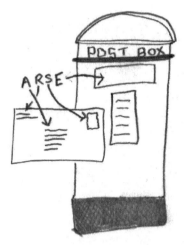

daddy reappeared. He staggered in smelling of something and slumped down on a bench and giggled. He said that he had been well hidden but Skip didn't say anything. Then Mel's mummy came in. She's a bit posh. She took one look at the whiteboard and demanded to know why it had "ARSE" written on it. Before

Skip could say anything Charlie's daddy said that Skip was teaching us an alphabet of sweary words and that by Christmas we should be on "Z" but for now we had only learnt "A." The scouts all sniggered but Mel's mummy said, "Well, we'll see about that," and she walked over to the whiteboard and rubbed the word out with her hand. "Now we're never going to get our envelopes delivered," Emily complained with a smile but Mel's mummy was looking really cross so no one laughed - except Charlie's daddy who was by now lying on the bench saying to himself, "There's loads of 'B' words; I can think of at least six," at which point he fortunately fell asleep.

Daddy has bottled the slow gin and he said that he now has to keep it in his office "to mature" and it should be ready by Christmas.

Saturday 3rd March
Shopping for mummy goes a bit wrong.
Mummy sent Sam and me to the supermarket to get a few bits of shopping for lunch. We were just about to put all our stuff on the conveyor belt thing by the cashier when Sam reckoned we had enough for extra sweets. "Leave the basket there," Sam said, pointing at the metal basket-rest ledge bit at the start of the conveyor belt, "so that no one pushes in and then we can get a couple of bars each." We were only gone about ten seconds but when we got back an old man had already pushed in. "I'm very sorry," he said, "but I thought the basket had been abandoned." We said that it was fine and then he said, "The thing is, I'm not very good at this shopping lark but I always insist on doing it. Women don't do it properly, you know. They come in for one thing and leave with a dozen extra bits. It drives me mad. Men do it much better. Organised. In - shop - out. Done." Sam and I just nodded. "For example," the man droned on whilst packing his bags, "I bet you

do the shopping better than your mother, that's why she's sent you." "That would be a bit difficult," Sam said. "'Cos she's dead." "Oh I'm sorry," said the man looking as embarrassed as I looked surprised. He didn't say anything after that. "Why did you say that Sam?" I asked, once the man had gone. "I was just getting bored listening to him, that's all." I then told Sam that he could have just said that she was ill. "Yeah, with a hangover," Sam chuckled. We then packed our bag before paying and leaving. "Come on," Sam said, we still have some change. Let's go to Sweet Sundae and get some gobstoppers. On the way out of the supermarket we went past one of our old neighbours so we said, "Hello." I don't know his name but we thought we ought to ask if he was alright. He was sitting on a chair behind the cashiers reading a newspaper and drinking a coffee. "I'm fine," he said. "Do you want us to help you with your shopping?" I asked. "Certainly not," he replied. "You don't get a dog and bark yourself. No way. I've got Mildred doing the shopping. Women do shopping so much better than men don't you think? So much more organised. Men, in my experience, make a proper hash of it so I just sit here and wait. That's the best way for a man to shop, don't you agree?" "Err, oh yes, probably," Sam said and then we bustled outside to eat our sweets whilst walking up to Sweet Sundae. I told Sam that it must be very confusing being an adult and believing different things. We both decided that when we were married we would go shopping with our wives although we would have to hide the sweets.

We went into Sweet Sundae and bought a mega gobstopper each with our change. I think that you're supposed to lick them but we put them in our mouths and then couldn't speak. We had only gone a few feet up the road when a man pulled over next to us in his car, wound down the

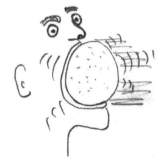

passenger window and asked where the nearest car park was. Sam put down the shopping bag and leant on the car window but couldn't speak. Instead he started to go a funny colour. "Slap him hard on his back," the man in the car commanded. "He may be choking." I didn't need telling twice to hit my brother so I thumped him smartly on his back between his shoulder blades. Sam coughed then gasped as his slightly smaller by now, but only slightly, mega gobstopper shot out of his mouth, bounced off the shelf above the dashboard and cracked the front windscreen. The man's faced changed to thunder and he started to unbuckle his seatbelt so we decided to run. We ran all the way home through the woods. When we got home mummy asked us where the shopping was so Sam told her that we had been mugged which might have been true had we not run although we did so we weren't but if we hadn't then we might have been so it was nearly true so that was okay.

Sunday 4th March
The everlasting gobstopper.
I finished my mega gobstopper today. I didn't keep it in my mouth all night, I put it on the carpet by my bed so that I could find it easily and start on it again first thing this morning but it wasn't as nice 'cos it was all fluffy like I was sucking one of George's fur balls.

Monday 5th March
268 bus takes a different route - for one day only.
Sam was really late for school today. The 268 bus has the relief driver who hates talking to people so he goes from Bexleyheath to Croydon on non-route roads so he doesn't have to pick anybody up.

Tuesday 6th March
Skip's been suspended.
Sam came home from school and said that Tanya had told him that Skip's been suspended from scouts.

Wednesday 7th March
Charlie's daddy comes clean.
Charlie told me at school today that he's found out from his mummy what happened to his daddy last Friday evening. Apparently he was so cold waiting for the scouts to find him that he walked to the end of the footpath and climbed over the back fence of the Lion's Head and went in for a drink or three. "It was a good hiding place, wasn't it son?" he said to Charlie with a smile. I don't think he's going to be asked to help again.

Thursday 8th March
The school photo suffers.
Oh dear. Sir said that the school photo is going to have to be retaken in its entirety "thanks to you and Charlie." Apparently the head teacher sir has seen the proofs and he's not very happy. Apparently sir told sir that he didn't want a couple of children in the photo that appear to have raided their dressing-up boxes and daddy was going to get a bill. Next year I'm going to go to World Book Day as me - again.

Friday 9th March
Archie the gentleman - nearly.
Patrick was in charge tonight. He said that Skip was "incapacitated" at present. Both Archie and Emily have colds. Emily sneezed a huge sneeze and so Archie leant her one of his cotton hankies. "I always keep a spare," he told her. After she had finished wiping her nose and all

around her face very thoroughly Archie said, "Sorry. I've given you the wrong hankie. That's not the spare."

Saturday 10th March

I'm a scout, not a guide.

We're doing "I'm a scout, get me out of here" today with the explorers and the district. You have to do certain tasks and one 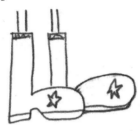 by one groups are evicted to another campsite. Tanya's group were evicted first and off they went through the countryside with Skip (who's still allowed to do district things) and another scout leader who wasn't very nice. "Look at that girl," the other scout leader said, pointing at Tanya from behind. "She's wearing wellingtons. She should be in the guides." "That's my daughter," said Skip. "Oh, er..." said the other scout leader, then shut his mouth.

Sunday 11th March

A new edition to the family - temporarily.

Big screams from the bathroom this morning. Sam had left his skinny jeans on the bathroom floor last night and was a bit bemused to find little bits of shredded denim on the carpet this morning. He put his jeans back on for Own Clothes Day and then screamed 'cos there was something crawling up the back of his leg by his knee on the inside of his jeans. He took them off slowly and shook them over the toilet without looking. When he opened his eyes there was no creature in the toilet and not on the carpet either so there is obviously still a live mouse in the house,

brought in by George probably. Everyone is on high alert and mummy spent the evening walking round with a kitchen knife in her hand.

Monday 12th March
'Phone issues at Explorers.
Sam isn't very happy 'cos explorer leader Chrissie has told him

that mobile 'phones are now allowed but must be kept in pockets throughout the whole of their meetings. Sam reckons that that's like having a packet of cigarettes in your jacket but not being allowed to smoke one, not that he would know. I did suggest that he leaves his 'phone at home but apparently that's not an answer. For some strange reason he would rather have his 'phone with him that he can't use but could sit on and break or melt round the camp fire rather than leave it safely at home (for me to play on but he doesn't know that bit).

Tuesday 13th March
Miscellaneous stuff in the freezer.
Mummy's been having a bit of a clear out of all the leftover stuff from Christmas that she had bagged up and put in the freezer. This explains why I was presented with a bag of stewed red cabbage to go on my porridge this morning. "I thought they were blueberries," mummy said. I asked her why anybody would want to freeze stewed cabbage. "No one eats it even

when it's freshly made so why bother freezing it? You might as well just make it and then chuck it away. Anyway, what was written on the freezer bag?" "Carrots" apparently. I don't understand.

Wednesday 14th March
Has mummy found the new addition to the family?
Mummy did "ladies who lunch" today. She put on her posh clothes and long leather boots and went off to the Italian up the road. She was only part of the way through her starter when she felt something move by her toes. She screamed so loudly that a man heard it from outside and across the road and came running in. One of mummy's friends took her boot off and once she had calmed down mummy said that there was something alive in her boot but whatever it was was probably squashed. Mummy's  friend, the one who's an Akela so quite used to little squeaky creatures, carefully removed the offending boot and tipped it up over the water jug. Out dropped George's clockwork mouse with a plop and then it started to swim around in the water. "Waiter there's a mouse in my water," said mummy's friend, the one who drinks too much, and they cackled. Mummy didn't though and she walked home with her boots in her hand and I had to recheck them this evening. I gave them the "all clear" and the real culprit is still at bay.

Thursday 15th March
"Knights of Weye" permit awaited.
Olivia came back from cubs tonight and told me that she's going camping soon, once Akela had renewed her "Knights of Weye" permit whatever that is.

Daddy took a teaspoon out of the kitchen tonight in a tumbler. He said that he's just checking on the slow gin and the tumbler is for keeping the spoon in so as not to make any mess.

Friday 16th March

Edward gets a new haircut.

Skip's back! He told us that "A-R-S-E" is a sweary word and not one that we should use when playing "Please Mr Postman." Now how is anyone going to remember the order? I hope Mel's mummy's satisfied.

Edward's turned up with a haircut that Skip called "sharp." Edward usually has a good haircut but this one is all styled with a shaved back and a gelled front. Skip asked him where he had it done. "Barry Gibsonne," Edward said. "He's up in London and is a designer hairdresser and it's really expensive." "Oh," said Skip. "How much does he charge?" "I don't know," Edward said, "but my mum goes to him as well and he charges her about two thousand pounds." "Really?" said Skip. "That's quite a lot." "She gets a glass of Champagne with that as well." "I should think for two grand she should get a case," said Skip.

Saturday 17th March

Good news for mummy - I'm alive!

Mummy's received a refund on her credit card from the ski hire shop in Samoens. She rang them up to query it and they said that the police had brought in my skis having found them on the Veroce piste. Apparently a skier had found one of the skis then the other sticking out of the ground and told a lift attendant. They then closed the piste for the rest of the day and used avalanche transceivers, sniffer dogs and an army of volunteers to dig the snow to try to find me before deciding that the body, i.e. me, was not frozen to death on the piste but safe at home in Chislehurst. I don't think mummy's going to tell daddy though as she doesn't want Matt to find out.

Sunday 18th March

The new addition to the family is no more.
Mummy came downstairs first this morning and screamed but not a big scream. She found a decapitated mouse by the front door. Sam said that cats often only eat the heads 'cos the brains are a cat delicacy. I'm glad I'm not a cat.

Monday 19th March

More 'phone issues at Explorers.
Sam's phone rang at explorers this evening. Chrissie tried to confiscate it but Sam said that she couldn't 'cos it was still in his pocket. Chrissie said that if it happened again she would make the explorer put the 'phone on loudspeaker. Tanya said that that was an invasion of privacy but Chrissie told her to just turn her 'phone off. I need to speak to Tanya.

Tuesday 20th March

Sam steals the school's Energetic Kids vouchers.
I am going to be in so much trouble! Miss asked me at school today if I would count up to see how many of the supermarket Energetic Kids vouchers we had collected so far. She let me bring them home to do it. She gave me a carrier bag and some elastic

bands. It took me all evening and I had a bit of help! I counted 15,455 points, that's the result of over £150,000 being spent! I put them in piles of a thousand each and then in elastic bands

before putting them back in the carrier bag and leaving it by the front door to take to school in the morning. Then they went missing and I've found out that Sam has stolen them! He took them up to explorers tonight 'cos 3rd Chislehurst are collecting and he put them in their collecting box with his name on them. Apparently the scout that collects the most gets a prize. Sam said that he's bound to win. When I told him that the vouchers belonged to the school he said that the school doesn't give prizes and only buys boring stuff like pom poms and dance scarves whereas Skip will get tents. With that number of vouchers I should think he'll be able to get a whole campsite. It the meantime, what am I going to do?

Wednesday 21st March
Things are looking up!
I have Tanya's mobile number. Result!

Thursday 22nd March
Mouse gets me into trouble even in death.
I told sir in biology today that mummy had found evidence of George's decapitation last weekend by the front door. "Oh dear, that sounds serious," said sir. "Did you call the police?" I said that I hadn't.

After lunch I had to go and see the

school's safeguarding officer and answer loads of questions. At the end when she asked me if I had anything else to add I said that I thought that it was quite a lot of fuss for one field mouse at which point miss slammed her folder shut and said, "So do I" and walked off.

Friday 23rd March
Injured Emily and a not quite scalped Edward.
We were whittling today at scouts. We had to make woggles from small blocks of wood by drilling through them and then smoothing them off, then we had to use a heated pen thing to burn our initials on them. First Emily whittled her finger then she burnt it so I was asked to do first aid. We have quite a big first aid kit at the scout hut which is just as well although it's always in a bit of a muddle 'cos people just pull things out quickly which is hardly surprising 'cos of having to deal with emergencies and stuff. I cleaned the wound, cooled it down under the tap, found and applied a padded sterile gauze dressing which looked quite thick and loads of tape to hold it in place. All in all it looked quite professional. I was very pleased with myself.

Edward's hair continues to intrigue Skip. Not one strand had moved since last week. "I look after it Skip," Edward said. "Obviously. Where did you say you had it cut?" "I have it cut by Barry Gibsonne but this time I had it done at 'Scissor Stanley's.'" Scissor Stanley is the local hairdressers' in the high street. Scissor Stanley doesn't so much dress hair as

scalp it. Skip looked at Edward a little disbelievingly. "The thing is," Edward continued, "Barry Gibsonne was having an exhibition haircut with a talk and advice and stuff and as I am such a good customer and 'cos he knows that I live in Chislehurst he invited me down to model my hair for him." "Oh I see," said Skip, but I don't think he did and I don't think Skip thought that Edward was telling the whole truth.

Saturday 24th March
Sam's football team gets beaten.
Sam's not very happy today. His football team that he plays in had reached the quarter finals of whatever cup they're playing for and they played their next game today and lost two-one. "It was so unfair," he complained to daddy. "Both of their goals should've been disallowed. One was a result of a penalty that wasn't a penalty and the other was clearly offside. All the spectators were screaming and shouting at the ref but both goals stood. Everyone was really angry apart from the other team of course," he said. "I'm surprised that there wasn't a pitch invasion," daddy said calmly. "How many spectators were there at this crunch match?" "Two dad." "'Two?' So the ref hardly needed police protection?" daddy replied. "No," said Sam, "but I called him a wazzock as we came off the pitch." "I'll expect he'll survive," daddy suggested.

Sunday 25th March
First-aid fiasco.
Mummy woke up with a "hurray" today 'cos the clocks have gone forward one hour. I didn't know why she was so happy 'cos we've all lost an hour's sleep  and we won't get it back until October and there was an empty

wine bottle on the kitchen table. But I found out later when we went for our spring walk and bumped into Mike the vicar. Mike said to mummy that she looked very well and she said, "That's because the clocks have gone forward and when the clocks go forward I can start drinking rosé and I can continue drinking rosé all through the summer until the clocks go back in October." "As good a reason as any," said Mike, but then I said, "What about skiing?" When mummy looked at me with a puzzled expression I said, "You know mummy, when we were at the teddy bear hotel in Samoens and you drank a magnum of rosé and that was in February." "Doesn't count in France," said mummy abruptly. Honestly, I don't know why she hasn't moved to France instead of making all this fuss about a funny-coloured wine. Mike was more interested in the magnum. "A magnum all to yourself, Karen?" he said. "That's quite impressive." "David had a couple of glasses," mummy said. "Well I know what your new year's resolution's going to be!" said Mike but I put him straight. "Maybe. But she always does the 'no drinking' one but it only lasts...well not very long." I didn't want to say how long 'cos I didn't want to get mummy into trouble and I didn't want to say that mummy hadn't even started her book club new year's resolution yet but then Mike suggested, "A week or two?" "Actually," I told him, 'cos then I didn't want to lie, "mummy normally only lasts until about lunchtime, and an early lunchtime at that, one that you could probably call 'elevenses.'" So I probably did get mummy into trouble but she will never know unless Mike tells and he won't 'cos he's not allowed and 'cos by this time mummy was halfway up the road and out of earshot so I said "goodbye" to Mike and ran after mummy who held my hand tightly. She said that she was feeling a little unsteady and so to reassure her I said, "It's probably 'cos you missed out on an hour's sleep," and mummy said, "Possibly but not probably," and gave me a kiss even though we were outside.

Later this afternoon Mummy had a call from Skip who's had a call from Emily's mummy. She wanted to say "thank you" for caring for Emily's burn on Friday but wondered why I had taped a sanitary pad to Emily's finger.

Monday 26th March

Supermarket conversation causes consternation.

Mummy sent me down to the local supermarket today to buy a few bits for dinner. I went through the till that had the meaty man on it. He's very friendly and his name is "Jock" and he says things like "Hallo young man, how are you today?" which is nice 'cos he looks genuinely interested and he smiles and he listens to you while you tell him. The problem is that he doesn't start scanning until you've finished speaking so if you have a lot of ailments it could take quite a long time to get your shopping packed and paid for. I normally just say "I'm fine thank you." That wasn't good enough for Jock today though 'cos he then said, "Oh that's good to hear. Better than me then. I've had a bit of a funny pain in my leg this week. It started a few days ago..." and off he went while I just nodded. The best bit though is when he's scanning your food. He talks about all the stuff you're buying. Everything. He says things like "Blueberries? I love blueberries. They're great on Weetabix or in a berry smoothie with some bananas." Or "Washing powder? That's a nice large pack. That should keep your mum going for a while. Everyone needs to keep their clothes clean although there are some people who never seem to ever buy any. I prefer the non-bio myself..." and so on. It's quite funny if you're not in a rush. There was a woman behind me who looked as though she was in a bit of a hurry which was fun 'cos she only had a few bits and started to tut as soon as Jock asked me how I was. Then he saw my venison sausages in red wine. "Oh," he said, "Are you over eighteen? Ha, ha! I haven't tried those. I wonder what they're like?" As I had plenty of time, well more time than the tutting lady behind me I thought that I would play him at his own game. "They are really yummy," I said. "I love the just-a-position of strong and weak, the embattled deer and the heady claret coming together in a sausage." I didn't know what I was talking about but daddy had said it once and it sounded good and meaty man rose to the challenge, totally ignoring the woman who was now not only tutting but sighing as well. "I bet they're nice in a toad in the hole," he suggested. "Oh yes, that's when the toad comes into its own with meat and wine and, um, stuff." The woman had had enough. "Next time you want to have a chin-wag you need to close your till and go and have a coffee. For now, that's what I'm going to do and I'M NOT COMING BACK!" she shouted as she stormed off. Jock was totally unfazed. "Well would you believe it?" he said to me, pointing at the woman's shopping that

was sitting on the conveyor belt. "You've got to be a bit of a cheapskate to buy that sort of chocolate bar. You can't do anything with that. It's certainly not edible. And look at that cereal. It's full of sugar. No wonder she was so short-tempered. I hope for the well-being of the baristas that there's not a queue in the coffee shop," and we both giggled like little schoolboys. Well I am a little schoolboy so I was alright. I hope I'm like him when I grow up. Not meaty though, just happy. I think that I'll always go to his till when I'm in his supermarket.

Tuesday 27th March
Great aunt Poppy and the passport.
Mummy's great, great aunt Poppy has a lovely little sausage dog called William and she brought him to tea today. Apparently he has his own passport. I wonder if it has his photo in it? Poppy said that when she applied she had to go and see a man in an office and fill in (or fill out - I'm never sure which) a long form. "Name?" he asked, full of pompous officialdom. "Poppy," Poppy

said. The man looked up. "Not your dog's name madam, your name," he sighed. "'Poppy,'" Poppy said. "My name's 'Poppy.' The dog's name's 'William.'" The man sighed again.

Wednesday 28th March
More supermarket shenanigans.
Whoops. Big problem today. I broke the large kitchen knife. The one that's mummy's favourite. I was trying to open a tin of baked beans and I needed to stab it with a knife 'cos the ringpull had broken and I couldn't find the tin opener. First of all I stabbed it to make a hole then I tried to prise the lid open by putting the knife tip in. Unfortunately there was a loud ping and the end of the knife broke off, quite a large end actually, so large that there was no way that mummy wasn't going to notice. I hid the knife 'cos she would just think that she had put it somewhere else like

in the dishwasher. Then, when daddy came home from work, I told him 'cos I needed to buy a new one but I had no money and I knew that he wouldn't be cross. Daddy said that he would have to come with me 'cos I'm too young to buy knives. Daddy told mummy that we were just popping out to the supermarket and mummy said that she needed some tights. When we arrived we got a basket and we found mummy's tights and then we found a really good-looking kitchen knife that was similar to the broken one.

We went to queue up for my favourite cashier but just as we arrived at the end of the conveyor belt a woman pushed in front of us. I thought she was with the people that were being served but she wasn't. She turned round and sort of beckoned to a man who suddenly appeared next to her with a basket full of food. The woman started to put their stuff on the conveyor belt. Neither of the couple would look at daddy who was just standing there staring at them with his mouth open wide. Then he suddenly said in a loud voice, "EX-CUSE ME!" The man looked at daddy out of the corner of his eye. That was enough for daddy and he said to the man, "Is she your runner? Do you follow her everywhere, being told what to do?" With that the woman turned round, looked at daddy and muttered, "How rude." Daddy put his basket down on the metal ledge at the start of the conveyor belt ready to remonstrate some more. But he needn't have bothered. The woman looked in daddy's basket and then looked at daddy. Then she started putting her husband's items back in their basket. "What are you doing?" the man asked and the woman just nodded in the direction of daddy's basket. The man said, "Oh," and off they went to the self-service checkout. "Never let someone push in front of you Horace, just because you're a child," said daddy. "And if they do in the future I'm going quickly to show you something that will be of great help. If you feel down here..."

"Hallo young man," said Jock, "and hallo dad. How are we today?" "Fine," I said. "They were a queer pair, weren't they?" he said nodding in the direction of the scarpering couple. "Maybe they were suddenly too embarrassed with buying long life milk - and skimmed milk at that. What is the world coming to? Milk is milk and it's blue top all the way for me. If you buy red top you might as well be buying water. Now what have we here today? Ah yes, a nice pair of tights. I expect these are for your lucky lady. And what else? Oh. Oh." Jock had seen the knife but he had to say something. "And, err, what are you going to be doing with the knife?" "The bank," said daddy without missing a beat, "once we've put the tights over our heads." In the distance a bell started clanging and Jock began to speak very slowly. "It's - nice - weather - for - the - time - of - year. Only - the - other - day - I -

was - saying - to..." "Can we just pay?" asked daddy impatiently as a security guard came and stood at the back of the till. Jock took daddy's money and started to count the change in small coins. "Keep the change," said daddy as he picked up the knife and tights and brushed past the security guard who held out his hand but did nothing more.

On the way up the high street a police car came whizzing past us towards the supermarket and as we went into the woods on a short cut it came whizzing back the other way with its blue lights flashing but no wailing.

When we got home I put the knife in the rack and mummy was none the wiser. Daddy presented mummy with her tights and she gave him a kiss and said, "Thank you." "And what did you do Horace?" mummy asked me. "Narrowly avoided getting us both arrested," said daddy without waiting for me to reply, not that I had anything much to say.

I think I'll give Jock's till a miss for a couple of weeks.

Thursday 29th March
Grandad's on the television.

Grandad went out today to see the Royal Family doing something. He loves all of them, past and present, and has been to all sorts of events where they've been and just stands and waves a flag. "I normally get to the front, you know and at least one of them always comes over and sees me. I don't need my wheelchair but it seems to help. 'I'm very old you know,' I tell them. That's what I said to them again today. Look," he said,

66

pointing at the television that happened to be showing the news. "There I am, look, waving. Fantastic. I'm on the tele!" "You should be careful dad," mummy said to grandad, "or Special Branch will be wanting to have a word with you." "Oh, don't worry about that," he said, "they've spoken to me already a few times. And I've been frisked." "I hope they didn't find anything." "Only my cherry brandy hipflask, but I was able to keep that once they'd smelt it and I told them that it was my medicine."

Friday 30th March
Eatwell plate and Edward eats some words.
We did food nutrition at scouts tonight. It sounded quite boring at first but then Skip gave each patrol an "Eatwell Plate" diagram.

It was a large circle or a dinner plate and it was divided up like a pie chart with blank sections for fruit, vegetables, herbs and spices, dairy, and protein and we had to fill it in with food ideas for each section. We were very pleased with our result. Skip wasn't. We had filled ours in with the following:

Fruit: Lemon sherbets, chocolate orange, strawberry doughnuts, blackcurrant millions, pineapple cubes.
Vegetables: Potato crisps (all flavours), coconut mushrooms.
Herbs and spices: Murray mints, glacier mints, spearmint gum, ginger beer.
Dairy: Milk bottles, cream soda, dairy-milk chocolate, butterscotch.
Protein: Jelly beans, port scratchings, doughnuts, sugar mice, foam shrimps, fried eggs, munchy maggots, starfish, jelly turtles, cream eggs, wiggly worms, jelly turtles, starfish, humbugs.

Edward's daddy was helping and Edward's hair was not all gelled tonight - it was quite fluffy. After the meeting Skip was complimenting Edward on his hair in front of his daddy. "A bit fluffier this week Edward," Skip said. "Yes," said Edward's daddy. "He looks after it well. But he's not allowed gelled hair at school and he didn't have time this evening to redo it. But I expect it'll be back to normal in the morning." "That's good," said Skip. "Now remind me. Who is it who cuts your hair?" Edward threw his daddy an anxious glance. "Oh, er, Scissor Stanley," said Edward. "Oh yes, that's right," said Skip. But it wasn't right and now Edward's having to live with the fully justifiable rumour that Edward's mummy also has her cut by Barry Gibsonne a.k.a. Scissor Stanley.

Saturday 31st March
The mini game gets too much for daddy.
We had a very pleasant day out today, just mummy, daddy, Sam and Olivia. And me. Mummy said that we could play the I spy mini game again after we had been banned since last summer. If you see a mini you have to shout "mini." The first one to do so scores a point. If it's a red mini and you say so you get five points. It all gets very competitive. Olivia sees minis that no one else does and Sam tries to bend the rules at every opportunity. If he sees a red mini he tries to claim six points by saying "Mini red mini" but

that's not allowed. Then Olivia said that we can't "mini" old minis 'cos she doesn't recognise them so it all gets a bit distraught also. We pulled out of the drive and Olivia shouts "Mini!" though no one can see one. "There's one on the next corner," she says. "You can't say it until you see it," said Sam. "Yes, I can." "No you can't." Then we get to the next corner and it's not there. "Minus one point," says Sam. "It's normally there, so it's plus one to me and I'm winning." It goes like this all the way to Bromley. Sam's on twelve and Olivia's on a disputed ten. Mummy refuses to play but had still shouted "mini" a few times. Daddy has a minus score. I just bide my time. We go past the Chinese, then the playing field and then I scream, "Mini, mini, mini, mini, mini, mini, mini, mini," and "twenty minis" as we go past the mini garage with all the minis on the forecourt. "You can't have twenty points for 'twenty minis' you have to say them all individually." "Alight. Mini, mini, mini..." "It's too late now 'cos you can't see them." "No, but I could see them and so did you so you know they're there." "That's not the point..." "Yes, it is. I'm winning." "No it's not and you're not." Then daddy intervenes. "As referee we are going to change the vehicle. From now on it's no longer minis but nineteen fifty-seven Jaquar XKSSs." That kept us quiet for the rest of the journey.

Sunday 1st April

April 1st - always a risky day.

I got very told off this morning and it was really, really unfair. I only crept down to the kitchen to get breakfast ready for mummy and daddy as a treat. I made them a mug of tea and poured out some orange juice. Then I did cereal and milk - all on a tray each. Then I boiled four eggs and I made some toast. Unfortunately the toaster had been turned up full so the bread went black and started to smoke so I had to turn it off. Then the smoke alarm started and then the upstairs one too and I couldn't easily stop them 'cos they were too high up on the ceiling so I got hold of the broom out of the cupboard and

poked the downstairs one with the handle but I think I poked it a bit too hard 'cos the casing cracked and bits of plastic fell to the floor but at least the noise stopped - well downstairs at least. Then mummy appeared in her dressing gown looking very sleepy and she wasn't very happy and, "How dare I set off the smoke alarm for an April Fool?" I told her that it wasn't an April Fool and I had made her breakfast. Then she gave me a cuddle and took her tray upstairs and I took daddy's. After a few minutes there was a scream and mummy appeared again, this time with blood coming down her chin 'cos she had cut the roof of her mouth on a shard of plastic while she was eating her muesli and she was going to 'phone up the cereal people and sue them but I told her that that wasn't a good idea and I would explain once she had come back from the urgent care centre.

The rest of us had red and green coloured milk at proper breakfast this morning. Daddy told us it was a new regulation and skimmed milk was now red and semi-skimmed milk was now green which seemed a very sensible idea.

Sam's explorers had a maintenance morning at the scout hut. They were just getting their briefing from Chrissie when Tanya's 'phone rang. She took it out of her pocket, looked at the screen and put her hand over her mouth. Chrissie told her to answer it and put the call on loudspeaker. Tanya said, "No!" but Chrissie said, "YES!" so she did. When Tanya said, "Hallo," this voice said, "Hallo Miss Tanya. This is the Bromley Pregnancy Clinic. We have posted your results but we thought that you would like to know as soon as possible so that is why we've called. We're pleased to advise you that your results are positive." All the explorers then put their hands to their mouths and Chrissie went very red and started shaking and told Tanya to take the 'phone off loudspeaker immediately but she didn't. She just said into her 'phone, "Thank you for that unexpected but welcome news. Can I take your name for reference? 'Miss - April - Fool?' Thank you," and turned the 'phone off. Chrissie had now gone from red to very white and Sam came home with a large bar of chocolate for me from Tanya and I'm now having second thoughts about the coloured milk.

I don't think I'll get up on April 1st next year. I think I'll stay in bed unless it's a Monday but it might be a Saturday which is a bit easier.

Monday 2nd April
Mummy gardening? Something's not right.
Mummy was in the front garden this afternoon when I came home from school today. She told me that she was doing a bit of weeding but she wasn't wearing any gardening gloves and had her high heels on and a nice jumper and was wearing bright red lipstick which is almost unheard of for a Monday. Just then a smart, friendly-looking man walked past. He stopped, smiled and said "Hello" to both of us and mummy blushed as well she might 'cos he's half her age and brown like he's been on a  beach for a long time. Mummy told me later that he had recently moved in down the road and that he's just come back from Tenerife and he's chatty and he has a few days off before he goes back to work and he's Italian and he has a cat. I asked mummy how she knew all this and she said that she had bumped into him this morning when he was walking to the shops and mummy had just got out of the car so he came over to introduce himself.

Tuesday 3rd April
Mummy gardening again? Something's very wrong. Action needs to be taken.

Mummy was in the front garden again this afternoon when I came home from school. She said that she was doing a bit of pruning but she wasn't holding any secateurs and had her high heels on and a nice jumper and was wearing bright red lipstick which is almost unheard of for a Tuesday. I told her that I had hurt my hand and she said that she would come inside "in a minute" to have a look at it so then I told her that I thought that it was broken. Then she said, "In that case I'll take you to A and E," so I asked her when and she said, "In a minute," so I gave up and went indoors and went into her bedroom 'cos I knew that she wouldn't be in for a few minutes at least and I found her red lipstick on her dressing table. I took it downstairs and pulled out the

shoe cleaning box from under the stairs and turned the lipstick so that it stuck out and I rubbed the top of it over the black shoe polish. Then I put everything back and went and had my tea and mummy still hadn't appeared.

Wednesday 4th April
Mummy gardening again and daddy's in a bit of a mess. Actually, mummy's in a bit of a mess also.
Daddy went to work today with a red streak across one of his

shoes like it had been gashed open. Mummy was in the front garden again this afternoon when I came home from school. She said that she was doing a bit of planting but she didn't have a trowel in her hand and had her high heels on and a nice jumper and was wearing bright red lipstick with black smudges over it like she was an apprentice clown. I stayed talking to mummy even though she said that I must go inside "NOW!" and get my tea otherwise I might starve, which is what I've always said to her but at last she might be listening. She even said that I could have two slices of cake but I still didn't budge. I told her all about school and the subjects and which teachers we had and I started to tell her about the Battle of Trafalgar and how it wasn't in Trafalgar Square but in Spain when the Italian man walked passed and mummy waved but he just nodded and didn't stop. Then I told mummy that I was going in for my two slices of cake and she said as she followed me in, "No, just one slice now." Typical.

Thursday 5th April

Twinkly wave day from someone who shouldn't.

Mummy was in the front garden today and she said that she was cutting the grass but she didn't have the lawn mower out and she wasn't wearing any lipstick so I thought things were sort of going back to normal. I started to tell her about Charles Dickens' The Pickwick Papers which was his first novel but she told me to go inside and get some tea "before it all goes." I asked her how many slices I could have so she said that I could have the whole [sweary word] lot if I wanted to. When I returned with half a Battenburg mummy asked me why I had come outside again and I told her that I wanted to finish off telling her about The Pickwick Papers but she wasn't listening 'cos she was staring at the road. Just then our Italian neighbour went past but he was driving and mummy gave him a wave but he didn't notice. It's just as well 'cos mummy gave him not just  a wave but a "twinkly wave" which is when you move all your fingers as well. This wave is reserved for friends you know really well or daddy does it at Tanya's mummy sometimes but I don't think mummy should be doing it at new Italian neighbours. Not men ones anyway. He might get the wrong idea. I'm glad he didn't see. I think I'll have to have a word with daddy.

Friday 6th April

Mummy's back to normal and Emily thinks she's (Emily not mummy) a cat.

Mummy wasn't in the front garden this afternoon. She was out the back in a baggy sweatshirt taking in the washing and she had her slippers on.

Emily was really told off at scouts this evening. Chislehurst's Real Ale Club had used the scout hut last weekend and we knew 'cos Charlie's daddy's a member. Anyway  they didn't clean the tables very well and when Skip came in he caught Emily licking one. He asked her what she was doing and she said that she was cleaning it. Then Skip asked her why she couldn't use a cloth and some spray like everyone else and she said that that would be a waste of beer. Skip had no answer to that one.

Then Emily said that the beer tasted 'earthy' and she had to leave scouts early 'cos halfway through she felt ill and her mummy had to come and pick her up. No one had the heart to tell her that in between the beer people and us the local gardening club had been in to make some wormeries.

Saturday 7th April

Point to point with a posh picnic.

We went to a point to point race meeting today. This is racing like you see on the television but with amateur horses. We were supposed to be meeting a family that mummy and daddy know but they didn't turn up. Apparently the mummy was expecting another baby which might have put a spanner in the works according to daddy.

Mummy had put together a really great lunch with smoked salmon and other things that we don't normally have. It was yummy.

Sunday 8th April
Who needs a point to point for a posh picnic?
Mummy's friend is a mummy - again! The daddy rang to say sorry that they weren't at the point to point but just as his wife had finished getting the hamper ready in the morning she announced that she felt that she was about to have her baby - two weeks early. The daddy put the hamper (and his wife) in the car and drove to the hospital. I think he thought that things would be "done and dusted," so mummy said, by lunchtime, but lunch came and went and there was no baby. The daddy got fed up and went and fetched the hamper from the car. He found a little room in the hospital that no one was using, sat down and opened the hamper. He popped the Champagne cork and poured himself a glass, tucked a large cotton napkin into his collar and took a bite out of a

fat smoked salmon with crème fraîche blini when a doctor walked into the room. "Blimey," the doctor said, "you're prepared." And he's not even a scout.

Monday 9th April

The new Scout Promise.

I can't understand why we have to have a Scout Law when Skip and Patrick and everyone like them don't have a Scout Leaders' Law. So I've written one based on ours. It goes like this:

1. A Scout Leader is large.
2. A Scout Leader is late.
3. A Scout Leader is sometimes grumpy and miserable (mentioning no names).
4. A Scout Leader belongs to a world-wide family of unusual humans.
5. A Scout Leader has Courage, but often prefers Stella or Fosters.
6. A Scout Leader makes good use of earplugs and is careful to make sure that he (yes, just 'he') gets enough sleep on camp and doesn't stay up half the night talking round the campfire and keeping the scouts awake and then blaming them for not getting enough sleep.
7. A Scout Leader always has an empty stomach and respect for bacon.

The problem is, I'm not sure what to do with it so I've emailed it to the authorities.

Tuesday 10th April

Holiday discussions start and Skip is in trouble.

I've had an email reply already! It says, "It seems as though you may not be having the best time in Scouting at the moment, and maybe there are some problems with your leaders. I've copied in my colleague Iona who is happy to help you sort out these problems with your leaders. Please could you let Iona know what group you attend, and any other information that Iona might find helpful to help you resolve these problems. We would like to let you know that you are not in any trouble and we are here to help." Oh dear! It was only supposed to be a bit of fun. Time to keep my head down I reckon!

Mummy and daddy have been discussing where to go on holiday in the summer. Daddy doesn't care so long as mummy's happy and mummy doesn't care so long as it's somewhere different, it's hot and away from loads of British people but who still speak  English and the hotel's a five star and there's sea nearby but the hotel needs a pool, and there needs to be some good walking routes and great views and decent bars and restaurants. They were talking all through dinner about it but still couldn't think of anywhere so afterwards I went upstairs and got my globe. I gave mummy a pin and said that when I spin it she should stick the pin in and that's where we'll go. I gave the globe a big spin and mummy jabbed at it. When it came to a halt we found that mummy had put a pin hole in Antarctica. "That'll be fun," said Sam. "It can get to minus ninety degrees C in August." I told Sam that it would be different and there won't be any British people there so it meets two of mummy's first three requirements but mummy and daddy just sat and stared at each other so I don't think we'll be going there.

Patrick has sent round an email. Apparently Skip has been suspended again. I was very careful not to put my name on the email that I had sent. I told Sam that I might've got Skip into trouble with an anonymous email. Sam said, "How can you be anonymous when your email is 'hhorrise' at whatever?" He has a point.

Wednesday 11th April
Holiday discussions continue with a little help from the children.
The whole topic of conversation was holidays again this evening. In the end daddy said that he would stick a pin in my globe and Antarctica didn't count. We all agreed that this was definitely going to be it and wherever the pin landed we would certainly go there. I span it round and daddy said again that we would definitely go where the pin landed as he made a wild jab at the globe. When the globe stopped I looked for a hole. "Bournemouth!" I declared. "Fantastic!" said Olivia. "We can go to a lovely sandy beach." "Great!" said Sam, "We can go kayaking in Poole." "Super!" I said, "We can go on the enormous zip wire." "That'll do," said daddy, thinking about his wallet - again! "It'll be warm and we haven't been there for ages." "The trouble is," said mummy gloomily, "it'll be full of British, they'll all be speaking chav and it's hardly different." "Let's have another go then," said daddy. "We can do a week in Bournemouth and a week somewhere else." I span the globe again and mummy jabbed at it with her eyes shut. When it stopped spinning I looked for the hole and announced "Cornwall!" "Brilliant!" Sam and Olivia cried and daddy smiled.

Surfing and pasties here we come! Mummy groaned.

Later on, when I was in my room, Sam and Olivia came in and they were both grinning. "Where had the pin holes really ended up?" Sam asked. We got the globe out and felt around. Finally we found them. One was in Barbados and the other in New Zealand. "Thank goodness mummy and daddy weren't wearing their glasses," Olivia said and we all smiled our secret smiles. "She wouldn't have liked either of those places though," I told them, "'cos they're so far away no one would speak any English at all and she would have to have spent the whole holiday pointing."

Thursday 12th April
Own clothes day - always a challenge for some.
Easter holidays have arrived. Yippee!

Olivia went to school wearing jeans with great big holes in the

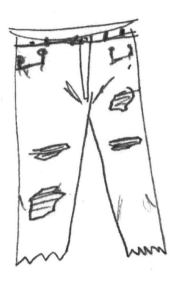

knees. Mummy asked her at breakfast, "Why are you going to school dressed like Worzel Gummidge? It's Own Clothes Day not World Book Day." Olivia looked at mummy and said, shaking her head at the suggestion that she looked like a scarecrow - at least the bottom half, with great emphasis on the "W", "I KNOW-WAH." Then she sighed a really heavy sigh. I don't understand girls. I really don't and I doubt I ever will.

Still, at least she did a bit better than Charlie who turned up in his underpants (and was sent straight back home again) 'cos he thought miss said that it was "no clothes day."

Friday 13th April
The car goes in for its annual service and mummy takes charge.

Mummy took the car to the garage today for its annual service and I went as well to be a witness. Normally daddy takes the car in but last year the service cost loads so mummy said that she'ld go and it would be cheaper 'cos she wouldn't be "messed about." I don't think daddy believes her. Mummy said that it was "Good Friday" for more reasons than one. When we got to the garage the man at reception asked if there were any particular items that needed looking at. Mummy said, "No but I've noticed that there's a bit of excessive play in the big end which appears to be developing a niggling left-tilt wobble." "Oh," said the mechanic and made a note. On the bus home I asked mummy how she knew all about the big end business and she said she didn't, she just made it up so that it sounded as though she knew what she was talking about and so wouldn't be ripped off. Even so, I thought the mechanic would know that it was all made up. When she picked the car up later on the bill was cheaper than last year but when mummy looked at the itemisation she found that she had been charged for "Investigating and rectifying cause of excessive play in the big end which had resulted in left-tilt wobble." She could hardly say anything. But daddy did when he saw the bill. "You can't get a left-tilt wobble from a big end. Someone's been trying to rip you off. I'll have a word with them in the morning," daddy said. "I'ld rather you didn't," was mummy's reply. "I think what mummy's attempting to explain," I patiently tried to point out to daddy, "is that by having a left-tilt wobble, even though it doesn't exist, it made the bill less." "Yes," said daddy sounding not at all sympathetic to what I was trying to say. But I bet mummy is the one to take the car in again next year.

Saturday 14th April
Daddy speaks French - I think.

The Horrise family went on a car trip to Calais - again - for the day. Daddy bought loads of wine in the hypermarket, mummy bought loads of wine in the hypermarket, Sam bought a packet of madeleines, Olivia bought some macaroons and I bought nothing. We went for lunch in the main square once more and

for a treat we were allowed to eat what we liked. When the waitress came over I asked her if she spoke English and she said, "Non." In a French accent I asked for a fillet steak 'cos I don't get steak much at home. I told the waitress that I would like the steak "well done" and daddy translated to "bien cuit"

'cos he can translate food. The waitress went off but came back to daddy and said something like, "Le chef dit que vous ne pouvez pas avoir votre steak bien cuit. Vous l'avez soit moyen ou avez choisi une coupe de viande inférieure." Daddy told me that the waitress had said that the chef says I cannot have my filet well cooked and that I either have it medium at most or choose an inferior cut of meat." I thought that daddy was joking so I decided to challenge him. "She didn't say that." "Oh yez, I did," the waitress said. I had a burger.

Sunday 15th April
Not a very happy day.

Easter Sunday and we had relatives and turkey! Mummy produced a lovely meal but she hid the salt 'cos salt isn't good for you and she thinks that if food needs salt then she'll add it while she's cooking and so we don't need it at the table. We only have turkey at Christmas normally and so I don't know why we had it today. I'm not sure how farmers do this 'cos all the turkeys are made for Christmas so the one that we had must have been quite old in turkey years. I don't think that they live very long so one year or so is about a human lifetime probably. That means that ours must've been about one hundred and fifty. It tasted okay though. Daddy said that ours was yummy because it was a female and everyone laughed except mummy but I don't know how daddy knew. He said that most turkeys that we eat are female. But we'd better be careful that we don't eat all of the girls otherwise we'ld have to have chicken and that wouldn't be quite the same on Christmas Day with mummy bringing out a huge great serving dish full of yummy roast potatoes and roast parsnips and pigs in blankets and in the middle there is - dar nar - a chicken. Imagine everyone's faces! When I asked mummy why she didn't laugh she said that daddy was just trying to "deflect criticism" but I didn't know what she was talking about but then she apologised to everyone that the pigs in blankets weren't pork chipolatas wrapped in streaky bacon but fat beef sausages wrapped in back bacon rashers that "my dopey husband bought when it was blindingly obvious that when I put 'bacon and sausages' on the shopping list it means 'streaky bacon and chipolatas' not 'beef sausages and back bacon.'" Daddy then said, "Not so much 'pigs in blankets' as 'hogs in duvets' then." Mummy still didn't smile but everyone else did so mummy just took a sip of her wine, well actually she

finished off a nearly complete glass in one and just stared down at her food. 'Cos I was sitting next to mummy, well sort of 'cos I was on a corner, I could see that she was looking a bit sad so I whispered, "I love you mummy," and then two big tears dropped off her face and plopped in her gravy and so I whispered, "Too much salt mummy," and then she looked at me and smiled and laughed then gave my shoulder a rub and it looked as though she was just laughing at nothing but she wasn't, she was laughing at me and so long as she can laugh at me then the world is all fine.

Monday 16th April

Easter egg issues with Emily.

I saw Emily today while I was out trying to climb the old oak tree on the Common. I was quite high and Emily was quite low but she didn't see me until she was halfway up and then I said,

"Emmmmmilllllly!" She looked up and waved which was a bit of a mistake when you're thirty feet up in the air but she only fell a few feet before she managed to land on a large branch that held her weight. I climbed down to see her and we sat on the bough and talked about yesterday. I asked her how many Easter eggs she was given and she said, "I had eleven. I had one from dad, two from mum, one from nan, one from Auntie P, two from Uncle John, one from our neighbour, I won one on the egg hunt, one from grannie and I was given one at church but that was only a mini egg. Will [brother] had eleven as well. Then, in the afternoon, we had to lay them all out on the carpet and mummy and daddy only had one each and they were big ones. Then we had to choose one each but mummy and daddy went first and they chose their own fat eggs and then it was our turn so I chose my fattest egg and so did Will. Then mummy and daddy chose two of the fat eggs that we had been given and then daddy took one of the best eggs that was given to me which wasn't very big but it had loads of sweets in it. We ended up with six each but I had started with eleven so it's not at all fair when you lose five 'cos that's nearly half of them and so I didn't have as good an Easter as I should've," then she sighed a great big sigh.

I wish I hadn't asked.

Tuesday 17th April

More grief at the supermarket.

Mummy sent Sam and me to the supermarket today to buy a few bits. We only needed a hand basket. It was very busy but Jock's till had just one person queuing so we went over to join him and

he smiled at us then craned his neck to see if he could see in our basket as we approached. We had just reached the back of the conveyor belt and Sam had put down the basket when a woman pushed straight in front of us just like happened before. She didn't look at us and she didn't say anything but Sam did. "EXCUSE ME!" he said in a loud voice but, still without looking at us, she said, "I'm in a hurry!" Sam said, "We were here first," but she said nothing else, she just kept loading more and more stuff from her TWO baskets onto the conveyor belt. "It's okay Sam," I said to him so that she could hear. "Move our basket and stand to one side to let her finish." The woman didn't even say, "Thank you," which meant that I was fully justified in then doing what daddy had shown me but I had yet to put into practice. I waited until the woman had put everything on the conveyor belt and Jock was just about to scan the first of her items. I felt under the counter and found the switch. I flicked it down one notch and, just like daddy said would happen, the conveyor belt stopped. Then I flicked it down further and the conveyor belt went into reverse. I then turned the dial next to the switch fully clockwise and the belt went into overdrive. The woman's shopping all shot away backwards from Jock's grasp, back along the conveyor belt to the start which was now the end and then started to shoot off the end and into the aisle. Shoppers that were passing by were being pelted with lettuce, strawberries, shampoo, bread rolls and loads of other stuff besides. Jock pressed an override switch and the conveyor belt stopped suddenly but by now the damage was done. The woman's shopping lay in a heap on the floor as if someone had simply upturned their shopping basket and then jumped on the contents. "Oh dear," said Sam and then looked at Jock. "Are you free?" he asked. "I'm free," said Jock and we all chuckled as the woman got down on her hands and knees and started to refill her baskets. "She won't be in such a hurry next time, will she?" said Jock and we all laughed.

Wednesday 18th April
Hike day today, some with Skip but most without.
Today we went on a hike. It was so much fun. We walked all the way to the Thames Barrier from Chislehurst along the Green Chain Walk. Then we walked to the dome thing at Greenwich and caught a bus back. We were meant to be map reading but when it was Emily's turn she decided to do Green Chain signpost reading until we got really lost. Then Skip explained that the signs should back up the Ordinance Survey map and not the other way round 'cos someone can (and had) turn a signpost round but you can't turn a map round. Well you can I suppose but then it would just be upside down. Melanie was map reading, ahem sign reading, with Emily and she asked Skip who would be so stupid as to turn a sign round and Skip said that he used to quite a bit when he was our age so Melanie said to Skip that he should be ashamed of himself and no wonder nothing got done in the old days 'cos everyone was walking around lost. Then Skip said, "That's enough," to Melanie but she hadn't finished. She told

Skip that the reason that the country was in such a mess was because people of his generation were too busy mucking about to do any proper work and now we, i.e. the Ravings and people our age, have got to sort everything out but I think by now Skip had stopped listening.

We had lunch in Oxleas Wood at the cafe with a fab. view right across to the North Downs. We were just about to leave, although Skip didn't tell us, when Mel went and bought a mug of hot chocolate 'cos her mummy had told her how good they were she but had forgotten and only just remembered. She asked for "one hot chocolate" but then the lady asked if she wanted cream and Mel said, "Yes please," Then the lady said, "Sprinkles?" and Mel said, "Yes please." Then the lady asked if she wanted marshmallows and Mel said, "Yes please," and then the lady asked if Mel would like a Flake and when Mel said, "Yes please," the lady asked, "Small or large?" and Mel said, "Large please." "Drink in or take-away?" and Mel said, "Drink in," and so she got her hot chocolate in a nice china mug. When the lady told her how much it was Mel didn't have enough money 'cos she didn't realise that all the extras cost more so then Mel said, "Sorry, but 'no thank you,'" but by then it was too late to take off all the extras so the lady just said, "Give me what you've got," so Mel got all the extras for nothing.

When she came outside Charlie had a good look at Mel's drink before asking her how much it was. Mel told Charlie that she got all the extras for free so Charlie thought that he would try and do the same. However, once Charlie had placed his order, the lady made him pay before she started to make his so he spent more than he had wanted to on a drink with extras that he didn't want unless they were free but he didn't tell the lady 'cos he said he thought he might get a bit told off. Then Skip said that it was time to go but Mel said that she couldn't 'cos she had only just finished the flake and still had the drink to go. When Skip asked her why she had her drink in a stupid china mug when we were on a hike and not a takeaway cup like he had for his coffee Mel told him that today's young people were looking after the environment instead of wrecking it like the last few generations had done. Then we had to sit and wait while Mel sipped her hot chocolate. When she had finally finished she said that she fancied another one but she wasn't allowed. Then she said that she needed the toilet. Skip knew that she might try and sneak back indoors so he went and stood guard outside the ladies' round the back of the cafe while Mel went in for a wee. Skip was waiting there for ages and at one point a lady came out and so Skip asked her if there was a girl in the toilet who had hot chocolate all over her face and the lady said that she would find out and went back in again. After about ten more minutes Skip felt someone grab his arms and it was two policemen and they handcuffed him and took him to their police car. Then the lady came out with Melanie and told her that it was okay now 'cos "the dirty old man's been arrested" and Melanie said, "Thank you for your help," and came and joined the rest of us and told Patrick about Skip's dilemma so Patrick had to go and rescue Skip but it was too late and Skip had been driven away so we had to do the rest of the hike without him and I think it'll be quite some time before Skip tells Mel and Em off again.

Thursday 19th April

Skip gets let off - again.

The word on the street is that Skip's been released from police custody "pending further enquiries." Apparently he told the police that it was a genuine mistake and he thought that his son had gone into the toilet and that he was waiting for him but that as he's dyslexic he thought the sign said, "Laddies." Anyway it was just in time 'cos we have scouts tomorrow.

Friday 20th April

Burgers on the campfire. Yummy!

We had a great campfire this evening and Skip is back, thank goodness. We made burgers from scratch with mince and onion and stuff and then had to cook them on a large wire tray on the fire. Then we put them in buns with ketchup. They were yummy even though they tasted a bit of smoke. Emily said that they are good enough for Restaurant Rating and we should try and get a listing. Emily was trying to deflect attention from when she had to light the campfire earlier. Edward told her that as she was left-handed she would have to get some left-handed matches from Skip. Skip said that he didn't have any, only right-handed ones, so Emily said that she  couldn't light the fire and Skip just walked off grinning. If I was Skip I would be a little bit more careful in what I was saying to Emily for a few more weeks at least.

Saturday 21st April

Daddy's face and minibus drained.

Unlike Sam, my football team reached the final in our league and it was today but it was a bit one-sided. We had to play a team up in Loughborough which was miles away and it was daddy's turn to drive the minibus that we borrow from another local scout group. Daddy's only one of a few people who can drive a minibus 'cos he's old enough to have a "Dee Won" licence although it's a bit odd 'cos he's not had much experience in driving minibuses. We met all the other boys on Royal Parade and it was really early but daddy said that we had to leave plenty of time for such an important match 'cos it was going to take three hours plus toilet stops. No one else came to watch from Chislehurst, I don't think, which was a bit of a poor show but it worked out for the best in the circumstances. The first thing daddy did, once everyone was on board, was fill up with fuel. Daddy said that there was some in the tank already but if he filled up then it should get us all the way to Loughborough and back.

After we pulled out of the petrol station the minibus started to jolt a bit but it was okay when we got on the motorway and seemed a bit better. Although daddy didn't want to stop until we arrived at Loughborough, everyone had drunk their elevenses and eaten their lunch by the time that we had reached the Blackwell Tunnel so when someone saw the toilet sign on the Toddington service station notice board on the motorway everyone said that they needed a wee and so we had to stop. We all jumped off, went to the toilet and jumped back on again. Then daddy started the engine but nothing happened. He tried several times but the battery was getting weaker and weaker so in the end daddy called the breakdown people. We had to wait about two hours but eventually a van turned up and a man jumped out and he was whistling. He asked daddy what had happened and daddy told him that the minibus hadn't been right since he filled up with fuel this morning just after he had picked everyone up. "Was it out of fuel," the man asked, "when you filled up?" Daddy said that the tank was a quarter full but he filled up so that he wouldn't have to stop again "but I didn't account for fourteen full small bladders." Then the man asked if daddy had filled the minibus with diesel and not petrol "because you're not covered under the policy for misfuelling." Daddy said that he wasn't stupid and he knew what to put in the tank but he had gone a little bit red. Then the breakdown man unscrewed the filler cap and sniffed it. "I'm sorry to inform you, sir, but it smells like petrol," he said, "so this is going to cost you a few bob." Daddy was adamant that he had filled up with what he was supposed to and I believed him so I told the breakdown man that my daddy wouldn't lie but it seemed like daddy was getting himself in a bit of a bad position so I wanted to help him out. Then my opportunity came. The breakdown man asked daddy when he had last filled up and daddy reminded him that he had just said that it was this morning. The breakdown man then looked at daddy very suspiciously and asked him if he could see his fuel receipt. Daddy went even redder and said that he never kept receipts and that he had thrown it away but I knew that he hadn't 'cos daddy had put the receipt in a little slot in the dashboard so that he would remember to claim the cost of the fuel back. I didn't want daddy to get into any more trouble so while he was talking to the breakdown man I went and got the receipt and gave it to the man. "Here it is," I said. Daddy's face suddenly drained of all colour. "Daddy must've forgotten that he had kept it but he needs it to claim expenses." The man took it and opened it up then said to me, "I think daddy is going to be in for a bit more than fifty litres of PETROL!" and then handed daddy the receipt back and daddy had to pay the breakdown man a load of money and then he went away.

At least the breakdown man had contacted a fuel drain company. A different man appeared after a couple of hours and he stuck a tube down the petrol tank which is actually the diesel tank and pumped all the petrol out and then put in some diesel. We then had to drive round to the petrol station and daddy filled up with diesel this time after he had paid the fuel drain man a load of money.

When we left the service station we had been there for over four hours and daddy drove as fast as he could to Loughborough but when we arrived we were too late and everyone was going home and the other team had been given a win and the cup and all that there was left for us to do was to go home. Daddy then said that no one back home need know that we had lost even though we hadn't really anyway so he stopped at another service station and had several goes on the cash machine. He then gave us all twenty pounds each to tell our mummies and daddies that we had WON! This is a great big lie but I think that it was justified 'cos the alternative would have been quite messy, that's what daddy said anyway.

When we got home daddy told mummy that we had won and she just said, "Well done, Horace," and that was that. Phew. Mummy suggested that we all go out for a meal to celebrate but daddy said he was a bit tired after all the excitement but mummy said, "All you've done is drive a minibus up and down the M1." Then daddy said he was a bit short of money and so mummy said, "Okay." If daddy thinks that what he's spent today is a bit then he must be even richer than I thought.

Sunday 22nd April
The herb and spice girls on practice hike and Skip dives onto an explorer in his tent.

Sam's just back from his practice hike. He's got a load of girls in his group. Apparently their names are Rosemary, Saffron, Ginger and Cassia. Sam 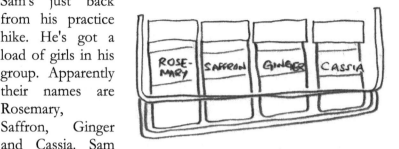 reckons it was more like walking with a herb and spice rack than a group of females.

They all had to sleep in expedition tents which are lightweight two (very small) man tents and Skip went along to help. He got his own tent but he didn't sleep very well. During the night one of the explorers went sleep-walking. Whilst he was wandering around the field Skip woke up and went for a wee. Unfortunately, while Skip was in the toilet, the sleepwalker sleepwalked back into his tent. Only it wasn't his tent - it was Skip's! When Skip returned he dived back into his tent straight onto the sleepwalker and woke him up. We don't know who the more surprised was but now Skip has to fill in a very long form.

Monday 23rd April

One, two, many.

Today is St George's Day. Daddy came home from work and said that to celebrate he was going to meet Patrick in the pub for a quick pint. Mummy said, "See you at closing time." Once daddy had left the house I asked mummy how daddy could be  hours in the pub having one pint that was quick. "You don't understand, darling," she said. "A quick pint can mean anything from two to about fifteen." I'm so confused. I know there are some things that daddy can't do, but I thought that he could at least count. Sam said that in the Greek numbering system it goes "One, two, many." One too many more like.

Tuesday 24th April
Olivia is germ-resistant.
Mummy was really told off today - by Sam. We were all eating breakfast together (for a change) when

Olivia dropped her toast on the floor, marmalade side down. She wasn't going to waste good food so she simply picked it up blew on it and was just about to stick it back in her mouth when mummy shrieked, "You can't do that - it's so unhygienic. You don't know what germs are on the floor." Olivia said that she had blown them off but mummy said that that wouldn't be very effective. Then Sam said, "What about Olivia's dummy? When she was a baby and she dropped it out of her mouth you used to pick it up, put it in your mouth and then stick it back in Olivia's." Mummy went very red and didn't say anything - but daddy did. "That's the third baby for you," he explained. "The first baby's dummy is rinsed under the tap and then put in a steriliser. The second baby just gets theirs rinsed under the tap and by the time the third comes along it'll be lucky if the dummy even gets in a mother's mouth. Often it will just be blown on, like your toast Olivia." "That's fine then," said Olivia. "I've been pumped full of germs all my life thanks to mummy and I'm still alive." She stuffed the toast back into her mouth with a smarmy smirk on her face. "And what am I supposed to do when I drop my toast mummy? Rinse it?" I suggested. "How do you think I feel?" asked Sam. "I'm going to have mine sterilised." Sam and I were sent to our rooms after that, but not for very long 'cos we were back at school and it would look a bit odd if we were late. "Why are you late for school?" miss would ask me. I would have to explain that I was sent to my room for suggesting that I should rinse my toast. Still, at least there are only three of us children. I expect if mummy and daddy had a fourth then they would automatically drop their dummy on the floor each time before giving it to them and then their toast when they were older.

Wednesday 25th April
3rd Chislehurst on Restaurant Rating.
I saw Charlie at school today. He has managed to get 3rd Chislehurst's campfire on Restaurant Rating. He has even posted a comment. He put, "Limited range of menu items (mainly burgers) but cooked to perfection with an authentic barbecue flavour and served by young, attractive staff in casual green tops with badges to signify seniority or rank."

Thursday 26th April
Spending a penny - well seven actually - in Harrods.
Looking back it was quite a fun Easter holiday and I didn't even write about our trip to London 'cos of the excitement of Skip being released. Last week he took us to Harrods as part of a scout hike round London. We had a competition to buy the cheapest thing we could. We had one hour. When we met back up outside, Charlie thought that he had won 'cos he had spent 17p and bought a grape. But I was the winner! I managed to buy one blueberry for 7p. And I got it in a Harrods  bag whereas Charlie wasn't allowed and so had to stick the grape in his mouth for safe-keeping and then swallowed it. At least he had the receipt.

Miss said that we have a new boy joining our class today but he didn't show up.

Friday 27th April

*Sonny starts at scouts and I get the feeling that nothing's ever going ↓
same again.*

A new scout has joined us. His name is "Sonny" and he's a bit of
a hard-nut. He's in our patrol. Skip said beforehand that he just
got a 'phone call from Sonny's mummy asking if he could come
along as a special case and Skip said, "Yes" although he didn't
know what sort of special case Sonny was and he didn't like to
ask. But he does now! Mel asked Sonny what his daddy did and
he said, "He's bin done for GBH." Mel didn't know what he was
talking about so just said "Oh." I think it stands for "Great Big"

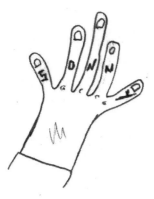

something so it's obviously
rather important. Sonny doesn't
call Skip "Skip," he calls him
"Mate." Still part of a ship
though.

So that everyone could make
Sonny feel welcome we had to
stand in a circle and tell him
our names in turn and then
something about ourselves. It's
amazing what we have in 3rd
Chislehurst that no one knew before other than each person
themself. One boy's a Harrods' model, another boy has written a
film, two girls have been on television, one girl has produced her
own perfume. I think Sonny was imagining that he hadn't joined
a scout group but an entertainment and lifestyle company - until
we got to Ravings. When it got round to Mel she said, "My
name's 'Melanie' or 'Mel' and the something about myself is that
my bestest ever friend now and forever and ever is Emily." Next
to Mel was Emily and she said, "My name's "Emily" or
sometimes "Em" and the something about myself is that my
bestest ever friend now and forever is, um..." In the slightest of

95

gaps that followed Sonny said, "Well it sounds like it's not Melanie." "I didn't not say that," said Emily confusedly. "I was just thinking to make sure before saying." But it was too late. Melanie had gone off to the toilet and Skip said to Emily that it was best if she didn't say anything further so she didn't - all evening. Then Melanie reappeared and spat out, "If you must know Sonny, my best friend is actually my cat," and then Emily went to the toilet. What is it with girls and toilets? As far as I'm concerned that's the last place that you would want to go to, especially a scout one, unless it was a matter of life or death and arguing over who your best friend is is hardly in that sort of category.

When everyone had had their go Skip then said to Sonny, Now you know everyone's name and something about them - it's your turn. We all know that your name is "Sonny" but tell us firstly, what's your surname?" "'Christy,'" said Sonny. "How do you spell that?" Skip asked, looking down at his notepad, ready with his pen. "'Christ why,'" said Sonny. Skip looked really cross and went quite red. "I only asked," Skip said, sounding very affronted but Sonny didn't say anything so Skip said, "Tell us something about yourself." Sonny said nothing. When Skip asked Sonny a second time Sonny looked at Skip and said, "I can't be arsed," and everyone gasped and looked really shocked 'cos there's no swearing at scouts and that word's a level two sweary word and Sonny's used it on his first day so he's not going to get invested in a hurry. That's what I was thinking anyway. Skip looked at him really crossly and said, "You'll have to change that attitude young man if you want to remain in 3rd Chislehurst." Sonny then said, "But I can't be 'cos it's about the others tellin' me about themselves not me tellin' the others about meself so I don't know why you 'ave asked me. That's all." Then Skip said, "Oh, you mean, 'I can't be asked?'" and Sonny said, "Yeah, that's what I said." Then he looked all slyly at Skip and demanded, "What did ya fink I said mate?" but Skip said that it didn't matter and it was

96

just that the acoustics were quite bad in the scout hut and we were given a five minute break even though we had just started and it was Skip's turn to go to the toilet and when he came back he had red eyes like Mel and Emily like he had been crying as well but I don't think he had 'cos he was in a jolly mood for the rest of the evening.

Saturday 28th April
Daddy gets a parking charge shock.
Daddy's in big trouble! The scout group with the minibus has been sent a penalty charge notice for loads of money from Toddington for parking in the car park for over two hours and not paying the parking charge. The minibus people rang up daddy to ask him why he was at Toddington services for so long when he had a match to get to and daddy said that he had an answer but it was confidential. Anyway daddy has now paid the charge and I reckon his little adventure with the fuel has cost him over one thousand pounds in

charges, fees, expenses and bribes. I don't think daddy will be wanting to drive the minibus again anytime soon.

Sunday 29th April
Parading, singing and awarding - all in a day's work for a scout.
St George's Day parade today. The district met in Petts Wood and we had to parade to a school field for a service. We held up all the traffic in the high street and we were allowed to walk along the road which was fun. When we arrived at the school there was a talk and some awards and stuff from the District Commiserator. We sung a song that was called "Jerusalem." When I asked Emily why we were singing about a foreign country

she said that we were singing in praise of English food, particularly an artichoke.

A very nice lady vicar spoke to us as well. She said her name was Helen Burn. "How appropriate," Patrick whispered to Skip.

Monday 30th April
Sonny starts at our school and I now know that nothing's ever going to be the same again!
Sonny's the new boy! He's just sort of appeared out of nowhere but he's living locally. When miss asked him how he spelt his name, Charlie said, "Here we go," and miss looked at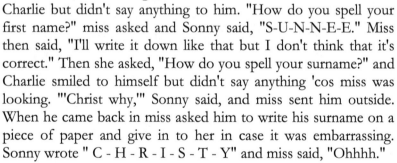
Charlie but didn't say anything to him. "How do you spell your first name?" miss asked and Sonny said, "S-U-N-N-E-E." Miss then said, "I'll write it down like that but I don't think that it's correct." Then she asked, "How do you spell your surname?" and Charlie smiled to himself but didn't say anything 'cos miss was looking. "'Christ why,'" Sonny said, and miss sent him outside. When he came back in miss asked him to write his surname on a piece of paper and give in to her in case it was embarrassing. Sonny wrote " C - H - R - I - S - T - Y" and miss said, "Ohhhh."

Charlie told me at school today that his brother, who's at uni., rang up on Friday to ask if his daddy could courier up his passport for Saturday as he needed it urgently. When his daddy asked him why he needed it so quickly he said that he was going abroad on a field trip. When his daddy asked him where he was going he said, "Wales." When I asked Charlie if his daddy got it to his brother in time Charlie just laughed and said it was okay because his friends managed to smuggle him in. I only hope that he manages to get out again at the end of the week otherwise I think his brother will have to try to find the British Embassy.

Tuesday 1st May

Birthday tea and no incidents - for once!

My birthday! I still had to go to school though. I got a few presents from mummy and daddy but they weren't very interesting. Birthdays aren't as much fun when you get to my age. I did have a birthday tea though which I enjoyed 'cos I had all my friends round. Well, some of them. Mummy also made me invite Sonny but I don't know why. He came round wearing a baseball cap. Daddy says that people who wear baseball caps have half average intelligence. There were ten of us. We had fish and chips from down the road and they were yummy. Sonny had a battered

sausage and Edward said that it sounded like one of his daddy's victims but no one laughed. The fish came in separate cartons and Sonny's sausage was wrapped in paper. Mummy wouldn't let us eat out of the cartons like we normally do and she gave us all a posh plate each. We had the ones that mummy uses at dinner parties and we all felt very grown-up. It's Royal Doulton Clarendon and it's very expensive. We were pretending to be posh and Emily asked mummy if she could have another fork 'cos hers had disappeared but she said "fork" like upper-class people do but she's not and it sounded like a sweary word and we all laughed, even Sonny. Then mummy asked us what we would like to drink and Mel said all poshly 'cos she is a bit, "Oh my goodness is it wine o'clock already? I think that I would like a large glass of chilled Sauvignon Blanc darling." She got squash but at least we all had the dinner party glasses.

Sonny said that his grandad had told him that when he was a boy fish and chips used to come wrapped in newspaper so once mummy had disappeared with the cartons Sonny said that he needed the toilet and came back with some sheets of paper from daddy's study 'cos he couldn't find any newspapers. He didn't know that NO ONE goes in daddy's study without permission. Sonny said that the papers were all over the floor so they couldn't be very important and they just had loads of scribble on them so we tipped our fish and chips (and sausage) on them and then put them back on our plates to keep mummy happy. After we had finished we just shoved all the paper and leftovers in the big box that the food came in. Mummy didn't know whether it should go in general waste, the paper recycling or the composting so Sonny took it outside and set light to it on the lawn. I don't know how he managed to light it though 'cos I think that carrying matches is illegal unless you're over forty or a scout leader. During the course of the tea Sonny turned his baseball cap round so that the visor bit was over the back of his neck. Daddy came up to me and said "quarter intelligence" but I didn't laugh in case I had to explain.

Everyone brought me a present and they were the best. Sonny gave me a cigarette.

Wednesday 2nd May
The morning after the night before.
I came down to breakfast today in my dressing gown. I slumped down on a chair and said to mummy, "That was some party. My head's pounding! I need a large Bloody Mary!" I then produced the cigarette from my pocket and asked, "Does anybody have a light?" I was speaking all posh now. Mummy told me to stop being silly and

to go and get dressed and "Where did that cigarette come from?" as she took it from me. I told her and she said that I could be friendly towards Sonny but that didn't mean that I had to be friends with him.

Thursday 3rd May

Birthday tea fallout but no one knows - except me.

Big problem this evening. Daddy has lost all his notes for a very

important speech that he's supposed to be doing at work on Monday. He said that it was on sheets of A4 paper all stacked neatly on his coffee table in the study. I told him that if they were all over the floor then someone might've tidied them up but he said that they weren't. Mummy's finger of blame was pointing at Sheila who's our cleaner and who comes on Thursdays. Personally I would be pointing the finger in a completely different direction but I didn't say anything. Mummy said that she would have "a quiet word" with Sheila. I'm keeping my head down.

Friday 4th May

A busy day with urinary issues.

We had a limerick competition at scouts. I won! Here's my effort...

"There was a young scout from Kent,
Whose nose was incredibly bent.
One day, I suppose,
He followed his nose
And no one now knows where he went."

101

We had a new girl starting tonight. She said that she was a brownie. Her daddy wanted to stay at the meeting. Skip said he could but the girl told him to go home. She told me later that he is quite protective of her.

Sonny asked me if I had enjoyed my cigarette. I told him that mummy had confiscated it so he gave me another. I've hidden it under my bed.

We made nettle tea as well this evening. We had to pick the leaves and then simmer them for a couple of minutes in twice the volume of water. It tasted a bit woody but Skip said that it's good for urinary complaints. No one knew what he was talking about but Sonny asked so Skip told us that it was things to do with urine like kidneys and bowels and tubes. It makes them all clean and healthy.

Saturday 5th May
Birthday tea fallout continues.
Mummy asked me how many of her Royal Doulton Clarendon plates got broken on Tuesday "because I'm missing two. And two glasses." I said that as far as I was aware none were broken. I expect mummy can't count either.

Sunday 6th May
Mummy considers a car boot sale.
Mummy bumped into Susie this afternoon. Mummy was in the front garden when Susie drove past, stopped and got out of her car. Mummy looked as though she was looking for something so Susie asked her what she had lost. When mummy said that she had misplaced a couple of her very expensive Royal Doulton Clarendon

dinner plates Susie said that mummy should try the local car boot fair which is where she had just come back from. Mummy looked a bit sniffy and said that she had never been to a boot fair in her life but Susie said that it was worth a visit, especially the vintage china and glass stall and then showed mummy some bits in her boot. Apparently Susie keeps going there to add to her dinner service and she's now convinced mummy to meet her at the next one in a month's time so that she can show her a couple of stalls.

Monday 7th May
Fountain pens - what a mess!
We've been practising with ink pens at school today. You have to

unscrew the pen barrel and stick the nib end in the ink and pull on a plunger then wipe the nib on some kitchen towel. It was all a bit messy. We were supposed to bring a pen and some blue or black ink but Sonny didn't bring a pen and so had to be given one. At least he had some ink but it was only a small amount in a tube and it was red. It didn't work very well either so in the end he had to use a biro.

I usually ask daddy if he's had a good day at work. I didn't ask him today. I hid.

Tuesday 8th May
Daddy gets found out and Sonny comes clean.
Oh dear! Daddy has received a postcard from the fuel drain people asking him if he was happy with their service. Unfortunately daddy was at work when the

post arrived and so mummy read the postcard 'cos everyone's allowed to read postcards. I think it's the law. It doesn't matter who they're addressed to. When daddy came home mummy asked him why he'd been contacted by a company that specialises in draining petrol from diesel vehicles and I expect by the end of this evening there will be fifteen mummies in possession of the full facts - at last. I also expect that the next time that daddy's asked to drive the minibus he will take all of us footballers on the train - at least they don't have tanks to pour the wrong kind of fuel in.

Sonny told me at school today that his pen ink wasn't ink it was red cochineal that he found in a cupboard at home. I told him that it was no wonder that it didn't work very well in the pen that he was using 'cos it was squashed insects but I don't think that he believed me.

Wednesday 9th May
Shark attack at Mel's.
It was a lovely day today so Melanie's mummy invited the Ravings including Sonny round to tea. We weren't allowed in the house. Mel has a swimming pool and we were permitted to go in

it but we were told that if we needed a wee then we should go in the outdoor toilet that was in the changing room in the pump house. This all seemed a bit unnecessary seeing as how all the water in the pool is filtered and has loads of chlorine. Sonny told Mel's mummy that it wouldn't matter 'cos we had all been drinking nettle tea so our "pee is pure" but she didn't smile, she just said that if anyone peed in the pool then the water would turn blue and the culprit would be sent home with a large water bill.

Mel has a tortoise and he's called Bulldozer. He's older than Mel's daddy and he likes tomatoes so we were feeding him. He's allowed the run of the garden 'cos it's all fenced in and that's why there's also a little fence round the swimming pool 'cos I don't think that he can swim - not very fast anyway.

When we were mucking about in the pool Mel was smiling and she said, "It's really nice that we're all in together in the pool," and everyone thought so too. Trust Sonny to spoil it. Next thing we know he's climbed out of the pool and taken his trunks off before jumping back in, leaving his trunks on the side. The girls all screamed and waded away from him. "What are you doing?" Archie asked. "Skinny-dippin', like the rest of ya," Sonny said. "There's no skinny-dipping in this pool," said Mel from behind Emily's back. "That's just for adults and you're not old enough." "You said that it's really nice that we're in the altogether in the pool." "Nearly," said Emily. "Now go and put your trunks back on whilst we all look the other way." "I'll be back when I'm eighteen," said Sonny as he climbed out and made himself look decent once more.

I was desperate to have a wee after we had been in the pool for about an hour and I was going to get out but suddenly it was a bit late. I was standing up at the shallow end and Sonny asked me what I was doing. I told him that I was just having a little wee and that it was an accident but the water hadn't gone blue so Mel's mummy was probably lying; that or someone had forgotten to put the stuff in that makes wee change the colour of the water. Sonny then told me that he was going to get out and go to the proper toilet. When he got back in with a smug smile on his face

Emily was at the top of the slide. She was just about to go down it when she stood up, even though there was only a tiny platform, pointed at the pool and screamed. I looked over to where she was pointing and the water had gone a very bright red and Sonny was in the middle of it. Sonny then screamed, "Shark attack!" and everyone jumped out of the pool screaming; all except Sonny who stayed in the pool shouting, "Help me! Help me! I'm under attack, aaaargghhh!" as the rest of the pool quickly turned red as well and Mel's mummy came running and then she started to scream as well. Edward pulled the lifebelt off the post beside the pool and threw it at Sonny but it sank. Then Sonny stopped screaming and calmly climbed out of the pool. He still had two legs and two feet so he was fine. "I just assumed there was a shark or somefing in there," he said to Mel's mummy, "when I saw all the red water." Mel's mummy demanded to know why the water had gone red. Emily said, "Well if it goes blue when someone wees in it then I expect that it's all gone red 'cos someone's pooed in it." Sonny suggested that Bulldozer had fallen in and would have weed red wee 'cos of all the tomatoes. This put Melanie and her mummy into a real panic and we all had to go and look for Bulldozer. Eventually Archie found him in the herbaceous border and so everyone sighed a big sigh of relief, no one more so than Mel and her mummy. But no one owned up to the red water (and Sonny wasn't a suspect 'cos he was actually in the pool at the time) so we all had to go home although we did get a bit of cake each and Archie was given two pieces so it wasn't a wasted journey.

Thursday 10th May
Cleaner issues and Sonny gets some proper ink.

I don't know what mummy or daddy have said to Sheila but we don't have a cleaner anymore and now mummy's going to have to do some real work.

Miss gave Sonny some blue ink today and asked him for his red ink in exchange but Sonny said that he had used it all up and had thrown the container away.

Friday 11th May
Skip's told to sleep with the scouts.
Interesting start to the camp this weekend with the cubs. We have the young girl who's just moved to 3rd Chislehurst. She told me that her daddy thinks that she needs "toughening up." Fat chance of that. When she turned up at the campsite her daddy was horrified to find out that the girls all share a tent with

no leader in with them. He said to Skip, "You must sleep in their tent. All night. I don't want my daughter being abducted." Skip told him that he would put a padlock on the girls' tent and organise for one of the leaders to stand guard outside. The daddy went home happy.

Charlie's brought two whole bottles of tonic water to camp. He said his parents drink it by the caseload. Then he drank a whole bottle. He says that he likes it 'cos it's really fizzy and has more taste than lemonade. Sonny had some as well.

Saturday 12th May
Skip's kept busy and the mess tent gets a new lick of something that's not paint.

Dinner took rather long time tonight 'cos we had to rebuild the fire. It was so wet when we were trying to light it that Skip said that he would do it under a tarpaulin. So he draped the fire with a huge sheet and disappeared underneath with a box of matches. He managed to get the fire going but unfortunately he got the tarpaulin going as well and by the time that he had re-emerged he couldn't remove the tarpaulin 'cos it was stuck to the wood so then it burnt with really black smoke and Skip said we couldn't cook on a melted plastic fire 'cos it was too carsinagenic, or something like that, so we had to start all over again.

When we were sitting round the campfire after dinner Skip told Emily to move further away because she was too close. "I'm trying to get a suntan," she told Skip. Skip suddenly stood up and walked off without saying anything but when he returned a few minutes later it looked like he had been crying. He was probably worried about how he was going to have to explain sunburn to Emily's mummy.

When she complained that all the camp fire smoke was blowing into her tent Skip suggested that she unpeg it and turn it round by ninety degrees. "Alternatively you could move it to the other side of the camp fire." That all sounds a bit like too much work," Emily replied. "Can't you just turn the fire round instead?" Oh dear.

Skip told a ghost story tonight whilst we were having hot chocolate in the mess tent. Unfortunately he forgot to tell us to put our mugs down before he got to the "BOO" scary bit. Now there's hot chocolate all over the inside of the tent and several of the younger cubs are in emergency nightwear having received crisis counselling from Akela.

Charlie was sick during last night and has had to go home. Sonny's been okay.

A mysterious slit has appeared in the groundsheet overnight. Sonny is number one suspect as the slit is furthest away from him and 'cos he's new and we've never had one before.

Sunday 13th May

Skip's kept even busier on camp.

We had a bit of an incident first thing this morning and Akela thought that we had a safeguarding issue. Yesterday we made a shower with a pallet to stand on and a solar panel to heat the water up that was in a watering can that we had tied up to a tree above our heads with a bit of rope to pull. Then we wrapped a large tarp around so as to give some privacy. There wasn't much pressure but it would be warm enough. However, at about six o'clock in the morning we all woke up 'cos one of the cubs was screaming, "No, grandad, no! Please leave me alone! Let me do it by myself!" We looked out of our tent and saw Akela running towards the shower area to see who was being abused. It turned out later that one of the cubs had his grandad with him and grandad was so keen to make sure that his grandson was clean that he went and got him up at the crack of dawn and put him in the shower. Grandad was then busy hosing his grandson with a hose, down through the top of the shower cubicle, not realising that the water was freezing cold. Had he used the watering can his grandson would have been a bit warmer, but it probably wouldn't have cleaned much mud off. So, warm and muddy or freezing cold and clean? I know which I would choose.

Skip found Charlie's tonic water bottle in the rubbish and so deduced the reason for his sickness. He had obviously picked a bottle from the wrong case because it was ready-mixed gin and tonic.

Emily's burnt her face and it was all red so now she's walking round like she's seen a ghost 'cos Skip has covered her head with antiseptic cream.

When new girl's daddy picked her up this afternoon he asked Skip about the guard. Skip said that he wasn't able to find anyone suitable so he had used an explorer. However, as it was a cold night he allowed the boy to go into the tent for the duration. "So I hope you're happy. As you can see she's in one piece but don't blame me if she's pregnant," he said which I thought was a bit unnecessary.

The mystery of the slit has been resolved 'cos another two appeared last night and Charlie's gone home. Sonny was questioned and he said that when he wakes up needing the toilet he must go "straight away" and 'cos the toilet's miles away he has to take evasive action. This involves him making an incision in the groundsheet and having a wee through it. "It's not a problem, honestly. I can't see why you're making that stupid face," he told me when I looked all disgusted. "All the wee goes underneath the tent so it's not like you're havin' to sleep in it." "No, but I'm sleeping over it, and that's just as bad," but I don't think Sonny agrees. I shall ask Skip for a tent transfer next time we go camping.

Monday 14th May
Mel wants a puppy.
Mel came to school today in tears. She told me that her mummy was pregnant with a baby. I told her that that was usual but Mel said that she had wanted a puppy. "I don't think that it works like that," I told her with my serious face.

Tuesday 15th May
Dartboard confusion.

Sonny told me this afternoon that when he got home later he was going to play darts. He likes to play a game called "Round the Clock" where you have to hit each number in turn from one to twenty. I said that I didn't know any other young person that had a dartboard although we have one in the shed somewhere, then Emily informed me that she had one and that she liked playing darts, especially Round the Clock. Her daddy  had bought it and it was a professional one and was really expensive. "It has red and green and black and white colours with a seamless playing surface and a unilock board levelling system," she said. Sonny then said that his was a really good board also but probably wasn't quite as professional as Emily's. "I also think mum prob'ly got it on the cheap 'cos all the numbers on it are muddled up," he told us. Emily then started to giggle but I don't know why.

Wednesday 16th May
Sonny v. Emily v. Sonny.

Sonny told me today that he was a bit tired as he had been up late with his mummy "drinkin' beer." When I told him that he was a bit young for drinking beer, especially on a Tuesday, he said that it had been alcohol free. Then Emily said, "What's the point in drinking alcohol-free beer? The whole idea of beer is that it has alcohol in it." Big mistake! Sonny looked at Emily a bit funny

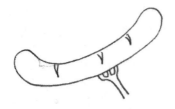

then said, "What's the point in eatin' vegetarian sausages? The whole point of sausages is that they have meat in 'em," and then chuckled to himself. I don't think Emily likes Sonny very much.

Thursday 17th May
Cleaning and footwear issues.
Daddy complained this evening that the house is looking "a bit of a mess" and that Thursday's were normally the day when it's looking its neatest and cleanest. Mummy's locked herself in her bedroom.

Sonny was told off at school 'cos he had a toe showing through one of his shoes. We had a supply teacher for maths who was quite strict and told Sonny that as far as he was aware sandals weren't on the approved uniform list. Sonny went all red and didn't say anything. I thought he was going to cry. I have never seen Sonny nearly cry before. Maybe

he likes his shoes with a hole in them and was thinking that maybe sir was going to confiscate them. Well, one of them maybe. Then he would have to hop everywhere.

Friday 18th May
Shoe catapult.

Chrissie came to scouts tonight to help put the mess tent away. "How did it get so muddy?" she asked. "That's not mud," Skip told her, "that's hot chocolate." "Do you think I'm stupid or something?" she asked him. Skip didn't reply.

We played "Shoe catapult" down past the farm later on this evening. It was great fun. We had to take off our shoes, lie down on our backs side by side in a line, put one shoe on top of our ankles then launch our feet up in the air sending the shoes over our heads. It's a good idea to keep your legs together as they go over your head otherwise you will end up with a black eye like Archie's. Edward was winning until it was Sonny's go. Sonny was wearing his school shoes a.k.a. sandals. He launched first one shoe then the other so far that they both ended up in the Kyd Brook and Skip shut his eyes and said, "Oh no!" Skip ran to see if he could get them out of the river but the level was quite high 'cos of all the recent rain and off they floated. Sonny declared

himself the winner "'cos my shoes'll end up in the Thames and that's miles away." Edward was having none of it. He picked up his trainers and dropped them into the Kyd Brook. "What on earth are you doing?" Skip asked incredulously. "Making sure that Sonny has some competition," said Edward. "Just think of it as a sort of long-distance Poohsticks." I don't think Skip was very impressed. We then had to walk back to the scout hut really slowly 'cos Sonny and Edward had to go on tiptoe so as not to cut their feet. Edward's mummy was really cross 'cos he had new trainers but Skip just shrugged his shoulders. I don't know what Sonny's going to do though. He didn't seemed too bothered 'cos he was smiling at Edward. He'll probably be at school on Monday in his socks.

The new girl has left 3rd Chislehurst scouts.

Sheila was at our house when I came home and she had a glass of wine in her hand but I kept out of her way and didn't say anything.

Saturday 19th May

Beaver sleepover.

Beaver leader Bramble had a sleepover at the scout hut yesterday with some of us scouts and cubs and Skip but she didn't get much rest. At about midnight she had just gone off to sleep when she woke up 'cos one of the littlest beavers was screaming the place down. She quickly got dressed and went outside to find this little boy standing outside his patrol tent wailing, "I WANT MY MUMMY! I WANT MY MUUUUM-MEEEEE!" "Sssssss. Ssssssssh," Bramble said, putting a finger to her lips.

"MUUUUM-MEEEEE!"

"Now why are you outside screaming?" "Well," the little beaver replied. "I didn't want to do it inside the tent because I would wake up all the others." But actually the others were awake so Bramble put the littlest one back to bed and then very naughtily told the others to "Be quiet as it's four o'clock in the morning!" But it didn't really matter that she had lied 'cos no one would know and it did the trick. Silence followed.

Sunday 20th May

Bonking Beaver.
At bedtime last night one of the beavers announced loudly, "If anyone screams tonight and wakes me up then I'm going to bonk them!" I don't know why Skip and Bramble both looked at each other and burst out laughing, but they did.

Once the beavers had all gone home and we were helping clear up this afternoon one of the beaver mummies turned up with the most enormous box of chocolates and a case of wine. "I would just like to say, on behalf of the parents, how sorry we are about your having been kept awake until four o'clock in the morning by our naughty little children." What could Bramble say? But we all got a handful of chocolates each so we're not telling.

Monday 21st May
Supermarket strategy.
Big news! Sonny turned up at school in brand new shoes! They were really posh and trendy which was a bit of a surprise 'cos we all thought that Sonny's mummy was very poor and he'd probably never had new shoes before.

I had to go with mummy to the supermarket today after school. Mummy only had to buy a couple of items but she insisted on starting by the entrance and going up and down all of the aisles in order. She met a few friends on the way and chatted to them each time before continuing. We went up and down all the aisles even though she didn't want anything at all in most of them. When we were back in the car she started to complain about how long it took "having to speak to everybody." I suggested that if she didn't go up all the aisles then she would meet fewer people and so would have fewer conversations. "Yes, but at least if I do it my way I'm not so likely to bump into the same person twice. Bumping into the same person more than once is really bad form and simply not on because you feel like you need to continue the conversation that you've just been having, even though you've sort of finished it. Or else you have to speak about something else which isn't very interesting. Or you say something stupid because you've run out of normal things to say. That's why not. If I go up and down the aisles like I do, if I do happen to bump into the same person again then at least I'll have the moral high ground as I'm going round the supermarket in a semblance of order, unlike the other person who's darting all over the place. If you're suggesting that it would have been quicker to have cut across the aisles to get the few items I required you may be correct but then I could theoretically bump into the same person - who is going up and down - several times and that is to be avoided at all costs, even if it would have been ultimately quicker," mummy said in reply.

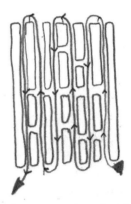

I wish I hadn't asked.

Tuesday 22nd May

Mummy makes a surprising discovery - to her not the rest of us.

We were on the common after school today when Christina from the stables came across on her horse. Her name is Bitney. She's not supposed to go across the common, she's supposed to keep to the bridle path. There is a big notice but Christina says she can't read. I don't know if she means herself or the horse but I don't like to ask. We were all giving Bitney a pat when she made a huge noise like a muffled rifle going off and then she put a huge poo on the path. Sonny just giggled but Emily looked horrified. "Don't panic," said Christina. "She's a vegetarian. It's only mushed up grass. Someone will come along before the day is out, scoop it all up and put it on their roses."

After Christina had ridden off Sonny looked at Emily a bit strange. "What you staring at Sonny?" she asked quite aggressively. "I was just wonderin', seeing as how you're a veggie like Bitney. Do ya get scooped up and put on the roses?" Sonny got a big kick from Emily for that one but I think he's got a point. When I arrived back home I asked mummy, "If you're a vegetarian do you think it's okay to put your poo onto the roses?" "I should think that you'ld be in danger of getting thorns in your bottom," was mummy's considered response, "but it would probably be fine." "I didn't mean go straight onto the roses like daddy does when he wees to keep the foxes away..." I was going to say that I meant put it in the compost bin and then on the roses but mummy was more interested in daddy weeing in the garden. I told her that sometimes daddy wees in the garden 'cos the foxes don't like it. When she said, "How revolting!" I told her that Sam and I do it as well. Mummy looked really cross. "I can't believe that you would do something so disgusting. What would you think if I was sitting at the dinner table and then I suddenly stood up and said, 'I think I need the toilet,' but instead of going to the downstairs loo and shutting the door I opened the back door and strolled down the garden before having a wee over the roses?" "There wouldn't be any point," I told mummy, "'cos daddy says it only works with male wee." I don't think mummy was too impressed. "I don't care who it is or what it is, I do not want anyone in my family weeing or pooing in my garden. And that's the end of the matter. I shall deal with your father later." "What about George?" I asked mummy. "You can't stop the cat going to the toilet in the garden," but I don't think mummy was listening and I haven't yet been given a proper answer to my question.

When daddy came home it was perhaps unfortunate that the first thing that he said was, "I need to go to the toilet." Mummy said, 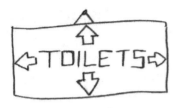 "I've been speaking to Horace so take your pick of three now - upstairs loo, downstairs loo or..." "I'm sorry," said daddy as he gave mummy a kiss. "I shouldn't have told Horace but even so it was wrong to have ever started to make it a habit to wee whilst in the shower." I looked at mummy and mummy looked at daddy and daddy looked at me. "That's four and counting then mummy," I said quietly, "and we haven't started on the shed yet."

Wednesday 23rd May

Croquet crisis.

We were allowed back to Mel's house today and her mummy said "Sorry" to us all about the red pool. She said that her husband had had the water analysed and the scientist people had found a large concentration of insect matter. They concluded that a huge quantity of red staining insects must have found their way into the pump and been squashed. We weren't allowed to swim today though which, in any case, would have been a bit difficult even if we had been 'cos the pool water had all been pumped out and the swimming pool men were taking the opportunity to give the walls and floor a good clean. So we turned our hand to croquet. We were each given a great big mallet like the ones for doing wooden tent pegs but with a really long handle, and a heavy ball like a cannonball only wooden, and we played four at a time in teams of two. I played with Sonny and we were blue and black. You have to knock the balls through the hoops in a certain order. Mel said that you have to hit the balls quite hard like in hockey. If you hit someone else's ball with yours you can put yours against theirs and hit yours. This can send theirs in the wrong direction and hopefully yours further in the right direction. It was a great game and was getting really tense as we went round the huge course. We didn't finish it however and had to go home. Emily had hit Sonny's black ball and so had put hers against his and sent his deep into the herbaceous border. He wasn't very happy. Mel said that there was no out of bounds and so Sonny had to rejoin play by chipping his ball back onto the lawn. He was determined to get Emily back but her ball was now on the far edge of the grass, about twenty metres away. He spent ages trying to find his ball amongst all the young flowers but eventually found the dark lump. Mel's mummy even came out to see what Sonny was up to. He told her that he was "in the bunker." She said that he must be careful of the foxgloves that Sonny was about to trample on and he said that he would be.

There was no way that Sonny was going to chip his ball back onto the lawn - he was going to drive it clean out of the border and hit Emily's at a hundred miles an hour. That was his idea at least. And so, instead of putting his mallet between his legs and gently swinging like you're supposed to do, he stood to one side and took a shot that was more like a golf swing or full cricket stroke. He missed. What I mean is he missed the ball and took out the head of some hollyhocks. Mel's mummy screamed. "Sorry, sorry," Sonny muttered. Mel paced over and from the edge of the lawn told Sonny to aim at the base of the ball and it would ping the ball out like a sand wedge does only faster. Mel stood back as Sonny had a second wild shot. But success! The ball flew out of the flower border and sailed clean over the entire length of the croquet lawn. "FOOOOUR!" cried Mel's daddy who had just returned from work and was walking down the garden to say "Hello" to us all. He had seen where the ball was heading and the swimming pool men were in immediate danger. They looked up as the ball came plummeting down towards them like a guided missile. One of them was going to take a direct hit but he got out of the way just as the ball crashed into the side of the pool. Who would've guessed what was inside a croquet ball? It had been, until then, a bit of a mystery, a bit like a golf ball with innards of elastic and rubber liquid. I thought that they were just wood. The ball shattered and lethal shards of something flew in all directions. There was soft gooey stuff everywhere and loads of red. It was as if someone had blown up a can of beef stew and baked beans on the camp fire. Everyone ran over to the pool, everyone except Sonny. Mel put her hands to her eyes as her daddy picked her up clean off the lawn and ran indoors. Mel's mummy screamed again only louder and also ran indoors  leaving a small trail of sick on the patio. We couldn't understand why initially but all was soon quite obvious. As the rest of us stared into the empty pool, one of the men bent down and picked up a tiny little head. "What a way to go," he sighed, "and after fifty-seven years." The silence was broken by Sonny who was still in the flower border scratching his head. "That's odd," he muttered, still looking down at the ground, "I've just found me ball."

Thursday 24th May
Sonny changes his diet.
Sheila's back. Mummy didn't say anything but the house once more looked very neat and clean when I returned from school. This only happens on a Thursday. Actually I saw Sheila on the way back from school. She was in a new car and I tried not to see in case she was cross but she was all smiley and waved so everything must be okay.

We were allowed back to Mel's tonight, mainly to apologise, but Sonny wasn't allowed indoors. We were playing down the bottom of her garden when Sonny said that he needed the toilet. Mel told him that he couldn't go indoors but that he could go behind the pump house. We had tea on the lawn which was fun and then we played cricket with Mel's daddy and her mummy came to watch as well but we were only allowed a soft ball. When it was her daddy's turn he hit the ball straight over the pump house. "I'll get it," said her mummy as she ran off round the back. When she returned her face was ashen. "I think you had better see for yourself," she said when Mel's daddy asked her what the matter was. We followed her round to the back. She pointed at an enormous human poo and beside it a small pair of boys' underpants. We all looked at Sonny but we didn't say anything. He did though. "It's okay, I'm a vegetarian now so you can just shove it on the roses." Now Sonny's allowed round Mel's but not indoors and not outdoors so there's not really much point for the time being.

Friday 25th May
Curly name crisis.
Sonny turned up at scouts today in new trainers and I caught Skip looking at them several times which was a bit odd. I wasn't alone 'cos halfway through the meeting Emily said to Skip, "Why d'you keep looking at Sonny's trainers? D'you fancy a pair?" Skip didn't say anything and looked away quickly but he was still looking at them later when he thought no one could see.

Skip showed us how to build a fence tonight 'cos one had blown down at the scout hut. We had a length of featheredge each and had to nail to a Harris rail. I don't know who Harris is - probably the inventor. Mind you there's not much to invent, just a triangular bar with a flat bit to nail onto. To make it a little more interesting Skip had bought some large plastic letter stencils so that we could spray our names onto our bit of featheredge. We had to draw round the plastic stencils and spell our name on a sheet of card. Then we had to use a craft knife to cut the letters out ready for spraying. Charlie was complaining that his first letter had a curve in it that was much harder to cut 'cos if you have a straight letter you can use a ruler as a guide. I know what he's making a fuss about 'cos he has nearly all curly letters. We were having a race to see who could finish first. The girls won 'cos neither MEL nor EMILY has a curly letter which wasn't fair. When I have children they're only going to have straight names like WILLIAM or ALEX or ELLEN 'cos if they're called QUODGROBS then they're going to have real problems.

When I got home I told Sam that Skip had been staring at Sonny's new trainers all during scouts tonight. Sam suggested that maybe Skip fancied a pair 'cos perhaps he was trying to rediscover his youth.

Saturday 26th May
Bath bed and breakfast.
We're all in Bath for the weekend. We've gone with Uncle Bill and his family and we all went down in his big car. Mummy thought that we were going to the Royal Spa Hotel but Uncle Bill

122

said that it was full up 'cos he's not very organised so we're now in a bed and breakfast on a farm which is really nice although there was a bit of a pandemonium when we first arrived because Colin the cockerel had disappeared. We went down in convoy with Uncle Bill's friend, Mark and his wife. They are staying at the Royal Spa 'cos they are organised and mummy kept moaning about it and even more about Mark's wife who kept on about how nice the hotel was and how expensive it was and how she was always treated with respect when she stayed there. Daddy then 'phoned the Royal Spa from the car and said that he was Mark and could he order some flowers for his room as it was his wife's birthday and maybe a bottle of Champagne and a box of chocolates?

We went out for dinner with Mark who said that he was received like an old friend at the Royal Spa. "It was by no means full and we've only stayed there twice before but they know how to look after their regulars. We found complimentary flowers in our room, and a bottle of chilled Champagne and a huge box of posh chocolates." "All we have are half-a-dozen eggs," mummy complained.

Sunday 27th May

Colin is found.

I woke up this morning at 4am with a cockerel cock-a-doodle-doing at close quarters. At breakfast daddy said that Colin had been found in the middle of the night - under their bed. Mummy said that if Uncle Bill hadn't lied about availability at the Royal Spa then she would have had twice as much sleep.

"And flowers, Champagne and chocolates," Sam added, not very helpfully. We were supposed to be coming home in convoy and having supper on the way but when we went to the Royal Spa to find Mark we were told that he was being spoken to by security so we left.

Monday 28th May

Sonny's shoe saga continues.

Daddy spoke to Uncle Bill today. Apparently, when Mark went to pay at the Royal Spa, the cost included flowers, Champagne and chocolates. "I haven't ordered these," Mark complained and so they crossed them off but then he was taken round the back and after a short while the police appeared and he sat in the police car for ages. But then they let him go. This all seems a bit of a hassle but sounds like an easy way to get something for nothing. Maybe that sort of thing is acceptable in hotels in the West Country.

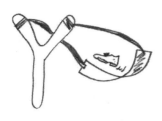

Sonny's new trainer mystery is solved. Sam told Tanya and Tanya said that her daddy (Skip) had had Sonny's mummy on their doorstep after the game of "Shoe Catapult" and demanded that he pay for Sonny's shoes to be replaced. Her daddy said that it wasn't his fault that Sonny had thrown them into the Kyd Brook but then Sonny's mummy said that she would contact the District Commiserator and make a formal complaint whereupon Skip went down to the cashpoint with her to get some money out. When Skip got back he and Tanya's mummy had a big argument and she said that she didn't know why he bothered being a scout leader and then asked how much he had given Sonny's mummy. When he told her she said that you could buy half a shoe shop for that and if that's what you have to do to get a new pair of shoes then she was going for a walk down to the river in a pair of kitten heels.

Tuesday 29th May

Mummy goes missing.

I had to go to the supermarket with mummy today. Mummy only needed some frozen burgers and buns. After last week's effort I told her to give me her debit card and stand at the back and I would go and get the bits 'cos it would be quicker. I was only a couple of minutes. When I went to pay the lady at the till asked me if it was my debit card. I told her it was my mummy's. Then she asked me where my mummy was. I looked over to where she should've been standing but she wasn't there so I said that I didn't know. Then a man with something in his ear came over and he said, "Follow me," and he took me to a little room out though a swing door in the far corner of the store and asked me why I had my mummy's debit card. I said that she had given it to me. Then he asked me where my  mummy was and I said that she was supposed to be waiting at the back of the store but she wasn't there when I went to pay and I went to the till that was by where she was supposed to be waiting. The man asked my name and mummy's name and I told him. Then he pressed a button on a desk and said, "Could a Mrs Karen Horrise please report to customer services immediately whereupon she may find something that she's misplaced?" He said that his announcement was all over the speakers in the store and that mummy couldn't miss it. Then the man said that he would take me to customer services and by the time that we'd got there, 'cos it's at the other side of the store at the front, then mummy will probably be there. She wasn't. I did try to explain to the man that mummy couldn't just come walking over from wherever she was 'cos she can't go from A to B, she has to walk up and down the aisles so that she doesn't bump into the same person twice and bumping into them several times is "simply not on." Then the man looked at me as if to ask for an explanation but I didn't given him one 'cos I didn't have one.

We had been standing there for a few minutes when Susie appeared. She said, "Hallo, Horace. I heard your mother being called over the loudspeaker system. Is everything okay?" I said that mummy had asked me to get her some burgers and buns and pay for them but that she had disappeared. Then Susie told the man that she would look after me and go and find mummy with me but the man said that he couldn't let me go 'cos I had tried to pay with someone else's debit card even though it was mummy's. Then Susie got really cross and said that the man was effectively kidnapping me and said, "Come on, Horace, let's go and find your mum," and she grabbed my arm and the man didn't say anything. We went to where mummy was supposed to be and - THERE SHE WAS! I went over and gave her a big hug and she said, "Well your system doesn't work, does it? That took twenty minutes. I could have done it quicker going up and down the aisles," and "Hello and goodbye Susie" but I got the impression that Susie wasn't going anywhere. I said that when I went to pay she wasn't there. She said that she had seen Charlie's mummy and was just helping her with her shopping in the car park 'cos I wouldn't be *that* quick but I was and "goodbye Susie" and this time Susie left. I explained to mummy what had happened and she went all red in the face and said that she would write a letter when we got home. She strutted out of the supermarket and I followed. Then she waited for me to catch up and we both marched up the road.

Halfway home mummy saw Susie in front who was also walking and mummy slowed right down. When I asked her why she said that Susie was going quite fast and so we would have to overtake her but then keep up the faster pace until we were well past her so it was easier to slow right down and keep behind. "Why don't we just walk near her?" I asked but mummy said that that was not something that people did. When we reached the duck pond we had to stop and talk to the ducklings even though mummy hasn't talked to the ducklings since I was about five.

Eventually we got home and mummy asked for her debit card and I said that the man with the thing in his ear at the supermarket had taken it from me. Then mummy sighed and took the burgers and buns from me which I had managed not to pay for but the buns were all soggy and the burgers had defrosted and had started to warm up so mummy chucked it all in the bin and we had fish and chips with her credit card and I don't think mummy's going to let me do the shopping again for her for a while so "Every cloud has a silver lining" as granny used to say.

Wednesday 30th May
Stowaways at Stratford.
No school this week as it's half term. We had a scout trip up to London to the Olympic Park and we went by minibus 'cos it was

quicker. We looked at all the sports buildings and we had a go on the big slide which was great fun. I think people in London are very fit with the huge places to exercise. On the way home Skip drove us into Stratford for fish and chips but I didn't say anything 'cos I was supposed to have had burgers last night. We weren't meant to get out of the minibus but Sonny got out of the back 'cos he said he had cramp then he was talking to a little beaver that was only about six years old and who was standing by a wall. He told Sonny that his name was Jake and that he was waiting for his mummy who was getting fish and chips for him as a treat as he had behaved very well at some presentation. He certainly looked very neat. Sonny was telling the little beaver that we had come from Chislehurst and that we were on our way home and that there are caves where we live. Then Archie got out to get Sonny back in and then Mel got out to get Archie back in and it was going on like this for a few minutes until Skip appeared with all the fish and chips and a sausage for you know who. Patrick sort of put his arms all around the scouts that had escaped and shoved them back in and we started off. Patrick was passing all the food down the minibus as Skip was telling him all about how he had met a beaver leader in the fish and chip shop and that she had been to a presentation with the beavers, including one who was her son. Skip said that we would go through the Blackwall Tunnel 'cos that was quickest. It was a bit dark in the tunnel and suddenly there was a huge scream and Skip shouted out for whoever was doing it to shut up. But then it happened again but Skip couldn't do anything 'cos there's no stopping in the Blackwell Tunnel without a huge fine. When we got out the other end Skip asked which of us it was but we all said that it wasn't us. We didn't get home until about nine o'clock and all our mummies were waiting for us at the scout hut. We all climbed out of the minibus and Archie and Mel had to clear up the litter. When they finally jumped out Patrick asked them if there was any lost property in the bus. Mel said that there wasn't but she had found a beaver. "Not a real one?" Skip asked, trying to be funny but then Mel said, "Yes, a real one." When Skip told her not to be so silly she said, "Not a real one like you get maybe in the River Thames but a real one that you might get before cubs." Skip climbed in the back of the minibus and then slowly sat down. He had found what Mel was talking about. It was little Jake who had been scooped up by Patrick along with all the other scouts outside the fish and chip shop in east London. "Why didn't you say anything?" Skip asked him crossly. Jake's bottom lip started to tremble. He said that he thought that he might see some caves but he wanted to go home now. Then he started to cry. Skip said to Patrick, "It would've been a good idea to check what you were shovelling up." Patrick said that he had only scooped up scouts and it wasn't his fault if he had an extra one from another group. Skip was wondering what to do when there was a "nar, nar" down the lane and two police cars appeared to give him his answer. Two policemen and a policewoman jumped out. They put Jake in the back of one of the police cars and Skip and Patrick have been arrested. Skip was shouting something at Patrick from the back of the police van that then showed up but no one could understand what he was saying.

Thursday 31st May
Alan gets his rucksack packed and loses an item.
Olivia and the cubs are having a camp at the scout hut tonight and they're in tents and Sam was sent to help until bedtime. Some of them have never camped in tents before. The red six leader told Akela that one of the new cubs hadn't brought his sleeping bag so Akela went to investigate. Red six were all standing outside their tent and they said that Alan didn't have his sleeping bag. "Okay, okay," said Akela. "You don't all have to tell me. Now then Alan, do you have your sleeping bag?" "No, I don't Akela." "Did you pack your rucksack yourself?" "No Akela." "Did your mummy do it for you?" "Yes Akela." "Did I not say last week that you need to pack yourself so that you know that you have everything?" "Yes Akela." "Why didn't you then?" "'Cos mummy said that she wanted to do it so that she was sure that I had everything." "Well she didn't do very well if she forgot one of the most important items of kit." "No Akela." "Do you mind if I just have a little peek in your tent?" "No Akela." Akela unzipped the tent and saw where Alan was going to be sleeping. He had a sleeping mat and the most enormous lump at one end. "What do you think

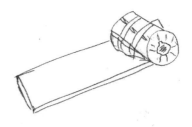

that is at the end of your sleeping mat Alan?" "That's my pillow Akela." "I think you might get quite a neck ache with that underneath your head Alan." "It's very soft Akela." "I expect that it is and I think that's because you'll find that that's your sleeping bag Alan. Have you anything to say?" "Oh, Akela."

Friday 1st June
Skip gets his eggs well done.
Skip and Patrick were at scouts tonight having been de-arrested. They weren't talking to each other though and Patrick had a black eye. He showed us how to prepare an English breakfast as part of 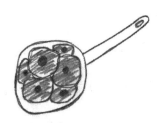 some sort of food badge. When it came to the eggs he told Charlie and me what to do and how to fry an egg - saucepan, bit of oil, make sure it's hot, flip the egg over. "How long should I fry the eggs for, Skip?" I asked. "Four to five minutes then turn them over and do the other side for the same amount of time at the most," was what I should've heard. Skip watched me expertly crack six eggs into the frying pan and put them on the gas then he went to find Patrick to get the bacon and other bits sorted but he got a bit sidetracked. After a while Skip came back to see what was going on. He took a plate of charred lumps that looked like those blackened funguses that grows on trees and that are commonly known as "King Alfred's Cakes." "What on earth...?" Skip asked. "Horace thought you said 'forty-five minutes,'" said Charlie who had been standing watching. How was I to know? And why didn't Charlie say anything to me?

Saturday 2nd June
Mummy tries a new dish at the Chinese.
Grandad took us all out for a meal at lunchtime. We had Chinese which was lovely. I had spare ribs, sweet and sour chicken,

mushroom rice, lemonade and ice cream. Mummy's found a new dish that she says she's never had before. Mummy asked the Chinese lady what sort of noodles she had been eating and the lady said that they were "Kuan Chi" noodles. Mummy said that they were lovely and she would have them again. I still don't know what they are though. It's like daddy always orders Singapore noodles but when I ask him what they are he just says "Well, they're sort of, umm, noodles from, um, Singapore." I could have told him that.

Sunday 3rd June

Shopping in a field and mummy makes a purchase.

Car boot fair day! I went with mummy and we met Susie at the entrance. It was a bit of a wet day but there were loads of people around. It wasn't at all sunny but mummy went round with her sunglasses on. Susie showed us the vintage glass and china stall. There was a large cardboard handwritten sign in black Sharpie stuck to the front of the table. It said,

BOWN CHAI - NA AND SILVEWEAR AN KUT GLARS

There were loads of things for sale and plenty of people having a look. Mummy pushed to the front and immediately saw two Clarendon Royal Doulton dinner plates. "I'll have those Horace," she said to me. "And those two Waterford glasses. They're the same as ours. And that knife and fork." Whilst mummy was having a good look

I pushed round to the side to go and speak to Sonny who I had just seen quickly going round to the back of the van - quicker than I'd ever seen him move before. "Hi Sonny," I said. "Do you work here? Come and say 'Hello' to mummy." Sonny said that he couldn't 'cos he was on his tea break. When I asked him how long his tea break was he said that it was for as long as my mummy was hanging around.

Mummy was in a good mood for the rest of the day and she gave me some money to buy a scooter which was really expensive but when I got home the back wheel fell off. I told mummy that it was the sort of thing that I could imagine Sonny selling and mummy said, "Oh, does Sonny sell stuff?" and I said, "Yes, mostly other people's."

Monday 4th June
A difficult R.E. test.
Test day today at school but they didn't go too well. My first one was R.E. That's short for Religious Education. At the top of the paper I had to write my name in the "My Name" box and then Miss Groves' name in the "Teacher's Name" box. Miss Groves is our R.E. teacher. I wrote my name okay but then I wrote "Miss Groves." Then I thought that I shouldn't put "Miss" 'cos she's married so I crossed off "Miss" and put "Mrs." Then I thought that   although
     there's a Mr around

TEACHER'S NAME: M̶i̶s̶s̶ G̶r̶o̶v̶e̶s̶   she usually calls

him "my boyfriend" so then I thought that they probably weren't married so I crossed off "Mrs" and put "Miss" again. Then I thought that if she wasn't married but had a boyfriend but someone who's probably more than just a boyfriend then she should probably be known as a "Ms" so I just crossed off the "i" and "s" in the middle of "Miss" but then it looked a bit of a mess so I crossed it all off again and wrote "Ms," which isn't a proper title and it sounds like "Miz" so I thought that maybe I shouldn't write that so I crossed that off. But then I just had "Groves" but now there was no space for anything else. Then miss called out, "You should have completed page one by now," and I hadn't even written her name. Still, that was the hardest question sorted out although I had spent so much time on it that I didn't finish the paper and there's no mark for getting your teacher's name right.

Tuesday 5th June
Sonny and the stroking nettles story.
"Did you know that you can safely pick stingin' nettles without being stung if you stroke them?" Sonny asked me today. Apparently it's the little hairs on nettles that sting you but if you pinch the leaf going from stem to outer, which is the way that the hairs grow, and then pick the leaf then you'll be okay. I don't think I'll try it though. I told Sam and he just nodded.

Daddy took a teaspoon out of the kitchen tonight in a tumbler. He said that he's just checking on the slow gin and the tumbler is for keeping the spoon in so as not to make any mess.

Wednesday 6th June
We find out miss' real name.
Miss (Mrs Ms) has marked the R.E. paper. I didn't do very well.

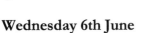

"Next time just write, 'Catherine,'" she said. "Is that with a 'C' or a 'K?'" Mel asked. "Just Horace and only in writing, not in conversation," miss said firmly.

Thursday 7th June
A cub has an imaginative idea in stone-painting - not!

Olivia's been stone painting at cubs tonight. They were supposed to be making the stones look like an object like maybe a piece of fruit or a face or something. One little cub just painted his dark brown. When Akela asked him what his was meant to be he said, "A poo." Akela said, "There's only one place for that," and threw it outside the scout hut door. It landed in the grass by the drain.

Friday 8th June
Stone-painting ramifications.
Mummy told us this morning that today is "World Naked Gardening Day." When I was at scouts this evening I said that I thought that I could do my naturist badge. Skip laughed and said that he presumed that I meant naturalist badge. I said that he presumed wrong and that today is "World Naked Gardening Day." He said that he couldn't have a load of naked scouts running around the scout hut garden for a naturist badge. When Emily's mummy picked her up Emily told her that Skip said that scouts have to take all their clothes off as part of their naturalist badge. Emily's mummy and Skip went and stood in the corner of the hall and were waving their arms around and having a very serious talk then Skip walked off and Emily's mummy made a 'phone call.

I told the Ravings about the cub stone poo and so, when Emily finally left, she picked it up and walked off up the path with it. I came out just after her and she shouted and waved and said that she was taking the stone poo home with her 'cos she said, "No one else will want it and I think it's really real-looking and Akela's 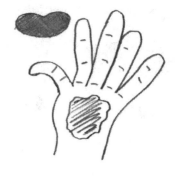 chucked it out and I can have some fun with it." She was about to have that alright. When I looked down I saw that the stone poo was still sitting in the grass next to the drain where Olivia had said that Akela had thrown it. I didn't say anything to Emily though. Then she suddenly came back down the path and she didn't have any poo in her hand - stone or otherwise - and she told me that it was all a bit odd but she had put it in her pocket so that no one else could take it and the stone was three things that you don't expect from a stone. One was that it was soft, another was that it was smelly and the third was that it was warm. Just then Archie's mummy appeared from inside the scout hut and she had rubber gloves on and a bowl of hot water and some cloths and a black sack. She said that Archie's dog had just had a "small, okay, rather large, accident" and that she was going to clear it up but "mysteriously, worryingly and totally inexplicably, the deposit has completely disappeared." When I told her that Emily would probably know where it was Emily looked at her muddy but not mud hands and was then sick. Very sick. So Archie's mummy had to clear that up as well and Emily's gone home in her knickers. So that's Emily's naturist badge nearly sorted.

Saturday 9th June
Charlie gets a wriggly feeling in his tummy.
The scouts had a stall at the Chislehurst Rotary Summer Fair today. We had our world's largest bagatelle board for people to

play on. It measures four feet by sixteen and it's such fun! We had a prize for the highest score for children and adults but no one went without. We had made up a hundred clear plastic bags with slices of carrot and peaches in them and then filled them up with water and tied them at the top. When you shook them they looked just like real goldfish. It was just for a bit of fun. But the really funny thing was that at lunchtime Melanie and Emily went and had a go on another stall and won two actual goldfish each and brought them back to compare and show us how real our carrot and peach slices were.

In the afternoon Charlie and Archie were looking after our stall when a man and his son had a go and were given a couple of carrot and peach bags. Charlie told the man that they weren't really goldfish but the man kept telling him that they were so Charlie said, "Watch this." He took the boy's bag, untied it, put his hand in, scooped up the carrot and peach slices and popped them in his mouth. They went straight down. Then he did the same with the man's bag. He told me later that he was sure that he could feel wriggling in his tummy which was no surprise to Emily and Mel when they came back and asked where their goldfish had gone "'cos we put them there and now they're not," said Emily pointing at an empty chair.

Sunday 10th June
Red dots at church and Sonny gets an unexpected windfall.
Church parade today. Sonny told Skip that he wasn't coming 'cos he had other more profitable things to do than go to church but Skip said that he had to. During his talk the vicar who's called Mike had a big world map and the children had to go to the front and stick small red circles on places where they had been. Soon the map was filled with little red dots all over the world. There weren't many countries that hadn't been touched. The scouts had all had a go - except Sonny. Mike said that it was so nice that the scouts were so well travelled; we even had beavers that had been to Canada and Japan. All Mike asked was, "Have all the scouts had a go?" when someone said, "Sonny hasn't," so Sonny had to go up the front and stick on a red sticker. He stuck his sticker on a place where no one else had - Chislehurst. "Yep, that's great Sonny, but we're supposed to be sticking on places where we've been." Sonny gave Mike a scowl and said, "Chislehurst is about the only [sweary word] place that I've ever bin to recently and as for where I've bin before - that no one's supposed to know," and

he went and sat down again. Afterwards someone came up to Sonny and gave him a load of

money and said, "Please use it to go on a nice long train journey with your family." With this Sonny's eyes lit up so quite a profitable morning's work for one scout at least even though we're not sure what he meant about his cover being blown.

I bet Sonny comes to church parade next time. I wonder if vicars can get suspended?

Monday 11th June
Mel gets locked out of home.
On the way to school today, when we went past the Lion's Head, who should we see inside but Melanie and her mummy tucking in to a full English? I said to Charlie that it's alright for some, but most of us have to put up with a bowl of cereal. It wasn't until Mel got to school that she explained that she had been out with her parents for most of Sunday but when they got home the electric gates on their drive wouldn't work and 'cos it was quite late there was nothing for it but to take a couple of rooms for the night at the Lion's Head. She said that her daddy wasn't very impressed at having to spend a load of money on a few beds for the night that were a stone's throw away from home. I said that she should've 'phoned up Skip and they could have arranged to camp at the scout hut but Mel said she wasn't bothered and she had two sausages in her breakfast.

Tuesday 12th June

Mel gets locked in at home.

Mel wasn't at school today so after school the Ravings all went up to her house to see if she was okay. Mel lives in a huge house at the end of the road with a big wall and big metal gates like at Buckingham Palace which were closed which wasn't normal. There appeared to be no way in but there was a metal plate in the side pillar and it had loads of numbers on it and blue button so we pressed all of them in turn. Then we heard Mel's mummy's voice so Emily said, "It's Emily. We're outside. We just wanted to know if Mel's okay 'cos she wasn't at school today." Then there was a pause and then Mel's mummy said, "You will be aware that I know that she wasn't at school. She's fine. We've just had a bit of a local difficulty, that's all. If you must know, it's all very embarrassing. The drive gates have failed. We finally managed to open them yesterday but now we're in we can't open them again so we can't get the Range Rover out and we've been incarcerated all day waiting for the gate man to come and let us out. We've tried everything. We've put in the emergency code, we've changed the batteries on the clicky thing but to no avail. Nothing. So we've had to sit here all day waiting." Just at that moment Charlie, who had been fiddling with the side gate, opened it. "How did you do that?" I asked. "I turned the handle, that's all," Charlie replied. Emily spoke into the metal plate again. "Are you still there, Mel's mum?" Emily asked. "Yes," came back the reply. "Charlie's just opened the side gate, so you could've escaped." "Yes, yes," said Mel's mummy irritably. "We know the side gate's okay, but you don't think I'm walking Melanie to school do you? We do have standards up this end of the road don't you know? I can't not take the car. June is summer dress - white, yellow and pastels. I might get dusty."

Wednesday 13th June

Sleepover preparations.

Mel's back at school today which is just as well 'cos she's having her first sleepover on Saturday for her girl friends. Apparently her mummy has finally relented. The gates still aren't fixed so she walked down to my house on her own and we went to school together which was fun and I didn't call for Charlie so he was late and it was sort of my fault but I don't care 'cos he needs to take a bit more responsibility for himself. I like Mel. I told her that I hope that she has a fun sleepover and Mel said that her mummy's getting really stressed with the caterers and getting the house spring-cleaned. I said, "It's a bit late for that seeing as we're in summer," but Mel said that she gets the house spring-cleaned every season, even the rooms that no one goes into unless they're playing hide-and-seek.

REMINDERS
TO DO
Spring cleaning
SPRING ✓
SUMMER
AUTUMN
WINTER

Thursday 14th June

More brownie defections.

A new girl has started at cubs. She's moved across from brownies. Olivia came home and said that she said that the reason that she left brownies was 'cos she didn't like her Brown Ale. "It's okay if you mix a bottle with a half of mild," was daddy's reply. I wish I knew what they were both talking about.

Friday 15th June

Bagatelle preparations - how low can you score?

Emily was really told off by assistant scout leader Patrick this evening. Patrick was late to our meeting 'cos he had to visit a friend and got stuck in traffic. Emily asked Patrick where his friend lived and he said, "Mottingham." Emily then told Patrick that her daddy says that he would never live in Mottingham after he saw a

banner hanging at the front of one of the houses that said "Happy 30th Birthday Grandma!" Then Patrick told Emily that he, Patrick, lives in Mottingham at present.

I wonder how old his grandma is?

We have a stall tomorrow at Saint Exuperance School's Summer Fair. Some 3rd Chislehurst scouts a couple of years ago made the world's largest bagatelle board and that's what's going to be on our stall again like we did at Rotary but with no goldfish. It's huge, like an enormous pinball machine but you play with golf balls and a broom handle for a plunger. Skip's a bit fed up 'cos no one puts their name down on a rota anymore and he didn't get many people last week so he has to think of other ways to get us to come out on a Saturday. He's come up with a great idea - we're going to get paid this time! We charge each person for a go and the scout that gets the money can keep it. Everyone gets a certificate with their name on it and their score. We had an entrepreneurial evening including a bit of a "brainstorming" session - which is where you have to think - 'cos we had to work out how much to charge. Emily suggested twenty pounds for five balls but then Skip drew a graph that showed twenty pounds - no customers, no pounds - everyone's a customer. We're going to charge one pound for eight balls.

We all had a practice this evening and Emily scored nought which is almost impossible to do. She reckons that we should have a prize for the lowest score but Mel pointed out that once someone had scored nought how could you go lower, how could you score a minus?

Saturday 16th June
Sonny scores at bagatelle.

We had a great day with the bagatelle board at Saint Exuperance School's Summer Fair. Our bagatelle board is very popular and having a stall at Saint Exuperance's School for Young Ladies is the pinnacle of achievement according to daddy. Mysteriously some of the numbers on the board had become minuses overnight. We had to make a rule that whenever you had a customer, (Sonny called them "punters"), you had to keep score and then do the certificate 'cos Sonny was trying not to do the adding up and certificates. He said that he was best at "front of house" but eventually he had to agree to add up the score for one of his customers / punters. It wasn't very difficult 'cos the numbers are all noughts or fives, like 150, 20, 75 and so on but Sonny was really struggling. He made the score three hundred and seventy-five for the first customer that he added up for but the customer's daddy said that it was four hundred and fifty. Sonny then said that his decision was final and took the balls out of the pockets and holes so no one could check but his customer's daddy was insistent. "Don't you know who I am?" he asked Sonny. "No," said Sonny. "I am the Chief Executive in the United Kingdom of one of Germany's largest banks, that's who I am." "So you should be able to add up," replied a completely unfazed Sonny, before adding, "Or then again, maybe not." In the end, when Sonny was writing out the certificate he put under SCORE - "About 400." I don't think the customer's daddy was very impressed. Then Sonny asked the girl what her name was and she said, "Holly" and under

NAME on the certificate Sonny wrote "HOLE." When he gave Holly her piece paper she looked at it and said, "That's not how I spell my name." Sonny said, "That's how I spell it." Holly said, "You've written 'hole.'" Sonny said, "Well that can be your name naw then can't it? In fact, if you like, I can put 'BIG CAKE' in front of it," as he walked off to find another customer. Sonny was allowed to just give out leaflets and get customers in after that although he had to pay ten pence to whoever was doing his adding up and certificates. Emily was managing quite well with the adding up but she was doing it on her 'phone so got it confiscated and then had to think.

When we were packing up Emily asked Sonny if he had trouble adding up. "Not really," he said, "although I'm better at doing minuses naw 'cos I do that with grandad and darts in the pub when we're playin' '301.'" "Oh," said Emily but that's all she said 'cos I don't think she knew what Sonny was talking about and didn't want to ask even though she has a dartboard. Despite Sonny having been paying out loads of ten pences to those who were looking after his customers he still had tons more money at the end of the day. He even had several twenty pound notes. "How did you get those?" Emily asked. "People here are very generous," Sonny said. "When you're asked, 'What's the money going to?' it's not very encouragin' if you say, 'In ma pocket' so I said that we were donatin' it to the poor of Chislehurst which is basically me but I didn't tell them that bit 'cos they didn't need to know anyfing more complicated than what I had said. Several people gave me a large donation and one woman gave me fifty pounds." Emily couldn't believe it. "That money should be shared!" she complained. "Don't worry," Sonny said. "I've taken out ten pence from each donation." "Yeah, but you've got over one hundred pounds and I only have a few." "Tough, tough, TOUGH," said Sonny. "Not tough," said Emily. "Go and get buy some arithmetic lessons." And that's why Emily has a large bruise on her leg and why Sonny marched off to the bouncy castle. She's at Mel's for a sleepover now so hopefully she can forget all about it otherwise she will just turn into a bitter person.

Sunday 17th June
The girls meet Alfred.
I saw Emily today. She said that the sleepover at Mel's was great fun. "We had food that I didn't even know what it was," she said. "And when it was time for bed we were all given a sort of control pad each and told not to make any noise but if we wanted anything we just had to press the button on the pad. We asked Mel what it was and she said that we would never know unless we needed something. So in the middle of the night when we were all awake we all pressed our buttons and this man appeared in our sleepover room and he was wearing a suit and he didn't smile and he was very posh and he had a name badge with 'Alfred' on it and he said, 'At your service, miss.' I asked, 'Could I have a Pimms and a box of Smarties please?' Then Alfred disappeared and came back in a few minutes with a tumbler glass that looked like it had fizzy blackcurrant in it and bits of chopped-up fruit that I said was very tasty, and a bowl of Smarties on a silver platter and put them down on a table at the corner of the room and then he asked, 'Is there anything else miss?' and I said, 'Not for now, thank you.' All the others were so shocked that they didn't say anything but I reckon it's just as well that the sleepover wasn't two nights otherwise I think that Alfred would've been a bit busier."

Monday 18th June
Making a catapult character during chemistry.
Did you know that you can make quite a good catapult from a plastic bendy ruler? You screw up a small piece of paper into a

ball then chew it to make it all wet then put it on the end of a

ruler and "flick!" They go for miles! Our classroom ceiling is covered with them. Charlie brought in some coloured paper today and is on a mission to flick a red smiley face onto the ceiling. He reckons by the holidays he will have it finished!

Tuesday 19th June
French test gets in the way.

Smiley face is progressing but Charlie had to stop during French as we had a test so we had to keep our heads down. Charlie's no good at French so I let him copy my answers. Unfortunately he got a bit carried away and where it says "Name............" at the top of the sheet of paper he copied my name. At least he

didn't put "Catherine" under the teacher's name bit. Only I'm allowed to put "Catherine."

Wednesday 20th June
Mummy doesn't get what she was expecting at British Hairways.

We didn't exactly laugh when we came home from school but we

all had a little smile. When I got home Olivia marched me up to my bedroom. She followed me in (which is something she normally has to ask to do so I knew that something was up) and told me quietly not to laugh at mummy's new haircut 'cos she said that she had laughed, more out of shock than anything, when she came in and she thought that mummy was going to cry. We went

144

downstairs together and found mummy in the kitchen looking a bit distressed. I smiled at mummy and she gave me a biscuit, in fact she gave me two without having to be asked which was odd, but I didn't say anything. We were both in the sitting room quietly munching and not saying anything when Sam came bombing in. Although Olivia ran out of the sitting room to try to stop him she failed as Sam was on a mission to get a biscuit. He went flying into the kitchen and headed straight for the tin. Nothing was going to stop his advance, nothing was going to get in his way between the front door and a handful of Bourbons. Except mummy's hair. Olivia was in the doorway with eyes wide open and hissing "Sam" through clenched teeth; I was looking at Sam telepathically urging him to look at me but to no avail. "Blimey mum," he exclaimed, "what's happened to your hair?" Then he added insult to injury by continuing, "Looks like Fred the Fork's [our gardener] attacked it with a strimmer!" He didn't wait for an answer. Having made his comment he continued his forward advance to the biscuit tin. The damage had been done however. Despite Olivia's best efforts it was too late. Mummy did something that I wasn't expecting. She burst into tears. "Oh mum," said Sam as he went over to mummy and put his arm around her, although he got his biscuits first, "what's the matter?" "I know it's a disaster," she spluttered through the tears. "First Olivia, then you. I knew exactly what I wanted when I went to British Hairways and was so looking forward to being pampered and having a really lovely restyle. I even tore a photo out of Trend. But Roger [the hairdresser] wasn't there and I had someone new." At this point mummy rushed out of the kitchen, picked up her jacket that looked like it had just been thrown onto the hallway floor and temporarily abandoned, fished around in one of the pockets, and came back into the kitchen holding a scrap of glossy paper. "Look!" she exclaimed, thrusting the photo of a glamorous woman at some event in front of a still-startled Sam. "Does that look like me?" "No, but it's not, it's Kate..." "Yes I know who it is. But look at her hair. Does that look like mine?"

Sam took the photo and scrutinised it carefully. "You don't have to look that closely," mummy complained. "I was just thinking how nice she looked," said Sam purring, "but 'no' it doesn't look like your hair. But why didn't you say something when you could see that it was starting to go wrong then they could have sort of readjusted or whatever?" But mummy just scowled. "You just don't understand. Once you've told your hairdresser what you want to have done and have given implicit instructions, you can't say anything if it goes wrong. You just have to sit there in silent sorrow as the hairdresser gives you a different haircut to the one that you had sought," mummy sighed. She's right on one thing though. We don't understand.

We all feared for daddy's arrival home. We imagined him coming through the front door, throwing off his jacket, loosening his tie and wandering into the sitting room to give mummy a kiss but then taking one look at her and saying, "Blimey, I've married a pulverised pixie!" But he didn't. We were doing our homework in our rooms when he came home. He was so quick that none of us had time to intercept him. We all fell down the stairs and stood in the kitchen doorway just in time to see daddy go up to mummy, give her a hug and say, "Hallo sexy. Nice hair!" "Do you think so?" mummy asked. "Yes," he said. "I loooove it. Fab. Fantastic. A new look for the summer. It's great." Then daddy turned round at looked at us staring; he winked and asked us what we were doing. "Nothing," we said. Mummy then told daddy that it wasn't quite what she was expecting. She said that she wanted it to look like Kate whatshername's new style but she couldn't find the photo. "I put it down here somewhere," she said, absently stroking the kitchen table. We found it later. Well I did when I went into Sam's room to borrow a ruler after Charlie and I had ours confiscated at school today. I found her taped to his bed headboard. "Are you thinking of getting a haircut as well?" I asked him but he didn't say anything, just smiled. Maybe he's considering buying a Versace dress.

146

Thursday 21st June

Personal hygiene issues at beavers.

Edward and Charlie were helping at beavers tonight. They were having a personal hygiene session and had to bring a wash kit with them. When it was time to clean their teeth one of the beavers burst into tears and said that his mouth tasted funny as foam poured out from between his lips. When Edward investigated he found that the beaver had squirted shower gel into his mouth before rubbing it in with his toothbrush. On pick-up beaver leader Bramble told

his mummy that he has "very clean teeth and a very clean mouth." "And rabies," Charlie added, not very helpfully.

Friday 22nd June

Emily has a surprise.

Joint sleepover at scouts this weekend with some other scouts in the district who have visited with a very bossy scout leader. I don't like him one little bit. We're practising putting up some new modern tents and then taking them down, sleeping in them in-between obviously. It's a really warm evening. Mel has been collecting scarves and has three and is wearing all of them. Mind you, she has quite a way to go to beat Archie's seventeen woggles.

Sonny wasn't looking very happy tonight and Emily wanted to know why. "Surely you can't be sad when you're rich, with all that money you got at the bagatelle?" "It's not that easy," he said. "I had the money in ma shoe for safe-keepin'. Then I decided as a treat I would have a go on the bouncy castle, while you were clearin' up, but I wasn't allowed my shoes on. When I came back to them they were still there but the money had gone. I can't believe it," he sighed. "Chislehurst is full of thieves." "Yeah, and since a couple of months ago we've had one more," she said. And with that Emily pulled out one hundred pounds from her pocket and waved it at Sonny.  "Here's our money Sonny," she said. "I followed you to the bouncy castle and then took it for safe-keeping, so shall I give it to you to buy some sums lessons or shall I give it to Skip which is where it should be going?" "I'm sure we can come to some arrangement," said Sonny. And they did. But neither will tell me what. And I thought that Emily was my friend.

Saturday 23rd June

It pays to listen carefully to what Skip is saying.
It was a really warm evening yesterday and it lasted half the night. It felt more hot than usual in our tents. Mel kept getting up and complaining to Skip, when he was sitting round the small camp fire with Patrick, that she couldn't sleep 'cos she was too hot. Skip asked her what she was wearing in her sleeping bag and she told him that she had all her clothes on. Well take them off and put your pyjamas on. "I don't have any," she said. "Then unzip your sleeping bag and lay it across you like a duvet." Five minutes later she was back, still hot. In despair,  Skip said, "Then strip to your knickers. Then you should be cool enough." Unfortunately for Skip, just as the horrible scout leader appeared, so did Mel once more - from her tent - stark naked but

148

for her three scarves. "Like this, Skip?" she asked, "'cos I'm still too hot."

Sunday 24th June
Skip gets suspended - again!
The District Commiserator paid us a visit today at our scout hut camp as we were packing up and Skip has been suspended.

Monday 25th June
Daddy's caught fibbing.
Sam told me that Tanya told him that daddy told Skip that mummy's new hairstyle was "horrible, like she's been run over by a lawnmower." When I told daddy that he had told mummy that he loved it he said I would "work these things out for yourself when you're older. Anyway," he added, "I had my fingers crossed when I said it so it didn't count."

Tuesday 26th June
Finger-crossing fibs.
I asked mummy today whether she had ever crossed her fingers. She said that she did when she was getting married and saying her wedding vowels. She then said that people cross their fingers for luck. I don't think daddy does, but I didn't say anything.

Wednesday 27th June
Emily has an expected visitor during her birthday tea.
The Ravings and few other lesser individuals went round to Emily's after school today for a birthday tea. Emily's house is really old and someone famous once lived there and she has a blue plaque on the front of the house but I don't know who the person is. While we were scoffing an old lady appeared at the front door and Emily's mummy had a long chat before admitting

her. Then she came in and she joined our tea party. She was such fun. She looked about two hundred years old and apparently she used to live in Emily's house years and years and years ago. She lives in north London now and was going down to the coast so asked her grandson if he would take her to look at her old house which is now Emily's, well Emily's mummy's or daddy's or both probably or maybe it belongs to all of them. Or the bank. Daddy says that our house is owned by the bank which is a bit weird. Maybe it used to be a bank but I'm not too sure. Maybe there were loads of banks in the old days so that people could put their cash somewhere instead of in their pillow, like I do sometimes. When the old lady saw that there were people in the front room she

decided to see if she could come in. She's related to the blue plaque person but she's not actually the blue plaque person as,
1. She's a woman and the blue plaque person is a man I think.
2. She's not dead. At least I don't think she is although she looks it.

I don't think that you get a blue plaque until you're dead.

She told us stories about what it was like living in the house years and years and years ago. Then she told us about the garden and the big climbing tree (that's still there only bigger) and the layout of the house. She remembered all sorts of interesting things about the house, the road and Chislehurst. She was really interesting. Then she suddenly stopped talking about whatever she was talking about and grabbed Emily's wrist and held on to it tightly. "Do you ever wonder why sometimes it gets really cold in this room?" she asked her cryptically - all the while staring at her.

Emily had said to us before that the room had sometimes been inexplicably chilly but she didn't tell the old lady. Emily just said, "Err, no." "Then did you ever find out about the unexplained event that happened in nineteen-eighteen with the little boy?" "Err, no," said Emily again, sounding more than a little nervous. "Or the blood in the room that's now your bedroom and the scandal regarding the woman who lived here who was hung although she was later adjudged to have been innocent and who then..." She suddenly broke off, seemingly now aware of the effect she was having on us with what she was saying and that she probably should not be telling young people 'cos we were probably all looking terrified apart from me. She let go of Emily's wrist and said without waiting for a response, "No and it's probably best if I don't say any more. And I have to leave now." The old lady stood up and left. It was all a bit weird.

Thursday 28th June
Emily's recovering.
Emily looked really tired at school today. I asked if she had seen any little boys in the night and she said that she hadn't and that it was highly unlikely as she had spent the night at Mel's house.

Mel said that she had enjoyed the party but that the party bags were a bit naff "'cos there was nothing in mine that you could plug in."

We're making nettle tea again tomorrow with Patrick. I hope I don't sting my tongue.

Friday 29th June
Tea and tarps.
Nettle tea with Patrick was yummy but I did add loads of sugar. Charlie said that it was a bit of a bother when all

we had to do was go down to the supermarket but I told him that you can't do that when you're in the middle of the jungle or up Mount Everest or have no money.

Then we made a waterslide down the slope with a kids' slide to start on. We put down loads of tarps with plastic sheeting on top. Then we poured water down the slide and squirted washing-up liquid on the water. We used up a whole litre from the kitchen. We all had tons of goes and it was great fun. When I got home mummy said that for the first time in my life I had come back from scouts cleaner than when I had gone.

Saturday 30th June
Flight stimulator - but daddy has a bigger problem.
We had a trip to Biggin Hill Airport today with Patrick and met the air scouts. They have a device that their scout leader said, "artificially re-creates aircraft flight and the environment in which it flies, for pilot training, design, or other purposes." When I asked their leader if I could be first he asked, "On what?" and I said, "Your flight stimulator." "Now there's an idea." he said. Sometimes I think grown-ups are on a different planet. My fears were further confirmed when I got home to find daddy in the sitting room looking particularly dejected. I went and sat next to him so that he could give me a cuddle. I then asked him what the problem was. Daddy said that he had been in the high street earlier and had bumped into Mike, the local vicar, who daddy doesn't really know. Daddy said that he never knew what to say to a vicar so just said, "What are you up to then?" Mike said, "Tomorrow I'm taking a small group to Lords." "Fantastic," said daddy. "Eat loads of pies, drink too many Pimms, then a dozen pints of Fosters and watch the Aussies get smashed for a successions of sixes all around the ground?" "No," said Mike. "Lourdes. In France. In the foothills of the Pyrenees. Where the Virgin Mary is said to have appeared to a local woman and where pilgrims can drink or bathe in water flowing from a spring.

They're seeking miracles."
"Same as at Lords then," said daddy as he went extremely red and hurried back home without looking up once. Why don't people just smile at vicars and walk quickly past rather than talk to them and say something stupid? Or maybe not even look at them at all?

Sunday 1st July

Chinese checkers.

Mummy and daddy went out this evening for a Chinese meal with some friends from down the road. Mummy told her friends that the special noodles were to die for. When the waiter came over mummy asked if she could have her favourite noodles. The waiter said, "Yes, of course. And which noodles are they?" Mummy said, "They are your excellent..." and at this point daddy said that mummy rather ostentatiously opened her mouth as if she were about to pop a large grape in it, pursed her lips, and said, "Kuan Chi noodles." The waiter snatched the menu away from mummy and said, "You taking the pith?" Mummy looked really shocked and said, "No, I just want your excellent noodles that I had last time." "You mean zees?" asked the waiter opening the menu and shoving it in front of mummy's face. "Oh, um, yes, sorry, I'm really sorry, but yes, they're the ones." When the waiter had gone off daddy asked, "What on earth was all that about?" Quietly mummy said, "I think we would pronounce them, 'crunchy noodles.'"

Monday 2nd July
Dandelions and nettles. Good and bad!

Sam did scavenger cooking at explorers tonight. They ate dandelions. You can eat all of a dandelion. You can make coffee with the root and put the stem and leaves in a salad. The yellow heads you can dip in batter and fry. Yummy! Free food! Sam said it was great fun. Unfortunately the rest of the evening wasn't so successful. Sam remembered what I had said about stroking nettles so he told Chrissie as they were making nettle tea. What he hadn't remembered was the direction in which you have to stroke them. I can't remember either now. Anyway, all the explorers got stung and Chrissie ran out of antihistamine cream. Then Sam said that all you had to do was pick a dock leaf, crush it, spit on it and rub it on the sting. Chrissie told him that she had enough of Sam's quackery and sent him home.

Tuesday 3rd July
Sonny changes his mind.

Tanya told Sam and Sam told me that Skip has been reinstated, thank goodness. In the meantime Melanie has been taught the difference between "knickers" and "neckers."

I told Sonny that he was responsible for all the explorers getting stung by nettles last night after stroking them. He said that it wasn't nettles it was dandelion leaves. I informed him that they picked those as well but they didn't sting. "See, it works then," he replied and walked off.

Wednesday 4th July
Sonny and his world of knots.

Emily's brought "The World of Knots" and a bit of string to school today and said that she wanted to learn some new ones.

She showed me how you can make handcuffs from a clove hitch which is quite good fun. I did ask her why anyone would want to handcuff her with a bit of rope but she didn't know. Then Sonny walked past and smiled. Emily reckons she knows about ten knots so I said that I thought that I knew about twelve. She then said that hers were definite and mine were only "thoughts" so each of mine counted a half so my total was just six. At lunchtime we asked the other Ravings how many knots they knew. Emily was still winning on ten definites when we asked Sonny. "I reckon about fifty at least," he said quite confidently. "What are they?" Emily asked, keen to learn a few more. "Start with the ones we all know." Sonny said, "Do not swear, do not be late for school, do not steal all the time, do not shout, do not kick, do not hit, do not..." No one liked to say anything so we just let him continue. Edward counted sixty-seven and so we made Sonny the winner. We called him the "Not knot winner," but we didn't tell him that.

Thursday 5th July

Balmy mint.

Mummy's been growing herbs outside the back door in a big pot. She wanted to grow some mint 'cos she said that she likes it on her potatoes but daddy said, "Funny that because it's also quite nice in Pimms," but mummy just scowled. We had boiled potatoes tonight and mummy added some mint 'cos it's been growing really well. The trouble was, it didn't make the potatoes taste minty, it just made them lemony. Then mummy said that it was probably lemon mint but she hadn't been looking too closely in the garden centre so daddy went and looked in a book. He then informed mummy that she hadn't bought mint, lemon mint or

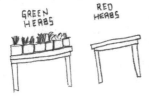

any other mint, she had bought lemon balm. Mummy said that it looked similar to mint "'cos it was green," but daddy then said that most herbs were green so that's no excuse. Anyway, now mummy's made some lemon balm tea and it's chilling in the fridge and we can have some later. She's made loads.

Friday 6th July
Fun with armpit fudge.
We made armpit fudge tonight at scouts. This involves taking fudge ingredients - icing sugar, butter, some cream cheese, cocoa powder and vanilla essence, measuring them into a freezer or sandwich bag, sealing it and then squishing and sliding it under the armpit until the contents have gone all doughy. The bag can then be undone and the fudge attacked with a spoon. It's a good idea to double bag as otherwise the bags would be in danger of popping  which would make quite a mess. As it was it was quite successful and we all went home full of sugar.

Emily told Skip that she knew ten knots but then Sonny piped up and said that he knew sixty-seven and the Ravings all laughed. Skip said that that was more than he knew and Sonny told him that that was because Skip was a "goodie-goodie" and we all laughed again. Fortunately Skip didn't ask Sonny to name any of them.

Mummy went to the garden centre today and found out that lemon balm is part of the mint family so doesn't know what book daddy had been looking in. I took a large bottle of mummy's lemon balm mint tea to scouts tonight so that I wouldn't have to drink it. Some of the scouts quite liked it but it didn't taste lemony so maybe mummy had just bought lemony potatoes.

This year our summer camp is NorWamBamJam and all the Ravings have signed up to it. It's going to be really exciting! The camp is an international jamboree and has thousands of people - scouts and guides - going from around the world and each group will be in a subcamp. We're in the 1940s which is the oldest one. Skip says each subcamp will have a gateway and it will be decorated with a load of similar mascots, one from the fifty or so groups in each subcamp. The best in each subcamp wins a prize. Ours is to be an aeroplane each and Skip showed us the template that we can use as a guide. It says that the dimensions have to be approximately four hundred by four hundred centimetres. Skip says that it's going to be a huge gateway and he's freaking out over the size and how he's going to get it built in time. It can be made from any material and we've all been told to put our thinking caps on. It can't be anything to do with the Second World War 'cos we have a German group on our camp and we don't want to upset them. Same goes for the fancy dress evening. I suggested to Skip that he speaks to Mel's daddy - 'cos Mel's not at scouts tonight - 'cos he did something with aeroplanes like build them or fly them or blow them up or maybe all three 'cos he was once in the RAF. Skip told us that we need to do a little bit of research on East Anglia and the cathedral at Norwich and stuff like that so that we have something to tell the Germans if they want to talk to us.

Saturday 7th July
The two jug trick.
I've kept my head down today 'cos mummy was starting the day all stressed. It was the Chislehurst School fair so I went there.

Daddy had to go to hospital today for a check up but there was a bit of a moment at breakfast time 'cos mummy couldn't find daddy's urine sample. "Where was it mummy?" I asked and she said, "I put it in the fridge yesterday to cool down." Fortunately Skip hasn't rung to say that everyone that was at scouts last night has died. Sam came to the rescue. He said that he had swapped a bottle 'cos he wanted the urine bottle 'cos he needed a green bottle and that he'd put the urine in a clear one and it was in front of all the others. Off mummy and daddy went. Once they had gone down the drive I said too Sam that whatever he had swapped over it wasn't the urine 'cos I'd already taken it to scouts yesterday. "I know," he said but I couldn't let mum find that out 'cos you would've been really told off and I owe you a favour." So "thank you" Sam.

At the fair Sonny's mummy was in charge of the bar and Sonny was helping but he was only allowed to do the children's drinks. There was beer and wine and Pimms for the adults. Pimms is a drink that is light red and it has loads of chopped up fruit in it and it's full of alcohol and makes parents speak all posh and giggle. Sonny's mummy had made up loads in large glass jugs. The Ravings weren't allowed any. We had a sort of fruit punch that was mainly cranberry juice and lemonade and it was a bit boring to start with and was in plastic jugs with no fruit. At least it was much cheaper than the Pimms 'cos sir said that we needed to be encouraged to drink to stay hydrated 'cos it was so hot. Sonny wasn't happy that his mummy wouldn't put chopped up fruit in the children's drinks so when she was in the toilet Sonny asked the man that was doing the Pimms if he could have a couple of handfuls of chopped up fruit from the bowl for the children's fruit punch and he said, "Yes!" Then the man got busy with having to sort out change for someone so Sonny put his hands into two jugs of Pimms and fished out all the fruit that was floating on top and stuck it in two of the fruit punch jugs. "That will liven it up!" Sonny thought. But it was worse than that! A bit of fruit soaked in alcohol wasn't going to do much damage; it was nothing worse than having a bowl of sherry trifle, but when Sonny's mummy came back from the loo she started to complain that the drinks were in the wrong jugs. "I had Pimms in the glass jugs and the kids' fruit punch in the plastic jugs," she grumbled. "Now someone's made up two jugs each with the wrong stuff in it." Sonny said that it was his fault and that he was only trying to help. (I think he's learnt that line from me.) Then the man said, "Don't worry. Sonny has been looking after things admirably, even suggesting a few tweaks here and there, so don't be too hard on him." Sonny's mummy just huffed and swapped the jugs over and Sonny came and found us. "Now's the time to get ya fruit punch! And you can buy me one Mel please," he told the Ravings and we all wandered over to the bar. "Seven fruit punches please!" Sonny asked the man. "And please can we have them out of the glass jug with no fruit?" "Of course," said the man, picking up a jug and starting to pour. "But why the glass jug?" "Not only is it a bit more grown-up but the plastic ones remind us of water wiv our school dinners." "Fair enough," said the man. After we had had our second glass each and had finished off both jugs things went a bit fuzzy and we were all getting confused and had to hold onto each other in the middle of the fair - apart from Sonny who seemed perfectly alright. At one point sir came over and asked us what the matter was. Emily said, "Please sir, can you tell us where we are?" and sir said, "Some place I reckon you definitely shouldn't be."

When Sonny's mummy found us she complained that she had been "removed from duties" 'cos "all the mums were complaining that I'ld been watering down the Pimms."

"At least the parents'll know where they are," said Emily as she ran off to what she thought was a camp toilet tent but unfortunately wasn't and that is how Sidney the sick sailor came to put in a sudden and unexpected appearance at the Punch and Judy show mid-performance.

Sunday 8th July

The Ravings go pick-your-own and Sonny and Charlie go help-yourself.

Daddy's check-up went fine but the doctor was a little concerned when he saw daddy's bottle of green lemon balm wee. "I don't want to alarm you Mr Horrise," the doctor told him, "but green could be the sign of a urinary tract or bacterial infection." Daddy has to ring up in a week.

Meanwhile the Ravings all went off to the farm to do pick-your-own 'cos it's strawberry season. Charlie brought a tub of clotted cream and Sonny had a packet of sugar. Needless to say I picked strawberries with Emily and Mel. They had money. We walked home with our heads held high. Sonny and Charlie had a ride home in a police car with their heads hung low. Charlie said that he was Sonny's brother so they both got dropped off at Sonny's house to avoid embarrassment on Charlie's mummy's part. When they got to Sonny's a policewoman went and told Sonny's mummy, that her children had been eating strawberries without paying for them. Sonny's mummy didn't bat an eyelid at the suggestion that Charlie was one of her sons. I know Sonny comes from a large extended family but you would've thought that his mummy should've known which ones were her children. I thought that Sonny and Charlie would get a big telling off but after the policewoman left Sonny's mummy said, "Well done boys. Did you save any for me?" With that Sonny produced the tub of what was left of the clotted cream that was stuffed full of strawberries. "There ya go mum," Sonny said and his mummy chuckled. "Yummy, my favourite!" I think Sonny is becoming a bad influence on Charlie. I shall have to keep an eye on him.

Monday 9th July
Axe-throwing idea.

Sam did axe-throwing at explorers tonight. That sounds like great fun but we haven't been allowed to do it in scouts. They use axes with pointy heads and long handles and they throw them at a wooden target. I'm going to have a go tomorrow. Daddy has an axe in his shed and I think that I'll use that. It will probably work the same.

Daddy wasn't speaking to mummy tonight. Maybe he's saving his voice 'cos he has an important meeting tomorrow and has to be up at five o'clock. He wrote mummy a note that said, "I need to be up at five o'clock in order to catch the 'plane. Wake me."

Tuesday 10th July
Axe-throwing preparation.

Mummy's been quiet today after daddy had a paddy at about seven o'clock this morning and stormed out of the house. Daddy hadn't been woken at five o'clock by mummy 'cos she had simply rolled over in bed and put a piece of paper on his head which read, "Wake up! It's five o'clock," before going back to sleep.

I made the tea tonight. I told mummy that I would and she said, "Okay." I knew that today was the right day to offer 'cos it's been quite hot so the next thing mummy said was, "We'll just have a salad."

All was fine until Olivia found a caterpillar and screamed, "There's nothing that I can think of that's worse than finding a caterpillar in my salad." "I can," said Sam. "Half a caterpillar," then everyone laughed.

I didn't.

I built my axe target tonight. I made a tripod using a figure of eight lashing that Skip has taught us, and put it on the back lawn. Then I found the old dartboard in the shed and screwed it onto the tripod. I'll be facing the house when I do it so that I can see if anyone's in the kitchen whilst I'm practicing and so can stop before I'm found out 'cos I don't think that I'll be allowed. I couldn't find an axe like Sam was describing but I did uncover a pick-axe so that will do. After all, axes are all the same, more or less, just different shapes and sizes. It's wooden with an iron top and it's old and rusty but it will be fine with a bit of prep.

Wednesday 11th July
Axe-throwing on hold and aeroplane taking off.
Couldn't do axe-throwing tonight as mummy was in the kitchen. I made more preparations though. I went into daddy's shed whilst he was still at work and still sulking and got out the pick-axe. I've oiled the wooden handle and now it looks much nicer.

Mel's daddy's come to the rescue with the aeroplane for NorWamBamJam. Mel says that he was previously something high up in the RAF so he will know what to do. Mel says that whatever he's planning it's going to be a winner 'cos the RAF is something to do with fighting planes.

Thursday 12th July
Axe-throwing finally.

Axe-throwing this evening. It didn't go too well though. It's not as easy as it sounds. I waited until mummy had taken Olivia off to cubs and before daddy had returned home. Sam was round at Tanya's. At teatime Sam told me that you have to hold the axe over your head and throw really hard. He told me that when he did it he shut his eyes but still managed to hit the target. I showed him the dartboard target and he said that it was a bit small and that they had used slices of tree trunk but I thought that it'ld be fine. I'm a better shot than Sam. Well, was. Once mummy had disappeared in the car I went and got the pick-axe. I had a couple of practice throws aiming at a tree but I missed both times however the tree is quite narrow and I wasn't throwing hard enough. I went and stood in front of my target, about five meters away like Sam said. It was really hard to lift the pick-axe over my head and throw it in a straight line like Sam had instructed so instead I did it like I was bowling a cricket ball but not round and down 'cos I would just hit the grass. I did round and up which was the other way round. It was underarm but I kept going in a circle a bit like a hammer throw but not over my head. I thought that I'ld be okay 'cos I'm a good shot and I would hit the target on the way up. I had a couple of practice swings then shut my eyes and then let go. It was more like a slip though 'cos the handle was quite oily. Then I heard  an enormous CRASH! and it's not the sort of crash that little boys like to hear. I opened one eye but the kitchen window and patio doors were still intact so I went indoors and hid. Mummy came home, daddy came home, Olivia came home and Sam eventually came home but no one said anything so I just thought that maybe it was a bad dream, but one that seemed very real nevertheless, too real maybe and the pick-axe is missing. I went to bed.

Friday 13th July
Axe-throwing ramifications.
This morning didn't get off to a very good start. I woke up at 00.15am according to my clock to the sound of mummy screaming uncontrollably in her bedroom. I put my head under my pillow and I heard my door open then close again but no one said anything. At breakfast I wasn't going to speak but mummy did. She said that when she went to bed she found that her large bedroom window was smashed to pieces with glass all over the carpet and daddy's sweary word pick-axe imbedded in the fitted wardrobe on the other side of the room. "What should I make of that?" mummy asked, looking at me very angrily. "Put him in the Olympics," Sam said, before I could even start to think of a suitable reply.

It was tie-dyeing tonight which was fun and a welcome distraction from the atmosphere at home. The scouts all tie-dyed a t-shirt and Emily tie-dyed her hair.

Saturday 14th July
Bag packing and sent packing.
My axe-throwing target has been dismantled. Not by me.

We did bag packing in the supermarket today to raise money for scout funds. I was packing with Sonny and he was great. We raised the most money. He would talk to all the shoppers and told anyone who would listen, and even those that didn't want to, that we were raising money for those who needed some joy and a bit of adventure in their lives. When I asked him who that would be he said, "Us." I told him that I had plenty of joy and adventure in my life already but he said that he was just using a well-known marketing tool. "It doesn't matter if what you're sayin' is one hundred percent correct, you just want to help assuage the guilt trip that the greedy shoppers are on, buying unnecessary items that they don't need." I said to Sonny that it sounded as though what he was saying had come straight out of a salesman's brochure. "It did," he said quite unashamedly.

Every hour we were allowed ten minutes off to go to the toilet and stuff. Sonny and I wandered around the store and Sonny spied the strawberries. "You can't take those," I told him. You stole enough last week." "That wasn't stealin'," said Sonny. "They were lyin' on the ground. The fact that the farmer owned the field and they were attached to the plants has nothin' to do with it. We can't all go around claimin' bits of ground as our own otherwise  eventually we'ld 'ave nowhere left to walk." By this time we were walking up the shampoo aisle and Sonny saw a small roll-on antiperspirant. "I could do wiv some of that," he said and helped himself. He took the top off and pulled out his t-shirt at the side and applied a bit under his arm. He then did the same on the other side. He then replaced the cap and put it back on the shelf. When he saw my face he said, "I haven't stolen it; I've just borrowed a bit. Look," he said, pointing at the label, "it says that it contains fifty millilitres. That's loads, and I've had not even one pence worth. Don't worry about it. The supermarket don't want smelly bag packers do they?" I thought Sonny had a point so I had some as well. Just then a man with a badge and an ear-piece appeared and to cut a long story short Sonny had to do the afternoon shift by himself.

We played Monopoly tonight and daddy cheated - again.

Sunday 15th July
Monopoly deceit.
Tanya came round tonight and told us that her father really approves of her going out with Sam. The reason she gave was that when her daddy rang her up yesterday evening at our house she heard our daddy say that he was just about to buy a hotel in Mayfair. She hadn't the heart to tell him that we had been playing Monopoly.

Monday 16th July
Tie-dye ramifications.
Emily's off school today 'cos she can't get the tie-dye out of her hair.

Tuesday 17th July
Daddy's test results.
Daddy rang up the hospital today to get the result of his green urine. He was told that he had no infections and that his urine was perfectly fine if somewhat alkaline.

Mummy celebrated with a Pimms and lemon balm.

Wednesday 18th July
How to avoid being injured when attacked.

Charlie told me at school today that if someone's about to attack you the best thing that you can do is crawl under a car 'cos no one can throw a punch if you're under a car so you're quite safe. You just need to  get your head and torso under the car "the legs aren't so important." "They are if the driver gets in the car and drives off," said Melanie.

Thursday 19th July
Olivia's found out where babies come from.
Olivia came home from cubs tonight and was really excited. "I've learnt something new," she said to mummy. "I know where baby's come from." This was going to be interesting 'cos there are certainly others in the Horrise family who are a little unsure, mentioning no names. Mummy asked her, "And where do babies come from?" Emily took a deep breath and said, "Their mummy's bladder!" Mummy didn't say anything so Olivia said, "Is that right mummy?" "Near enough darling," said mummy and walked off. "Near enough?" What sort of answer is that? Can you imagine going into hospital and saying "I'm about to have a baby," and the doctor says, "Where is it?" and the mummy says, "It's around here somewhere," pointing at her tummy and the doctor says, "Near enough."

I'm glad I'm a boy. And some are still unsure.

Friday 20th July
Sonny gets invested - just and then drops a bombshell.
Sonny was invested tonight. We lowered the flag and Sonny had to put his left hand on it and make the scout sign. "Repeat the Scout Promise," Skip told him. Sonny looked all serious and said,

"On my honour," and then put his hand down. "There's a bit more to it than that," Skip told him. "My dad always said never to promise nuffin then you can't get into trouble for not keepin' your promises, mate," Sonny retorted. "The thing is Sonny," Skip replied gently, "the promises that we make are things that we aspire to. No one's going to get cross if you've tried your best to do your duty. The monarch isn't going to get you into trouble, God isn't going to tell you off. As long as you try to help others and aim to keep the scout law then everything's fine." "It's all a bit of a nonsense then isn't it?" said Sonny and we all gasped but he still got his scarf and woggle. I think Skip made an exception.

Skip's growing tomatoes in his greenhouse and we know 'cos he brought a tomato plant in to show us 'cos not all the scouts had seen one. "Looks to me a like a cannabis plant," said Sonny  without being asked for his opinion. "How do you know that?" asked Skip looking a bit surprised. "'Cos that's what my dad grows when he's around to make a few bob but he doesn't have 'em in a greenhouse he has 'em, hundreds of 'em, in the roof of a house that no one lives in." "And where is this house?" Skip asked. "I'm not stupid," Sonny said. "I'm not tellin' you 'cos I know what you're like an' you'll probably try and nick a few but I can bring one in for you in the next week or so if I can get hold of one, if ya like, and do a swapsies 'cos I've always fancied growing tomatoes."

At the end of the meeting Sonny somehow managed to go home with the tomato plant and Skip's refused the offer of a swap. I think that maybe Sonny's considering a more honest way to earn a living.

Saturday 21st July

Charlie doesn't have a key - and not much garden by the sound of it.

Charlie came round to play which was fun but he wasn't in any hurry to go home for his lunch. "Mummy isn't in so she's going to come and get me when she's home." "Why don't you have a key?" I asked him. "'Cos I normally lose them." "Get your mummy to stick one under a flower pot." "We don't have any flower pots." "Why not?" "'Cos the flowers all die." "Get your mummy to stick one under a plant in the garden." "We don't have any plants in the garden." "Why not?" "'Cos the plants all die."

Charlie stayed for lunch.

Sunday 22nd July

Sonny's tomato plant at risk temporarily.

Sonny's house has been raided but the police found nothing more suspect than Skip's Moneymaker tomato plant that Sonny had planted in the garden. The police profusely apologised to Sonny's mummy and said that tomato plants weren't what they were after and someone had obviously misheard a conversation about highly lucrative cash crops.

Monday 23rd July

Emily gets in an A to Z muddle.

We did a London hike today. We were put in teams of four and given an Ordnance Survey map for London North (Explorer series) and a compass. We were set off at ten minute intervals from the underground station at Hampstead Heath and had to get to Charing Cross using as much green space as possible and on foot. My team did really well and if we hadn't diverted into Covent Garden for an ice cream and to watch an acrobat then we probably would've won. Archie's team didn't do so well. One of Archie's team members (ahem Emily), told Archie that she could never understand Ordnance Survey maps so had brought along an "A to Z of London" street map book. Apparently things were going quite well to start with. They went south down Haverstock Hill and then Emily turned the page as they continued into Chalk Farm Road and that's where it went terribly wrong. Chalk Farm Road went below the bottom of the page but instead of finding the new page somewhere else in the book to carry on their journey, Emily assumed that if you turn the page you would be able to continue on down. She told her team, "I know what I'm doing," so they just followed. Instead of going down south they started going sideways east - first to Hackney Marsh then Forest Gate and by the time they got to Ilford in the middle of the afternoon Archie decided to ask a policeman. He said something about turning Emily's book sideways and then they got a ride in a police van to Charing Cross where Skip and Patrick were waiting with the rest of us. As they were climbing out of the van Skip went running over and asked the driver what the scouts had done wrong. The driver said, "Nothing," and so Skip disqualified Archie's team for not walking even though they had probably walked further than any of us.

Tuesday 24th July

A welcome addition to the family.

Daddy's bought a caravan. Just like that! It's on the drive 'cos there's space with the car and there's a few centimetres to spare. It's white and it's brand new. It sleeps five. It has seats that turn into beds and there's a toilet and a shower and a kitchen. We're going to take it to Bournemouth on holiday this year. Daddy says that it'll last for years and although it cost loads we (that means he) will save a lot of money 'cos there will be no more expensive hotel bills. I've been inside and it makes me wonder why we all have such big houses when five people can fit into something the size of a large van. After all, if we can live in it for one or two weeks then we can live in it forever. It's probably going to be as much fun as a hotel but mummy says that there's no bar. Well daddy can just jolly well park it outside a pub then can't he? We're sleeping in it tonight, that's me, Sam and Olivia, but daddy says we're not allowed to touch anything 'cos not everything's ready yet but we can go to the toilet.

Wednesday 25th July
Crazy golf, crazy satnav and caravan capers (maybe).
We went to play crazy golf this evening somewhere in Lewisham. Mummy took me and Charlie in the car. She wasn't sure of the way so we had to put the postcode in the satnav. We found the car park was shared with Lewisham Crematorium. Mummy's lady on the satnav managed to get us all the way without a hitch. When we turned into the car park she said, "You have now arrived at your final destination," to which mummy replied, "I hope not love, at least not yet."

We can sleep in the caravan again tonight and so can Charlie and we can cook breakfast. Mummy's given us some bacon and eggs and beans and said that it's fine 'cos daddy's gone away for a few days.

Thursday 26th July
The new addition suffers.
Not such a good day today. This morning Charlie and I cooked our bacon and eggs and beans 'cos mummy said that we could so long as we didn't plug in or unplug anything. Daddy had said that the cooker hob didn't have the gas plumbed in yet 'cos there's one canister for the hob and one for the grill and daddy has only bought one so far for the grill. We had a small gas stove with smaller gas bottles in the garage so we used that. We put it on top of the hob and grill and I did bacon and eggs in the frying pan on one gas ring and the beans on the other. Charlie did the knives and forks and plates and put them on the dining table which was where we had been sleeping but the beds become seats and a cupboard becomes a table. Just as it was all ready Charlie wanted to have a wash so had to go indoors. I put his fairly full English under the grill and turned it on to keep it warm and ate my breakfast on my own. By the time that I had finished Charlie still hadn't appeared so I went to find him. He was in the hallway talking to mummy and telling her how much he had enjoyed his sleep in the caravan and how he was going to see if his daddy would buy one. Mummy was saying that his family could always borrow ours 'cos we would have it for many years when there was an explosion outside the front door and it sounded like someone had blown up a petrol station. Mummy rushed to the front door and opened it and then screamed. The roof of the caravan was smouldering in the road, the side walls had collapsed

and what little there had been on the caravan floor was all smoked black. There were piles of smouldering stuff all over the front lawn and beyond. It was like someone had dropped an atomic bomb on our garden maybe but I don't know. The explosion was really loud 'cos it woke Sam up. He came down the stairs and said, "Cor, it's just as well that dad's away," whereupon mummy said, "It makes no difference, you stupid boy. We're not going to magic up a new caravan in a couple of days are we?" "We don't have to mummy," I told her. "We just tell daddy the truth."

Friday 27th July
Campfire custard crisis.
Susie popped round today. She said that she had found a dirty frying pan in her garden and was it ours? Mummy said, "Possibly." This evening we had the last meeting of term before the summer holidays. We had a camp fire and did some cooking. Each patrol had to do one course and we all went down to the supermarket to buy the ingredients. Eagles did starters, Hawks did mains, Ravings had pud and Woodpeckers did cheese and biscuits which wasn't very difficult. For pudding we had baked apples and custard. We cored the apples and filled them with raisins. Then we wrapped them individually in three layers of silver foil and put them in the embers. Whilst the apples were cooking we did the custard. Sonny was in charge and he had said that he was going to buy ready-made 'cos to make real custard was really complicated with eggs and things and Sonny's not allowed eggs at home without an adult.

We told Skip that we had tinned custard and he said that that was fine and we just needed to make sure that we pierced the can. When he went off to look at what Hawks were doing Sonny said that we didn't need to pierce the can and he knew. Mel told Sonny that we did 'cos otherwise the air would get too hot inside and the can would explode. Sonny then said that that would happen if you left it too long but that he wasn't going to. "It's like a pressure cooker," he explained. "The tin'll cook stuff really quickly and ya just 'ave to be ready, that's all. When you hear the tin fizzin' it means that it's ready." Archie asked if it was the same for custard powder which is what Sonny had actually put on the fire - four tins of it. "Oh yes," said Sonny, "it works the same way. It will just sort of melt when you heat it up." No one was sufficiently knowledgeable to say anything, apart from Emily who said quietly that you needed to add milk first but Sonny wasn't listening so when, after a couple of minutes, the Ravings leant over the tins to listen for any fizzing, there was a massive explosion as bad as the caravan one and Sonny and Archie took the full impact of a tin each. Everyone - apart from Emily - was more than a bit surprised. Skip came running over and was presented with the rather bizarre sight of two of his scouts who looked, he said later, "as though you'd both fallen into a vat of yellow talcum powder." Emily said that all we had to do was douse them in milk and then we could lick them down but there were no takers. Then Charlie said that he couldn't find his baked apple and neither could anyone else. If the truth be told we couldn't find much of the campfire either.

Saturday 28th July
Daddy stays calm.
Sam washed the car today and was paid! No one asked me. I can make things clean again - apart from myself maybe. It was all a bit of a waste of time though 'cos there's not much left of the car after Thursday.

When the taxi drew up outside our house we all had to go into our bedrooms whilst mummy spoke to daddy. After he had been home for about an hour we were allowed downstairs and daddy asked me what had happened so I told him. I didn't mention (although I told grandad so someone knew, just not the right person), that in keeping Charlie's breakfast warm I had, in grandad's words, "heated up the gas canisters to well beyond safe tolerances." Now daddy's going to be on the 'phone to the caravan people in the morning.

Daddy's been away for a few days at a place called Brac which is, he told me, one of Croatia's larger islands. He said, "It's still relatively untouched by mass tourism with the interior home to not much other than a million olive trees and loads of rock." He said that he had a very nice time. When I asked him what the best bit was he said, "On a hike through a sleepy village and in need of lunch I stopped outside a rather run-down cafe with a table with

 chequered tablecloth outside and in the shade. There were a couple of chairs and inviting smells were wafting through the door. I asked the old lady who stuck her head out of the door if I could have a menu. She disappeared, coming out after a couple of minutes and saying, 'No menu,' handed me a bowl of what tasted like fish soup. A mixed meat platter with chard and potato followed, then some excellent ice cream. She gave me a couple of glasses of rose wine, that she said was 'me.' I assumed she had made it. Likewise with a glass of killer grappa that I had with my extremely strong Turkish coffee. One of my best meals ever. 'The bill, please.' 'No bill.' 'No bill? You have an interesting restaurant.' 'Not restaurant, my house,' she said and shuffled back

indoors." I think daddy'll be returning again and after what he came back to, sooner rather than later.

He looks / did look very relaxed after his mini-break and mummy also said how well he looked. I expect mummy will be going on her own mini-break soon.

Sunday 29th July

The hire car has an unscheduled clean.

Today mummy decided to go the gym and "do a circuit," whatever that means. I had to go with her 'cos everyone else was out and I'm not allowed to be left at home on my own just at the moment. Mummy parked the hire car and as we were getting out a man came over from the car wash that's in the corner of the car park. He asked mummy if she would like him to wash the car whilst we were in the gym 'cos he wasn't very busy. Mummy looked at him rather crossly and said, "No I do not - it's perfectly clean!" and we went inside. When we came out an hour later after I had sat and read my Tintin book and had a hot chocolate and mummy had done her circuit which had made her all hot and red

and we had walked over to the car, mummy squealed 'cos the car was covered in mud like someone had been rallying in it! Two cars away the man from earlier was busy cleaning another car. "Not so clean now!" he shouted when he saw us. Mummy shouted back, "And you're not going to be paid to clean it - he is!" pointing at me. On the way home mummy went to the automatic car wash to clean the car and still paid me! This seems like a very sensible arrangement, but I don't think that it's likely to happen again any time soon.

Monday 30th July

Things are looking up.
The caravan insurance people came round today and saw mummy. I think we're going to get a new caravan and loads of money in compensation.

Tuesday 31st July
George gets a haircut and I get told off.
Mummy told me off today for something that wasn't really wrong. Not properly wrong anyway. Then she told me that I was very badly behaved which wasn't very nice 'cos all I was trying to do was give George a haircut 'cos he looked very hot and was sitting outside in the shade. I told mummy that I wasn't badly behaved - just defiant and then she smiled which isn't the right thing to do when you're trying to tell someone off.

Wednesday 1st August
Pinch and a punch gets out of hand.
"Pinch and a punch" day today. I don't do it on Sam anymore 'cos it's too dangerous and I don't do it on Olivia anymore 'cos she always cries. However I saw Sonny in the high street so I went up to him and said, 'cos I didn't want to pinch and punch him if he didn't know what I was up to, "Did you know that it's 'pinch and a punch' day today?" and he said, "Yeah," so I thought I was safe. I gave him a tiny pinch and a little punch and then he pinched me really hard, then he punched me even harder, then I was flicked, then kicked. After that he punched me again, then he thumped me. Then I was slapped and finally I was smacked. As I was lying on the ground and he was standing over me he said, "A flick and a kick for being so quick! A punch in the eye, for bein' so sly. A thump in the 'ead 'cos I've just said. A slap on the bum for bein' so dumb. A smack on the nose 'cos anfing goes." It really, really hurt and had mummy been there I would've cried

but she wasn't so I didn't. After he walked off I got up and I ran home but I had to go the long way so that I wouldn't have to bump into him again and mummy wanted to know what had happened 'cos I had loads of bruises and red marks. I told her that Sonny had attacked me 'cos it was "pinch and a punch" day. Then Olivia said, "Now you know how I used to feel," which wasn't very helpful.

Thursday 2nd August
Daysack drama.

Mummy has bought me a new daysack for camp. It's for stuff that you need during the day but not at night. I filled it up with all my stuff. It was a bit of a squeeze. Then I put it on the wrong way by mistake so it was at the front 'cos I got the straps all muddled up and looked as though I was really said that maybe all to carry something simulate being they know what it mummy said, asked, "What about are you going to

Sam said that it was pregnant. It was really uncomfortable! He men should have similar around to pregnant so that feels like. Then without being Caesareans? How simulate those?"

We certainly couldn't do anything while on camp 'cos we're not always allowed penknives.

Friday 3rd August
A quiet trip to Hastings.

Mummy and daddy aren't talking to each other at the moment - again! We went out today in the hire car to Hastings and mummy was talking all the way down but not to daddy, just to us children or herself. When we got to about Tonbridge daddy suddenly spoke. He said that he knew of a man who was driving down a motorway when he was stopped by the police. The man wound down his window and asked what the matter was. "I haven't done anything wrong have I?" The policeman said, "No sir, however I just thought that you ought to know that your wife fell out two miles back." "Oh, thank goodness for that," said the man. "I thought for a moment I'd gone deaf." Mummy said, "Even if I had been talking to you before then I wouldn't be now." Then it was really quiet 'cos mummy stopped talking completely, even to us children. Sam took advantage and when we were having our fish and chips at lunchtime he ordered a drink that he's not usually allowed to have

and mummy couldn't say anything and daddy didn't. Mini-golf was a bit more difficult. Mummy did play but she wasn't trying and when we handed in our scores the man in the booth said that mummy had just beat the course record for the highest score but she just smirked and scowled at the same time but still didn't speak.

Saturday 4th August
Our holiday in Bournemouth begins.
Off on holiday today! We're in Bournemouth but we're having to stay in a hotel. I asked mummy about the animals this morning and daddy said, "The cat's in the cattery and the chickens are in the oven." Just as well they didn't get that the wrong way round.

We're looking forward to sand, kayaking and zip wires and mummy's already wearing her sunglasses even though it's evening. I asked mummy if we could have an ice cream when we arrived and went out for a short walk but she said, "No," which was a bit mean 'cos it's our holiday too. But at least she's talking again even if it's only one word at a time.

Sunday 5th August
A day out in Poole.

We had a very nice trip today to Poole. We wandered round the harbour and went to a place called Sandbanks which is really cool. Mummy wasn't wearing her sunglasses even though it was quite sunny. There's a hotel by the harbour and when you walk through the reception there's the beach on the other side. How super cool is that? We had lunch there and mummy was asking loads of questions about the wine but she was only speaking to the waiter and after a while he was getting a bit bored. Then mummy said in a loud voice that she could have a drink or two 'cos, "We can walk home because we only live round the corner. In fact we only live a few doors away." After that the waiter was very attentive and mummy loved it and was even able to sample some wines by the glass. Later on he asked mummy which was her house and she said, "Oh, it's number seventeen," but the waiter looked a bit confused and said that the houses in Beach Road all had names. Mummy then had to think before saying that her house name was "Number Seventeen" but by then we had a different waiter and we were asked to move off the veranda and onto the beach.

Daddy didn't love it when the bill came. On the way back to Bournemouth mummy became chatty again and wanted to play

"I spy." She said, "I spy with my little eye, something beginning with 'S.'" The answer was probably quite obvious but we had all learnt quite a bit in the hotel restaurant so Sam said, "Sauvignon Blanc," and I said, "Sauternes," and Olivia said, "Sambuca." Then mummy said, "It's not 'I spy mummy stuff,' it's 'I spy stuff out there,'" as she waved her arm across the front of the car and wacked daddy in the head. "I think they realise that," said daddy, "otherwise they would have said 'sozzled.'" Mummy then said, "I'm not sizzled," before falling asleep in the car and daddy left her there when we got back to the hotel and I think she's still there but I know daddy will get her in before bedtime 'cos he's not going to waste her side of the bed not being used.

Monday 6th August
A very inexpensive meal.
Free food today. Mummy and daddy went out by themselves and gave Sam loads of money to spend on dinner for the three of us. We went to a very nice hotel called "The Suffolk" and had a yummy set dinner. When we were given the bill the waiter asked Sam, "What room number shall I put it on?" and without a moment's hesitation I said, "Eleven," 'cos that's about my  age. We divided the money up between Sam, Olivia and me and we walked back to our hotel very full and very rich and mummy and daddy don't know and we're going to be able to have ice cream whenever we like now.

Tuesday 7th August
Back to The Suffolk but we didn't go in.
Bad day today. We went to The Suffolk on the way to the beach to show mummy and daddy where we had had dinner and as we walked past daddy asked why there were large grainy photos of the three of us "CHILDREN" stuck to the front door with

"WANTED" written underneath. "Maybe you left something behind," said mummy and Olivia said, "Only the bill." We came back the long way.

Wednesday 8th August

Olivia tries to be helpful.

Shopping this morning. Eugh. We went into a large, posh department store so that mummy could have a good look around. We finished up on the sunglasses' counter. Mummy and daddy were wandering round so aimlessly that they sort of forgot about us and left. Olivia noticed that mummy had left her expensive Dior sunglasses on the counter so she picked them up and ran to catch up mummy who had already crossed the road and was by now heading towards Central Gardens. "Mummy, mummy you forgot your sunglasses," Olivia cried, waving them wildly in the air. "No I haven't," mummy said, patting hers comfortingly. "They're on my head, look." Everyone went quiet for a few seconds. Then Sam spoke. "Oh dear," he said to Olivia. "That's another window your photo's shortly going to be appearing in." "Can I borrow your sunglasses mummy?" Olivia asked. "Which pair?" I wondered aloud.

Thursday 9th August

Daddy's in danger of getting armpit fudge for lunch.

We went out for lunch today. Unfortunately the waiter was from Poland and he has just arrived in our country and spoke no English which was a bit of a problem in a restaurant. Daddy said that he would like a chicken dish and when the waiter looked at him like he didn't understand daddy stuck his hand under his armpit and wagged his elbow up and down, trying to be a chicken. "Be careful daddy," I said, "or you may end up with armpit fudge." Apparently that's what it tasted of when it arrived unfortunately.

Friday 10th August

A bit of a boring morning.

We were going to go on the beach this morning for Olivia but it

was so hot that by the time we had managed to park the beach was full up. I said that I would like to have a go on the zip wire but once we finally found the place I was told that I wasn't old enough. We then drove all the way to Poole so that Sam could have a go kayaking but was told that he couldn't 'cos the sea was too rough so we wandered round the town - again! We did suggest to mummy that we could go on the beach at Poole but the tide was out and it was out miles. At least we managed to buy an ice cream each when mummy wasn't looking. Then we spent the rest of the day in the car 'cos we had to get back home to prepare for NorWamBamJam tomorrow. At least I'd packed beforehand. I'm so excited!

Saturday 11th August

NorWamBamJam is here!

Hurray! We're at NorWamBamJam - East Anglia's premier international scout camp! Daddy drove Sam and me and Sonny all the way to Norfolk in his new car. We had one stop on the way and we were allowed a drink and a doughnut. Sam and I know that when you eat a doughnut in the car you have to eat it over the bag but no one told Sonny and 'cos he was in the back with Sam, 'cos Sam said a sweary word yesterday so wasn't allowed to sit in the front, daddy couldn't see and Sam didn't say anything. We're not sure how Sonny could afford to come and he's got a brand new posh

rucksack. Maybe he stole it but I didn't say anything. When we got to Norwich daddy made Sonny hoover up his sugar mess with his portable vacuum cleaner that he keeps in the boot. "I don't know why you're botherin' mate," Sonny said to daddy much more calmly than I would've expected, "'cos when we come back it'll be with somefing far worse - mud!"

Some of the scouts and all of the other Ravings have come on the train but Skip asked mummy if she would take Sonny in the car and mummy said, "Yes," and daddy said, "Thanks Karen." Mel's mummy organised for the other five Ravings to go on the train from Chislehurst via London with a bus at the end. Personally I would've preferred not to have had a new rucksack and gone on the train instead but no one asked me - I was just told. Even Mel came by train 'cos her daddy had to take control of the aeroplane delivery. Mind you it's probably better that I didn't go on the train after what happened.

On the train from London to Norwich, four of the Ravings were sitting at a collapsible table with drinks and food; Mel had to sit with someone else on the other side of the aisle 'cos she was last in 'cos she was trying to get a first class upgrade but she wasn't allowed 'cos it was full 'cos someone important had booked it all. Edward had bought a large raspberry ripple yoghurt from the supermarket outside the station in London. When he was sitting at the table the plastic lid that sometimes you get on the yoghurt

 pot and sometimes you don't (mummy always makes sure any large yogurt that she buys has a lid) was partially off and hanging down the side once Edward had taken the silver foil off. For some reason known only to him, Edward tried to flip the yoghurt pot over and back onto the lid but missed and all the yoghurt went over the table and over Emily who spilt her

skinny decaf. macchiato coffee with a caramel shot all over herself as well in shock. She said that she didn't care and she had only ordered a skinny decaf. macchiato coffee with a caramel shot 'cos she liked the sound of it 'cos the barrista called it a "Skid-ma-Cocas" but the ticket inspector did care and when he came along the carriage to check their tickets Emily had to go into the corridor for the rest of the journey. Then Mel came and sat in her seat but not before she had got Emily's towel out of her rucksack and quadruple-folded it up over the mess on the seat. Unfortunately Emily had decided to put her towel at the bottom of her rucksack and not the top 'cos she wasn't listening to the recent "How to pack a rucksack" evening 'cos Skip said, "Put important things - LIKE TOWELS - at the top." Mel didn't want to get Emily's rucksack down from the rack in case she couldn't get it back up again so she stood on her seat and then half on the table and reached up like they had to to get their rucksacks up there in the first place although Archie didn't want to put his up 'cos it would've been too far away from where he was sitting so he sat with it on his lap the whole way so now he has a large bruise.

Anyway, Mel reached up and undid Emily's rucksack and started ferreting about inside. She was just about at the bottom when she felt a bit of towelling so she pulled 'cos she thought that she could pull the towel up the side of everything else but it didn't work. When it got a bit stuck Mel gave it a big yank and the towel came out but it was huge and it pulled all Emily's clothes and sleeping bag and stuff out with it like loads of hoodies and warm stuff so then Archie, Charlie and Edward ("A.C.E." I've never noticed that before) and the people opposite were rained on with loads of Emily's underwear and stuff and Archie, Charlie and Edward all went red and Mel had to pick it all up and shove it back in with the rucksack still on the rack. It didn't all fit back though so she stuffed the rest in the top of Archie's 'cos he had loads of room 'cos he had been listening to Skip and had packed his sleeping bag separately and his rucksack was still on his lap. So that is why Archie has such a big bruise 'cos some of Emily's stuff is quite heavy, especially the hairdryer and iron although they probably don't work now 'cos they both took a direct hit on the table when they fell and made two huge dents. Mel found a free newspaper and covered up the dents although it was Emily's fault but the ticket man couldn't have done much more to Emily 'cos she was already in the corridor and he could hardly throw her off the train 'cos by now it was non-stop to Norwich.

When they arrived at Norwich they tried, but failed, to collapse the table. Archie looked underneath and said that something was cracked so they left the paper all over the table and ran.

When they went past the first class carriage a load of old people with scout shirts on and loads of badges that no one recognised got off and no one had any idea who they were so the Ravings didn't say anything and Emily hid her scout shirt 'cos it looked like someone had tie-dyed it.

Once everyone had arrived we had to put our rucksacks in the mess tent that Skip and Patrick had already erected whilst we put up our troop tents and Emily took herself and her towel off for a shower. Emily said that they're eco showers and run on solar so that's a bit daft 'cos everyone knows how much sun we get in August. Emily cold-showered herself and her scout shirt and her towel and then had nothing dry to dry herself with and so had to come back to our site wrapped in a wet towel. On the way back she was stopped by a man on a golf buggy with a clipboard who told her off 'cos he said that she was supposed to get dressed in the shower area and then she burst into tears and said that she had had an accident on the way to the campsite and it wasn't her fault and she wanted to go home. So the man with the clipboard put her on his golf buggy and took her to the first aid and she had to wait there whilst he went off to something called "The

SuperDooper Store." Then a nice grey-haired lady with a smile appeared and gave Emily an even bigger towel AND a NorWamBamJam t-shirt AND sweatshirt AND shorts AND a beanie AND a snood AND a baseball cap AND a big bar of chocolate. The lady said that Emily would get her towel and other wet stuff back later once the lady had had it washed and dried properly and she could keep all the other stuff for free.

Once we had put our tents up Skip said that as he had recently ran an evening on "How to pack a rucksack" and 'cos we were all at the meeting we would remember that we were to pack light and important things at the top. This would mean towel, small torch and stuff. Skip lined us up and said that he wasn't going to get all of our kit out but we needed to open up our rucksacks and produce the first three things from the top. I went first. I produced a towel, my small torch and a book. Skip smiled and said, "Well done." Next was Sonny. He brought out an axe, a full bottle of Tozer with a cap that had been undone and with a yellow colour that wasn't Tozer, and a packet of cigarettes. Sonny and his rucksack then had to go off with Patrick to see someone. Everybody else's rucksack was fine apart from Emily's which was a bit of a mess with a hairdryer and loads of warm stuff 'cos she told me later that she thought she was going to Norway not Norfolk, and Archie's. Archie was last. When he pulled out three pairs of girls' knickers that was bad enough but when Emily shouted, "Those are mine!" and snatched them back it was a whole lot worse and Archie and his rucksack had to go off with

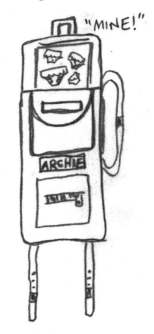

"MINE!"

Patrick, once he had returned with Sonny and his rucksack that came back half empty, to see someone also.

An exciting day all round - and it wasn't even lunchtime. But it was set to get a whole lot worse. Or better.

After lunch one of the subcamp leaders came and asked us for  our aeroplane but Mel's daddy hadn't arrived with it although he said to Mel yesterday that it should be there first thing 'cos he needed a police escort up the M11. The subcamp leader looked a bit puzzled but Mel said, "My dad was a top brass in the RAF so he knows what he's doing." The subcamp leader, whose name was Larry, said, "That's fine; I was expecting a bit of friendly competition but it seems that your father may have moved things on to a whole new level."

At about five o'clock there was a bit of a commotion. Actually quite a big bit of commotion. One of the security people from the south gate radioed Larry to say that he had an RAF low loader at the gate with four military personnel, two police Land Rovers with four police officers, seven journalists, one of the scouts' fathers and a 'plane for the 1940s' subcamp gateway and "Can we come up to your base? It's rather large." Larry said that that was fine but I think that he soon changed his mind. Up the main drive came two huge police cars with flashing lights. Everyone stood aside as between them was sandwiched the low loader with, on top of it, packaged as if it were made of glass and strapped so that it wouldn't move a millimetre in a monsoon was - a Spitfire! A real Second World War Spitfire! Then we realised that no one had told Mel's daddy about not upsetting the Germans. Oh dear. Everyone looked round at them nervously.

Larry was speechless and so was everyone else, mostly. The Germans were laughing which was a bit odd. One of the RAF men jumped from the lorry with Mel's daddy who went and gave her a kiss and a hug. The RAF man went up to Larry and asked him where he wanted it. "Err, just here please," he said, pointing to a large patch of grass that was supposed to be part of the communal play area but no allowance had been made. The RAF men pulled a small crane out that was tucked neatly into the back of the lorry and slowly winched the 'plane off the back and down onto the grass. They then propped up the wings and hammered in some metal poles and wrapped KEEP OUT tape around and between them. "No touching please sir," said one of the RAF men to Skip who was still standing open-mouthed and had yet to say a word. "It's insured for three million pounds and I don't suspect you are," he said with a wink.

By now a small crowd had gathered and Mel and her daddy were already the talk of the camp. "So where's the competition?" asked Mel's daddy. Larry feebly pointed to the subcamp gateway frame that had a few assorted planes already tied to it. "They're a bit small aren't they?" he suggested. "It's more a case of yours is a bit big," Larry countered cautiously.

"John told me the template specified four hundred centimetres. I know the Spitfire is slightly bigger but not by an excessive amount and it's the specified shape. In fact the shape that the subcamp people gave us was of a Spitfire." Larry went pale and looked like he was was having trouble saying anything so another of the staff spoke. "Forty centimetres. Forty not four hundred." Larry turned to Skip and squawked, "The original template had '400 cms by 400 cms' on it but a few days later someone pointed out the error so I sent out another email saying that it should be forty centimetres. Didn't you get that email John?" Larry asked although he probably already knew the answer. When he received no response he turned round and found John had suddenly gone missing. "Where's he gone?" asked Larry hurriedly to no one in particular. "He's gone to help himself to my beer and fags that got confiscated from my rucksack I expect Larry mate," said Sonny with a smirk.

"Where did you get it from?" Archie asked Mel's daddy whilst everyone else was still in shock and didn't know quite what to say. "It's the one from outside the old RAF Biggin Hill," he said. "It hasn't been moved for years but a bit of a restoration's in the pipeline and so it would have to have been moved anyway. I've managed to pull a few strings and take it on a bit of a detour. That's all. I hope you win." he added hopefully. "Whether or not we win, I think you've won 'top dad' for this camp already," said Sonny who then totally unexpectedly burst into tears. It was probably the lager.

Sunday 12th August
More fun at NorWamBamJam as we meet the Germans.

NorWamBamJam is enormous and we've all been given maps so that we don't get lost and a pass with our photo on it and other stuff for different activities and our age like "under 14" 'cos if you're over fourteen you can go to the milkshake disco and do the quad-bikes and probably shoot stuff and talk to girls that you don't know. Sonny's pass was done in a bit of a rush - and not with a passport-sized shot of his face - that Skip had to email. Sonny's has been zoomed down and his photo comprises a field and all you can see of Sonny is his left ear. "It's my ear though," said Sonny, "'cos Skip took the photo outside scouts the other day and you can recognise the field 'cos it's the one at the farm down the road and those are the sheep in the background and you can see the dent on my ear lobe where I tried to do a piercin' for nuffin when I was seven."

We all had to check our passes today 'cos some of them were wrong. Sonny's now found that his has 18+ on it but he said nothing, just nudged me, pointed at it and smiled. "Who needs a dodgy Tozer bottle when you're eighteen-plus?" he asked me, somewhat cryptically.

All the scout and guide groups have been put into subcamps. Our 1940s is really dowdy saved only by our light khaki brown Spitfire which totally dominates the entrance; our scarves are mud-coloured which we have to wear all the time along with our passes and the subcamp leaders are all dressed like they've just been bringing in the harvest. Opposite we have the 1960s subcamp. It's all multi-coloured and snazzy and psychedelic flashing bright lights and Beatles music and beads everywhere and lots of wigs of really long hair and bright red, blue and orange scarves. Whilst Emily and I were looking at the Spitfire with Skip one of the scouts from the 1960s' camp wandered over to have a look. Skip said "Hi" and the girl said, "Our subcamp is really bright and cool and yours is all brown grass and smelly. Do you know why?" Skip said, "Yes of course. The 1940s were a difficult time with half of the decade dominated by the Second World War. The 1960s were a period that ended the coming out of twenty years of that war and the austerity that followed with continued rationing and loans repayments that could have bankrupted the country." "Er, no I don't think so," said the girl. "It was because in the 1960s everyone was on drugs." Skip looked a little bit shocked but Emily wasn't at all fazed. "Yeah, and that's why all the people who lived in the 1960s are now dead and those that lived in the 1940s are all fit and well," she said. Now it was the girl's turn to look shocked. She turned round and walked back to her camp without saying anything further. Skip looked at Emily and smiled. "The more I think about it, the more completely illogical what you have just said is," said Skip. "Yeah, but don't forget Skip," said Emily, "the people of the 1960s were also mainly zombied out so wouldn't see an illogical argument if it slapped them in the face. One-nil to the 40s Skip!" and Skip smiled. I think we have the best subcamp.

Everyone has mostly green and white tents. The mess tents are white and are for eating in and the troop tents are green and are for sleeping in and hiding. We have two huge troop tents, one for the boys and one for the girls. We also have a green toilet tent for changing in. We call it the "Punch and Judy" tent 'cos you can stand up in it but it's only one square metre in floor space. Skip and Patrick have an orange tent each. The Germans have one enormous black tent, like a castle. Their site is next to ours and we have a group from a place called "Lichfield" which is Staffordshire on the other side. Skip asked the leader in charge of the Lichfield scouts what Lichfield was near. He said that one of the big cities was Walsall. "And where's that?" asked Mel who had just appeared with Emily. "It's the capital of Poland silly," she told Mel. "I would've thought that you would've known that." This is a bit odd 'cos they don't sound Polish although I'm not sure what Polish sounds like - probably nearer German than English. The Germans are also very friendly; the Ravings have been playing with them and they speak to us in English and to each other in German. Sometimes when they're speaking German it sounds like they're saying a rude word in English which is quite funny but I don't think that they are. It's just that with only twenty-six letters in the alphabet it must be the case that sometimes words in one language sound like completely different words in another.

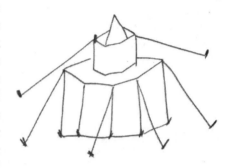

Sonny has made friends with the Germans also. Apparently he told them that he could speak German and so when they asked him to say something he stood up straight and barked out, "Vot iz your nim?" He's been giggling as well and he was then invited to look at the inside of their black tent by a nice girl with two long pigtails who said, "My nim iz Heidi," but actually she speaks English better than Sonny. He said that he wished that he still had his axe but he came out alive. He wasn't in there for very long 'cos the Germans were having their tea. Sonny said that they were having sausage which is a bit odd 'cos sausages are English. I asked him if he found anything out about them that we should know. He said, "Yes. Heidi told me that a road in German is a fart." We all squealed! No one can tell us off now 'cos we can just say we're learning German. Emily asked Sonny what he had been talking to them about. Did he tell them about Norfolk or the cathedral or any of the history of East Anglia like we had been told to find out? Sonny said that he hadn't but he had mentioned other things of interest - he had told them all the sweary words that he knew but they knew them already so he made some up.

In the evening Heidi and some of the German scouts visited us in our mess tent and brought with them some nice badges and German biscuits which we ate. We were all there apart from Sonny who had gone off under cover of darkness with his eighteen-plus ear photo pass. He said that he was going to find out what he could get for eighteen-plus that fourteen-minus couldn't. Heidi told Skip that our tent was a bit of a mess and Skip said, "That's why it's called a mess tent." Mel then told Skip that if that was true then it would be called a "messy tent" which is, I suspect, what it's going to be called from now on.

Skip asked Heidi how they - she and the other Germans - managed to get away with bringing just one tent, albeit a large one. "We do everything in it. We cook in it, eat in it and sleep in it," she said. "Scouts, explorers - boys and girls - and leaders." Skip nearly choked on his coffee but didn't say anything. When I grow up I want to be a scout in Germany; I'm fed up sleeping with boys. Edward asked Heidi what they would do if one of their scouts was gender neutral - would they get their own tent?

193

Heidi said that no one in Germany is gender-neutral so it's not something that they would ever have to consider. Maybe we have a lot of catching up to do. Edward then asked Skip what he would do if he (Ed) announced that he was gender-neutral. Would he get his own tent? Skip said, "Probably."

Heidi asked us if we all liked our Spitfire. Emily and Archie didn't put up their hands. They both said that they thought that it was a bit insensitive. Now Emily and Archie have been invited to go and help show the Germans around Norwich tomorrow afternoon during free time which is a bit unfair. We're not allowed out of the campsite unless we have an adult with us. The only time that John and Patrick go out is to visit the supermarket nearby to buy the food for the following day's meals. I suppose that we could try and take eighteen plus Sonny with us but we don't have much money so probably wouldn't get very far. I would ask him but it's now eleven o'clock and he's not back in our tent yet. I expect he's having a great time.

Monday 13th August
Spitfire causes a stir.
Sonny was in his sleeping bag when I woke up this morning and he was fast asleep so we left him there. Then he appeared late at breakfast with no pass round his neck. "Pass!" we all shouted. Sonny told us that he was "temporarily without my pass" but

wouldn't say why so Skip told him to go and speak to him after he had eaten. Neither would he tell us what had happened last night.

Someone's spayed a big white sign on the German's tent which isn't very nice 'cos I think it's banned. Skip saw it and looked very cross. He said, "Whatever scumbag's done that has got it all wrong 'cos it's only got three legs instead of four and the

194

bottom bits aren't sticking out and they look like feet." I wish I knew what he was talking about but he wouldn't say any more.

Edward has been thinking about the Germans 'cos he asked Skip how wars start. Skip said, "What do you think everyone?" Mel said, "The longest journeys start with the smallest step." When Skip asked her what she meant she said little things become big things - that countries fight each other over land and before that the inhabitants argue over food and before that football supporters hit each other at international matches. "So football's to blame?" suggested Edward. "Pretty much," said Mel. "It's the general acceptance of low-scale violence at a lower level that escalates and then, if left unchecked, turns into guns, tanks and bombs." "And aeroplanes," added Archie. "What we should be looking at is 'Focolare,'" said Mel, "which comprises people who share the aim of building a united world." Sonny tried to repeat the word but was told to "sssh" by Skip. Maybe Mel just made it up. At lunchtime the Germans asked us if we would like to have a football match on the playing field and we all said, "No," which seemed a bit mean but we had all remembered what Mel had said and no one wanted to explain.

Our Spitfire has appeared in a local newspaper! The headline reads, "SPITFIRE SIGHTED IN NORWICH!" The tagline is, "German scouts upset at WWII hero appearing at international jamboree!" This is a bit odd as I haven't seen any upset Germans. They've all been smiling and taking photos.

After lunch Emily and Archie went into Norwich with the Germans. When they returned they didn't say where they had been, only that it was a surprise and they had had ice cream. The nearest we got was when Mel asked if they had shown them round Norwich Cathedral but Archie said, "No, we've been to an industrial park." I suppose the Germans like things like that 'cos they're all engineers and mechanics and stuff.

The rest of the Ravings did activities at our subcamp base. We had a craft session and my favourite was that we made big plastic poppies using bamboo sticks and the top parts of plastic drinks bottles. We had to paint the stems green and the bottle red with a black blob in the middle of each. Then we had to stick them all together using big reels of sticky tape. On the other table someone dropped a reel and it rolled along the grass. "Oh look," said Mel, "someone's dropped a Camembert!" The subcamp leaders that were helping all laughed but I don't know why.

Edward has told Skip that's he's now gender-neutral and that he needs his own tent. Skip said that he can have the toilet tent but he would need to sleep standing up. Edward then asked, "What would happen if I was sick?" 'cos we normally have a sick bay tent on camp. Skip told him he would have to go and be gender neutral in the medical centre.

It was Raving's turn to cook today. We had cereal (Coco Pops), orange juice, Danish pastries and fruit for breakfast; for lunch we had ham and cheese sandwiches with lettuce, cucumber and tomatoes, and fruit; for supper we had chicken slices with olives, lettuce, tomato, cucumber, bread and butter, and yoghurt. Who needs to cook when you're on camp? Skip and Patrick looked a bit cross but Mel said, "You told us that Ravings had to 'do' the meals on Monday, you didn't say that we had to cook them." From now on at least one meal a day has to be 'cooked' but we're alright 'cos our next day is Saturday and we're going home after breakfast so I expect we'll choose lunch for cooking!"

Sonny has a new pass. It has a photo of him scowling outside the information and administration centre. He is now fourteen minus.

Archie was serving dinner this evening and he had loads on his plate. Sarcastic as usual, Skip asked, "Don't you find it a little bit strange, Archie, that the meal that you serve ends up with your having twice as much food on your plate as anyone else?" Archie said that it wasn't at all strange as far as he was concerned and that he had an allergy. "An allergy to what?" asked Skip, probably concerned that he had an undisclosed medical issue. "Small portions," said Archie.

The white spray on the Germans' tent is still there but there is now a sign next to it which reads, "Twinned with Isle of Man."

We're having a fancy dress party tomorrow and we've all brought a costume from home. We've been told not to wear anything that might upset the Germans. I'm going as a 1940s' golfer. It's basically long trousers tucked into my long socks and a jacket and shirt and tie and a baseball cap. I also have a golf club and it's called a driver. It's the one golfers use to hit the ball off the tee. Mummy found it in the charity shop. I think she was expected to buy all of the clubs that were in the bag and the bag but she said that she only wanted the driver. The lady in the shop said that most golfers use a complete set but mummy said that she didn't need a complete set, only the driver. Then the lady looked at mummy a bit funnily and said that most people who are attacked by a golf club are attacked by a driver but mummy didn't say anything. Mummy's also given me a pipe. She said that it works 'cos it used to be her grandad's and she's kept it for "sentimental reasons" whatever they are.

Tuesday 14th August
Fun with fancy dress.
Today we went to one of the other subcamps to meet a group of special needs scouts. It was a bit scary 'cos some of them don't speak much and they had special wheelchairs and stuff. However there were loads of friendly carers so nothing horrible was going

to happen and they could shake our hands though we weren't sure if they were able to at first. One of the special needs scouts asked us, "Who's the cleverest?" and we all said, "Mel!" but she didn't. The scout then asked Mel, "What do you call a baby swan?" and Mel said that she didn't know 'cos she thought that it was a joke but she didn't know anyway. The scout then said, "A signet!" and all the special needs scouts clapped and we came away thinking that some of them may have some difficulties in some areas, but in other areas they were ahead of even normal scouts. And then we had to decide what normal meant and we gave up 'cos we're all people of God, that's what Mike says anyway. We all decided that next time we saw a special needs person when we were out and about then we would just say hallo and talk to them and shake their hands.

Today we had our fancy dress party. All the sub-camps were involved. We had 1940s, 1950s, 1960s, 1970s, 1980s, 1990s, 2000s and 2010s. It was all a bit weird. I wore my golfing clothes and loads of people said how good I looked with my golf driver and pipe. Sonny was dressed up as Hitler with a little black moustache which was the sort of thing that I would've imagined would fall into the "might upset the Germans" category. But I got in trouble first for  putting the pipe in my mouth. Some bossy scout leaders told me that there was "No smoking on camp" even though I had nothing in it. They were going to confiscate my pipe so I put it in my pocket. Then they saw Sonny in his Hitler uniform and I think that he was going to get really told off but it was a bit difficult 'cos Sonny was talking to the Germans. The leaders kept watching him but he was with the Germans all the time so I went over to tell him. Sonny then asked me where my pipe was and I said that it was in my pocket. He wanted to borrow it so I gave it to him 'cos then I couldn't get it confiscated. I whispered to him that he was probably in trouble for dressing as Hitler but he said he wasn't, he was dressed as Charlie Chaplin without the hat. In any event some of the Germans were dressed as British airmen 'cos, they said, they wanted to be on the winning side. As we were

both talking to the Germans for so long the bossy leaders came over to speak to Sonny. They quietly asked him what he was doing dressed as Hitler. Sonny was going to say that he wasn't and that he was dressed as Charlie Chaplin but then one of the Germans said that Sonny made a very good Hitler and the Germans all laughed and they all had pipes and so the bossy leaders all left and we went back to the Germans' tent which was the huge black tent and then Sonny did fill his pipe with something and coughed a lot but he didn't get told off 'cos the Germans said that no one goes into their tent 'cos everyone's too frightened of what they might find - like a pipe smoking Hitler without his moustache and some British airmen with funny accents saying things like, "I zay chaps, vee are effing a wery wunderbar time here vot?!" and one with a

Hitler moustache. I like international camp and I like the Germans and the special needs scouts best.

Wednesday 15th August
Street Food Square doesn't go to plan.
Hawks did dinner tonight which was very tasty. We had lamb chops for mains. For veg. they chopped up potatoes and carrots and steamed them with peas but they made far too much and

they had loads left over but they couldn't clear up straightaway
'cos there was something more important going on shortly. More
food! This evening was Street Food Square. Each group set up a
table at the front of their site and cooked and served taster food
for everyone else. It was supposed to be a regional speciality but
Chislehurst has no regional specialities. We do have caves in
Chislehurst so Edward suggested we do rock cakes but we
couldn't really do those whilst people waited and anyway the

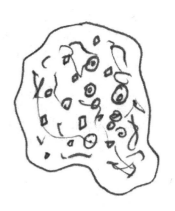

caves aren't rock, they're chalk
and flint I think so we did mini
pancakes. 'Cos we were the
1940s to make it more authentic
we used dried egg instead of
fresh egg. The problem was we
couldn't get hold of any dried egg
so we decided to hard boil some
eggs beforehand and then mash
it all up with a fork and then we
mixed it in with the milk and
flour. It made a really good
batter mix but was very, very
lumpy so no one wanted pancakes from us therefore we left it
and went in search of more food even though we were full up.
We had scones with jam and cream, blue stilton on crisps,
beetroot yoghurt and much more besides.

We all had to help clear up later 'cos there was so much mess.
Skip poured the lumpy batter mix into the billy can with the
leftover potatoes, carrots and peas and Edward had to go and
pour it down the slops drain. He didn't get very far though. He
was on the communal path when he dropped the billy 'cos it was
so heavy even though he had told Skip it wasn't and loads came
out but he didn't tell anyone. He just picked up the billy with the
little bit that was left still inside and continued on his journey.
Emily was coming up behind with a bin bagful of rubbish and

stopped by Edward's mess 'cos there were several people there staring at it. Just then a man approached and he had a clipboard. "Whose is this?" he demanded with fierce, glaring eyes and so Emily said, "Edward from 3rd Chislehurst," 'cos she didn't want to get into trouble. Emily caught up with Edward, they deposited their loads and walked back to our site. When they passed Edward's mess there was red tape all round it, on poles. By the time that they had returned to us there was a man with a green florescent jacket on with a big white cross on the back in our mess tent. "Are you Edward?" he demanded. "Yes," said Edward quietly and he wasn't given the chance to explain. Edward had to go with the man and he had to put a face mask over his mouth and Skip and Patrick were nowhere to be seen.

Now there's been a leaders' meeting and Larry has said that our subcamp may have a Norovirus victim and no one can leave the subcamp for one day. It's been suggested that we all go to bed early especially as it's a new moon and so very dark outside and in the morning there will be an update. Given what all the scouts have had to eat I reckon we'll all be Norovirus suspects by the morning.

Thursday 16th August
Night time manoeuvres at NorWamBamJam.
No one was in a hurry to get up this morning, but when they did it wasn't the return of Edward having been given the all clear that was the major news. Nor his comment that when the medical staff were filling in an admission form for him and they asked, "Sex?" he said, "Neutral." ("We don't have a box for that," the doctor said so ticked both boxes.) It was the Spitfire! It has been transformed! No longer is it a muddy green, blue and brown camouflage colour with bull's-eyes. It's now striped pink and yellow and red and green, orange and purple and blue, like someone's been singing, "I can Sing a Rainbow," whilst painting it. It even has a face on the front. A huge crowd had once more

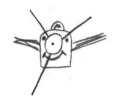

gathered. Everyone loves it! Apart from Mel. Suspicions have fallen on the Germans 'cos the Spitfire has "TWINNED WITH ISLE OF MAN" on the side and the Germans have been taking loads of photos - more than anyone else. Also Archie said that they showed them where to buy metal paint in Norwich the other day and had been sworn to secrecy. I don't think the Spitfire's going to be back on display at Biggin Hill for a while.

Friday 17th August

Gender neutral issues for Skip.

All the 3rd Chislehurst scouts to a boy and girl and Edward have told Skip this morning that we're now all gender neutral so can sleep in the same tent. Skip has said that we can all sleep in the mess tent tonight, gender-neutral girls at one end and gender-neutral boys at the other.

That's enough gender-neutral diary for one day...

Saturday 18th August

Time to go home - for one night.

It was freezing in the mess tent last night and was no fun at all 'cos the girls made it stink of talcum powder and stuff like Olivia's bedroom so we all had to have showers first thing to wash the smell off. We won't be doing that again! Edward told Skip last night at bedtime, once the rest of us had settled into the mess tent, that he was no longer gender-neutral and that he is now a boy again, so had to sleep in the boys' troop tent. Still, at least he managed to get it to himself which was more than the rest of us succeeded in doing and what I think he was trying to achieve in the first place. I'm now back at home with very happy memories of international camp. I hope Mel's going to be okay.

The RAF men turned up to pick up the Spitfire, took one look at it and then refused to take it. (The first time they drove up to the subcamp they drove straight past it.) After Mel managed to borrow a subcamp leaders' 'phone and made a few calls to her daddy the RAF men loaded it back onto their lorry but then they went all round the camp getting loads of tarpaulin which they put over the plane and tied down so that no one could see what was underneath. A bit like when the police cover up a car on a recovery vehicle after a police chase or an accident - but this was no accident.

Mummy came to pick Sonny and Sam and me up in the new car. Daddy's put plastic sheeting all over the seats and floor 'cos of the mud that Sonny was threatening but we've had little rain all week so there was no mud anywhere. However just as we were wondering where Sonny was he appeared out of nowhere and he was holding Heidi's hand and it looked as though she wanted to and not because Sonny had something sticky on his palm so was stuck. He was soaking wet from head to toe and covered in mess and so was Heidi. And they stank! Mummy bundled him into the car and off we went. On the way home we found out what had happened. He and Heidi had decided to go for a walk after we had packed up now that they were no longer confined to the camp. They found themselves in a farm that was next door and they were being chased by the farmer 'cos they shouldn't have

been there and they jumped into a big trough to hide but unfortunately it was the sheep dip. Sonny absolutely stank!

We had to have the windows open and no aircon 'cos mummy said that that would've just made "cold stink." Still, things could've been worse. Heidi had to go back to Heathrow and then go on a plane. I bet she said she was gender-neutral.

A quick shower and sleep and it's off to Cornwall tomorrow. What a life I lead! (Well, in August at least.) But I still don't know why Sonny was holding Heidi's hand and he wouldn't say although I did ask.

Sunday 19th August

Mummy's packing goes awry.

Big problems in Cornwall. We've been collecting old clothes to raise money for stuff at scouts. It comes mainly to the scout hut in black sacks and then we send it off to Phil the Bag who recycle it. At the beginning of the holidays Skip asked daddy if he could  store the bags for a "couple of weeks" 'cos we have a big garage. As a result we've been having all sorts of odd packages dumped on our doorstep and Olivia and I have been earning extra pocket money by putting them in the garage. We drove down to Penzance early this morning after daddy had loaded up the car the night before with our suitcases, holdalls and rucksacks having taken out our rucksacks and sleeping bags and kit and sprayed the car. There were bags everywhere! When we arrived at the hotel this evening daddy got all the bags out of the car whereupon mummy said that her suitcase looked a bit bashed. "I was very careful loading it," daddy said. I hadn't been in our room with Sam and Olivia for more than five minutes when we heard a blood-curdling scream from our parents' room next door. We thought that daddy was strangling mummy. We all three rushed out of our room and barged into theirs. On the bed was the opened suitcase - full of old, smelly clothes, and they weren't mummy's. "Now what am I going to do?" she wailed. "David, you'll have to go home and get my suitcase." "No chance," he said. "You should've checked. You can get the train back." Mummy had dinner that night in the outfit that she was wearing when we drove down. She wasn't very happy.

Monday 20th August
Mummy makes do but it won't last.
Mummy came down to breakfast and was still in the outfit that she was wearing when we drove down and she had dinner in. Daddy said that he had looked at the clothes that had been brought by mistake and, although they weren't mummy's style, they are mostly her size and so daddy's put them all into housekeeping. We then spent most of the morning buying the other bits that were in mummy's suitcase (at home) like make-up and underwear. Sam said that mummy didn't really need either on holiday and daddy looked at him like he was a bit  odd but he didn't say anything. In the afternoon we walked to the beach and daddy went red because mummy had the suncream in her suitcase (at home) and they hadn't bought any new so whilst we sat in the shade daddy sat in the sun and sulked and now he's

burnt. Mummy came down to dinner in one of her "new" - i.e. cleaned by the hotel - outfits. It really suited her and she looked very pretty and elegant and we told her so. She reminded me of someone but I don't know who, probably someone famous, and she smiled - for the first time this holiday.

Tuesday 21st August
The racing island.
Today we went to an island with a castle. We thought that we were going to a racing stables 'cos that's what daddy said then he told us that the island was called "St Michael's Mount" and he laughed but it wasn't that funny. Mummy tried to buy a dress in a gift shop but daddy caught her and told her that it was a chancers' emporium for millionaires with more money than sense so she had to have dinner in another "new" outfit which didn't suit her quite as well but she still looked really pretty and it was certainly too good to throw out.

Wednesday 22nd August
Daddy's rich!
The insurance money has arrived today into daddy's account so that daddy can buy a new caravan. There's also a large amount for compensation. Mummy has told daddy that he can sleep in the new caravan "with the children" and she's going to use her bit of the money on the poshest hotel that she can find whenever the caravan goes out for a trip. I don't think that mummy's going to have as much fun though. Still, at least she won't be blown up.

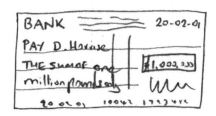

Thursday 23rd August
PIN problems.
Mummy's been for coffee with one of her friends that she's made at the hotel. She's one of those people who knows everything or at least thinks she does. Not mummy - the other lady. She doesn't though. She doesn't know my shoe size or what my favourite

colour is and she never will 'cos whatever she says, even if it's right, I'll change it. This could be a bit tricky with feet 'cos there's

only a few sizes I can be but there's thousands of colours, especially if I use the RGB colour chart. Then I can say that my favourite colour is 72, 75, 19 and she would never know that. She might guess "red" but she would never know what type of red. She told mummy that if you're being robbed at a cash dispenser, if you put in your PIN the wrong way round such as 4321 instead of 1234 then the cash dispenser will start taking photos of the suspects, the cash will be retained and the police will immediately be alerted. "That's a great idea, but what if your PIN's '1111?'" Sam asked. "Then I expect the police will come each time you try to take cash out," said daddy. However that would only be true if the PIN was put in backwards.

Friday 24th August
The family discusses horrorscopes.
Olivia's been reading horrorscopes (that's what daddy calls them) in one of mummy's magazines. She says that they tell you what's going to happen before it happens. This is a bit stupid 'cos if you know what's going to happen and it's not going to be very nice then you're going to do something else aren't you?

Olivia says that everybody has star sign and mine is Taurus. I told mummy this over tea and then I asked her what hers was. She said that she's Gemini and "Geminis don't believe in star signs 'cos they're cobblers." Then I asked daddy and he said that he was Pisces then said, "and Pisces are warm, generous and romantic." So mummy said, "See what I mean?"

Saturday 25th August
Mummy tries to cover daddy up.
We left our lovely holiday behind today and came home in one hit, but not before a major incident in the "tackle department" which is what daddy called it and I don't mean fishing. We had just put all the suitcases in the new car when mummy said that there was water or something on the ground under the engine. Daddy had a look and said that he thought that it could be a leaky radiator and told mummy to go back into the hotel and have a cappuccino whilst he sorted it out 'cos it might take a bit of time and he didn't want an audience. But daddy had no idea what was wrong so went along to the garage on the corner and found a mechanic who said that he would try to help whilst daddy looked round a vintage car that the garage had for sale. When mummy came out with a cappuccino for daddy she was a bit alarmed to 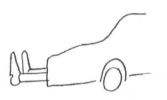 find daddy under the car with his legs sticking out and his bits on display 'cos he did have very baggy shorts on and had run out of pants. Mummy told Olivia and me to look the other way whilst she tucked him back in. When daddy then appeared walking through the car park I thought mummy was going to have a heart attack. At least my level three first aid skills were of use and the mechanic only had to have three stitches in his forehead.

Sunday 26th August
Mummy likes some of her new old clothes.
Back from holiday. Mummy's suitcase was the first thing to greet us as it was inside the front door by the console table just waiting to be picked up. The funny thing is, after all the hoo-ha with the

second-hand clothes, mummy said that she actually quite liked some of her "new" outfits once they were cleaned and is thinking of keeping many of them and donating some of her existing dresses in her wardrobe to Phil the Bag in their place to make some room.

Monday 27th August
Daddy gets his wires crossed.
Big trouble with Susie next door. She had unbelievably invited us all to a barbecue at her house tomorrow. She asked daddy before we went on holiday and daddy said, "Yes," 'cos mummy and daddy had nothing else on. Apparently it's a "meet the neighbours" event so it's not like it's just mummy and daddy and the children. Mummy wasn't too impressed when daddy told her but he said, "What's done is done but we won't have to stay long." Then, this evening, one of daddy's oldest friends rang up and apologised for the short notice but asked if would we like to go to a barbecue at his house tomorrow? Daddy said that he would but he would just have to uninvite us all from Susie's. Daddy then rang Susie and said that we couldn't come because all three children were unwell and she wouldn't want mummy and daddy passing on any germs to her or the other guests. Susie said not to worry and put down the 'phone. Daddy then dialled his friend back and after a voice said, "Hello," daddy said, "It's all fine - I've managed to talk us out of the old crow's barbecue next door thank goodness." There was no answer so daddy said, "Hello, hello?" Daddy could hear deep breathing on the other end of the line so said, "Can you hear me?" "Loud and clear," said the voice. "Is that you Nigel?" daddy asked. "No it's not, it's the old crow from

next door. Next time just make sure that the line's been cleared before redialling. Goodbye." Whoopsie! Whoopsie! Whoopsie!

Tuesday 28th August
Sonny gets a shock.

Sam's got a job in a local cafe but just for one week. He had a trial today but he didn't pass. In the afternoon Sonny came in and asked for a peppermint hot chocolate. Apparently this is a speciality of the cafe and what they do is melt a peppermint Aero bar in some hot milk. However, 'cos they were really busy Sam just did a hot chocolate and when Sonny said that there was no peppermint in it Sam had a look at the syrups and found a peppermint one so stuck loads of that in. Then Sonny wouldn't leave and was making a lot of noise and the owner asked Sam what Sonny was drinking. When Sam told him the owner said that no one had asked him for any peppermint Aero recently and Sam pointed to the peppermint bottle but it wasn't peppermint syrup it was peppermint Bols which is really alcoholic and Sam was sent home and by the time that he had got all his stuff together and left Sonny was asleep and the owner had put him in the staff toilet.

Mummy's had a huge clearout of clothes to make way for her "new" wardrobe and Sam took her old ones in a black sack down to the charity shop 'cos they're too good for "Phil the Bag" and mummy paid him! She said to Sam to tell the shop that they were all of excellent quality and well-looked after but she felt that she needed a complete change of style.

Wednesday 29th August
The Spitfire gets in the paper!

I went round to see Sonny this morning to see if he was okay. He said that he had a bit of a headache but he was fine but it was very nice hot chocolate. Whilst I was there he told me that he had been sent a copy of a German newspaper by Heidi and he showed me. On the front page there were two photos of our Spitfire. The first shows it when it first arrived at NorWamBamJam with all the Germans in front of it and they're grimacing; the second and main photo shows it as the rainbow Spitfire with all the Germans in front of it and they're smiling. It looks like this second photo was taken in

KUNDSCHAFTER SPUCKEN EIN SPITFIRE IN EIN FRIEDENSFLUGZEUG!

the middle of the night with a flash and the Germans are holding paint brushes and tins of paint with EMILY and ARCHIE in the photo!!! The headline is KUNDSCHAFTER SPUCKEN EIN SPITFIRE IN EIN FRIEDENSFLUGZEUG! which Sonny tells me means SCOUTS TURN A SPITFIRE INTO A PEACE AEROPLANE although how he knows I've no idea.

Thursday 30th August
Funfair frolics.
We had a great trip to All the Towers which is a theme park and my favourite ride was called "Soar" where you go up in a little carriage on a train really high and then down again and it was soo fast. There was a fat woman in our train who said that her name was Angela and Sonny was chatting to her daughter in the queue who was very sweet and Angela had not much on 'cos it was so hot. What I mean is she had on what she should've had on, just not much of it. When the train came flying down the track her top became misplaced and everyone on the ground was laughing.

When you go down the super fast bit there is a camera that takes your picture and after you can go to the little booth and look at a souvenir of yourself looking really cool or more likely exceptionally frightened. Skip said that we could have a picture each and he would pay. All we had to do was order the number and there were two pictures to choose from for each carriage.

When Skip went to pay he said to the woman in the booth that there must be a mistake as all the scouts had ordered the same photo - photo number thirty-two. The woman told Skip that  there was no mistake, sixteen number thirty-twos had been ordered. Then Skip demanded to see a copy of the photo and when the woman showed him he found out that number thirty-two was of Angela and Angela had by this time lost all of her top and Skip confiscated all the photos from us and he didn't get his money back either so none of us got an ice cream and photos number thirty-one and thirty-two quickly disappeared from the screen and Skip threw the photos in the bin and Angela was left looking unsuccessfully for her and her daughter's photos on the display.

Sonny was sitting next to me on the coach home and he said, "Look what I've got," 'cos he had something rolled up in his hand that had been sticking out of his rucksack all afternoon and he told Skip that it was a poster of the park. But it wasn't a poster of the park it was photo number thirty-two and sixteen of them and Sonny said, "Guess where I got these from?" I said, "Do you go scavenging in bins often?" and Sonny said that it could sometimes be quite profitable. "Where there's muck there's brass mate," he told me.

Friday 31st August
Washing-up continues to be a problem.
Mummy's not happy that the washing-up's not been done much by us during the holidays. It's all Olivia's fault. I think scouts and explorers are quite used to washing up but cubs less so, probably 'cos they break stuff. Mummy got really cross with Olivia this morning and told her that there was a washing up bowl full of

plates and bits from breakfast. She told her to do a third and then Sam and then I would do a third each whilst she did some gardening. This is mummy-talk for sitting in the garden with a glass of wine and a magazine even though it was only elevenses. When she came back indoors she found all the plates and cutlery lined up on the work surface. Olivia had cleaned exactly one third of each item. Mummy said that it would have taken her less time to wash the whole lot than work out one third of each thing and clean just that bit. Olivia said that mummy should have given her clearer instructions. Mummy told her that with that sort of attitude she should have been born a boy. Olivia said, "Yes, I would have preferred to  have been a boy but I couldn't do anything about that, but YOU COULD'VE!" and glared up at mummy and then ran upstairs. I don't think mummies and daddies can decide whether to have a boy or a girl each time otherwise there would be loads more boys in the world and there's about half and half 'cos most people get married and if there were loads more boys then they would have to marry each other and I don't think that's allowed which is a good thing 'cos otherwise the washing-up would never get done.

Saturday 1st September
Susie gives mummy a fright.
Susie from next door came round today. Mummy still doesn't like her very much. She made some excuse to come in and daddy went and hid after the barbecue incident but Susie wasn't taking much notice 'cos she was more interested in going on about her holiday in Santorini and how she stayed in an exclusive hotel on the island with a "stunning sea view." Mummy said that she thought that Santorini was an old volcano but Susie said nothing. She got out her 'phone to show mummy loads of photos. Then mummy said that we had all been to Cornwall and stayed in one of the top hotels in the county and in the shadow of a tidal island

that is a "Site of Special Scientific Interest." She didn't mention that it was a two star even though a two star may be a "top hotel" for Cornwall. I think mummy may have meant "top" to mean "high up" but she didn't say. Mummy showed Susie some of our photos but mainly the ones from when we were on the nice island with a castle. Susie was taking a very great interest in them and then suddenly remarked, "It's a funny thing, Karen, but you seem to be wearing clothes that are just the same as some that I used to have before they got a bit tatty and I threw them out. In fact the dress that you're wearing right now is very similar to the one that I used to have. How very strange. Do you mind if I have a look at the label? Where did you buy it from?" Mummy looked really flustered. She turned off her 'phone even though she wasn't even halfway through the photos and asked  Susie if she would excuse us but she had to go to Waitrose to buy some Duchy organic lemon shortbread and then take me to John Lewis for "a few bits" and so Susie left. But we didn't go.

Sunday 2nd September

Mummy throws her "new" clothes out.

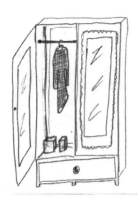

Mummy put all her "new" clothes in a black sack, threw it in the back of the car and daddy had to drive it round to Skip's when it got dark. Now mummy has no "new" clothes and few old clothes either and she said that she could hardly ask for her old ones back so now she has a nearly empty wardrobe and whose fault is that? "Not mine!" she told daddy and glared at him. Daddy opened his mouth and then closed it again like he was doing an impersonation of a goldfish but he wasn't.

Monday 3rd September

Mel's mummy gets a bill.

Back to school today. I've been so busy I'd almost forgotten what it was like! Emily told me at break that I had a bit of a tan and that it suited me. I don't know how I managed that as I have been keeping out of the sun but at least I'm not red like daddy. Charlie asked, "What about me?" but Emily said that he was still pink. I don't think Charlie was too impressed. I like Emily.

Oh dear! Mel's mummy's received a bill for a replacement table from the train company and Mel's been really told off 'cos it's very expensive 'cos it's not like at home when you just get a new one and chuck the old one out. Train tables have to be fitted so that they can withstand all the use and abuse like when people stand on them Melanie. Still, it's not as much told off as her husband's going to be when she sees the bill for repainting a Spitfire.

Tuesday 4th September

Pop-up presents.

First lesson today was R.E. Sir asked us a question that I didn't even understand then expected me to answer it. He just kept looking at me until I said something. In the end I thought I would give the answer that every question seems to end up with in R.E. I cleared my throat and said, "Whatever the question is, God is the answer." Before sir could open his mouth Emily said, "The question is, 'What is 'dog' spelt backwards?'" Everyone laughed - except sir. Emily and I had to stand outside the classroom until the end of the lesson. At least we couldn't be asked any more difficult questions whilst we were out there and

Emily had one more friend with her than she had in the corridor with her on the Norwich train last month.

Mel says she's fed up having to put up tents on camp and spending ages over it so she's asked for a pop-up tent for her birthday. I told her that they're a nightmare to pack away and that's why they're called a "pop-up" tent and not a "pop-down" one. Sonny said that they can't be that bad but how would he know? Her mummy's told her that they're quite expensive but Mel said that they're not as bad as the dinghy that her mummy's bought her daddy. Melanie said that she told her mummy that if she didn't agree to buy her a pop-up tent then she would tell her daddy about the accident with the Range Rover. I don't know what the accident with the Range Rover's all about but apparently it did the trick and Mel will be the proud owner of a pop-up tent for her birthday. Given how much the Spitfire's going to cost to repaint I'm surprised Mel hasn't got her daddy to agree to buy her a pop-up house. Now there's an idea.

Wednesday 5th September
Sizzled sausage during the night.
Sam's just come back from his expedition. He said that the group was divided into scouts and explorers (those that know what they're doing) and others (those that don't). They had to camp in a green field (that means no running water and no toilet). Fortunately Sam and the explorers had a toilet shovel so they knew what to do: dig a hole, do your business, fill the hole in and mark the spot with a cross of small stones to warn others. As for the "others" none of them went to the toilet on the first night and they all waited until the group was back underway whereupon they went into cafes and community toilets

throughout the day. The second night they were back at the greenfield site when one of the "other" boys who had very neat hair, according to Sam, asked him where he could find an electrical socket so that he could plug his hair dryer in. Without a moment's hesitation Sam told him that out in the countryside sockets were buried so that they weren't used by those not "in the know." "How will I know where they're buried?" the boy asked. "'Cos they're all marked by little stone crosses and you sort of have to dig down a bit," was Sam's not very nice reply.

Sam then told the "others" not to go for a wee near the stone crosses in case they electrocuted themselves. This unfortunately led to a real electrocution 'cos one of the "others" decided to have a wee over a metal wire fence into the other field during the night. At about three o'clock in the morning the other campers were woken up by screaming. Sam jumped out of his tent and saw that part of the wire fence was flashing blue sparks. Apparently the "other" hadn't realised that the wire fence was electrified and so had sizzled his sausage for five seconds before he could run back to his tent. Sam never did find out which "other" it was and no one said anything in the morning. Their leader had to do an accident report but no one owned up so where it said "Name" he put "Anonymous (boy)."

Thursday 6th September
Cinema, Chinatown and Charing Cross.
We were supposed to be going to see the new James Bond film that Sam wanted to see this evening but we missed one of the best bits that is right at the beginning and it was all mummy's fault. We all - apart from daddy (who thinks he is James Bond so

that would be a bit of a waste) - went to Leicester Square in London to see it on the very big screen but we missed the train and mummy doesn't drive 'cos of the cost of the constipation charge. We were all ready to go to the station and were at the garden gate waiting for mummy to lock up when Susie walked past and asked us what we were doing 'cos she's nosey like that. Olivia said that we were walking to the station to get the train to Charing Cross. Susie then told us that she

was getting that train as well and "see you at the station." When mummy had finished locking up she asked us what Susie had wanted so we told her. Mummy looked very carefully at what she was wearing then said that there was no way that she could get the same train as Susie and she could hardly get on a different carriage 'cos that would be rude but she said that there was no way that she was going to sit with Susie so we had to go back indoors for twenty minutes even though it would mean that we would be late for the start of the film. Eventually we were on our way. We walked down to the station, bought our tickets and went and sat on one of the platform benches. We had just put our bottoms down when the railway line started to click, so we knew that the train was approaching the station, at which point mummy suddenly announced, "I'm sorry that we're going to be a

little late for the film children but at least we won't have to sit and listen to that old moo going on about how fabulous she is for half-an-hour," when a voice behind mummy said, "Which particular 'old moo' are you trying to avoid Karen?" Mummy turned round to see Susie staring at her with a sarcastic expression and a big smile on her face. "Oh, oh, just someone that I used to know quite well until she was very rude about Sam and who I bumped into earlier today quite by chance and who said she was going up to London earlier this afternoon," mummy replied not particularly confidently. So not only did mummy tell a great big lie and we also missed the start of the film but we also had to sit and listen to Susie talk all the way up to London non-stop about her new fitted kitchen that she probably doesn't even cook in in case she gets it mucky.

Mummy wasn't the only one to tell a big lie though. When Susie took her coat off on the train mummy looked at Susie's dress and almost hiccupped and put her hand to her mouth. "That's a fabulous dress Susie," mummy said. "Oh yes," said Susie, lifting up her chin superiorly and stroking the red and grey checked dress that she was wearing. "It came from a fantastic boutique that I know of in London that specialises in new copies of classic vintage clothing. It was reassuringly expensive," she purred. "I think I know different," mummy said to me later but didn't say anything further so I decided not to ask.

At the end of the film mummy said that she had an idea. As everyone else was leaving their seats we stayed put and waited for the next showing so that we could watch the first ten minutes that we had missed. Some usherettes came round clearing up but we just sat there not saying anything but then it started to get quite busy with more and more people coming in. Then a couple came and stood in the aisle looking at us and they were holding tickets for the seats that Sam and I were sitting in. Then an usher appeared and asked mummy for our tickets but mummy didn't have any 'cos we had used them as cardboard scoops to eat our tubs of ice cream with after mummy took all the lids off and threw them in the bin without realising that the spoons were attached on the inside. Next thing we know we're being escorted from the cinema by a very big fat man with an earpiece with wire dangling from it and everyone was watching 'cos by the time that we had reached the front door we had four very big fat men -

each with earpieces with wire dangling from them and they were escorting us and gently shoving people out of the way like we were celebrities but we weren't anything of the sort and we were going in the wrong direction.

We then went into Chinatown and had a very nice dinner. While we were eating our prawn crackers I asked mummy if she heard the woman who was sitting behind me 'cos the film hadn't really started properly when we sat down and James Bond got a large tear in his shirt and the woman made a loud "Ohhhhhh-aH!" sound. Then Olivia said that she had heard it too and she had turned round and "Horace, it wasn't a woman who was sighing, it was a mannnnnn!"

We were very late getting home 'cos mummy said that she couldn't risk having to sit with Susie again so when we got to Charing Cross we didn't go on the Chislehurst train we went instead to Sidcup and then we caught a bus. Unfortunately, just as the train pulled out of the station Susie appeared out of nowhere, sat down and started to tell us about her new bathroom. When she stopped for breath mummy asked her why she didn't catch the Chislehurst train and Susie said that it was because there was someone on it whom she was trying to avoid and "You know how difficult it is to avoid someone on the train who you know without seeming rude." Mummy said that she did have an idea of what she was talking about. So we had the train to Sidcup with Susie, the bus to Chislehurst with Susie and a walk up the road with Susie at the end of which there wasn't much that we didn't know about the last three months of Susie's life including the fabulous barbecue that we hadn't been to.

Mummy said that next time we go to London she's going to drive and stuff the constipation charge.

Friday 7th September

Fence painting.
We had to paint the fence in the scout hut grounds tonight with wood preserver. Skip said that it stains the fence as well as helping prolong its life. It was great fun and the fence looks almost like new now! Although we used loads of preserver we still had a bit left over so Charlie asked if he could take it home as his daddy had a bit of fence to do in the back garden. I asked him when he was going to do his fence and he said, "Tomorrow." I said that I would come round and help him but he told me not to which was a bit odd.

Saturday 8th September
No fence painting.

I went round to Charlie's with my paint brush today 'cos I thought that I would help him anyway. He wasn't in but his daddy was so I told him that I had come to help wood preserve his fence in the back garden but he looked at me as if I was mad and said that they only had bushes and I wasn't going to paint them.

Mummy went down to the charity shop today in her sunglasses to ask whether the red and grey checked woollen dress with the sewn in silver necklace that she had seen "just a few days ago" had been sold. "Oh yes," mummy was told. "That went almost straightaway to one of our regular customers." "I knew it," mummy said when we were having dinner. "How do you know it was the same one that Susie was wearing?" I asked. Mummy said, "Because I changed the stitching round the necklace to a different colour. I can't believe it! Susie in a charity shop!" "Yes mummy," I said, "but you were in there yourself the other day." "I was browsing; Susie was BUYING!" mummy spat out.

Sunday 9th September

Archie's assurance causes an accident.

Whoops! Archie's in trouble now! He was helping his daddy get a worktop from Ikae in exchange for fish and chips and a Daim bar pud in the cafe. Archie had to measure the length of the inside of his daddy's car and it was exactly the length of the worktop. After they had paid for the worktop and were sticking it in the car with the worktop front resting on the dashboard the back stuck out by five centimetres. This was because the worktop was still in its box and it had a  thick polystyrene strip at each end. Archie told his daddy that it would be okay 'cos the polystyrene would just squash up so his daddy slammed the boot door shut - and cracked the windscreen.

At least Archie had made sure to get his Daim bar pud first.

Monday 10th September
Charlie missing.
Charlie wasn't at school today. Miss said that he wasn't very well and had been in hospital. On the way home I went to his house but his mummy said that he didn't want to see me but at least that means he's at home which is a good sign.

 Sonny came to school with loads of money. When I asked him how he got it he said that he had been selling mucky photos. "Who to?" I asked. "Angela," he said.

Tuesday 11th September
Sonny causes havoc at Melanie's birthday.
It was Melanie's birthday today so it was all round to Buckingham Palace - that's what mummy calls her house - for tea. Sonny was invited as well 'cos Mel said that her mummy feels sorry for him.

There were loads of presents in the hallway but all Sonny was interested in was how the pop-up tent worked. Mel said that it was in a blue bag in the hallway but that she wasn't allowed to open it indoors without adult supervision and so neither was he. That wasn't a good enough reason for Sonny so whilst we were all having our tea outside Sonny said that he needed to go to the toilet. He waited until the one by the swimming pool was occupied and then said that he needed to go urgently so that he had to go inside. But instead of going to the toilet he found the blue bag and took it into the drawing room - I think that's where they do art and stuff, unlocking the door with the key that was conveniently in the lock and shut the door. The blue bag was very heavy and Sonny struggled to get it onto the table so that he could see a bit more clearly what to do. Unfortunately this was no ordinary table, this is the large antique table that Mel's daddy bought in France and Mel's mummy's always talking about it and it's really valuable (or should I now say "was") 'cos it has loads of carvings on the legs and it's dark reddy brown polished wood. Mel's mummy had put her expensive cut glass and decanters and things on it up the other end that she was in the process of cleaning. Sonny wasn't sure how to open the tent but he said later that there was a tab sticking out that said, "Pull to inflate." Sonny gave it a tug and immediately there was a small "pop" followed by a loudish whooshing sound and the tent burst into life only it wasn't Mel's tent it was Mel's daddy's self-inflating six-man dinghy that expanded from a tiny package to a ginormous craft that inflated with more whooshing and unfolded and self-inflated and spread itself over the table that all the glassware was on. Sonny tried to stop it inflating but there was nothing that he could do. Wine glasses fell to the ground and broke, sherry glasses shattered and decanters were decimated. Soon the table and carpet were covered in thousands of pieces of glass that sparkled an array of beautiful rainbow colours like a disco ball but it wasn't in the ceiling. It was carnage. When I went inside for a real wee and to find Sonny, I went to investigate what all the crunching noise was. I found Sonny pinned against a wall in the drawing room with the huge dinghy sitting across the table whilst all that he could do was stamp up and down on the glass that was all over the large cotton handmade rug that Mel's daddy had made in Tunisia and imported home at considerable expense. "Move it Horace or deflate it," he demanded breathlessly. I couldn't see any plug like you get on lilos or a deflate button so I went round to the other side of the table, put my 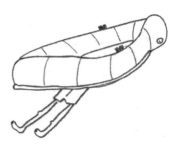 arms over the side of the huge beast and pulled. It only moved a few centimetres 'cos it was really heavy and cumbersome and I could hear horrible scratching noises under it where the glass bits were gouging into the table. "I didn't realise pop-up tents were so big," he said now that he could breathe, as he walked slowly to the door. "Come back over here," I said, then I explained what it was that he had been playing with and that you couldn't just pop-it-down. Suddenly there was a large BANG followed by more whooshing as the dingy deflated itself almost as quickly as it had gone up and there it sat, a huge flat piece of collapsed industrially thick plastic, across the table. "I think that we should leg it," said Sonny so we both retreated back to the garden, Sonny with a big stain on the front of his trousers even though he hadn't wanted the toilet. Sonny opened one of the windows slightly then locked the door from the inside, removed the key and then slid it back under the door. "That should give us enough time and Mel's folk enough confusion for us not to be chief suspects," Sonny said. "Not 'us' Sonny," I said. "'You.'"

Wednesday 12th September
Charlie found. Mel missing.

Charlie is back at school and oh my goodness does he have a tan! Emily asked him if he had been on a secret holiday to the Sahara or somewhere but he said that he hadn't and that he had been experimenting with a self-tanning lotion. Emily suggested that next time he used it he use a little less 'cos at the moment he looks like an Aborigine. I asked him why he had been in hospital but he said that it wasn't anything serious and that he had just had a minor skin complaint.

Mel wasn't at school today.

Thursday 13th September
Sonny has some questions to answer.
Sam's friend's older brother starts uni. in two weeks. He told his daddy yesterday that as his daddy has had to pay his hall fees, social club membership, society fees, discount card fee and sports hall membership, he doesn't want much for his birthday - just a new laptop, a new iPhone and a double pack of Oreos. I think I know what he'll be getting.

Mel was back at school today. She said that her family had suffered a break-in that was discovered yesterday morning just as she was about to be brought to school so she had to stay at home whilst her mummy 'phoned the police. Then they had to wait for the police to come which took all morning and then it was lunchtime and then it was too late to come to school and anyway her mummy had a hair appointment and... "Mel," I said, "tell us about the break-in." "Mum couldn't find the key to the drawing room so she went and got a spare from the safe. When she unlocked the door she found a key hidden under the door but that was just the start. All her glassware was smashed and the antique table was wrecked. There was also a window wide open. Mum thinks that someone broke in through the window, found the key and locked the door before making good their escape but it doesn't look like they've stolen anything. Although," she added queryingly, "for some reason that my parents can't fathom we have found the remains of dad's dinghy floating in the swimming pool with loads of small holes in it. It was all very odd and quite disturbing."

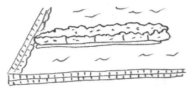

When I got Sonny alone later and asked him whether he had returned to Mel's house he said that he had. "But that's burglary," I told him. "No it's not," he said. "I had been invited, it's just that I went home in-between." "And what happened to the dinghy? Did you steal it?" "No, I didn't steal a dinghy," Sonny said, "I took a big bit of plastic and I was doin' Mel's parents a favour by gettin' rid of it for them. However it was so heavy that I only got it as far as the pool before I gave up so I pulled it into the pool 'cos I thought that it would sink and no one would notice." I explained to Sonny that even if it had sunk Mel's family would have seen it at the bottom of the pool but Sonny just said, "Oh," and walked off.

Friday 14th September
Skip gets told off.
Skip told Charlie off tonight 'cos Skip had been told off by Charlie's daddy 'cos Skip had given Charlie the rest of the wood preserver last week and not told his daddy so Charlie put it in his bedroom and on Sunday he got his flannel and wiped it all over his face to give himself an instant tan so that Emily would like it but instead a dreadful rash came up on Monday and he had to go to A & E looking like an Aborigine that had been super-sunbathing I would imagine.

Daddy took a teaspoon out of the kitchen tonight in a tumbler again. He said again that he's just checking on the slow gin and the tumbler is for keeping the spoon in so as not to make any mess. He keeps doing this.

Saturday 15th September
Sam scores at football.
Sam's all smiles today! It was his first full football match of the new season and he played the whole ninety minutes. What's more he scored a goal. "The final score was two-all thanks to me scoring the last goal against a much better team." Daddy said "well done" and gave him extra pocket money. Just for scoring a goal. How unfair.

Sunday 16th September
Sam's goal is clarified.
I saw Charlie today and he said, "Pity about Sam's goal." I asked him what he was talking about 'cos Sam had been really pleased about it yesterday. One of Charlie's brothers plays in the same team as Sam. Charlie said, "Without Sam's goal his team would've won

the game two-one. "How does that work?" I asked. "Sam said that he scored the goal that tied the match." "That's right," said Charlie. "He scored an own goal, a goal against his own team." When I told daddy he asked Sam for his extra pocket money back plus a fine for lying. Sam said he hadn't lied and it wasn't his fault if daddy just made assumptions. He has a point there I'm sure. I think Sam'll be a lawyer when he's grown up not that that's going to happen any time soon.

Monday 17th September
Vexatious Vegan.

Mummy had a bit of a meltdown today. She had a load of people round at the weekend for a dinner party and was sweating all day over starters, mains and puds and choices and cheese and decorations and everything. Daddy had to sort out the table, the wine and aperitives, the digestives - the list went on and on. Then it turned out that one of the guests was a vegan so mummy had to do some spaghetti thing for them which was a bit of a pain 'cos vegans don't eat much more than lettuce leaves. Unfortunately, when she was draining the water off she dropped the spaghetti in the washing up bowl but she just scooped it all out and rinsed it and threw it on the vegan's plate. When mummy asked the vegan person what it was like she said, "Mmmm. Lemony." Mummy felt really embarrassed but said later to daddy that she took the comment as a compliment as to her choice of washing-up liquid.

Mummy was really tired yesterday and still had all the washing up to do. Then today she read this in Trend magazine under:
"The New Dinner Party Rules:
Food - No one cares. Not really. Sharing plates on the table or help yourself from the side are preferable to staff trembling under the weight of enormous platters - too feudal and too self-conscious-making. Any guests with any kind of vegan tendency or intolerance should eat before and never mention it."
She agreed with the "vegan tendency" bit. That or risk / suffer your food having been washed.

This evening mummy just dumped dinner on dishes on the work surface and we had to help ourselves.

Mel said that her daddy was going to raise the dinghy up from the swimming pool over the weekend but when he went to have a look at it on Saturday morning it had disappeared.

Tuesday 18th September
Cockerpooshoodle - a new cocktail.
Charlie told me at school today that his mummy is getting a puppy for her birthday. When I asked him what type she was getting he said that it would probably be something like a Cockerpooshoodle. I told daddy when he came home from work and he said that it sounded like a Dutch cocktail drink. Sam added that it would probably look like one.

Wednesday 19th September
Mr Lillie runs out of waterproof repair tape.
I told Charlie what daddy said last night and he said that his daddy had said something similar.

I went to The Workshed which is our local hardware shop today and saw Mr Lillie who runs it. I told him that I was after some waterproof repair tape 'cos I had a tent that I needed to patch up after my friend had made several incisions in the groundsheet due to his mistaking it for a toilet. Mr Lillie told me that unfortunately he had run out 'cos "a boy came in earlier and bought six rolls." When I described Sonny to him he said, "That's the boy. Maybe he's going to patch up the groundsheet for you?" "No, Mr Lillie," I said. "I think he's got a slighter larger job on his hands."

Thursday 20th September
The Cockerpooshoodle is no more.
Charlie told me at school today that his mummy isn't getting a Cockerpooshoodle. She's getting a cat. I didn't dare ask what type. Probably a Tabbygingitortipuss.

Friday 21st September
Live lobsters cause a panic.
Hurray! We have a new fishmongers' in Chislehurst! It looks really posh and there's a big sign outside saying, "Fresh fish and seafood." Mel told me at scouts this evening that her mummy went out to have a look and ended up buying four lobsters which she brought home and put in the fridge. Mel was really looking forward to having lobster and her mummy was going to heat them up in the microwave but when she got them out of the fridge and undid all the packaging she screamed 'cos they weren't pink like she had expected, they were sort of brown and they started to move. Mel's mummy got the bin under the work surface and pushed the lobsters off the edge with the dustpan and into the bin. Now Mel is yet to have dinner 'cos her mummy suggested fish and chips but Mel said that she would just have a salad when she got home.

Saturday 22nd September
Mel's daddy's dinghy resurfaces.

It was a really sunny day today so the Ravings decided to go and do kayaking at Danson Park where there's a huge lake. We all went apart from Sonny who said that he was busy. But guess who was on the lake when we got there? Sonny! And he was in the most enormous dinghy - one that I thought that I had seen before, albeit not on a lake - and he was in it with a man that none of us had seen before  and some other people that we didn't know. Mel was jumping up and down with excitement. "Thief!" she shouted. "Thief!" "Sssh, Melanie," I said. "You don't know that it's the missing dinghy." "Yes I do," she squealed. "Dad named it after me and that's why it has 'MELANIE' printed down both sides in rainbow colours." Melanie lowered her voice and said in a conspiratorial whisper. "He hasn't seen us yet, let's go and get him! But what are all those black strips of tape doing all over it?" "Holding it up?" Archie ventured. He wasn't wrong. We were supposed to be having a kayaking lesson but once we got on the lake Melanie simply took off. "Come back here!" the instructor cried, but it was too late. She paddled like a maniac over to the middle of the lake and then, coming up behind the back of the dinghy, made not a sound on her final approach. Once she was right behind the dinghy she leant over and peeled off two of the largest strips of tape that she could reach and quickly paddled back to us. We watched with a mixture of excitement and fear as the dinghy slowly deflated and mass panic broke out amongst Sonny and his guests. As the dinghy began to sink and the occupants started to swim for the bank, Melanie paddled over once more with the rest of us following. Our instructor said that it was like a mini-Dunkirk evacuation but I wasn't sure what he was talking about. She shouted at Sonny, "You little thief! I should've known better than to invite you round my house again!" "I'm not a thief!"

Sonny protested between mouthfuls of water. "Where did you get my dinghy from then?" Melanie demanded. "I picked it up at a car boot fair last weekend," said Sonny innocently. "Oh," said Mel, sounding not very convinced. Sensing her suspicion Sonny looked at me then back at Mel, then at me again as if expecting me to say something, all the while treading water. Finally he said to Mel, "Ask Horace. He was with me." "Well thanks Sonny!" I thought. I was in half a mind to tell Mel how I had caught Sonny pinned to her drawing room wall the other day but I imagined things could get quite complicated, especially as Sonny had an answer for everything and if I wasn't careful he would probably make sure that it ended up with me looking like the thief so I just nodded. Melanie was so taken in by Sonny's explanation that she then let him climb on the back of her kayak and we all made our way to the bank. Then the instructor said that he needed to go and report the sinking of a dinghy and whilst he was gone I asked Sonny who all the other people were who were in the dinghy with him. "What people?" Sonny asked and we looked all around but there were no wet people to be seen, apart from Sonny so we all started to believe that we were going mad, but we had all seen them so we knew that we weren't. Something didn't add up but, as with most things that involve Sonny, rarely anything does.

Later on, after we had had our lesson, Sonny came home with us on the bus and he sat beside me and told me, without saying more about how he had acquired it, that he had put the dinghy for sale on an online auction site and the people in the dinghy were prospective purchasers. This still didn't explain why they had all disappeared and where they disappeared to.

Sunday 23rd September
Dinghy for sale.
I told Sam today all about the Danson Lake incident and that Sonny had said that he had sold Mel's daddy's dingy on an online auction site so Sam said, "Let's see shall we? You can still look at

stuff even though it's been sold." "I don't think it was sold," I said. "I think the people were testing it out." Sam found the site on daddy's computer and typed in the type of dinghy and colour and stuff and pressed "Enter." Up popped several photos of Mel's daddy's dinghy that was being sold by "SunneeEnterprizes." "That'll be him," I said, "and that's the dingy 'cos you can see all the tape stuck onto it. I don't think I would describe it as 'new' though." "Well I suppose it's not very old," said Sam, "although I see he's put on the delivery bit, 'Buyer collects.' Doesn't he realise how deep Danson Lake is in parts?" "Knowing Sonny," I suggested, "he'll pull the plug out of the lake so as to drain it and get the dingy out." Then Sam said, "Shall we search 'SunneeEnterprizes' and see what else he has for sale?" but in the end we didn't dare.

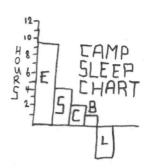

Monday 24th September
Sleep chart.

Sam told me today that Chrissie's done a sleep chart for camp. He said that she's calculated that explorers get about ten hours' but usually starting at breakfast time, scouts get four, cubs get two, beavers get one and leaders get minus four. How that works I've no idea.

Tuesday 25th September
Temporary traffic light colour meanings.

Shopping with mummy this evening after school. We had to wait for ages at some temporary traffic lights. When we finally reached the front of the queue the lights had already turned red yet about five cars in front had still gone through - and then mummy did - and then three more cars followed on behind. When we went reached the cars

waiting by their lights to come in the opposite direction I looked in my wing mirror and saw that the lights had already turned to green. "Mummy..." I said. "Red doesn't count on temporary lights," she said, without even waiting for my question. "Green means 'go,' amber means 'go' and red means 'just another ten cars or so.'" "What about if you're coming in the opposite direction?" I asked. "Then the lights all mean 'wait,'" mummy said. How confusing. I'm glad I don't drive.

Wednesday 26th September
Pasta overload.
Mummy and daddy and grandad went out for dinner tonight and left me in charge of dinner. We had pasta with bacon and pesto and broccoli. Mummy left out a one kilo bag of Fusilli, which is the curly one, some bacon to chop up and fry, a jar of pesto and some broccoli to steam. I put the biggest saucepan that I could find on the hob with loads of water in it and when it started to boil I added half the pasta. Then Sam came in and looked in the pan and said that it didn't look like very much and so he tipped the rest of the bag in. After ten minutes it certainly did look very much 'cos the pasta was now coming over the top of the saucepan and we don't have a bigger one. I went over to the sink and removed the bowl and wiped all round the sink, turned the hot tap on for a few seconds, let the water drain away and then tipped in the cooked pasta. Once that had drained I put the plug in and added the bacon, pesto and broccoli. Then I stirred it round with a big spoon and served it up on three plates with

some grated Parmesan. It was yummy but then everyone was full and it didn't look like the pasta had gone down at all. We could hardly leave the pasta in the sink even though it was stainless steel so keeping it nice and warm but then Sam had an idea. He took the big plastic vegetable tray out of the fridge, having emptied the contents into the fruit section, scooped up the pasta using the washing-up bowl and then poured it into the vegetable container. Once it was full up we filled six cereal bowls with pasta and then there wasn't much left. Sam pulled out the plug and squished the rest of the pasta down the plug hole. It took a bit of time but at least mummy wouldn't find it in the bin.

Thursday 27th September
Lobster and hamster breakout.
Cold pasta for breakfast and dinner today.

There was the usual noise at breakfast 'cos Thursdays are bin days and the bin men make a real racket doing what they do. I wandered up to Mel's 'cos she had to walk to school today 'cos her mummy has her car in the garage and I was surprised, just before I reached her house, to find four very dozy lobsters crawling slowly down the verge towards me looking very pleased with themselves. I had to rub my eyes to make sure that I wasn't

dreaming. I wasn't sure what to do so I picked them up and put them in my rucksack 'cos otherwise the bin men would probably have run them over. We went on a school trip to the aquarium today so then I knew what to do! It was a bit fortunate that I couldn't find my daysack earlier so had my sixty litre rucksack with me and it didn't have much in it apart from a sweatshirt, a coat and my packed lunch (fortunately in a food container) so there was plenty of room. I told Emily on the coach and she said that I had to liberate them so when we got to the aquarium and were being shown round I waited until we found a fish tank that had an open top. I had my chance in the small fish room. It was really dark and there was a big tank with loads of tiny shiny discus fish in it that our guide said were extremely rare. I was at the back of the line and when no one was looking 'cos we were going to the next room I took off my rucksack and Emily helped to put a lobster each in the tank. Unfortunately Emily didn't hold hers properly and squealed 'cos she was pinched and so everyone stopped and turned round but I managed to get the two in the tank with a small splosh. Sir was up the front and he came back to see what the problem was. I told him that my rucksack was hurting 'cos it was heavy but he just tutted and told me to stop sounding like a girl. As we started to go again Emily screamed and this time miss came to see what the problem was but Emily just said that she was getting frightened of the dark so had to go back up the front with miss. I didn't realise that Sonny had been watching what was going on but when we started off again he said, "Look at that tank that you've dropped a couple of lobs in." I turned to inspect my handiwork and soon worked out why Emily had been screaming. The discus fish were being eaten! Chomp, chomp, chomp! I decided that I needed to be up the front with Emily so overtook everyone in search of her with Sonny not far behind.

When we went into the next room Sonny asked me what I was up to so I explained about the lobsters and that I had two left. Sonny said that he would liberate them 'cos he had an innocent face and so that no further suspicion would fall on me which was kind of him so we stuck them in his rucksack when no one was looking. Sorted! Although I don't know what happened to them 'cos I didn't see him put them in any tanks. He had suggested that he took them home and stuck them in Mel's swimming pool but we thought that that would be a bit mean. Given what we had for dinner - again - this evening lobster would've been a very nice change but it wouldn't have been very kind to have brought them home and eaten them so I forgot about it and moved on.

Crisis at beavers! Sam enjoyed himself helping at beavers this evening, but that wasn't the crisis. They went on a visit to Pet World, which is a huge local pet superstore, as part of one of their badges. The beavers were allowed to pick up and cuddle some of the animals which they all wanted to do. Their favourites were the hamsters and a black kitten. They all wanted to play with the hamsters. Sam said that he didn't think the lady in charge was ready for so many beavers but she did her best. There were some very expensive Syrian hamsters in one cage which one of the beavers wanted but his mummy, who was helping, said that they were too expensive. "It's okay, mummy," the little beaver said, "you don't have to pay cash, you can just put it on a card," but his mummy still said, "No."

There were also some very cheap hamsters - so cheap in fact that they were free. They were in a "Bargain Basement" cage and were second-hand hamsters that people hadn't wanted anymore and had given back to the shop. Then there were the other hamsters that were in two huge cages and the beavers were allowed to hold the hamsters from one cage (although one of the beavers was holding one from the other cage when the lady wasn't looking) but then one of the beavers was fiddling with the lock when the lady was dealing with the black kitten and two beavers who both wanted to hold the kitten and were fighting over it. Then one of the other mummies who was helping suddenly screamed and jumped onto a rabbit hutch 'cos the beaver had unlocked the cage and all the hamsters were escaping and running around the store. They went everywhere and the mummies were no use 'cos they were all standing on cages and one was on the counter and screaming and screaming and screaming. Then the beavers were told to look for as many hamsters that they could and return them to the cage. Sam said that it was chaos and then the kitten scratched the beaver that was holding it and the kitten joined in the hunt but it wasn't returning the hamsters to the cage, it was pouncing on them and then chewing their heads off! It did two like this before the lady caught the kitten. She put the kitten back in its cage and picked up the headless hamsters and put them on the counter. Then the lady who was standing on the counter started screaming even more and then she was shaking even though the hamsters at her feet were probably dead unlike chickens that still run around although they can't think if their heads are missing. Well, their heads can think still but they can't make their body move 'cos they're not telepathic unlike worms.

Eventually as many of the hamsters that could be found were returned to their cage and the beavers had to go home. On the minibus the beaver who wanted a Syrian hamster told Sam that he had something in his coat pocket. When Sam could see the pocket moving Sam asked him what it was and was told, "It's my Syrian Hamster. His name is Sam, like you, 'cos it could be a boy or a girl." Sam was a bit confused that his name was being used for a hamster but he was more interested in the fact that the beaver had managed to get his hands on a very expensive hamster that his mummy had already said that she couldn't afford, and stuck it in his pocket. "Does your mummy know?" Sam (my brother) asked the beaver. "No," he replied. Sam then worked out that the hamster must have been stolen 'cos otherwise his mummy would have known 'cos she would have had to have paid for it or at least shown her card. "So you stole it?" "No," said the beaver. "While everyone was screaming and stuff I picked Sam out of his cage and put him in the Bargain Basement cage. That made him free so I then put him in my pocket."

Sam said that after all that he didn't ever fancy being a beaver leader. Nor work in a pet store I should imagine.

Friday 28th September
Safety with knives, saws and axes.
Cold pasta for breakfast and dinner.

We did "safety with knives, saws and axes" tonight. We used penknives, bow saws and hand axes. Skip said that it was quite dangerous so we had to listen to everything that he and Patrick said otherwise we could be in danger and may lose a finger or two. It was really interesting and we loved chopping wood up with the hand axes. This is something that we would never be allowed to do at school. We got so carried away that we ran out of wood but Skip found some upstairs where we store the tents and stuff. They were old bits of timber like broomsticks but shorter and they had been painted. Skip thought that maybe someone had once been doing some Morris Men dances. Now we could really go to town. We chopped the mini  broomsticks, we sawed the mini broomsticks and we made feather sticks. This is when you shave a stick with your penknife but don't shave the slivers off so that the stick looks like a palm tree. This means that you can make tinder out of a log (or a broomstick). At the end of the meeting, once all the parents had arrived for pick-up, Charlie put his hand up and said, "Axe stuff is really great fun Skip, but can I have my finger back?" All the scouts giggled but not before Emily's mother had fainted in a heap on the floor and had to be revived. Just as well she hadn't been on the aquarium trip.

Sonny's mummy picked him up tonight and asked me why I looked so forlorn. I told her that food wasn't much fun in the Horrise household at present and all that I had had for dinner today was pasta - again. "Oh," she said brightly. "That's a bit dull. We 'ad lobster."

Saturday 29th September
New burger recipe doesn't go down well with everyone.
Pasta for breakfast.

We were doing some backwards cooking today by patrol at the scout hut 'cos we're having a one night camp and so we had to go to the supermarket to get some food for dinner. Thank goodness. I was getting more than a bit fed up with pasta. We were given a budget by Skip. We had a good look round and found that onions were so much a kilo for loose ones or so much for a plastic bag of onions. Which were cheaper? How could we work it out 'cos the bagged ones were so much a bag and not done by weight? Fortunately Charlie was on hand with his pocket calculator so we weighed the bag and it worked out that the loose ones were cheaper. The only problem was that there weren't many loose ones left so we weren't sure what to do until Mel came to the rescue. We took the onions out of their silly little sealed plastic bag, got them weighed at the checkout, paid less and left the little plastic bag behind. Sorted! Emily got some very cheap tinned meat even though she's a veggie. When we got back to the scout hut we grated the onions and mashed up the meat, mixed it all together and made some burgers which we put in foil and placed in embers for ten minutes. Then we got them carefully out of the fire, opened up the packages, put them in buns, put

CAT
FOOD
(BUT
GOOD
4
BURGERS!)

some cheese slices on them, added a bit of ketchup and ate them. They were really yummy! Emily and Mel said that they didn't want any 'cos they're now both vegetarians which was news to me 'cos it used to be just Emily until an hour ago. We gave theirs to Skip and Patrick who were very pleased and said how impressed they were. They scoffed them down. When it came to the results it was Ravings' turn to be very pleased 'cos we were told that we had won. Patrick said that the burgers were a bit salty but that he had quite enjoyed them and wanted to know what meat they were but Emily wouldn't tell him and said it was a secret recipe and the tins had gone missing. When Emily went to the toilet Skip looked in her rucksack and found four empty tins of Whiskas chicken and jelly and was promptly sick all over the scout hut floor and Ravings were disqualified for serving up animal food although no one said we couldn't and it tasted alright to us.

Sunday 30th September
Triple breakfast.

What's the best breakfast on camp? I bring you the "Horace Horrise Triple Tickle!" When Skip's not looking you have a bit of each cereal - all in one bowl. This morning I had Alpen and Waitrose Wholegrain Apricot Wheats at the sides with Co-Op Maple & Pecan Crisp in the middle. Add a bit of milk and tickle your taste-buds - three times! Yum!

When we got home mummy wasn't looking very happy 'cos the drains had all been blocked up and daddy had to get an emergency man in. He pressure-hosed down the plugholes and cleared the blockage but they don't know what the problem was. I think I do but I didn't say anything.

Monday 1st October

Cats and fish and no dogs.
Pasta for breakfast and dinner.

Charlie's mummy bought her kitten at the weekend. She has a
 British shorthair and she's called it
Jennifer but spelt "Jennifurr." How the
cat's going to know I've no idea. Charlie's
sister wanted her mummy to get the dog
and cried when a kitten appeared so their
daddy had to go out and buy her
something but not a dog. So now she has
a fish. Unfortunately her daddy forgot to
buy a fish tank and so Bubbles is living in
a flower vase until they get a tank. Charlie
told his sister to beware of me when I'm at their house in case
I'm carrying a lobster or four around but she had no idea what he
was talking about fortunately and he didn't explain.

Tuesday 2nd October
Pasta - for the last time this year hopefully.
Pasta for breakfast and that's the last of it, thank goodness.

Wednesday 3rd October
Semaphore - Sonny style.
Today at school we learnt semaphore.
Miss gave us each a couple of sticks
with flags on them and told us that we
were going to have a lesson on how we
can sign with them. At that Sonny made
his into a "V" sign and then pointed
them at everyone, waving them up and
down, before announcing, "That was
easy. Now what are we goin' to do until
lunch?" Miss then explained that each
letter and number were represented by a different position. She

started with the easy one - "D" which is right flag straight up and left flag straight down. At that Sonny pipes up, "Stuff 'D'. What's 'F', 'U...'" After that we all learnt how to semaphore our names. Sonny had to learn "D-E-T-E-N-T-I-O-N." Emily only managed EMLY 'cos she told miss that she wasn't going to do "I" 'cos the flag positions for that letter made her look like she was a matador and miss couldn't make her 'cos of her human rights.

Thursday 4th October
The slug trap goes missing.
Sam (brother) said that the beaver hamster thief had been told by his mummy that Sam (hamster) would have to be returned to the pet store "after all the fuss has died down."

Olivia came back early from cubs tonight. Apparently she arrived at the scout hut and found a jam jar of something that "smelt nice" so whilst Akela was downstairs she drank it all. Then she felt a bit funny but didn't say anything. However, later on in the meeting when Akela was talking about how to grow stuff in your garden and avoid pests she suddenly asked, "Where's my slug trap?"

She picked up her empty jam jar and explained to the cubs that beer was a good trap for slugs as they are attracted to the yeast, climb in, submerge and die. "Here's the trap that I have in my garden," she said, "but the beer and little slugs seem to have disappeared. Does anyone know what's happened to them?" "Please Akela, I think Olivia's looking after them but it's okay 'cos they'll slide out of somewhere in an hour or two," said one of the cubs.

Friday 5th October
Rockets and axes - a fun evening!

We made some stomp rockets this evening in scouts. We're going to have a stall at a community event soon and have to represent a country. 'Cos our rockets went up a long way but they were all wobbly Charlie said that we should be North Korea but Skip didn't think that that was a good idea and he said that even Britain has the occasional problem.

We had an introduction to axe-throwing at the end of our meeting. I think I needed it. Skip showed us some small steel throwing axes and we were allowed to hold them but not to throw them. You have to hold the axe handle firmly but not tightly so that it's easy to let go when you're throwing and you don't throw too hard. Skip says we're doing axe-throwing in two weeks' time, after family camp. I can't wait to do it properly!

Saturday 6th October
Archie goes for a family meal and his daddy gets found out.
The Horrise family went out for dinner at a new place this evening and Archie was there so we sat near to him. It's at the end of the high street and it's Turkish. They do a beer called Efes Draft but it's in a bottle. Archie's daddy said that that didn't make sense 'cos if it was in a bottle then it couldn't be draft, but what does Archie's daddy know? Archie wanted steak and so was given a different knife that was sharper and pointier so the people in charge probably knew that they were going to give Archie a bit of tough meat. Archie said that you always get a sharper knife when you ask for steak which is very useful 'cos you can do a bit of whittling while you're waiting for your food if nobody's looking. When I asked him what he whittles he said, "Sticks mostly. It's always a good idea to smuggle in a small stick or go to a Chinese 'cos they eat with sticks. Alternatively you can carve your name

on the underside of the table. If you have a long wait you can usually carve your whole name but you have to make sure that you do it the right way round 'cos it's upside down." I told Archie that that was vandalism and he could go to prison but he said that it didn't count if it couldn't be seen. Later on he told me quietly that if you're going to carve your name it's best to carve someone else's just in case, especially if you have an unusual name. So it is vandalism. Anyway he didn't get much of a chance to use his steak knife - either for whittling or eating 'cos it was confiscated. Whilst his daddy, who was sitting opposite him, was looking at the wine list, Archie's sister was asking Archie about axe-throwing. Archie decided to do a demonstration with his steak knife. He gripped the handle firmly like it was an axe and told his sister, "Not too tightly so that it's easy to let go when you're

throwing and I think you have to throw quite hard," 'cos Archie hadn't been listening properly to Skip when he was talking about the throwing bit. He flicked his wrist which you're not supposed to do and that's when the trouble started. Archie said that his mummy doesn't realise why his daddy is being so secretive when it comes to choosing which bottle of wine to have with their meals. She thinks it's 'cos he's buying a really expensive bottle and doesn't want her to know the price whereas the truth is that he's buying the cheapest bottle and doesn't want her to know the price and that's the reason why he holds the wine list up in front of his face so no one else can see. Anyway on this occasion it was just as well that he was. Archie's grip was nothing near firm enough and he threw far too hard 'cos the steak knife shot out of his hand, did a couple of quick rotations, and embedded itself in the wine menu with the point going all the way through and stopping just before Archie's daddy's nose as he was ordering a bottle of particularly cheap Turkish red. I don't know who was more shocked, Archie or his daddy, but his daddy dropped the wine list to tend to his unscathed nose and Archie's mummy picked it up. She apologised profusely, extracted the knife and handed it to the waiter then looked up the wine that her husband had just ordered to make sure that the waiter had written down the correct bottle. Starting at the top with the most expensive, she found her eyes going down and down and down, then onto the opposite page, down, down, down until finally she reached the absolutely last bottle listed. And there it was! "I think my husband had the wine list upside down," she spluttered, before ordering a bottle of Chateauneuf Du Pape at more than three times what her husband was preparing to pay. "I hope this was a one-off," she said to him once the waiter had gone.

Archie had moussaka and was given a spoon.

Sunday 7th October
Olivia takes a dislike to her dead hair.
Olivia's been complaining about her hair 'cos it's starting to go all curly when once it was straight. "There's not much you can do about it," I told her, "'cos hair's all dead anyway. The only bits that are alive are the ends where the hair starts and they're in the head so you can't see." Olivia didn't believe me and had to ask mummy. Mummy said that I was correct and that the hair on your head is dead. "So why doesn't it just all break off?" Olivia asked. I told her to think of a bit of dead wood. "First it dies and then it goes all dry, then it crumbles and rots and finally falls apart." "So my hair is going to rot if I leave it long enough?" "Probably," I said. "That's why you have to have it cut from time to time." When I went to bed Olivia asked to borrow my penknife. "Be careful," I said to her as I handed it

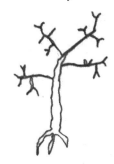

over, "it's very sharp." "Good," she said, "that's what I need." I hope she's not going to try penknife throwing in her bedroom.

Monday 8th October
Mummy takes a dislike to my penknife.
Olivia came down to breakfast this morning and mummy screamed. Olivia has cut, or more like hacked, most of her hair off with my penknife and then finished it off with Sam's razor (that I don't think he's ever had to use) and now her head's  bleeding in several places. "At least my hair's not going to rot, unlike everyone else's," Olivia announced. "You can't go to school like that," mummy told her. "You're right mummy," said Olivia. "I'll have to stay at home for the day." "You can't stay at home just because you've cut your head," mummy then said. "Oh make your mind up!" Olivia replied, before bursting into tears.

Anyway, Olivia did eventually go to school - once mummy had cleaned up her head and dabbed TSP all over - with a note in a sealed envelope. Olivia didn't think that she should have a note 'cos she didn't need to be excused from anything and the only thing that was different was that she had a dodgy haircut and, as she explained to me, "There are plenty of people at school with more dodgy haircuts." After school and once we were back at home I did try to explain that hers was less of a haircut and more of a hair removal but she wasn't listening 'cos she was busy getting mummy's note out of her bag whilst mummy was in the toilet. "Take a look at this," she said, thrusting the creased and opened envelope into my hand. "Don't let mummy see that you have it 'cos she thinks that I've handed it in." I took it up to my room to read it. I pulled out and unfolded the sheet of paper and read,

"I am sorry that Olivia has come to school today without any hair but we've just discovered that she is suffering from a very unusual type and severe form of alopecia which manifests itself suddenly and without warning. We are trying to shield Olivia as much as we are able from her deep feelings of insecurity over her physical appearance so would be grateful if you don't mention her hair loss to her directly whilst we try to get this matter resolved. The prognosis is good and she should start to see new hair growth within a few days.
Yours sincerely
Karen Horrise"

Downstairs Olivia was busy telling mummy that she had handed in her note telling miss that she was sorry that she had cut her hair and that it was an experiment. Mummy went white and said, "That may be your opinion Olivia, but your hair may just have fallen out." "No, mummy, I cut it, as I told you and as I told miss." Olivia told me later that obviously lying was in mummy's genes and therefore we can't help it if we do it also.

Sam came home from explorers and said that most of them had wet themselves laughing although I don't know what's so funny. This is what Sam said:

Explorer Scout (pointing to large "plaster" on leader's bare arm): What's that Chrissie?
Explorer Scout Leader: That's my contraceptive patch.
(Pause. Explorer Scout looks puzzled.)
Explorer Scout Leader: Everything okay?
Explorer Scout: Just wondering. How do you get pregnant up there?

Tuesday 9th October
Missing note and Bubbles.

Olivia was called in to see miss this morning at school. Apparently mummy had 'phoned up the school and spoken to the secretary to let her know that her note regarding Olivia's hair contained a "big error." The school secretary asked, "What 'note?'" and mummy put the 'phone down.

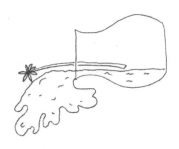

Charlie's daddy bought a fish tank at the weekend but it was too late. When he went to put Bubbles in his new home he found that the flower vase was on its side with water all over the sitting room carpet and Jennifurr was nearby licking her lips.

Wednesday 10th October
Sonny escapes for being Greek.

Sonny was very quiet during English today but he wasn't doing any writing and he had his hands under his desk for ages and he looked like he was really concentrating. Halfway through the meeting miss asked a question and told Sonny to come and write the answer on the whiteboard but when he got up Emily gasped and she sits behind Sonny and Sonny usually sits at the front of class but we don't know why. When miss came to investigate she found an open penknife on Sonny's chair and so it was confiscated and Sonny was sent out immediately to see sir. I don't think Sonny was really bothered 'cos he told me that he didn't even understand the question that miss had asked let alone know the answer. However he had a lucky escape 'cos at break the caretaker, who's called "old Mr Gregory", came in to examine Sonny's desk

249

for any damage but he couldn't find any.

Old Mr Gregory is older than the school and I think he lives at the school. He has his own room at the corner of the building. No one else has their own room apart from the head sir. Everyone else has to share so I think he's quite important 'cos he keeps everything working. Normally his door is shut and there's loads of smoke coming out of the window when it's open slightly. He's always whistling although sometimes it's his kettle. I told old Mr Gregory that Sonny wasn't a vandal and was probably just whittling. Old Mr Gregory said that he couldn't find any damage to the desk apart from someone had carved YNNOS on the underside. Melanie said that that was a Greek word and was probably a middle name or something of the boy who was from 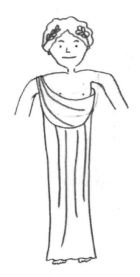 Cyprus and who had left last term so Sonny was allowed his penknife back at the end of the day but sir put it in a sealed envelope and told Sonny that his mummy was aware and he was to hand it to her when he got home. But he didn't and his mummy didn't ask for it.

Thursday 11th October
Sonny the Greek and wellie stick wars.

I asked Sonny what he was doing with his penknife in class yesterday 'cos he was surprised that he got it back. He said that if I look underneath his desk I will find that he's carved his name. And that is how Sonny came to be known as "Sonny the Greek" - but not by the teachers. He's also added what looks like a stick man running and he told me that it was for Mr Gregory.

Big trouble at cubs tonight. Olivia came home in tears to say that Akela was on the warpath 'cos someone had chopped up all the wellie sticks that the cubs had started on the week before. "We had painted all the sticks and Akela had put them upstairs to dry but when she went to get them she said that they had disappeared. Then we had a hunt all round the scout hut and when we couldn't find them we went outside and had a hunt and then we found them. They were all chopped up and on the woodpile," Olivia wailed. "They were chopped up into halves and quarters. Akela is furious." Olivia looked at me suspiciously. "Was it the scouts, was it you?" she asked me distrustfully. "You could use them as wellie sticks for midgets," I told her. "Was it you?" she snarled at me. I didn't answer. It wasn't my fault.

Friday 12th October
Family camp and the flags cause alarm.
Hurrah! Family camp! This is when mummies and daddies come and camp and we can show them that they don't know everything after all. We've all been put into teams and each team is a country. Last week we were allowed to choose eight countries for the teams based on their having "happy flags" and Sonny said that he wanted past or present Mozambique, Guatemala and Haiti and no one else was really bothered so Sonny was allowed those three countries then we had some countries that other people had heard of. We thought that Sonny was being really clever and now we know why. Well, he was being really clever but for the wrong

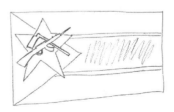

reasons. Akela looked a bit shocked when we were hanging the flags up in a line over the entrance to the camp. She put up Sweden which is a nice blue and yellow colour, then it was Sonny's

251

turn. First he put up Mozambique which has an AK-47 Kalashnikov assault rifle on it, then Haiti that has a whole load of weapons like cannons and swords, then Guatemala which has a couple of rifles. It's a nice blue and white colour though. I don't think Akela brought any spares so now she's busy up a step ladder with some Sharpies. There's so much going on that I'm going to have to write a separate diary later just for this weekend.

Saturday 13th October
Argentinean flag break and bacon press gets misused.
Too busy to write much stuff and it's very late. Akela's sorted out all the flags although it looks like she's drawn some of them. Unfortunately, despite having eight foreign flags, she's forgotten to bring a Union Jack so we had to do flag break with the Argentinean flag which was first choice after the Union Jack 'cos it's got a sun in the middle of it. But we didn't salute it. Daddy said that it was just as well that we didn't have a Union Jack 'cos it would probably be put up upside down but Mel told him that you can't put the Union Jack upside down, only the wrong way round. No one else is sure if she's right or not and a few daddy's got their 'phones out to check but there's no reception where we are so it's one-nil Mel and Akela's confiscated six 'phones 'cos it's no 'phones on camp, not even adult ones.

Mummy decided she wanted to iron her new and very expensive yellow jumper to wear tomorrow and asked Skip if he had anything that she could use 'cos it was all creased. Skip just laughed and said that he had a hand  iron that he used when doing the breakfasts but it was okay for her to use and that she just had to put it in the embers to heat it up then wipe it with a cloth before ironing. Mummy did as she

252

was told but the iron got too hot and she didn't realise. Now she has a new and very expensive yellow jumper with "BACON PRESS" and an imprint of a very fat pig burnt into it.

Sunday 14th October
Some daddies cause a bit of sadness.

A few of the daddies had a secret meeting this morning and they were shown a picture of the Union Jack by one of them and after Scouts Own when we prayed for peace and harmony in the world, one daddy went up to Mel and told her that she was wrong and "Union Jacks aren't symmetrical and can most certainly be hung upside down so maybe you should check your facts before opening your mouth." Then Mel started to cry and I've never seen Mel cry before I don't think and she ran off to her tent and I expect one daddy's been suffering from sleep deprivation and now another daddy's had his 'phone confiscated.

This has been the worst camp ever. Mel says family camp is an anagram of My Fail Camp. I don't think family camps are much fun. I'm going to make some more notes when I have a bit of time so that I can warn other scouts that if they have a family camp then the best thing to do is just stay at home and send the parents.

Monday 15th October
New year's resolution finally gets going.

Mummy's finally got round to implementing her new year's resolution - join a book club and she's only 280 days late. Daddy says that most people start their new year's resolution on 1st January and give up on it about a week later. Mummy on the other hand has made a new year's resolution but it's taken her nine and a half months to start. She'll probably unjoin tomorrow and then tell everyone that she kept her resolution until the middle of October. Her reason for taking so long is that she's been arranging to start a book club from scratch. She's been speaking to the Ravings' mummies and they've all joined! They're calling themselves "Ravens" which is a bit unoriginal. Mummy said that it stands for "Read A Volume Every Night Sisters" which is going to be interesting 'cos mummy hasn't even read a volume ever I think although maybe she did when she was at school. "We're not stupid," she told me when she was tucking me up. "I always have a book on the go." I don't know where though, I've never seen one. And magazines don't count 'cos most of hers are just pictures.

REFRESH
ARGUE
VINO
EAT
NUTS
SAUVIGNON

When we went into class this morning Sonny's desk was upside down at the front of class. Miss asked who had carved a swastika on Sonny's desk and she said that she knew that it wasn't Sonny 'cos "he wouldn't be so stupid." Shows how much she knows. Then she looked at me and said, "Horace?" and raised her eyebrows. I told her that it looked like a stick running man so miss then said, "Well it's not. It's a swastika, a symbol which is associated with ideas of racism and anti-Semitism." "Actually miss," said Mel, "the swastika was a pre-Nazi symbol that represents the north pole, the centre - and the axle - of the world, and the activity of the absolute God of the universe shaping the world."

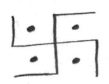

Sonny got his desk back.

Tuesday 16th October
Book club gets moving.
All the Ravings' mummies are definitely in the new book club!
And it's not just my mummy who doesn't read much. From what
I heard today at school none of them do. I'm not at all certain
how well this club is going to go. What's also uncertain is what
their club name really stands for. I told Melanie what mummy
had said and she laughed. "It may be that," she said, "but I reckon
it's more like, 'Refreshments And Vino Excites Non-Scholars.'"
Archie said that they should be called "Ravings" but no one could
think of words for that. They've also chosen their first book.
Emily told me that they had but I don't know what it is 'cos
mummy wouldn't tell me.

Wednesday 17th October
The first mummies' book club is chosen.
Sonny told me today that the
mummies' first book club book is
called "Lady Chatterley's Liver" by D
H Lawrence. I asked him how he
knew and he said 'cos his mummy
was allowed to choose first. It
doesn't sound very interesting 'cos
it's probably about surgery but Mel
thinks it's more likely to be about the
perils of drinking. Charlie tried to get
hold of a copy from the school

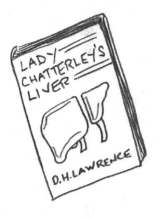

library during break but miss said that they didn't have any copies
in school 'cos it wasn't suitable so I think I'm probably right and
it's all about surgery.

Thursday 18th October
Hamster invasion.
Sam (brother) said that apparently there had been a bit of an
incident at the pet store. Sam (hamster) had been returned by the

beaver mummy but the people at the store were not very pleased with the mummy when she said who she was. Apparently three of the escaped hamsters had chewed their way into a huge bag of hamster bedding and made a little nest. Well, quite a big one actually. When a lady subsequently picked up the bag and popped it on the counter to pay, the hamsters scampered out. "I want to buy it FOR hamsters. I don't want to buy it WITH hamsters," she complained. But that wasn't the worst bit. Apparently the beaver who had taken a hamster from the cage that he wasn't supposed to and then returned it to the other cage with all the other hamsters was responsible for all the other hamsters getting pregnant and now they were giving birth and "It's your fault and what are you going to do about it?" So although his mummy gave back one stolen Syrian hamster she's returned home with two very large cages, two food bowls, two water bottles, two exercise wheels, two toys, two sand baths, one scales, food, bedding, two hamster houses, a pair of nail clippers, a set of scales and SIXTY hamsters with their mummies.

I hope Bramble has plenty of space in her garage.

Friday 19th October
Wellie-stick reparations.
We made wellie sticks at scouts tonight. Not for ourselves but for the cubs. Skip said that there had been a misunderstanding when we were doing our safety with knives, saws and axes and that the old bits upstairs - weren't.

Axe-throwing was cancelled.

Saturday 20th October
Quiz night.
It was 3rd Chislehurst's Annual Quiz Night tonight. We had over one hundred people taking part including parents and the other sections in teams of six or eight. The Ravings had a team and so did Hawks, Eagles and Woodpeckers. The questions in some of the rounds were quite hard but we had established a marking system that helped us considerably. At the end of each round we

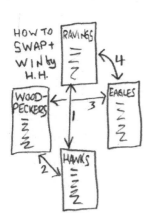

swapped with Hawks who then swapped with Woodpeckers. Then Woodpeckers, who had our paper, swapped with Eagles. Then Eagles who then had our paper swapped with us and we had Hawks' so it ended up with Eagles having Hawks, Hawks having Woodpeckers and Woodpeckers having Eagles, and we had our own paper back and nobody else realised. That was convenient. We won.

Mel's been into the bookshop and bought seven copies of "Lady Chatterley's Liver." I think that she's got the wrong book 'cos the liver's now a lover but it's by the same person (who doesn't appear to have a first name) so we'll see. The man in the bookshop looked a bit surprised but Mel told him that her mummy and her friends were reading it for book club. He then said, "In that case it's okay." He double wrapped them and told Mel to "take them straight to your mother." Mel's going to give our copies out at school.

Sunday 21st October
Sonny meets Tanya and makes her smile.
Sonny met Tanya today for the first time I think. He had come round to my house to borrow something and Tanya was there

and Sonny was chatting to her like boys do to girlfriends and Tanya was smiling so Sam got a bit cross with Sonny and then Tanya got a bit cross with Sam and she went to the toilet. Then Sonny said that she was really nice and Sam said, "Yes, I think so." Sonny asked Sam how long they had been going out and Sam said, "Ages." "Then you know her really well?" and Sam said, "Yes thanks." Then Sonny said, "Well if you've been goin' out with her for a long time then you've probably gone some way with her," and Sam said, "Yes, we went down to Worthing for the day back in the summer holidays," and Sonny smiled. He was probably thinking that they can go a whole lot further than that when they have a bit more time.

Monday 22nd October

Sonny gets a lift and has an accident.

Sonny wasn't very well this afternoon towards the end of school so Mel's mummy said that she would take him home in her car. No one's normally allowed in Mel's mummy's cars 'cos they're leather and the one that she has now she only picked up on Saturday. Sonny was allowed to sit in the front and as they were driving down the road Sonny picked up a huge golfing umbrella that was nestling down the side of his seat. "Put that down please Sonny," said Mel's mummy. "Okay," he said, but he was in no hurry to do so. "What does this do?" he asked, pointing at a big button just below the umbrella handle. "PUT-IT-DOWN!" said Mel's mummy through gritted

teeth as Sonny pressed the button. The golf umbrella sprang into life, bursting open across the front of the car dashboard and promptly cracked the windscreen. "Why can't you keep your hands off other people's property?" asked Mel's mummy to the opened umbrella. But it was too late. Sonny was already out and walking home.

We don't have our book club books yet. Mel's still individually double-wrapping them.

Tuesday 23rd October
The Ravings receive their copies of the book club book.
Mel gave us all our copies of "Lady's Chatterley's Lover" at school today. We put them in our bags to take home, apart from Sonny. During lunch break he opened his and we were all gathered round him in the pit when sir came over to see what was going on. Normally someone reading a book at break would not attract much attention but 'cos it was Sonny it did 'cos Sonny doesn't really do books and Sonny's now had his copy confiscated but we don't know why. Mel said that Sonny could always look at his mummy's copy when she wasn't around but Sonny said that she hasn't got the book. "I thought it was she who chose it," said Emily. "It was," said Sonny, "but she's got the audio version 'cos she's too busy to read so she can listen to it while she's driving." "You mum doesn't have a car," said Emily. "On the bus then," said Sonny threateningly. "On the bus to where? Not work?" "My mum has enough work to do looking after me EM-LY," said Sonny making a semaphore "I" matador sign at her. That shut her up.

Wednesday 24th October
The Ravings start on the book club book.
We've all started to read "Lady Chatterley's Lover" today and Sonny's listening to the audio version. He asked his mummy after school yesterday and she said that she had listened to it already so

gave it to Sonny. "You may learn that just 'cos they're posh don't mean they don't 'ave the same feelings," she told him, somewhat cryptically.

Thursday 25th October
Olivia packs a bread roll.
Olivia said that they learnt how to pack a rucksack at cubs tonight. Everyone had to bring one item from the kit list. Olivia took a small loaf of bread from the kitchen and I supposed it was 'cos she was doing emergency rations or something, but no. When she came back home she said that she had been asked to

bring a bedroll. "Sorry, Akela," she said rather pathetically I bet, "I thought you said that I was to bring a bread roll."

Friday 26th October
Camp fire cooking.
Patrick put a large log on the camp fire this evening and Skip was very impressed 'cos he said that he himself could hardly lift the log. "In fact I was trying to chop it up with my expensive new axe earlier before you arrived," Skip told him, "but it was getting dark so I gave up in frustration." "It was easy," said Patrick, "as it had a thick chopped-off branch sticking out from it that I was able to hold onto to pick it up and throw it on the fire."

"What's that glowing bright red in the fire Skip?" asked Edward as we were cooking sausages and roasting marshmallows later on. Turns out it was Skip's axe head. No prizes for guessing what Patrick's sticking-out branch actually was.

As Emily doesn't eat marshmallows 'cos she's a vegetarian still and marshmallows have meat in them supposedly, she was given some bread and jam. After she had stuck the bread on a stick and held it close to the embers for about a minute before trying some she declared that it was really nice and tasted like toast. That girl has a long way to go. Funnily enough, although she won't touch marshmallows she will touch sausages now. Apparently they're okay for a vegetarian 'cos "they don't have any meat in them."

Saturday 27th October

Hold your breath.

Sometimes we play a game in the car called "Hold your breath." It's really easy rules 'cos all you have to do is hold your breath when daddy drives under a bridge or through a tunnel. Bridges are easy 'cos often it's only a second or two but we had a bit of a problem today 'cos we were going to Lakeside through the Dartford Tunnel. If daddy's going really fast we can just about manage it but today there was a bit of a traffic jam halfway through so no one bothered 'cos we were moving so slowly. Or so we thought. Sam suddenly announced, "Olivia's gone all red!" so mummy turned round, saw Olivia's eyes about to pop out and thought that she was having a fit so told daddy to stop the car. Then Olivia exhaled dramatically and said crossly as daddy screeched to a halt across both lanes before jumping out and opening her door, "I'm never going to win now!" "And neither's daddy," said Sam as a Highways Agency man appeared at the side of the car from nowhere to tell him that he was already causing a five mile tailback.

Sunday 28th October

Day out in Calais - the usual disaster.
The Horrise family went on a car trip to Calais for the day.
Mummy and daddy like Calais although I'm not sure when we'll
be back after today's little incident. We went to the hypermarket
and mummy stocked up on wine as usual. But not much rose 'cos
the clocks have just gone back. And cheese. Then she said that
she was going to buy loads of fruit and veg. 'cos they sold nicer
stuff than back home. I don't understand 'cos a tomato is a
tomato in my book but mummy said that it didn't have to travel
so far in France so the flavour is better. I don't know what she's
talking about 'cos we've still got to take it home so it will have
travelled just as far eventually only in our car and not a lorry.
When we finally got to the till 'cos it was quite busy and mummy
was tut-tutting all the time 'cos she was now in a hurry and didn't
want to miss the ferry, the wine and cheese went through fine but
when it came to all the apples and oranges and courgettes and
peppers and things the woman looked at mummy and shrugged
her shoulders and said "posy" in French so mummy shrugged her
shoulders too. Fortunately there was a little French girl with her
mummy behind us and her name was "Amalie" 'cos I asked her
and she was eleven-years-old and she was very nice but mummy
told me off for talking to her. Mummy just wanted to know what
"posy" meant and Amalie said that mummy had to go and weigh
the fruit and veg. and salad bits over by where she got it all from
and put it in plastic bags and then tie them up and put a sticker
on each of them. Mummy wasn't very happy 'cos she said that
she was trying to stop using plastic bags and in Chislehurst you
can just dump your stuff at the till and the sales assistant simply
weighs it all loose and what's the point of having to do it all
yourself and whatever happened to service? The lady on the till
didn't understand but Amalie did and she said that it was to save
time at the checkout and to stop English people moaning so we
all laughed except mummy. We had to put everything back in the
trolley and go back to find the scales. I said "good-bye" to Amalie
and said that if ever she came to England she could come and

visit me in Chislehurst. Then she said that she lived in England already but she lived in Bournemouth which was a bit odd 'cos she looked far too young but I didn't say anything and she was definitely French. I'm glad I said "Good-bye" 'cos of what happened next. Mummy found the scales and put on the tomatoes in a plastic bag then had to press in a code next to "Tomates." Oranges were next and that was easy enough as was "Courgettes" 'cos they're English words but then we had a problem with "Apples" so then mummy tried "Peppers" and they weren't listed either 'cos it was all in French and mummy was getting very agitated. "You would have thought that they would have put everything in English, wouldn't you David?" she said, sounding very exasperated. "After all, everyone here speaks English, even the kids, apart from the checkout people, so why don't they make it easier for us?" Mummy got no reply 'cos daddy had wandered off so mummy told Sam to go and find out what "potatoes" were in French and so he wandered off as well. By the time that he had come back mummy had stuck all the other fruit and veg. and salad bits - all the stuff with foreign names that we didn't know - into the largest plastic bag that she could find and pressed "Pommes de terres." That made everything a lot cheaper as well, especially all the posh stuff. Mummy then tried to go through the self-service but was told by a man, "Non," and he pointed at all the shoppers with hand-baskets. Mummy said, "What sort of idiot goes shopping in a hypermarket with a hand-basket?" but got no reply and we went back to our cashier lady and had to queue again.

When it came to the large plastic bag with all the food with funny French names in it the woman took one look at it and said, "Non," and waved mummy away having given mummy a handful of plastic bags. "I have an idea," she said to us. "I'll pay for everything except the big bag and you wait over by the window whilst I sort the extra fruit and vegetables out." Which is what she did. Well, tried to do. We wheeled the trolley through and sat by the window and waited as mummy didn't go and rebag everything separately but went and got a hand-basket, put her plastic bag in it and marched over to the self-service, swinging it in front of the man. Mummy scanned the bag label and was just about to pay when mummy's till started to vibrate. Then it made a very loud peeping noise and a red light above it started to flash. Everyone and I mean EVERYONE turned round. The man went over to mummy and beckoned for her to follow him. By the time that daddy had reappeared, having spent the last twenty minutes tasting Beaujolais, we had to explain that mummy had gone off somewhere with a man which wasn't the best explanation but it was all we knew at the time. Anyway, she reappeared after another ten minutes and she was still with the man. As she walked over to us with a very red face she turned round and said that she didn't want his (very sweary word) vegetables anyway and then said, "Come on you lot," to us and walked out of the store.

Things didn't get much better once we were all back in the car. Daddy told mummy that he felt a bit squiffy 'cos of all the Beaujolais he had drunk so mummy made him use the emergency drink-driving breath detector thing that we had to buy at Dover and it said that daddy was not allowed to drive so mummy had to drive down to the port and she hadn't driven on the wrong side of the road for years so that was rather exciting. When we got to the roundabout by La Quai de la Loire mummy had a bit of a meltdown 'cos she was trying to go round the English way but the road was pointing her round the wrong way so she just drove over the middle of it. She left four rather obvious tyre tracks in the flower bed and then got tooted at by another English car as she bumped down off the roundabout on the other side. "I thought we were friends!" she shouted at the woman in the Volvo who was driving but the woman just tooted again and drove off. At least it meant that mummy managed to stay on the right side of the road, by that I mean the wrong side, 'cos we were able to follow the tooty woman so that mummy could "regain her bearings" and she drove to the ferry port so that was okay. What wasn't okay though was that we had missed our ferry and 'cos daddy hadn't bought a flexi-fare he had to pay a load more to get on the next ferry and we weren't allowed in the club lounge so had to "sit with the chavs" which is what mummy said. Daddy didn't sit with mummy though 'cos he wasn't very happy that all the money that mummy had saved by buying her wine in Calais he had spent on the excess ticket. Mummy said that she had to bite her lip in the toilet when a woman came up to her and said, "It's called a 'roundabout' not an 'overabout,'" and then walked off. Daddy came back eventually and said that he had met a man who had been in a bar in Calais and he had missed his ferry also. He had wanted four straws for his drinks and asked in French which apparently is, "Je voudrais quatre pailles." The waiter disappeared and didn't come back with the straws. Then the English family decided to drink their drinks out of the bottles and told the waiter not to bother but he wouldn't let them

A PAILLE

go. Then the English family stood up and so the waiter locked the door and looked angry. Eventually, just as the Englishman pulled out his 'phone, pointed at it and said, "Police!" another waiter appeared with four huge plates of meat pie, chips and vegetables. "SIT," he commanded and they did. And they ate the pies even though they had just had lunch. He wasn't talking to his wife on the ferry either. Dover-Calais ferries are usually full of noisy Englishmen getting drunk at breakfast time whilst on the Calais-Dover ferries in the evening everyone's asleep apart from the French children all going to England for a holiday. Their first impression of the English must be that everyone snores. Still, I was okay. I met Amalie in the Duty Free although I was only buying chocolate and she said that she would write to me. That will be nice.

Monday 29th October
National Happy Day.
Daddy's off work today and it's half-term for us but I still got up at the usual time. Mummy was in the kitchen and said brightly, "Good morning Horace, and how are you today?" I told her that I was very fine and asked her why she was so happy. She told me that it was "National Happy Day" and so she was going to be even happier than normal which was nice. When daddy appeared mummy said, "Good morning darling, and how are you today?" all brightly like she did with me but daddy just said, "What's the matter with you?" When Sam and Olivia appeared I think that she had already forgotten about "National Happy Day" and was back to "Oh Dear, The Kids Are Off On Half-Term - What Are We Going To Do With Them Day"? Anyway, we got scrambled eggs on toast with ketchup for breakfast so things weren't all bad.

Tuesday 30th October
Mel's mummy gives birth in the swimming pool.
Mel's mummy's had her baby. It's a boy. She had a home birth and she had it in the swimming pool. Just as well Sonny hadn't put the lobsters in. She has a birthing pool but all her posh friends have had one so she wanted something bigger and Mel's daddy said that you can't get much bigger than a swimming pool. Well I suppose you could give birth in the sea and you could go down to Dover or somewhere but you'd have to get the tide right or the baby might float off to France and then you would have to get the ferry to Calais and then it would be a French baby and you'd need to get it a passport to come home and you would have to call it a French name and you couldn't just give it an

English name 'cos you just can't call your baby anything in France like you can in England and I bet they've banned all the English names. Mind you, given that some people call their children Bus Shelter or Nutella this is probably not a bad thing.

Melanie's daddy was in attendance although he didn't want to be and Mel was at home 'cos it was half-term. Apparently the midwife brings gas and air which is supposed to help but it's for the mummies and not the daddies. Unfortunately Mel's daddy got hold of it and Mel thinks that he had a bit too much 'cos he took all his clothes off and jumped in the pool with Mel's mummy. Then he asked the midwife for a Pina Colada and a back massage and when the midwife asked him if he was okay he said that he would look after his wife and would the midwife go and get him a Chinese 'cos he was getting a bit peckish? He then climbed out of the pool, turned on the music system and played "The Hokey Cokey" singing, "In, out, in, out, shake it all about..." at full volume before saying he felt sick and went indoors to bed. The baby is fine but it's only being called baby so it doesn't have much of a name at present. Nor much of a father.

Wednesday 31st October
Book club book - read!
Oh dear Emily! Emily wanted to have black fingernails for the

Halloween party but her mummy said that she didn't have any black nail polish and even if she did Emily's "not going out looking like a witch" so she took matters into her own hands and bought a taster pot of black gloss paint from Mr Lillie at The Workshed in the high street and applied it with a cotton bud.

The Ravings have finished "Lady Chatterley's Lover" and now we all know why no one would tell us (apart from Sonny) what our mummies were reading for book club. If this is the sort of yucky stuff that's going to be going on with the mummies then next time we're going to have to get our own book. My mummy said that she's finished her book too and she's been smiling a lot. She said, "I've finish our first book club book," but still didn't tell me what it was. I haven't seen her copy though and I haven't seen her reading it. Sam said that if I look hard enough I'll probably find it. I'm not going to though 'cos I don't know what else I might find.

Thursday 1st November
The ceremonial, ahem, lighting of the wood burner.
First of November is always an eagerly awaited day in the Horrise household 'cos it's when daddy lights the wood burning stove for the winter even if it's not cold. We don't really need it as we have central heating but daddy likes looking at the flames and mummy says that daddy likes looking at his gas bill after Christmas so the more wood that we can burn the better. As I had done "safety with knives, saws and axes" in September daddy said that I could finish chopping up the wood when I came home from school. Once I had loads of wood ready I started putting it in the stove. I started with tinder then I added kindling then a few logs. Having done all that I didn't think daddy would mind too much if I lit it. Olivia found some matches that were stored with the emergency candles and I tried to light the kindling but it kept going out. I think that it was probably because it was a bit wet. In the end, just as I was about to give up, Olivia suggested that I could start it with mummy's crème brulee blow torch but that soon ran out of gas so then Olivia suggested that I use one of the camping gas backpacking stoves that Sam had in his room from his expedition. That lit okay so we put it in the wood burner in the ash tray so that it was underneath the tinder. That worked and the tinder started to burn quite well but then it started to smoke

so we had to shut the doors and open the little vent things at the front. The fire burst into life and soon we had a great big fire going. Olivia suggested that we open the doors to retrieve the gas cylinder but the door handle was too hot and anyway we didn't want the smoke coming back into the room. Just then mummy came in and asked who said we could light the fire. We said that we thought that it was a natural progression from getting all the wood ready but she said that lighting the fire was daddy's job although it was burning fine so "well done" but "How did you get it going so well when most of the wood was damp?" Olivia said that we had used a bit of gas and mummy saw her crème brulee blow torch on the hearth and said that that was fine and "well done" also for using our initiative but that was the last time that we heard mummy say "well done" today. We thought therefore that the gas cylinder would be fine 'cos it was probably built to withstand heat so we both left the roaring fire and went upstairs to our rooms to do our homework.

You hear of homes that have gas explosions and see pictures on the news on TV of buildings with walls and roofs missing but that's mains gas not a little camping gas cylinder despite our previous problems with the caravan. Or so I thought. I had just got to the bit in Tintin's "King Ottokar's Sceptre" where Thompson and Thomson were nearly blown up when a bomb explodes in Tintin's flat when I was aware of an accompanying sound effect. My bedroom shook and a picture literally fell off the wall. I opened my door and I couldn't see a

thing. The landing was full of smoke and mummy was screaming. I slid down the stairs as quickly as I could to open the front door. To be more accurate, I went to open the front door but I didn't need to 'cos it was already open 'cos it had opened itself. In fact it was in the road. Sam ran past and went to calm mummy down in the kitchen so I went to check on the wood burner in the sitting room. Unfortunately it wasn't there, well not where it normally was, and was now on the other side of the room embedded into the sofa. It was just as well grandad had decided to sit on the other sofa this afternoon otherwise he would have taken a direct hit. As it was grandad appeared to be fast asleep. I thought he may have been killed but he told me later that he was having a dream about the war and being attacked by a flying bomb. I told him that that was about the right description of what had actually just happened.

Daddy's not home yet and I've offered to take Olivia to cubs this evening. If we come home slowly enough hopefully daddy will be in bed.

Whilst I was waiting for Olivia to get ready I found mummy's Lady Chatterley book. It was under a cushion on her favourite chair in the sitting room that no one else is allowed to sit on. It looks as though she's read it more than once and several pages have been earmarked which is something that she's always telling me not to do. It also looks a bit bomb-damaged now though. I also found a cracked bottle of Sauvignon Blanc (empty).

Friday 2nd November
Emily joins the arsonists' club.
Daddy came home quite late last night and I was already in bed. Mummy and daddy were having a big discussion downstairs then Sam came and told me that everything was okay and there must've been a fault with the wood burner with a blockage or

something so that's a relief and daddy'll get some decorators in to clean and redo the downstairs. Phew!

Emily's in big trouble. Again!

Last week we roasted sweet chestnuts on the camp fire. First we went into the woods and collected the chestnuts all up. We had loads! Then we had to cut crosses in all of the skins which we did. We were told that this is so that the chestnuts would cook all over. Then we roasted them. They were really yummy!

Emily's daddy had a bonfire at the weekend and Emily collected loads more chestnuts from outside her house but she didn't bother to cut crosses in them 'cos she said that she had wanted them to cook quicker. She just put them all on the bonfire when her daddy wasn't looking but then the bonfire started to explode and it caught her neighbour's fence alight and Emily's daddy called the fire brigade who came and put the fire out and now her daddy's going to have to buy a new fence. I told her that at least it would be cheaper than a front door and a complete downstairs refurb.

I think Emily will be putting the crosses back in next time.

Saturday 3rd November
Emily the Witch.
Emily's in big trouble. Again! She still has black finger nails and Emily's mummy wants to know where she got the paint from but she's not telling.

Sunday 4th November
Mel's baby brother gets a name.

Mel's mummy and daddy's baby has a name. It's going to be "Arthur Stourton Barclay Ormerod." Daddy said to me when I told him that it was a pity that they hadn't checked out its initials first.

Monday 5th November
Bonfire night - more explosions.
A special scout meeting tonight as it's bonfire night. In previous years Skip has bought a load of rockets, we've had a safety talk and then we've been allowed to set them off - one each. It's such good fun but it does get a bit boring if you're the first to go 'cos then you have to wait whilst all the others do theirs. This year was different and for all the wrong reasons. Skip had bought just one firework but it was enormous. It was the size of a couple of petrol cans stuck together and was called "Triple Terror." We had the camp fire going with a bucket of water on the side just in case and we were all enjoying sausages in buns and some mulled wine - which was really Ribena with bits in it - when Skip produced Triple Terror and told us to stand back. Up it went, pop, pop, poppity pop, exploding in the sky and throwing coloured stars everywhere. It was great but thirty-six tubes of gunpowder didn't last long. However, the best was yet to come. Skip did something we know that you should never do: he threw Triple Terror on the camp fire. We returned to singing some bonfire night songs. Suddenly the fire started to hiss and so we ran up to the gate and just in time, thank goodness. For Triple Terror was a three-layered firework and Skip was supposed to have lit three fuses at the same time but he had only lit one. So instead of Skip lighting fuses two and three and retiring a safe distance, the camp fire lit them both then the whole of layers two and three of Triple Terror went up more or less together. Layer two sent up its thirty-six tubes of gunpowder all at the same time,

sounding as if an over-staffed firing squad had taken over then

layer three simply exploded, bang, bang, bangidy, BANG as it threw the fire all over the scout hut grounds. It wasn't a bucket of water we required, it was a whole flipping reservoir.

I think we'll be doing sparklers next year.

Tuesday 6th November
Daddy plucks a pheasant.

Daddy's friend's been out shooting recently and has been round with a pheasant for him. It's disgusting. It has big fat maggots coming out of it but daddy says that that is how it should be according to his friend. Daddy spent the whole evening trying to pluck the pheasant. Every single feather had to come out. He started with the large ones and ended up with the tiny fluffy ones. It took hours! The baby feathers are very, very soft. He had a huge pile on the work surface and no one was allowed near him. Once he had finished he came and found us in the sitting room (on dust sheets) and said that we could come and have a look before he threw the feathers away and gutted then put the pheasant in the freezer. We were told not to breathe! We crept quietly into the

kitchen and were admiring his handiwork when suddenly catastrophe struck! Olivia went, "A...a...a...CHOOO!" and sneezed the biggest sneeze you've ever heard in your life! The feathers went everywhere! The whole kitchen was covered and mummy and daddy stared at Olivia but didn't say anything and she ran to her room. I said, "Don't worry daddy, I'll clear up the feathers." It was the least that I could do.

Wednesday 7th November
The One Minute game.

We were so noisy in class today that miss made us do the "One Minute game." This is where you have to sit still for one minute and then stand up when you think the minute's up. The one who stands up nearest one minute is the winner. This evening I went into the sitting room and found that mummy and daddy were playing a longer version of the game but I don't know who was running it. Theirs went on for over two hours then I went to bed.

Thursday 8th November
The One Minute game continues.

Mummy and daddy were still playing the "One Minute game" this morning although they were grunting from time to time over the breakfast table so I think that they're both out. Also mummy was writing things down and giving them to daddy. This is also not allowed I think. This evening things were back to normal and they were hugging each other a lot which is obviously another game but I didn't ask.

Friday 9th November
Rock climbing? It was a relief to get out of Skip's car.

This evening we went indoor rock climbing at The Reach in Woolwich. It's such fun. They have a cafe there that sells yummy cakes. We all needed one by the time that we arrived, I can tell you. Skip gave us a lift in his Land Rover. I was in the front and Melanie was in the back with Darek from Poland. We call him

"Dalek" 'cos he always needs us to "Explain! Explain!" He doesn't seem to mind though. On the way to Woolwich Skip asked us all what we were doing for Christmas and was Dalek going back to Poland? "No," he said, "I'm staying in England. But I am going back to Poland for all of next summer to stay with my grandma. I don't want to go but mother says that I must." "That's a long time to go away for, Darek," said Skip. "I know," said Dalek sadly, "but mother says that I must go because she is having another baby soon and I expect I'll just be in the way." "I'm sure she doesn't think that Darek," said Skip who looked like he was thinking hard. Then he said, "How many siblings do you have?" "How many what?" "'Siblings.' Brothers and sisters." "Oh. Four and then the new one." "Hmmm," said Skip, "your parents must have to work hard?" "Yes, they do. Father has a small job and mother has three jobs and she has to look after all of us as well. She doesn't get much sleep. I am a bit worried for her." Skip decided to change the subject. "What about you, Mel? Are you away for Christmas?" "No Skip. I have to look after my kittens. They've been to the vets." "Oh dear," said Dalek. "How many do you have?" "Two, Dalek. Their names are Cleopatra and Ptolemy. Dad named them." "And what is wrong with them?" he asked. "Nothing really but they both have fur missing and scars. They're brother and sister so we had them spayed and neutered." "'Spayed and neutered'? What is this? It sounds nasty." "As this is Mel we are talking to Darek, I fear we're about to get a very fulsome elucidation," said Skip. And we did. "Well Dalek. It's like this. Cleopatra has been spayed. She has had a length of fur removed

"EXPLAIN!"

and has a long scar where the vet cut her skin and then tied a tube together to stop the boy's sperm from reaching her womb." Silence. "Are you okay Darek?" Skip asked. "Just about," said Dalek. "What about the boy?" "Ptolemy has been neutered but he hasn't had quite so much fur removed. Just a little bit and a little scar." "What did they do to him then?" "Oh, they just cut off his tes-tic-les," said Mel matter-of-factly, speaking slowly so that she would do the word justice by pronouncing it correctly. "Ohh. Ow," said Dalek. I think that Skip thought that that was that - until Mel looked at Dalek and added, "I bit like your dad should be having done."

I have a feeling that Dalek's next summer with this grandma in Poland may be his last.

Saturday 10th November
Mummy wants a car wash - but gets a bit more.
Mummy took me shopping today 'cos she's hurt her back and needed me to carry her bags. We didn't go to our usual supermarket 'cos they hadn't sent her any vouchers recently and she's trying to save money for Christmas so we had to go to a cheaper supermarket in Sidcup and mummy wore her sunglasses even though there's no sun. The supermarket's in an industrial estate with loads of workshops and stuff along one side. Mummy parked the car and gave me the keys and told me to go and tell the car wash people that she wanted the top wash and clean and everything. "Tell them I'll pay when I come out with the shopping. It'll be fine, I've used them before." There was a bit of a queue but I went and told the man in the office at the side that mummy wanted everything done and she would pay when they're done so he took the keys from me and said that he could get started straightaway and what colour would I like? I said, "Blue Trees," 'cos mummy always gets the Royal Pine tree air freshener which I hate and Ocean Breeze is much nicer. Then the man drove mummy's car into the garage and then it went into another

garage at the back and a shutter came down and I thought, "That's because mummy has a nice new car, not like all the others lined up!" I waited for about half an hour but mummy's car didn't reappear so I went to find her in the supermarket and she was just finishing paying. "Quick," she said to me, pointing at the huge trolley that was full of shopping bags, "I'm stocking up for Christmas." "There's stuff for the fridge and these have the frozen items that we need to get home promptly before they start defrosting." When we got outside mummy walked to our car parking space but there was another car there. "Where's our car?" she asked. "It hasn't come out yet," I told her so mummy stuck her head inside the garage. "Where's my Audi?" she asked a man but he just shook his head. I told mummy that I had given the keys to another man but I couldn't see him and then mummy looked a bit cross and said, "Do you think, for one second, that you might have given my keys to a man who's just stolen it?" "Oh no mummy," I said. "It's at the back of the garage behind a big shutter where you're getting everything done." "Show me!" she demanded and so I took her next door and pointed at the shutters at the back. "It's behind there mummy." Mummy pushed her trolley through the garage and then stopped and turned around. "Is this some kind of joke?" she demanded. "What do you mean?" I asked. Mummy pointed at the large notice on the front of the shutters. It read,

DO NOT ENTER. PAINT SPRAYING IN PROGRESS

Mummy didn't look very pleased at all. "What in the name of Frances of Rome have you done with my car?" Mummy went back to the car wash people and asked what was going on next door. "They do car resprays," said the owner. "And where is everybody?" "At lunch until two o'clock." Mummy looked at her watch. It was a quarter past one. "Shall I get someone to call a taxi?" I asked mummy quietly.

When mummy finally got through to the respray people she told them to stop work on her car immediately and she would come and pick it up "because there has been a big mistake." "As you wish," said the man, "but we've sanded most of the top layer off already." "And if I tell you to keep going when will the car be ready?" "End of the month," said the man. So mummy doesn't have much choice and I haven't been told off 'cos I was only doing what I had been asked to do.

Sunday 11th November
Roast potato palaver.
Mummy told me off today although I don't think that I've done anything wrong. We had a lovely roast dinner with all the bits including some yummy roast potatoes which are my favourite.

We all had loads to eat and seconds and then there was just one roast potato left. Daddy asked everyone in turn if they would like to have it. "Oh, go on," he would say encouragingly. I was last to be asked so I knew that no one else wanted it. "Thank you daddy," I said and as the roast potato was in a dish in front of me I speared it with my fork, put it on my plate and started to cut it up. Then mummy said, "You shouldn't have done that Horace - daddy wanted it." "How could he want it?" I asked. "He was asking all of us." "He was just being polite." "What's the point of being polite if you're going to get an answer you don't want? Why didn't he say, 'No one else wants the roast potato do they because I would quite like it?' Then we would all know and he could still sound polite but we would all know what to answer." Next Sunday when we have a roast dinner and there's one potato left I'm going to make sure that I ask if anyone would like it first before daddy asks. That way I can be polite AND get the potato.

Monday 12th November
Maths test mayhem.

A bit of a funny day today. I've been revising for my big maths test for ages now but there was still loads that I couldn't remember. I told Sonny before the test and he said that if you make out that you're stupid then you get extra credits added on. I told him that I wasn't stupid and the teachers knew that and so he said that the other thing that you could do was to pretend you're sick and then you will get the mark that they expect you to. "Wait until the test starts and then start moanin'. Don't do it before then 'cos it will look too obvious. Put your hands on your lower tummy 'cos there's all sorts of things that can go wrong inside down there. And be as dramatic as you dare; remember, the aim is to get outside the hall as quickly as possible." We went and sat down and the test started. I waited until we were about five minutes into the test when I grabbed my tummy with both hands and started to scream extremely loudly. I screamed so loudly that I managed to even force out a tear. Miss came running over looking very alarmed. "Horace, what's the matter?" she asked quietly but firmly as if she were expecting me to give an instant diagnosis to a condition that I didn't even have. All I

could say was, "It's something inside my tummy. It really hurts miss," and I put a very painful expression on my face. All the other children looked very alarmed - except Sonny who had got out his calculator which was banned for the test but miss had other things to worry about. Then miss pressed a button that was on one of the lanyards round her neck.

Next thing sir burst into the room and he helped me to my feet. He put his arm around my waist and helped me to the door. I started to limp as well although I was not sure whether I should've been doing so with the non-existent condition that I had but it gave Sonny a few more precious seconds to do several more sums before he had to put his calculator away. Outside in the quad I kept up the groaning just to make sure that I wasn't sent back into the test but I didn't know how long I should go on for. Looking back I obviously went on too long 'cos just as I was thinking of stopping an ambulance man appeared, asked me where it hurt and when I pointed to the bottom of my tummy took one look at sir, mouthed something to him and then said aloud, "We'll take care of him, we'll go straight to A and E. Please ring the parents." The ambulance man then picked me up, carried me out to an ambulance that was waiting outside the school with its blue light flashing and next thing I remember is waking up in a very comfortable hospitable bed with loads of white sheets and big white pillows and mummy looking over me. "What's going on?" I asked. Mummy took hold of my hand. "Everything's fine," she said. "You've just had your appendix removed. But you'll be home tonight once you've woken up properly." And I am. I hope I get a good mark in maths. I know Sonny will.

Tuesday 13th November
Maths test results.
I wasn't allowed a day off from school so I went in but mummy drove me in the hire car so it wasn't too bad. We had the results of the maths test and I did fine but I think that I could've done even better if I had actually sat through it instead of taking Sonny's advice. The shock news, however, was who came top so I suppose that I should be grateful that I've done someone a favour. As miss gave out the results from the bottom Sonny's name, that is usually amongst the first few names, was nowhere to be heard. Up and up the list she went until there was only the top three left. Sonny came third! Miss said that he was the only one in our class to get a particularly difficult, and consequently high scoring, calculation correct. Question: For whose benefit did I have my appendix removed? Answer: I'm still wondering, but it wasn't me.

Wednesday 14th November
Ravings' mummies have their first proper book club meeting.
Mummy was in a bit of a rush when I got home from school so I had to go to the supermarket to help her with the normal shopping. She pushed the trolley round really fast and just grabbed at stuff. She didn't have a list so when she wasn't looking I grabbed some stuff as well. When we got to the checkout I had to put the items on the conveyor belt and mummy was bagging up. I was trying to put all the freezer items together, then the fridge items and so on but mummy told me to hurry up. At the other end mummy was shoving everything into bags without even looking properly. We loaded the bags back into the trolley, mummy paid and we wheeled it to the hire car, loaded up and drove off. On the way home we kept hearing a beeping noise but we didn't really pay much attention. Once home I had to put everything away whilst mummy went upstairs to get ready to go out. Whilst I was unloading I came across something which mummy hadn't wanted and hadn't even paid for -

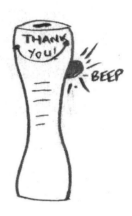

it was a charity collecting tin. It was really heavy. When mummy came downstairs I showed her and she just said, "Well it was probably on the side of the till so no wonder I packed it; I'll take it back in the morning."

Thursday 15th November
Beavers learn a new word.
Mummy hasn't taken the charity collecting tin back to the supermarket today. It was sitting on the console table in the hallway and every hour or so it beeped. Sonny came round for tea and he told mummy that he would take it back tomorrow 'cos his

mummy always goes to the supermarket on Fridays. So he wrapped his scarf around it and went home with it.

Archie was supposed to be helping at beavers this evening so he could start preparing for being a Young Leader. Unfortunately he couldn't make it so he asked Charlie and me if we wanted to go instead, which we did. Bramble was a bit surprised to see us 'cos she was expecting Archie but we told her that two of us added up to more than one of Archie so we were allowed to stay. Well, I was allowed to stay but Charlie had to leave. He didn't even make the drink and biscuit time. Lisa, who is a Young Leader, was playing a ball game with the beavers at the beginning of the evening. They had to stand in a circle and Lisa stood in the middle with a sponge ball. Starting with "A", the beaver who was thrown the ball had to catch it and shout out the name of something that they could eat beginning with that letter. It then moved on to "B" and so on. Charlie and I were allowed to play. When Charlie was thrown the ball we were on "K." "Carrot," shouted Charlie and the beavers all laughed. The funny thing was,

Charlie didn't know why. When it was his go next we were on "Q." Charlie shouted out, "Cucumber!" and the beavers all laughed again. Then we got to "S" and it was Charlie's go for the last time. "Celery" was his answer and the beavers all squealed with delight but Charlie wasn't happy.

"Stupid letter 'C,'" he cried. "How can C sound like anything other than C yet still be pronounced 'cee?' C is a stupid letter. Any word that starts with C is a stupid word. In fact, I don't think that there are any proper 'C words.'" Charlie looked around the circle, eyes open wide. "Does anybody know any 'C words?'" he challenged. The smallest beaver, who happened to be Sonny's little sister and who's called "Misty" shouted out without any prompting, "I know a 'C word,'" and then said the rudest word that you can ever imagine in the whole wide world ever that you can't even say on television unless you want to go to prison. Charlie was unfazed. "That doesn't begin with a 'C,'" he said. "That begins with a K." Then Bramble sent Charlie home and Lisa had to sit with Misty Christy for the rest of the evening just to make sure that she didn't enlighten any of the beavers with her word again.

I got Charlie's biscuit.

Friday 16th November
Go-karting pileup.
Sonny hasn't taken the charity collecting tin back to the supermarket yet. He said that his mummy wasn't feeling very well so they weren't going shopping today. I said that if he gives it back to me at scouts then I would return it in the morning but Sonny said, "No," - just a little too aggressively for my liking.

For a special treat the scouts went to Woolwich again, this time to do go-karting indoors. We went in a huge warehouse and they had laid out a track with lots of bends in it and the go-karts were very fast. Archie didn't bring his go-kart 'cos he said that the track "couldn't have handled it" but I think that's it's Archie that can't handle the go-kart 'cos Emily told me that Archie's daddy had told Emily's mummy that it was the most expensive Christmas present that Archie had ever received but it didn't last five minutes and it wasn't even insured. Apparently it's in the River Thames somewhere but Archie just said that it's been stored safely away but didn't say where. Mind you if it ended up in the Thames it could now be in Calais with Mel's mummy's baby.

We had to have a safety talk and then we were allowed to race in groups of ten. We had to wear enormous padded crash helmets and Charlie was complaining that they made his head really hot and weren't at all necessary as the go-karts "don't go very fast." How wrong he was. The first ten walked along the pit lane and climbed into their go-karts. The pit lane was sort of by the track on a bend so you could get to it without crossing the track. You could drive into it from the track and out onto the track from it. The winners of the first races went through to a final where it was the first to complete ten laps. I didn't manage to make it through to the final race but Charlie  and Archie did. Charlie was at the back and he was so determined to win. As he came round the bend before the final lap Charlie was still behind Archie so decided to take a short cut - through the pit lane. Unfortunately the pit lane men had started to store the other go-karts as there were no more races after this one. Charlie came flying round the corner and instead of going round the pit lane went straight into it thinking that he would come out in front of Archie. Which he didn't. The final count was two broken bumpers, one cracked steering wheel and three punctures. Charlie received five thousand penalty points and came last. At least he now knows why crash helmets are needed.

Saturday 17th November
Mel and her mummy discuss Lady Chatterley.
Mel asked her mummy how their first proper book club meeting went. "Very well thank you," she said. "The book that we read has a theme of individual regeneration that is explored through,

in the main, class differences between an upper class lady and a working class man who form an unlikely bond after another person is left suffering with mobility issues." Mel said to her, "When you look at the rather brutal relationship between the gamekeeper and his sadistic wife and also that with the man who has no wife but who's rather taken by the gamekeeper one could draw the conclusion that it is, in the final analysis, just a very rude and violent book." Then Mel's mummy went really red but didn't say anything. She just changed the subject completely which is what grown-ups usually do when they're wrong or they've been found out. She said, "I'm choosing the next book. I'm going to learn all about you lot and what makes you tick. It's called, 'In You Go! A year or two in the life of a scout leader.'" "Let's hope it's suitable for children this time," said Mel. "Probably not," said her mummy.

Sunday 18th November
One day I'll get the last roast potato.
Roast chicken today. Yummy! As daddy was carving I said, "Would there be any chance that when it comes to one roastie left that someone might like it?" Mummy said that I couldn't ask until there actually was only one left and that when it came to it there might not be one left. When daddy served me (and I get served last apart from Olivia) he asked me how many roast potatoes I would like. There were nine left and I usually have four and so does Olivia. So just to make sure I said, "Five daddy please." He looked at me a bit oddly, probably 'cos he only had three, but he gave me five leaving four for Olivia. Then once he had given me my plate I took one off and put it back with the other four that were on the chicken dish. "Now there will be one

left over mummy," I said and smiled to myself 'cos I knew it was as good as mine and I had been polite. Then daddy asked Olivia how many roast potatoes she would like and she said, "Five please daddy." And I said, "You can't have five 'cos one's mine 'cos it's a leftover and Olivia said, "It's not a leftover yet and it's not going to be 'cos I'm having it." And she did.

Monday 19th November
Mummy gets her car back.

Mummy's car was ready today and she went down to pick it up. But she's not happy. "Not only has it cost me several grand, but LOOK AT IT!" she screamed when I came home from school although I couldn't look at it 'cos for the first time ever in its relatively short life it had been put in the garage. "Why have you done that mummy?" I asked quietly. "I can't have Susie seeing my

was lovely beautifully coloured car that's now a sort of manky yellow with loads of blue marble streaks all over it. According to the paint sprayers you had asked for 'blue cheese.'" "No mummy," I said, even more quietly. "I said, 'blue trees' and even then I was only referring to the air freshener."

"Things could be worse," I said. "Sonny wasn't at school today." When she asked me why that was a problem I told her that the reason was that I thought that he had been arrested.

Tuesday 20th November
Charlie and I skip to school and get whistled at.

Walking to school with Charlie sometimes has its problems. As there's two of us we can never work out the best way to get to school. I mean we have to go by feet but feet can do different things. If we walk then Charlie goes too slowly and so there's always a risk that we're going to be late and so get told off. If I leave home earlier then Charlie's not ready but if I didn't wait then he would be late and then he would tell me off although that's probably better than miss telling me off. If we run then we get all hot and sweaty and smelly. We are allowed to get smelly but it's best to wait 'til home time; getting smelly *before* school is probably not on. Jogging wouldn't look right in school uniform and anyway we would still get hot but not go very fast. Today, after I had to wait three minutes and twenty seconds for Charlie to be ready and after I told him that we were going to be late he looked at me and said, "Skipping." "'Skipping?'" I repeated. "Yes. Skipping. It's very good exercise and it's very efficient on the feet 'cos we're like bouncing on one foot each time so we go further than jogging and running but don't get sweaty. And it's quite quick." We did look a bit silly, at least I felt a bit silly, skipping up the road to school. On the way some men in a white van whistled at us. They went, "Whit, wheeo." We stopped skipping 'cos we thought that they might've wanted directions or something but I don't think that they did 'cos they drove straight past. We then skipped up to school and when we arrived Sonny, who was waiting by the main gate not looking like he had been arrested, said that he was surprised that we weren't holding hands. I don't know why he thought that that would be a good idea 'cos we  needed both our hands to stop our backpacks jumping around too much. I told Sonny that some men in a white van had gone "Whit, wheeo" at us as they drove past and he said that he wasn't surprised that they had wolf-whistled us. It seemed that Sonny knew what he was talking about so I asked him why the men didn't stop 'cos they obviously wanted something from us. "You may've got more than you bargained for if they had," he said. I've no idea what he was talking about again but I didn't like to say.

At lunch break I was still wondering what a wolf-whistle was. I told Emily 'cos I thought that she would know but she didn't. "How does it go?" she asked so 'cos I can whistle quite well I did a "Whit, wheoo" and it was really loud. I don't know why miss got so cross 'cos I wasn't doing it at her and it wasn't my fault that she walked round the corner just as I was showing

Emily. She went all red and said that it wasn't appropriate for school and Sonny just laughed. I said "Sorry" to miss and explained that it was only a wolf-whistle and she said, "I know what it is Horace," all cross-like but then smiled. I told her that some people had whistled at me and Charlie this morning on the way to school from their van. Miss asked me if they were men or women and when I told her that they were men she said that maybe mummy should drive me to school for the next few days.

I asked Sonny if he had been arrested and he said that he couldn't talk about it 'cos it was an "ongoin' police investigation" although he didn't explain what "it" referred to.

Wednesday 21st November

I'm not alone in having my appendix removed.
Sir was patrolling the corner of the road down from the school this morning as Charlie and I skipped

288

past and he told us, "Walk properly." I said, "At least we're not holding hands," and he just said, "Whatever."

Sam had a few friends round to plan some Christmas activities. There was Tanya and some of her friends and some boys as well. I was going to get turfed out of the sitting room but then Sam said that I could stay 'cos I was still recuperating. When one of Tanya's friends asked me what I was recuperating from I told her that I had had my appendix removed. Then she asked me if I was a genuine case or was I trying to get out of a test or exam and all the others laughed. I lifted up my shirt to show them all my genuine scar and then all the boys did the same. Apart from Sam they all had scars as well! None of the girls did though or if they had they weren't showing. One boy said that as exams were so important these days it was vital to use as many tricks as you could. He knew of one of his older brother's friends who had got out of a whole A-level paper by having his appendix removed one week and his adenoids the next. I suppose if you were desperate then by this way you could pass all of your exams that you ever had to take but there wouldn't be much left of your insides by the time that you'd finished.

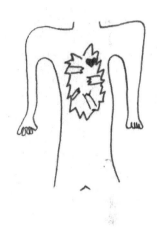

Just as Sam's friends were leaving the police appeared and wanted to speak to mummy. She has to go to the police station tomorrow.

Thursday 22nd November
Mummy gets arrested.

Mummy went to the police station today and had to have her fingerprints taken. She then had to wait for a couple of hours after which she was suddenly arrested for "handing stolen goods." When she asked what goods she was told "a charity collecting tin." Mummy then said that she had put it in her bag by mistake. "So you're not denying it? Jumped off the till by itself did it Mrs Horrise?" asked the policeman. When mummy said nothing the policeman said, "We traced it to the house of a one Sonny Christy who said that he had just taken it from you and was about to return it to the supermarket." When mummy asked how one could trace a charity tin the policeman said, "Due to a high incidence of charity collecting tin theft in the area they mostly now have trackers fitted and we tracked yours to Master Christy's." "Didn't it dawn on you that it might be Sonny that's stolen it?" mummy asked. "It did cross our minds," said the policeman, "but Sonny's fingerprints are nowhere to be found - but yours are." Mummy's now at home with a glass of rosé even though the clocks have been gone back nearly a month and she's not even skiing.

Friday 23rd November
"Runners and Riders" takes a bit of time.
We had a bit of a drama last night. We were doing maps and chestnuts and slows and a wide game and we met in the car park of Scadbury Park which has a two mile circular nature trail. We found some chestnuts which we're hopefully going to cook next week, then we did some map work. Skip's also got us to pick loads of slows to make slow jelly which is like jam. Funnily enough he asked us to do the same thing last year. He took them home and said that they had to be frozen first but we didn't see

them again. Daddy did, but we didn't. Whilst we were picking them a man came along and said to Skip, "Leave some for everyone else," but Skip said that he wasn't picking slows, he was picking poisonous berries to keep the hedgerow safe from people who didn't know what they were doing, in case they inadvertently tasted one. "That'll keep him well away," said Skip, once the man had gone. When it got dark we played "Runners and Riders." You

pair up in a circle and then the last pair to carry out an instruction, like "Mount" which is piggy back, and "Runners" which means the runners have to run round the circle, is out. The game ended rather suddenly when Skip called, "Mount," and then, "Once round the car park." Emily was on Melanie's back and Melanie misheard and set off "once round the park." She went so quickly that no one could catch her and she wouldn't listen to our shouts. It took the pair an hour to get back, what with getting lost and tripping up and stuff and we all had to wait until they had returned. Skip said that if anything good had come from it it was that Melanie had got a quarter of one hikes away activity badge. Personally I would have suggested that she had her ears syringed.

She didn't win the game either after that little episode.

Saturday 24th November
The Hop Farm - not what it seems.
Bramble took the beavers on a trip to The Hop Farm today and Olivia went along to help. She said that it was all going fine and there was plenty to do 'cos Bramble had got an "access all attractions" pass. However she didn't appreciate that this

included a history of beer making followed by beer tasting. Apparently she hadn't realised that she had bought adult tickets by mistake so the beavers missed out on cake and sweet-making but I don't expect any of them minded although one of the daddies who was helping said that it would be a waste not to sample the beer that the beavers had all paid for. Unfortunately he and a friend drank all the beavers' samples and then Bramble wouldn't let them back on the coach and told them to get the train home. There was only one other incident and that happened at lunch time when the beavers were all eating their sandwiches. The youngest beaver went up to Bramble and said, "Excoose me Bwamble, but where are the bunnies?" Bramble had to explain that there weren't any bunnies. Then the beaver said, "But it's the HOP Farm! I thought I was going to see loads of bunny wabbits!" and then burst into tears.

Sunday 25th November

More roast potato manoeuvres.

I went last at dinner today. I told daddy that Olivia shouldn't always be last and she smiled at me but I had a good reason. When daddy asked Olivia how many roast potatoes she would like she counted the potatoes round her side of the roast pork and then stood up and walked round to the other side still counting. Then she sat down. "I would like nine please daddy." There were only nine on the plate but I didn't say anything. Then daddy asked Olivia, "Isn't that a bit excessive?" She said, "Yes, but you asked me and so I've told you. If you had in mind a number why didn't you say so or just dish me up that number?" Anyway she got five and I had four and there were none left over so no one could be polite.

Monday 26th November
New Wine Nightmare.

Archie said that his daddy had a very red face on Saturday. He was invited to a "New Wine Taster" at his local church. Archie said that he went along with a big smile on his face, several pals and a half-case of Beaujolais Nouveau. Archie's daddy said that when they arrived they were very surprised to find that they wouldn't be tasting the latest and most popular French *vin de primeur* but experiencing an introduction to the New Wine organisation's ministry of worship, teaching and prayer.

Tuesday 27th November
Sonny gets a free haircut - again.

Sonny came to school today with a very smart haircut. It looks as though he had been somewhere very posh. And he had. But he didn't say where. What he did say though was that it was free. Of course we all wanted to know how to get a free haircut so he told us, but we're not allowed to tell anyone else. He went somewhere posh after school yesterday with one of his grown-up relatives. They went into the hairdressers together and the man went first and had a wash and a cut and some styling gel from the top stylist and a glass of Champagne. Then he said that he was just popping out to get a newspaper and put some more money in the parking meter. Sonny then had the same treatment but without the Champagne. When the stylist had finished with Sonny he went to leave but the lady on the reception said that he couldn't go until his father had come back and paid. Sonny then said, "That wasn't my dad." When the lady then asked who it was Sonny said, "I don't know; he just came in with me havin' asked me if I would like a free 'aircut." When the lady told Sonny to, "sit down whilst I call the police," Sonny told her that that would be kidnap and child abuse as he wasn't an adult and anyway he hadn't asked for a haircut, they had just given him one and if they made a fuss he would tell the police that they had physically assaulted him. When the lady  suggested that cutting someone's hair wasn't a physical assault Sonny suggested that she wouldn't mind if he took a pair of scissors to her hair then. At this point he was shown the door and told never to come back. Which I don't expect he will.

Apparently Sonny hasn't paid for a haircut for over four years. However, he's a bit short-sighted in what he's doing 'cos eventually he'll run out of hairdressers to cut his hair for free and then he won't be able to get it cut at all and when he gets to eighteen he'll probably be arrested - several times. And that'll be just for the hairdresssers.

Wednesday 28th November
Mummy gets a squeaky voice.
When I came home from school today mummy spoke to me really strangely. She was speaking slowly and clearly but with a very high-pitched voice. I didn't say anything 'cos I didn't want to get told off. I thought that maybe she had seen or read something so I merely asked her what she had done today. "Just a bit of shopping," she said. I can't imagine why shopping would give you a squeaky voice. I wonder if mummy will sound the same tomorrow. I hope not; it doesn't sound like her at all.

Thursday 29th November
Bramble gets told off.

Olivia helped at beavers again tonight. Apparently Bramble has been sent a letter from the littlest beavers' mummy saying how disappointed she was that her daughter didn't get to see any rabbits at The Hop Farm. At the end of the meeting Bramble gave the littlest beaver something that was the shape of a giant sausage with floppy ears that was all wrapped up in a carrier bag. She told the littlest beaver to take it home and "open it with your mummy." Given that Bramble's husband's a butcher I think that it's likely that Bramble's going to be getting another letter before too long, if not a knock at the door or a visit from the District Commiserator.

Mummy's still squeaking.

Friday 30th November

Archie gets sent home.

We've been practising for Christmas at scouts. Skip has been teaching us "Deck the Halls." When we sang, "'Tis the season to be jolly," Archie then added, "Skip's still off his (sweary word) trolley."

He got sent home after that. But not before he told me that he thought that mummy was going to get arrested at the supermarket on Wednesday. When I got home mummy had some shopping not from her usual supermarket so I knew that something was going on but I didn't like to ask. She's not squeaking quite so much today.

We're making a big catapult next Friday and we're going to fire water bombs. Skip's given us ten each to fill up and bring with us next week 'cos he said that he wasn't going to fill up several hundred by himself.

Saturday 1st December

Poppy dies but it's not too bad.

Mummy came home from shopping (not at the supermarket) to be told by daddy, very straightforwardly, some very sad news. "Poppy's dead." Mummy put down her shopping as a tear come to her eye. Poppy was her great, great aunt who was ninety-four and apparently in very good health.

"Oh dear, poor Poppy. She was a great age though. How old was she?"

"Ten or eleven," said daddy.

"Don't be silly David. I know you didn't like her that much but she was hardly immature. What did she die from?"

"Parvovirus probably."

"'Parvovirus?' What's that?"

"An illness caused through the sniffing of bottoms. She did enough of it. She was always sniffing mine."

"I can't believe that you can be so rude about poor old Poppy. Who told you that she'd died?"

"Susie, next door."

"'Susie?' How on earth would she know?"

"Well it was her dog."

Mummy's voice is almost back to normal.

Sunday 2nd December
Roast potatoes are no more.
We had boiled potatoes today and there were loads left over 'cos
I didn't have any and neither did Olivia.

Monday 3rd December
Things are going downhill and it's nearly Christmas.
We had cold potatoes today.
Not on their own; we had some
cold chicken as well but mummy
said that had we eaten all of the
potatoes then she would have
made a curry today with the
leftover chicken. Now who's not
being polite?

We had a water bomb fight on the way to school today.

Tuesday 4th December
The truth comes out and it's not too bad.
When I asked mummy at breakfast what she was going to be
doing during the day she said, "Going shopping." Not much of a
surprise there then. Without thinking I heard myself saying,
"Don't get arrested." When mummy gave me her funny look I
took a deep breath and said, "Archie said to me last week that he
thought that you were going to get arrested in the supermarket."
That's when it all came out. Mummy couldn't find her debit card
and so had borrowed daddy's. It was just unfortunate that when
she went to pay and put the card in the machine a security notice
flashed up which read, "MANUAL CHECK." "This happens
sometimes," said the cashier. "We just have to get you to sign a
receipt so that we can check the signature." The cashier took the
card and had a good look at it before announcing, "Well, I must
say, you don't look like a man." Why mummy couldn't have just

said that she'd simply borrowed daddy's card I don't know. Instead she said to the cashier, "I am David Horrise. I am having gender realignment surgery." "I can see that you have some way to go," said the cashier, "but your voice is getting there. If I shut my eyes I would put you down as a man." Now I know why mummy has been all squeaky for a few days, she's obviously retraining her voice to be properly female again. It also explains why she's been avoiding that particular supermarket.

Wednesday 5th December
Expanding bodies.
Women have wombs. This is so they can have babies. Mummy said that wombs are in a woman's tummy area so I suppose women must have smaller tummies and probably that explains why men can always eat more 'cos they have more space.

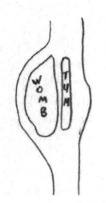

We had another water bomb fight on the way to school today. When you fill a water bomb up it looks like some daddies' tummies. Or women's wombs when they're being used.

Thursday 6th December
Miss gets a cold sore.
Miss has got a funny mark at the side of her mouth and she said that it was a cold sore when Emily asked. I told mummy when I got home from school in case it was infectious and mummy said that it wasn't catching unless I kissed miss which I haven't. I asked mummy what a cold sore was and

she said that it was something called "herpes, and you usually get it down under."

Friday 7th December

Miss has not been down under.

I asked miss today whether she had been to Australia recently but she frowned a little bit and said that she hadn't so I told mummy when I got home that miss hadn't been to Australia. Mummy just smiled and said, "No, probably somewhere a little closer to home then," and smiled some more. I'm glad it was scouts tonight so I could forget all about herpes for a while.

We were supposed to be making a huge catapult tonight and firing it but no one brought back any water bombs that Skip had given us last week to fill up 'cos we had used them all up during the last few days. That is except Sonny who brought his ten along in a carrier bag. The trouble was Sonny's weren't all squishy like they had water in them. Skip had to ask Sonny several times but eventually he said that his were full of bright orange paint that he had found in the shed. Skip then had to ask Sonny several times why he hadn't put water in his like he was asked. First of all Sonny said that Skip had just told us to fill them up and he didn't tell us what with. Skip said, "It's in the name stupid," then had to apologise for calling Sonny stupid. Sonny looked like he was going to cry so Mel said to Skip, "At least he's filled his up unlike the rest of us." Eventually Sonny said, or more like shouted, "'Cos we don't have any water at home at the moment alright?" Skip didn't say anything after that, he just told Sonny to take his water paint bombs home with him - and carefully. Sonny was really upset 'cos he was looking forward to doing catapults with his bright orange paint although they would've made quite a mess. We had to do signing instead.

Signing is so we can speak to deaf people. You do stuff with your fingers to make sort of pictures. Skip said that signing is a visual means of communicating using gestures, facial expression and body language. We learnt to say, "Hallo, good morning. How are you?" Sonny wasn't taking much interest and he was sulking so Skip said, "Come on, Sonny, there's no reading involved. It's just sign language." "I can read and I can do sign language already mate," Sonny said. "I can do this...and

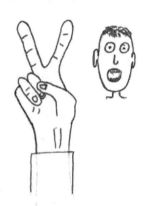

this...and this. Oh and this..." Each time the comments were accompanied by hand actions. One I had seen before but the other ones were new. "Yes and thank you Sonny but I don't think we need to do those at deaf people." "No mate, but my uncle does 'em all out of the window at motorists when he's drivin' an' I don't 'spect any of them are deaf," said Sonny looking very smug. But Sonny wasn't told off probably 'cos he had at least brought some bombs to scouts, albeit paint and not water. And he was smiling when we went home so Skip looked relieved.

Saturday 8th December

Performance enhancing drugs don't agree with me.

I found out today that there's no minimum age for performance enhancing drugs. Now I knew how to beat Charlie at football. I asked mummy at breakfast if she had any performance enhancing drugs and she said "Yes, Marmite." So I ate half a jar before today's match. Unfortunately I

had to come off after only ten minutes and go home 'cos I was really sick all down the goal post 'cos I was hanging on to it, all brown and smelly. Charlie reckoned that I had been eating poo. I might just as well've been.

Sunday 9th December

Chaos at Christmas - and there's still two weeks to go!
Sam's in so much trouble! He went round to Tanya's for a sort of early Christmas family gathering and everyone was there! All of Tanya's aunties and uncles and people that Tanya didn't see at any other time of the year were altogether for a buffet supper and a natter. Even Great Aunt Audrey, whom Tanya said had been permanently old for at least a hundred years, was in attendance in "her" favourite wingback chair by the fire. Sam and Tanya were a bit late arriving so there were no more sherry glasses left which was a pity 'cos Tanya said that she liked sherry though mostly in trifle. They were still allowed sherry but with added lemonade and

Tanya had to have hers in a mug and Sam was reduced to the absolutely last glass - the one that's normally kept right at the back of the cupboard. After he had been handed it by Tanya's mummy - it was like a balloon brandy glass, Tanya said, "Don't be fooled 'cos that's the joke glass. It has a double skin with a brandy coloured liquid inside it. When you go to drink it nothing comes out and everyone will laugh at you." "We'll see about that," said Sam. He looked up and everyone was indeed staring at him; little did he realise that this was probably only because, being Tanya's new boyfriend, he was something of a novelty and not because they were all waiting for him to take a sip of his sealed-in drink. Without saying anything and before anyone could stop him, Sam marched over to Great Aunt Audrey, who was very deaf, and said in a loud voice, "Hallo Great Aunt Audrey. I've heard you like a drink!" and then swooshed his glass at the *grande dame*. No one will ever know who was most surprised: the guests who wondered why Sam had greeted Tanya's Great Aunt in such a way, Sam who found that the joke glass was still perfectly usable as a drinks' receptacle, Tanya who couldn't understand why anyone would want to use the glass for anything other than a prank or Great Aunt Audrey who stayed perfectly still as if in severe shock, soaked from head to waist in sticky lemonade-diluted sherry. By the time that the guests were departing later in the evening, ("You've made a great impression!" chuckled one of the uncles to Sam), Great Aunt Audrey was still none the wiser as to why Tanya's new boyfriend should have greeted her by throwing a sickly concoction over her. "Maybe it's what the youth do these days," she suggested to Tanya's mummy whilst she was trying to explain for the umpteenth time that there was a perfectly rational explanation. Sam soon got over the shock however and has been given the glass as a souvenir. He's hidden it somewhere in his room. I don't think that's it's the last time that we will be seeing that particular glass.

At least Sam's not a suspect in the attack on Skip's house. When he was leaving to come home and was chatting on the doorstep Skip's wife let out a huge scream 'cos on the front wall of their

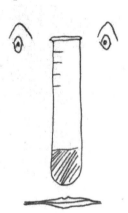

immaculate white house there were eight enormous roundish explosions of bright orange paint and two on their car.

Monday 10th December
Family secrets.
I'm sure Sonny has family secrets. I asked him today what he was doing for Christmas and he said that he would be at home with his mummy. There are definitely some things about him that we don't know. Things that most

people know about others. Most people have mummies and daddies. Actually everyone has a mummy and a daddy even if you're born in a test tube or stuff like that. We're not sure about Sonny's daddy. No one's seen him. What I mean is Sonny may have done and he has mentioned him occasionally and Sonny's mummy probably has but none of the Ravings has. Sonny doesn't look like he was born in a test tube. Probably people who are born in a test tube are long and thin. I asked mummy tonight if she had any family secrets. I was expecting her to say, "No Horace," but she didn't. She just smiled and said that it was time for bed which it wasn't 'cos it was only half past six.

Tuesday 11th December

Sonny and his grandad's secret.

I decided to ask Sonny today if he had any family secrets and he said "Yes!" I asked him what they were and he said, "I'll tell you if you tell me." I told him that I thought that we had some secrets but I didn't know what they were. "Why not?" "'Cos they're, well, secrets." "Yeah," he said, "but that's the point. If they're family secrets then they're known only by the family. They're not kept secret from the family, they're kept secret from the rest of the world. You have a right to know Horace. Demand to be told." "In that case," I said, "I shall ask daddy when he's in a good mood, which is most of the time, although if they're family secrets then I shouldn't be telling you." "It doesn't count with children Horace. We can't be held responsible for what we know until we're eighteen. That's why we children know so much and adults don't realise how much we know." "So what's your secret?" Sonny took a deep breath and said, "My grandad's missin' two fingers." "That's not much of a secret," I said. "He could've just had an accident." "That's what I was told to start with," said Sonny. "I don't remember a time when grandad had all his fingers and thumbs but the first time that I realised that he didn't have all of 'em was when I was with 'im at home in, um, wherever. We were walkin' down the local high street and he stuck two fingers up at a policeman and he got arrested. I remember it well 'cos I had to go to the police station and mummy came and picked me up and grandad was charged with makin' an obscene gesture but 'e got away with it 'cos he made the v-sign with not two fingers but two stumps and the magistrate said that you can't make a proper v-sign with your two fingers missin' and grandad could've been tryin' to cross his fingers like for luck but no one would know as he couldn't do the crossin'. Then the magistrate asked grandad how he came to have two shorter fingers and grandad said that he had had a nasty accident when he was child when his daddy had left him alone with a very sharp saw. The magistrate told the court that far from condemnin' grandad we should be sympathisin' with his plight but 'e was still told not to take advantage and he was bound over not to stick his stumps up at a policeman again. And that was that until quite recently when mum told me that grandad hadn't had a childhood accident at all. He 'ad chopped off both fingers with an axe only a few years ago so that he could make a huge insurance claim from his work. However he was found out and he had to go to prison."

That's certainly a big family secret but even bigger is where Sonny's "wherever" home is / was, but I think that that's definitely going to stay a proper family secret for now.

Wednesday 12th December
Partial family secret.
Daddy was in a good mood this evening and he was out in his shed so I went out to find him 'cos I didn't want mummy to

know. It was really cold so he had the heater on and he had his jumper on but I wasn't wearing much so I said, "Daddy, please be quick but I need to know, do we have any family secrets that I don't know about?" Daddy smiled and said that if there were any family secrets then surely I would know them. I thought daddy was starting to sound a bit like Sonny which was rather worrying. I then said, "I mean secrets that should be family secrets like missing or chopped fingers but aren't 'cos not all the family know them," and daddy smiled and said, "Sit down Horace." Now I was worried and as daddy held out his hand to direct me to the sofa I had a quick look to make sure that he had all his fingers which he had so I wasn't so worried. "There is one thing, but it was more of an embarrassment than anything else. You will remember when you were a bit younger and grandma died but you and your brother and sister didn't go to the funeral which was fine? Grandma wanted to be buried and so they had dug a large hole in the churchyard for her coffin to go into. When she was being lowered in one of the mourners lent over a bit too far and, just as the coffin had come to rest and the undertakers were removing the lowering-straps, his mobile 'phone fell out of his pocket and into the grave. Everyone looked a bit shocked and pretended that they hadn't seen. Then one of the grave-diggers was summoned to jump down and retrieve it, which he did. However instead of allowing  himself to be pulled out of the grave as discretely as circumstances would allow, he held up the 'phone and shouted,

"No one's answering!" Looking back on it it was quite funny but no one was laughing at the time and mummy felt that her family name was going to be mud around the village for a generation. So that's about the only family secret that we have, but don't tell mummy that you know." "In that case daddy," I told him, "it's only a two-thirds' family secret if only you and mummy and grandad and I know and Sam and Olivia don't." "Sorry Horace," said daddy, "but that's the closest that I can get." After that I went and told Sam and Olivia so at least we all knew that family secret even though some of the family didn't know that other parts of the family now knew. A sort of secret family secret then. And soon to be a Sonny secret also.

Thursday 13th December
Uncle Tom pays a visit.

I told Sonny our family secret and he laughed. "I can't believe that you've kept that to yourself for so long!" he exclaimed. I told him that I had only been told it yesterday and the only people that knew were my family and him.

Uncle Tom's come to visit for the day! I like Uncle Tom. He's always very jolly and can say things that I would get told off saying if I did so I don't. Uncle Tom's always very smartly dressed with a sports jacket that he never takes off. He "likes a drink," that's what mummy says. She should know. She always hides her Sauvignon Blanc when Uncle Tom visits as she says it's wasted on him. She puts out really cheap wine on the dinner table and then goes into the kitchen every five minutes to top up her glass from what she calls the "proper stuff." I always think it looks rather odd like she has a weak bladder or something but there's always something to be checked on in the kitchen. Anyway, she didn't tell anybody that this time, instead of keeping the Sauvignon Blanc hidden in the fridge, she poured two whole bottles into the stone water jug that she bought years ago and which you can't see what's inside, 'cos she knew that Uncle Tom never drinks water with his meal. Unfortunately Sam, Olivia and I all do but mummy forgot to tell us and by the time she remembered we were halfway through our chicken and she couldn't say anything at the table. She simply stood up and said that she had to go and fill up the water jug but daddy got to it first and he didn't know either so mummy's been drinking very watered down Sauvignon Blanc and Sam's now fast asleep on the sofa, Olivia's been sick and I'm sitting in bed with a horrible headache even though it's only seven o'clock. Uncle Tom, meanwhile, has drunk two bottles of the cheap stuff all by himself and has been discussing with grandad the theory of wormholes and the dangers of sudden collapse, high radiation and dangerous contact with exotic matter. I wonder if drinking dodgy wine makes you more intelligent?

Friday 14th December
Visit to Vertigo Village.
3rd Chislehurst scouts, cubs and beavers went to our local care home this evening. It's a complex called "Verito Village" but we all call it "Vertigo Village." We were there to do some carol singing to the old people. I think

they enjoyed it but they didn't say much. We had fun though. It was lovely and warm and we had squash and ate all the biscuits. One of the beavers told one of the old ladies that he could sing "Silent Night" in French. The old lady said, "That's very impressive. How old are you?" "Seven," the beaver said. "Go on then," said the old lady. "I need the words and the music," the beaver said. "Well that's no good. Anyone can sing 'Silent Night' with words and music," said the old lady. "Even I could." No wonder the beaver burst into tears, but the old lady was right. Old ladies are always right. While we were there they had a raffle and we were allowed to buy tickets. Arnold (in cubs) won a signed Vera Lynn poster, Noah (in beavers) won a bottle of sherry and I won a Mrs Brown's Boys DVD which mummy has confiscated. (I expect she'll wrap it up and give it back to me in my stocking.)

Saturday 15th December
Christmas shopping starts but doesn't last.
Christmas shopping today! I went into Bromley to buy mummy some perfume. Daddy scribbled the name down on a bit of paper and gave me loads of money. I went into a posh perfume shop and asked them if I could buy some channel number five but they told me that they don't sell televisions. I said that I could have worked that out for myself. I went and bought some doughnuts and a Christmas coffee instead 'cos daddy had given me too much.

Sunday 16th December
Christmas shopping doesn't get much better.
Back in Bromley with instructions from daddy to show the perfume lady the bit of paper. When I found out how much it was I told the lady that I could have bought a television for less, although not at her shop. I said that I didn't have enough money after yesterday and what was the cheapest thing that she sold?

Mummy is now going to be the proud owner of a pair of black false eyelashes and I bought myself some aftershave for when I'm older. I haven't told daddy.

Monday 17th December
Sam's not sure about my purchase.

I showed the eyelashes to Sam who said that they looked like a couple of anorexic caterpillars and maybe I should have got her some eyebrows as well. "At least they're dead," I told him. If they do make false eyelashes from caterpillars I hope that they are dead. It would be a bit embarrassing otherwise 'cos if you were walking down the road and then your eyelashes started to wriggle, especially if they wriggled in opposite directions you would go all cross-eyed and walk into things.

Tuesday 18th December
Money-making idea.
In order to make some money I got Olivia to cut off my eyelashes and eyebrows. We don't know how to stick them together so I've just put them in an envelope. They're now for sale on an auction site under the heading, "Eyelashes and eyebrows - loose." We haven't had any bids yet.

I think Sonny's been spilling the beans. Everywhere I go people get out their 'phones and wave them at me saying, "No one's answering!" and laughing. Soon the Horrise name is going to be mud all around Chislehurst as well. Thanks Sonny.

Wednesday 19th December
The phonetic alphabet.
We've learnt the phonetic alphabet at scouts 'cos it's useful when you need to speak to the police and stuff. It goes "Alpha, Bravo,

Charlie" like that. However I don't think mummy's learnt it. She's been getting a bit frustrated over the last few days because "a very important parcel" keeps arriving while we're all out despite a note to "Leave it under the hedge by the garage." Finally today mummy got through to the courier people on the 'phone and mummy's side of the conversation went something like this. "Karen Horrise. Horrise. HORRISE! H - O - R - R - I - S - E! H Half-witted, O Out to lunch, R Rude, R Ridiculous, I Idiot, S Stupid and E um Eric." When mummy came off the 'phone she said that she felt much better "after that" so I asked her who Eric was. "I don't know," she said. "I just couldn't think of a suitable word that began with an 'E.'" "How about 'Eczema?'" I suggested. "Don't be silly," mummy said. "I needed an 'E' not an 'X.'" I'm beginning to think that I'm becoming better read with my Tintin books than mummy with her magazines.

Thursday 20th December

First aid at the circus.

About three hundred scouts, cubs, beavers and parents went to the circus this evening in an event organised by our local district. It was such fun! Along with our mummies and some daddies we took over the Big Top. There was juggling and horses and some clowns, the latter mostly in the audience. The last act was a woman who was strapped to a large round table that was then put on its side and lifted off the ground. It then rotated like a wheel whilst one of the clowns threw large knives at her. I couldn't watch. Suddenly there was a scream and I opened one eye. The table had stopped revolving and the lady was bleeding. "Please," cried the ringmaster, "is there anyone here who is first aid qualified?" That was a bad request. About three hundred (less parents) scouts, cubs and beavers all surged forward to help.

Some leaders had even brought first aid kits which were pressed into service by scouts wishing to do their best. By the time that

the ambulance arrived and the scouts had all stood back the lady was so bandaged up that she looked like an Egyptian mummy like you see at the British Museum with only her nose sticking out so at least she could still breathe. The ambulance lady took one look at her patient and asked, "Are we supposed to be treating her or embalming her?" She cut all the bandages off to tend to the small cut and I understand our revolving lady is making a full recovery.

Sonny told me that when his mummy was younger she had once run off to join a circus. She said to him, "It weren't much fun. I was in bed every night by ten o'clock with a steaming cocoa." Then she cackled and Sonny said that he smiled. I don't quite know what's so funny. I shall have to ask mummy in the morning. Hot chocolate and a sleeping bag seem like heaven to me.

Friday 21st December
The last scout meeting of the year.
Mummy looked at me closely this morning then asked me where my eyelashes and eyebrows were so I told her that they were being auctioned off. She just tut-tutted and walked off after telling me that I should maybe see a little less of Sonny and definitely keep out of his mummy's way after I told her about her joining the circus when she was younger.

We did safety in stoves and lamps tonight. Skip showed us how to light matches properly and how to use a Tilley lamp which burns paraffin then we had a go. He told us that paraffin burns really well which is why I put some in an empty plastic water bottle and brought it home. You never know when you're going to need to heat or burn something. Apparently paraffin is ninety-five percent alcohol which is why the people in charge of the world put poisonous stuff in it and colour it purple to stop us drinking it after it's been mixed with a bit of tonic water.

Sonny was sent home early after he hit Emily halfway during the meeting. Actually he flicked her ear but Emily fell to the ground clutching her leg so there was no way that Sonny was going to get out of it. Sonny had just told us that you can also use paraffin to blow things up so Emily told him to stop being stupid 'cos we don't blow things up in scouts - not intentionally anyway. Then Sonny got all aggressive and showed Emily his fists. "My dad's a boxer," he said. Emily wasn't at all impressed. "Yeah, and your mum's a poodle." Then he growled and flicked her ear and that's Sonny's scout meetings over until next year.

Saturday 22nd December
Bag packing today. Unfortunately Charlie came too. Still, it could've been worse. It could've been with Sonny.
I've been bag-packing today at the local supermarket with the scouts. I thought daddy was the only one who behaved like a spoiled brat at the tills. (Mummy says he's 'anal' whatever that means.) Now I know differently. "No thank you," the daddies

would say when we asked if they would like help. They would have all their food on the conveyor belt with all the heavy stuff at the front and all the light stuff at the back. They would put all the fruit and veg. stuff together and all the freezer stuff together. They would then line out all their bags in the shopping trolley and then fill them up in order as the stuff came out on the other side from the cashier. They would ignore us completely then give us twenty pounds saying, "Thank you for not interfering."

The mummies on the other hand would be stressed out and gratefully accepted our offer of packing for them. We just shoved it all in as it came down the conveyor belt. Crisps would have four-packs of baked bean tins on top, tomatoes would go under the cat food and Charlie even put a hot chicken next to some frozen prawns and some ice cream. That would've made a bit of a mess of their car (and their stomachs) later on. They would say, "Do you think you could help me take the bags out to the car?" Then we would have to wait ten minutes while they spoke to a friend that they had bumped into in the entrance and to cap it all they wouldn't give us any money! By the time that we got to lunchtime Charlie had had enough. One woman had TWO trolleys and wide ones at that and she spent over THREE HUNDRED pounds! We bagged it all up and then Charlie had to push one of the trolleys to her car. When he got to next to her boot and she clicked the key thing and the boot popped up the woman said, "Sorry, but I don't have any change." Charlie said that we accepted notes as well but she just gave him one of those silly little smirks like some women sometimes do, so Charlie tipped over the trolley he was pushing and all the bags split and the bottles broke and all the food was rolling over the car park and then some people came running over and helped themselves and then they ran away again and the woman started screaming and then the security man came and Charlie wasn't allowed back in the store after that and had to go home.

Still, the rest of us raised over £400 so that's more go-karting sorted out for next year. Charlie will probably be a spectator and Sonny won't be allowed 'cos he hasn't been bag-packing.

Sunday 23rd December
A bit of fun with the carol singing.
Carol singing round Chislehurst this afternoon with the cubs and beavers. We were told by Skip to dress smartly which is a bit difficult when you're only eleven. We only know one carol which was fine 'cos people were paying us just to go away so no one was hanging around on their front doorstep to listen. It was rather cold anyway. We learnt "Good King Wenceslas looked out..." but the scouts had a new version so all we sang was,
Good King Wenceslas looked out
On a cabbage garden.
Bumped into a Brussels sprout
And said "I beg your pardon."
These are all the words we know
Can't learn any mo-re.
Give us ten quid now to go
Or we'll kick in your festive doo-oo-or!
(That last bit Sonny had made up but he wasn't allowed to come out with us so we sang it for him.)

No one seemed to notice and afterwards we all went back to the scout hut for drinks and mince pies. Charlie went and made himself a Horlicks with boiling water from the water boiler but it came out sort of creamy burgundy colour but he said it tasted alright then started to slur and went all floppy and Akela thought of F.A.S.T. and was Charlie having a stroke but I said that all he had had was seven mince pies and a Horlicks with water from the water heater. Then Akela said "Oh, that's alright then," but it wasn't alright 'cos Charlie's had half a pint of mulled wine with extra brandy.

Monday 24th December

Carpet laying capers in Chislehurst.

Sam helped daddy's friend out today on a carpet rush job 'cos it needs to be done by Christmas which is actually tomorrow so it had to be right first time. We call daddy's friend "Casper the Carpet" and he had to fit a large sitting room carpet and Sam had to help carry the roll which was really heavy. Once they had finished Casper reached in his pocket for a cigarette then realised that he couldn't find one because he had given the packet to Sam to look after but Sam couldn't find the packet. Then Casper told Sam off 'cos there was a bump in the middle of the carpet so Casper said that Sam had to be more careful and ensure that there was nothing under where they were laying and definitely not his cigarettes. 'Cos Casper was in a bit of a rush and totally stressed out, rather than take the newly-laid carpet up he just hammered away at the lump with his rubber mallet until it was flat. At that point Mrs McMillan came into the room clutching a

packet of cigarettes and said, "Lovely job boys." She held out the packet. "Sam, you left Casper's cigarettes in the kitchen when you were having a cup of tea earlier. Now, has anyone seen my gerbil?"

Let's hope the carpet doesn't start to pong too soon.

Tuesday 25th December

The best day of the year has arrived!

Christmas Day! We all went to church this morning as Tanya was going so Sam was going so mummy and daddy decided to go. It was called an "all age" service and mummy said that it wouldn't be like a usual service and she was right! It was full up which I don't think happens all the time but it was great fun and everyone was happy and some people were waving their hands in the air like they had had their Christmas dinner already and were onto charades. The vicar who's called Mike said that the Bible doesn't tell us when Jesus was born and that some astronomers reckon that he was born about the middle of June which would mean having to celebrate Christmas like the Aussies do at the moment and they would have to do it in the snow.

Tanya said that we all had to take a present, either an unopened one or an opened one, as Mike likes to get some people out the front with their presents and then talk about them. As we don't open any of our presents, except stocking ones, until the afternoon, we had to take unopened ones. Mummy and daddy refused to play so we took one for each of them from their secret box that was in their bedroom. It's secret 'cos they hide it but we know where it is 'cos it's always in the wardrobe and they have one every year but we never see what the presents are. When Mike picked on mummy to go up the front with her present she said that she didn't have one with her to open but I told Mike that she did and that she just didn't know about it. As she was being dragged up the front I produced the small parcel from my rucksack. It had on the label, "To my darling candy Karen. With love and kisses from your expectant Dave the Knave. xxx" I took it up the front and gave it to Mike.

When I got back to my seat daddy asked me where I had got the parcel from and I told him that Olivia had got it out of the box in the bedroom. Then daddy went all pale and had to leave to get a glass of water.

Whilst he was gone mummy opened the parcel and inside there was just underwear but there wasn't much of it but it was all red and silky and mummy seemed quite pleased and smiled a big smile. Then it was the turn for Mike to go all pale and someone had to go and get him a glass of water.

Mike didn't have much to say about that particular present but his wife did 'cos she was talking to daddy for ages after the service whilst we were having squash and mince pies in the hall. Mummy got quite cross 'cos daddy had stayed in the church bit and then he had loads of women talking to him, not just Mike's wife, but he escaped eventually and we walked home.

On the way home mummy asked daddy why he had been so panicked by the opening of some Amour Chéri underwear and he said, "You don't know what else is in 'that' box that you could have opened in front of a churchful of Christmas worshippers."

Christmas dinner was fab. but we had a bit of an upset with the pudding. Mummy had been steaming it for hours then, when it was ready, she plopped it out onto a plate and Olivia had to go into the garden and cut a bit of holly. Daddy warmed up a load of brandy and poured it over the Christmas pudding and lit it with a match - only he didn't 'cos the brandy wouldn't light. Then he had another go and then said that we had run out of brandy. He had a look in one of the cupboards that doesn't get looked in too often and brought out a bottle of what daddy referred to as, "some dodgy spirit" and it had a raffle ticket still stuck on it so we know what someone thinks of that don't we? Daddy went into the kitchen to warm some up but I wasn't sure whether I wanted brandy and dodgy spirit Christmas pudding so I went up to my room and brought down my bottle of paraffin and poured a load on the pudding 'cos it's mostly alcohol. I told grandad it was purple brandy and no one else was taking much notice. Mummy and daddy reappeared and poured the warmed up dodgy spirit on the pudding and daddy lit another match. He hardly had touched the liquid when there was a great big "WOOF" and the pudding exploded and it went everywhere and we still haven't found the sprig of holly. No one was very hungry after that but all the adults decided to have a glass of dodgy spirit and a mince pie anyway. It was just as well that no one was smoking.

Mummy said that it would be nice to have a glass of daddy's slow gin with their coffee but daddy said that he couldn't find it so 'cos I knew where he had been hiding it, which was behind some tall books in his bookcase, I went to get it but all the bottles were empty. When I brought out three empty bottles daddy looked very embarrassed and mummy was quite cross. "I didn't realise slow gin could evaporate so quickly," daddy said but I think we know what's really happened to it but I didn't say.

In the evening when everyone was asleep I went to see what else was in the secret box but all the presents were missing. I had a good hunt around but didn't find anything new that had been opened so I gave up.

I don't think mummy liked her false eyelashes 'cos she just said, "Oh," when she opened them and now they've disappeared also. I could've done with them 'cos mine aren't growing. Maybe eyelashes don't grow like proper hair but it doesn't matter 'cos it's not like they do anything like keep your eyes warm.

Wednesday 26th December
Boxing Day and daddy still has stubble.

Mummy and daddy stayed in bed for a long time this morning. They were so long getting up that I went to wake them but daddy was already awake 'cos he was shaving, albeit in the bedroom, so I left them alone. When they finally appeared for breakfast at about lunchtime I told daddy that I knew what mummy had bought him for their secret Christmas 'cos I could hear the buzzing noise. Daddy looked like he was shaking and asked me what it was and I told daddy that it was an electric shaver. It was a bit odd though 'cos daddy still has his stubble. No wonder he seemed worried 'cos probably it was a train set.

Thursday 27th December
Monopoly madness.

Things have come to a pretty pass with the Horrise family as daddy is now threatening to start CCTVing the Christmas

Monopoly game. He says that money gets stolen, the sitting room gets secret visits during a tea interval after everyone has had to vacate for ten minutes, properties get mysteriously swapped over, hotels disappear and the number of moves stops corresponding to the numbers thrown on the dice. Daddy's threatening to get Mike over for an exorcism unless someone owns up. In the midst of it all, a young lady that Sam is texting (not Tanya) asks him what he's doing. "Buying an electricity company," he replies. Five minutes later she's back. "My dad says that you sound like the sort of guy worth hanging onto." "Tell him I'm only playing Monopoly," was his honest reply. I wonder if Tanya's told her daddy yet that my daddy wasn't buying a real hotel in Mayfair in the summer?

At least daddy's now had a shave.

Friday 28th December
Olivia gets rabies - but only for a few seconds.

Olivia came downstairs at breakfast time in just her knickers and

she was crying and foaming red at the mouth like something inside her had exploded or she had severe rabies and she couldn't speak. It looked pretty serious and mummy immediately jumped up and went to her aid. It was all a bit odd at first 'cos she had had her breakfast and had only gone back upstairs for a bath a few minutes earlier. Who could've known how dangerous baths were? Through the sobs and after mummy had given her a glass of water and she had spat blood-coloured stuff all over the kitchen floor she explained that she had sneaked out a huge strawberry muffin from beneath the Christmas tree to eat in the bath but when she bit into it it had started to fizz so she chewed it and tried to swallow but she couldn't and then it kept fizzing and her head started to shake and then she couldn't see straight and then her mouth started to froth and she felt really sick and quite dizzy before she finally managed to stagger down the stairs. "That's not a strawberry muffin, Olivia," said daddy from behind his newspaper, sounding very unconcerned, "that's one of mummy's bath bombs."

Saturday 29th December
Eyelashes FOUND!

When I was doing some stuff in the garden I found the eyelashes that I had

given to mummy for Christmas that were still in their box. I also found some false eyebrows that weren't in a box. I got some superglue from daddy's shed and stuck the eyebrows on me whilst my new ones are growing underneath.

Sunday 30th December
Wine bottle wars.

My eyebrows started moving today and Sam said that they are in fact real caterpillars. Apparently they woke up. In the afternoon I had to go to A & E to have them removed.

Uncle Tom came for dinner. Mummy has got fed up with him "getting plastered" so has bought two bottles of alcohol free wine and decanted them into the empty bottles that Uncle Tom had last time and kept the Sauvignon Blanc in the fridge. He still got drunk though. Daddy says that it's a miracle but Sam told me the reason is a little more grounded. Uncle Tom never takes his jacket off because it's stuffed full of small bottles of home prepared quadruple strength gin and tonic. Sam caught him pouring one into his wine glass this evening whilst mummy was taking the soup bowls away and daddy was getting the beef out of the oven. He told Sam that he can't stand the wine that mummy puts out and can't work out how she can drink it. So no one drunk the dodgy wine that was in fact alcohol free and Uncle Tom got plastered and mummy got plastereder. Now daddy's saying that if Uncle Tom can get drunk not drinking alcohol free stuff then next time he's going to save himself a packet and put elderflower cordial in the wine bottles. "Good idea," said mummy, "and you can then buy me some even more expensive Chablis." I don't know what it is about adults and wine. If it gives them all a headache why on earth do they bother?

Monday 31st December
Swimming pool setback.

We're in Sussex in a posh hotel for a New Year's party. We're not going to a party in the hotel, we're going to mummy and daddy's friends later who are called Ali and Charlie and they live in a place called Horney Common which always makes daddy laugh but I don't know why. There's also a big party in the hotel tonight and loads of people are  walking around looking very smart. When we arrived we went into the bar for a sandwich. Daddy has been looking forward to using the swimming pool and had been talking about it all the way down in the car. When the waiter brought our drinks over daddy asked if he could use the swimming pool after lunch. "Yes sir," said the waiter pointing out of the window, "if you want to break the ice on it." "You could always go ice-skating," said mummy just as a very glamorous lady walked into the bar. Mummy and daddy both looked at her, then back at each other, then burst into laughter. The lady looked surprised and I thought that they were being very rude. Mummy later explained that the lady was Jayne Torvill. I am none the wiser. Maybe next year will bring more wisdom.

All I can say is, I think we'll be glad to see the back of this year. Things can't be any worse next year. My new year's resolution is to do my best. Again. And I hope that I won't be saying this in a year's time. Again.

***

If you've enjoyed "The Very Secret Diary of Horace Horrise" then please check out www.johnhemmingclark.com or www.amazon.co.uk for details of my other Horace Horrise books.

Please also leave a Goodreads (www.goodreads.com) or Amazon review. I would be very grateful. On Amazon - find "The Very Secret Diary of Horace Horrise" at www.amazon.co.uk and scroll down to and click on "Write a customer review" then "Submit."

**